And Here

And Here

100 Years of Upper Peninsula Writing, 1917–2017

Edited by Ronald Riekki

Michigan State University Press | *East Lansing*

⊛ The paper used in this publication meets the minimum requirements
of ANSI/NISO Z39.48-1992 (R 1997) (Permanence of Paper).

Michigan State University Press
East Lansing, Michigan 48823-5245

Printed and bound in the United States of America.

26 25 24 23 22 21 20 19 18 17   1 2 3 4 5 6 7 8 9 10

LIBRARY OF CONGRESS CATALOGING-IN-PUBLICATION DATA
Names: Riekki, R. A., editor.
Title: And here : 100 years of Upper Peninsula writing, 1917-2017 /
edited by Ronald Riekki.
Description: East Lansing : Michigan State University Press, 2017.
Identifiers: LCCN 2016049664| ISBN 9781611862591 (pbk. : alk. paper)
| ISBN9781609175412 (pdf) | ISBN 9781628953107 (epub)
| ISBN 9781628963106(kindle)
Subjects: LCSH: American literature—Michigan—Upper Peninsula. | Upper
Peninsula (Mich.)—Literary collections. | Michigan—In literature.
Classification: LCC PS571.M5 A53 2017 | DDC 810.8/097749--dc23
LC record available at https://lccn.loc.gov/2016049664

Book design by Charlie Sharp, Sharp Des!gns, East Lansing, MI
Cover design by Erin Kirk New
Cover image: Miners Falls in the Upper Peninsula of Michigan
(© csterken—stock.adobe.com).

Michigan State University Press is a member of the Green Press Initiative and is
committed to developing and encouraging ecologically responsible publishing
practices. For more information about the Green Press Initiative and the use of
recycled paper in book publishing, please visit *www.greenpressinitiative.org*.

Visit Michigan State University Press at *www.msupress.org*

Nimbwaawinanigoomin.
We are still here.

⌐

JIM NORTHRUP,
Rez Road Follies: Canoes, Casinos, Computers,
and Birch Bark Baskets (1999)

Contents

A NOTE ON DATES: The parenthetical year denotes the earliest draft completed by the respective author. When that information is not available, the earliest publication year is used. In some cases these dates do not indicate the actual year of composition. William Jones, for example, collected Ojibwe narratives more than a decade before the publication date.

1957–2001

2001–2017

Foreword

Thomas Lynch

When I was a boy, I went with my dad to take a body home for burial. It was 1957. I was nine. My brother, Dan, riding shotgun, had just turned eleven. I remember the long drive sitting between them. We were headed for a place called the Keweenaw Peninsula.

My dad had been doing some trade embalming to supplement his income as the licensed man of a Romanian funeral director in Highland Park, a job he took when he came home from the war, after he'd been to mortuary school on the GI Bill. One thing always led to another, and my dad was taking the trip up to the U.P. for Noah Potti, who did all the Finnish and Swedish funerals in Detroit, many of them transplants from that far country.

The boy in the box in the back of the car—a Plymouth station wagon with blackened windows—had been the worst case that Noah had ever seen. "Split his face down the middle with a thirty-aught-six, the poor client, over a girl, of all things," he told my dad when he called him. "Still, his people insist on seeing him." He'd done it out at the Finnish camp on Loon Lake in Wixom and lay in that June heat for a couple of days before anyone thought to check on him. He'd been drinking and threatening his fellow campers for days before laying himself out on the bed, taking the gun barrel into his mouth and pulling the trigger with his big toe. I'm thinking my father gave me these details in age-appropriate doses, over the years, the narrative accreting over time like ice shards shoving themselves ashore until a story becomes frozen in memory.

Noah had hired my dad to drive the poor client up to Copper Harbor for graveside services and burial. The Lutherans had had a funeral for him downstate, but he was to be taken back to the family plot in Houghton or Hancock for military honors and burial. My dad was to read a psalm, say amen and nod to the honor guard, who'd do taps and fold the flag and do three rifle volleys more or less in unison much the same as Native Americans shot arrows in the air over their dead to keep malevolent spirits away. The downstate pastor had written out Psalm 51 for my father to say to the assembled. It all seemed easy enough, and the pay was good. In addition to the mileage and per diem and his professional fee, he'd get the little stipend for the clergy stand-in for the graveside service. And he'd make a little vacation out of it, early in June as it was. He took Dan and me out of school and brought us along for the ride, telling our mother to tell the nun that we'd learn more on the road trip than we would in school.

I can still see him astraddle the crapper in the riverside cabin in Indian River, reciting the scripture in hopes that he'd have it by heart in time. "Create in me a pure heart, O God, and renew a steadfast spirit within me."

ON WE WENT PAST TOPINABEE AND CHEBOYGAN, UP THE STRAITS Highway to the State Dock at Mackinaw City, where we waited with other pilgrims for the ferry to make the crossing. The town was packed out with workers building the bridge that would span the four-mile divide between Michigan's Lower and Upper Peninsulas.

There was a sense, in that decade after the war, there at the tip of the mitt, that we all stood on the brink of a future where no expanse or expense could keep us from our American dream. We'd won the war, bombed the Germans and the Japanese out of competition with the Motor City and the arsenal of democracy. Factories that had turned out tanks and dozers, bombers and Corsairs, were cranking out new Chryslers and Caddies, Lincolns and Fords. Everything looked like rocket ships—bright chrome and fins and flashy parts. Even the dead wagon glistened in the bright sun, hot and humid, waiting in line.

Out on the water we could see the ferryboat, *Vacationland,* which worked the Straits between Mackinaw City and St. Ignace, coming and going with its cargo. When it opened its great jaws and stuck out its tongue, dozens of cars and trucks were disgorged from the dark interior for their onward journeys south. Then the northbound pilgrims drove forward, parking bumper to bumper in rows.

Once parked, we went up to the deck and counted seagulls and looked at the islands, Bois Blanc to the east, and Mackinac with the white patch of the Grand Hotel. In the distance was the edge of the U.P., to which none of us had ever been.

"Why do they call them Yoopers?" I asked my father, "instead of Uppers?" He hadn't a clue.

OUR MOTHER'S PEOPLE CAME FROM UP THERE: NANA AND POP O'HARA. She was Marvel Grace from Munising and he was Pat O'Hara from Manistique. They'd met in Ann Arbor, where she was studying music and he played clarinet in the marching band. It was late in the gay and gilded age that bridged the gap between their births and matriculations. They married in 1917 and remained downstate to make their futures and raise their family.

Except for the three weeks she'd allow him in the fall to go hunting and fishing back up at his camp near Kitch-iti-Kipi, the "Mirror of Heaven," he spent the rest of his days in Detroit living the abstemious, respectable life of the paterfamilias.

He'd return from these adventures to regale us with stories of excess and peril, ferocity and serenity, stargazing and moon-shadows. I remember still this aspect of the man, my grandfather—though he died when I was not yet four, at an age years younger than I am now—that the real him, his authentic self, bided in a mysterious place that hovered over the life he lived in southeastern lower Michigan; that his real voice, his primal, wild being stalked the woods and rivers, beaches and scrub acres of his Yooper boyhood, where what Walt Whitman and Robin Williams called his "barbaric yawp" still echoes and to which the bridge we saw them building that summer of '57 promised easier access in the sparkling future.

As bridges do.

KEITH TAYLOR AND I ARE AT THE DAM SITE INN ON THE MAPLE RIVER in the Pellston Plain. It is early August, and the bright blue heat of the day is cooling into the sumptuous light of northern Michigan; gold finches and hummingbirds at the feeders, round bales of silage baking in the meadows, sweet corn coming to markets, peaches.

After the radish and green onion relish tray, after the coleslaw and side salad course, they bring the platter of chicken, noodles, mashed spuds, and peas, whereupon we fall into our earnest gobbling, counting the blessings of another Michigan summer, not least among them this breaking bread, this companionship, we two old pals, if not fully retired, still not required elsewhere for anything anytime soon, like a run-on sentence we pray never to end.

For years now we've found ourselves on the south end of our respective lakes, at the north end of the Lower Peninsula, proximate enough for such repasts and colloquies.

Keith spends his summers at the U of M Biological Station on Douglas Lake teaching scientists how to write in a way such that ordinary humans can make sense of their esoterica.

His desk allows a view of the water in all its moods and incarnations. His poem "Upper Peninsula Fires," in this anthology, was written there, in his pale green lakefront cabin, that August a decade ago, when the Sleeper Lake fire burned bog and forest for most of the month up in Newberry and sent the breath of its disaster south of the Straits to waft in the nostrils of the poet-naturalist who wrote: "A hundred miles north the forest is burning."

"What," I asked Keith betwixt the drumsticks and thighs, "What do you know about Stellanova Osborn?" I was trying to stump your man with the name of a poet I'd only myself lately heard from Amy Moore, a filmmaker I'd met in the library on Mackinaw Island.

Keith is surely one of Michigan's most bookish men—a sort of wiki-Keith, whose research, curiosity, and the hold his brain box keeps on anything he places there for safekeeping makes him perfect company for a long road trip or walk in the woods or chicken dinner. But Stellanova Osborn was a new star, and the story of her romance with the only governor from Michigan's Upper Peninsula seemed like a movie waiting to be made, whence, I suppose, Amy Moore's deep interest. Chase Salmon Osborn was sixty-five and Stella was thirty when they met in 1924. He was going ninety when he died two days after they married.

In the library on the island, Amy Moore has read Stellanova's poems in *Here: Women Writing on Michigan's Upper Peninsula*, Ron Riekki's companion anthology to this one. The voices that volume returned to life, like those made audible by this one, are essential to the singular peninsula they reference or hail from.

A BOOK BROUGHT INTO BEING, LIKE A BRIDGE TO A MYSTERIOUS PLACE, offers us access to voices stilled by time or disinterest or obscurity.

Which is why Keith Taylor knew what there is to be known about Stellanova Osborn.

"I have a book of her poems I'll be happy to loan you," he told me, and we agreed to drive north to Sault Ste. Marie in the morning, take the short ferry ride across to Sugar Island and drive to its narrow southern end where the three-thousand-acre bequest of Chase Salmon Osborn to the University of Michigan surrounds the graves of the governor and his bride not far from the cottage ruins and derelict library where they watched the summers come and go on Duck Island and the St. Mary's River.

TWILIGHT MIRROR

The moon and the evening star
Peer over the alder's shoulder
And even the littlest clouds
Are admiring themselves in the water.

(from *Summer Songs on the St. Marys*, by Stellanova Osborn)

The U.P. occupies a space in our imaginative geography beyond the pale of the open palm of our habitation.

My mother's father and his stories of black bear and gray wolves, brown trout and bald eagles and bottomless springs of freshwater churning, of ghost towns, mystery spots, copper miners and barroom brawlers, still haunt me now, beckoning from the rich hinterland of imagination we Michiganders share.

In the 1830s the Toledo Strip with its harbor at the mouth of the Maumee River seemed worth fighting for and the distant country beyond the Straits of Mackinaw, the province of Anishinaabe and white pine, a place of such unspeakable desolation that nineteenth-century folks felt they were getting the short end of the deal when they settled for it in trade for statehood.

They'd be proven wrong, of course, as rich deposits of copper and iron ore, comingled with the great natural waterways and standing timber, produced a frontier of prospects that attracted Finlanders and Swedes, Irish and Cornishmen and women to bide with and breed with the indigenous tribes so that we soon knew the joke was on the Ohioans.

The poems and stories, essays and oddments gathered here are rich with the arc of our peninsulas' becoming—from camp to coastline, village and town—the singular place that it remains in Michigan's geography and imagination.

So, these are thanks and here is to acknowledge the debt we all owe to Ron Riekki and MSU Press, for collaborating on this well-wrought bridge, transport and metaphor across a century—this access to voices old and new, living and dead, hovering overhead and under the radar from that mysterious yoop we're all connected to.

1917–1957

nthologies share a secret held as close to the vest as a royal flush. In a treasured splay of stories and poems, the first part of *And Here* gives us tantalizing glimpses of that ancient mystery.

"Now Great-Lynx" thrums so deeply in our chests we swear it's the hard beat of knucklebones cast in a game of chance. The Great-Lynx lives as something in dire need of killing, and, after the storyteller teaches us a few facts about that truth, we notice how the story ends. *That is all.* But, as soon as those three words are out of the storyteller's mouth, we're quite sure he winks at us. Did you notice? Before we can give his wink much thought, Sarett talks to us about graves. "Copper bones tossed in a hole." Death surely stands as the ultimate end.

Then that wily Hemingway thrusts us into the small town of Hortons Bay. And here, five houses live and breathe. Five-card draw. He leaves Jim asleep on the dock—story over—but as we learn in his poems that follow, Hemingway isn't always so good with a poker face. "They must have ended somewhere." Ha! Hear his doubt?

Walker's *Fireweed* brings us to 1934, and here she tells us about the end of things, especially the end of trees and of iron ore. Now that's a poker face. In *Loon Feather*, Fuller takes up the same theme, but she adds a sly contradiction.

"For the wash of the waves on the pebbles is something that . . . will always be." Then Niedecker, 1950, reminds us "we can always play."

And finally here, we understand a secret that trumps all others, whispered to us by the glorious amalgam we call the anthology. No story well told ever ends. *That is all.*

—*Sue Harrison*

1918

The Blue Duck: A Chippewa Medicine Dance (excerpt)

Lew R. Sarett

Hi'! Hi! Hi'! Hi! Hi'! Hi! Hi'! Hi!
Hee'-ya! Hoi'-ya! Hee'-ya! Hoi'-ya!　　*Faster and louder*
Keetch'-ie, Má-ni-dó, Má-ni-dó　　*—with abandon*
I place this pretty duck upon your hand;
Upon its sunny palm and in its windy fingers.
Hi-yee! Blue and beautiful is he, beautifully blue;
Carved from sleeping cedar
When the stars like silver fishes
Were a-quiver in the rivers of the sky;
Carved from dripping cedar
When the Koo'-koo-koo' dashed hooting
At the furtive feet that rustled in the leaves,
And seasoned many moons, many moons!—
Ho! seasoned many, many, many sleeps!
Hi-yee! Blue and beautiful is he, beautifully blue.
Though his throat is choked with timber,
And he honks not on his pole,
And his wings are weak with hunger,
Yet his heart is plenty good!
Hi-yee! Hi-yee! His heart is plenty good, plenty good!

Hi-yee! Hi-yee! Hi-yee! His heart is good!

My heart like his is good!

Ugh! My tongue is straight!

Ho!

Ho!

1919

Now Great-Lynx

William Jones

LONG AGO PEOPLE OFTEN USED TO SEE SOMETHING IN PLACES, ESPE-
cially where the current was swift. The people feared it; and that was the reason
of their practice of sometimes throwing offerings to it into the water, even
tobacco. Now, once yonder, at what is called Shallow-Water, was where some
women were once passing by in a canoe. Accordingly there happened to rise
a mighty current of water, nearly were they capsized; exceedingly frightened
were they. While they were paddling with all their might, they saw the tail
of a Great-Lynx come up out of the water; all flung themselves up into the
forward end of the canoe in their fright. Now, one of the women that was
there saw that the canoe was going to sink; accordingly, when she had gone
to the stern, she raised the paddle in order to strike the tail of Great-Lynx.
And this she said: "While I was young, often did I fast. It was then that the
Thunderers gave me their war-club." Thereupon, when she struck the tail of
Great-Lynx, she then broke the tail of Great-Lynx in two. Thereupon up to the
surface rose the canoe, after which they then started on their way paddling;
and so they were saved.

Now, one of the women was seized by Great-Lynx. Therefore she it was
who had told at home that Great-Lynx was continually harassing the people.
And though the master of the Great-Lynxes would always speak to his son,
saying, "Do not plague the people," yet he would never listen to his father.

Once, yonder at the Sault, together in a body were the people living.
Once against a certain wigwam was leaned a child bound to a cradle-board;

and then the child was missed from that place. They saw the sign of the cradle-board where it had been dragged along in the sand. Thereupon they heard the voice of the child crying beneath a rugged hill. Even though the people made offerings in the hope that Great-Lynx might set the child free, even though for a long while they besought him with prayers, yet he would not let it go. So at length the people said that therefore they might as well slay Great-Lynx. Accordingly they began digging straight for the place from whence the sound of the child could be heard. And after a while they had a hole dug to the den of Great-Lynx. They saw water coming in and out (like the tide). It was true that even then they spoke kindly to Great-Lynx, yet he would not let the child go. Still yet they could hear the voice (of the child) crying. Accordingly they said: "Therefore let us dig to where he is, that we may kill him."

Truly they dug after him, following him up. By and by out came the cradle-board floating on the water, together with the child that was bound to it. And when they caught hold of the cradle-board, they observed that the child had a hole crushed into its head; Great-Lynx must have slain it. Thereupon they followed him up, digging after him; and one man that was famed for his strength said that he would kill Great-Lynx. When drawing upon him, as they dug after him, round towards them turned Great-Lynx. Thereupon him struck he who said that he would kill (Great-Lynx). Sure enough, he slew him.

And when they pulled him out, they saw that his tail was cut off. That was the one that had been struck at Shallow-Water; by a woman with an oar had he been struck.

That was what happened. Only not long ago was seen the place where the people had once dug the hole; (it is) over toward the Big-Knife country, over by the Sault.

That is all.

Beat Against Me No Longer

Lew R. Sarett/Lone Caribou

A Chippewa Love Song

Ai-yee! my Yellow-Bird-Woman,
My né-ne—moosh, ai-yee! my Loved-One,
Be not afraid of my eyes!
Beat against me no longer;
Come! Come with a yielding of limbs.
Ai-yee! woman, woman,
Trembling there in the teepee
Like the doe in the season of rutting,
Why foolishly fearest thou me?
Beat against me no longer!
Be not afraid of my eyes!
Cast the strange doubts from thy bosom!
Be not as the flat-breasted squaw-sich
Who feels the first womanly yearnings
And hides, by the law of our people,
Alone three sleeps in the forest;
Be not as that brooding young maiden
Who wanders forlorn in the cedars,
And slumbers with troubled dreams,
To awaken suddenly, fearing

The hot throbbing blood in her bosom,
The strange eager life in her limbs.
Ai-yee! foolish one, woman,
Cast the strange fears from thy heart!
Wash the red shame from thy face!
Be not afraid of my glances!

Be as the young silver birch
In the Moon-of-the-Green-Growing-Grasses—
Who sings with the thrill of the sap
As it leaps to the south wind's caresses;
Who yields her rain-swollen buds
To the kiss of the sun with glad dancing.
Be as the cool tranquil moon
Who flings off her silver-blue blanket
To bare her white breast to the pine;
Who walks through the many-eyed night
In her gleaming white nudeness
With proud eyes that will not look down.
Be as the sun in her glory,
Who dances across the blue day,
And flings her red soul, fierce-burning,
Into the arms of the twilight.
Ai-yee! foolish one, woman,
Be as the sun and the moon!
Cast the strange doubts from thy bosom!
Wash the red shame from thy face!
Thou art a woman, a woman!
Beat against me no longer!
Be not afraid of my eyes!

1920

The Electric Giant

William Paris Potter

A mighty giant cleft the air
O'er chasms broad and dark and deep;
His fiery tongue hissing, sissing—
Red lightning writing on the clouds;
His booming voice rising, falling
O'er vale and hill in Titan roar;
Peal on peal in tones of steel
That set the brain in dizzy whirl!
But science tamed this giant old,
Bold demon of the earth and sky,
That rushing rivers hide and hold,
To turn the wheels of commerce wide
And blaze on cities' great white way,
Undimmed by clouds that gather near—
A messenger from earth to sky,
To cross the ocean dark and drear!
Lo! Like God's scepter set on high,
Its light is dazzling to the eye;
Its Titan power moves the world:
To air above the dimming earth—
Beneath the deep and heaving sea;

From the Land of the Midnight Sun
Afar to land of tropic heat,
Our wireless messenger now goes!

1921

The Box of God (excerpt)

Lew R. Sarett/Lone Caribou

III: TALKING WATERS

Of eagle whose whistling wings have known the lift
Of high mysterious hands, and the wild sweet music
Of big winds among the ultimate stars,
The black-robes put you in a box of God,
Seeking in honest faith and holy zeal
To lay upon your lips new songs, to swell
The chorus of amens and hallelujahs.
O bundle of copper bones tossed in a hole,
Here in the place-of-death—God's-fenced-in-ground!—
Beneath these put-in-pines and waxen lilies,
They placed you in a crimson gash in the hillside,
Here on a bluff above the Sleepy-eye,
Where the Baptism River, mumbling among the canyons,
Shoulders its flood through crooning waterfalls
In a mist of wafted foam fragile as petals
Of windflowers blowing across the green of April;
Where ghosts of wistful leaves go floating up
In the rustling blaze of autumn, like silver smokes
Slenderly twisting among the thin blue winds;
Here in the great gray arms of Mont du Père,
Where the shy arbutus, the mink, and the Johnny-jump-up

Huddle and whisper of a long, long winter;
Where stars, with soundless feet, come trooping up
To dance to the water-drums of white cascades—
Where stars, like little children, go singing down
The sky to the flute of the wind in the willow-tree—
Somebody—somebody's there . . . O Pagan Joe . . .
Can't you see Him? as He moves among the mountains?
Where dusk, dew-lidded, slips among the valleys
Soft as a blue wolf walking in thick wet moss?
Look!—my friend!—at the breast of Mont du Père! . . .
Sh-sh-sh-sh! . . . Don't you hear His talking waters? . . .
Soft in the gloom as broken butterflies
Hovering above a somber pool . . . Sh-sh-sh-sh!
Somebody's there . . . in the heart of Mont du Père . . .
Somebody—somebody's there, sleeping . . . sleeping . . .

Up in Michigan

Ernest Hemingway

JIM GILMORE CAME TO HORTONS BAY FROM CANADA. HE BOUGHT the blacksmith shop from old man Horton. Jim was short and dark with big mustaches and big hands. He was a good horseshoer and did not look much like a blacksmith even with his leather apron on. He lived upstairs above the blacksmith shop and took his meals at A.J. Smith's.[1]

Liz Coates worked for Smith's. Mrs. Smith, who was a very large clean woman, said Liz Coates was the neatest girl she'd ever seen. Liz had good legs and always wore clean gingham aprons and Jim noticed that her hair was always neat behind. He liked her face because it was so jolly but he never thought about her.

Liz liked Jim very much. She liked the way he walked over from the shop and often went to the kitchen door to watch for him to start down the road. She liked it about his mustache. She liked it about how white his teeth were when he smiled. She liked it very much that he didn't look like a blacksmith. She liked it how much A.J. Smith and Mrs. Smith liked Jim. One day she found that she liked it the way the hair was black on his arms and how white they were above the tanned line when he washed up in the washbasin outside the house. Liking that made her feel funny.

Hortons Bay, the town, was only five houses on the main road between Boyne City and Charlevoix. There was the general store and post office with

---

1. Based on edits made by Hemingway, Scribner's *The Complete Short Stories of Ernest Hemingway* refers to "D.J." throughout, but the original 1923 version uses "A.J." I use the original version here.

a high false front and maybe a wagon hitched out in front, Smith's house, Stroud's house, Fox's house, Horton's house and Van Hoosen's house. The houses were in a big grove of elm trees and the road was very sandy. There was farming country and timber each way up the road. Up the road a ways was the Methodist church and down the road the other direction was the township school. The blacksmith shop was painted red and faced the school.

A steep sandy road ran down the hill to the bay through the timber. From Smith's back door you could look out across the woods that ran down to the lake and across the bay. It was very beautiful in the spring and summer, the sky blue and bright and usually whitecaps on the lake beyond the point from the breeze blowing in from Charlevoix and Lake Michigan. From Smith's back door Liz could see ore barges way out in the lake going toward Boyne City. When she looked at them they didn't seem to be moving at all but if she went in and dried some more dishes and then came out again they would be out of sight beyond the point.

All the time now Liz was thinking about Jim Gilmore. He didn't seem to notice her much. He talked about the shop to A.J. Smith and about the Republican Party and about James G. Blaine. In the evenings he read *The Toledo Blade* and the Grand Rapids paper by the lamp in the front room or went out spearing fish in the bay with a jacklight with A.J. Smith. In the fall he and Smith and Charley Wyman took a wagon and tent, grubs, axes, their rifles and two dogs and went on a trip to the pine plains beyond Vanderbilt deer hunting. Liz and Mrs. Smith were cooking for four days for them before they started. Liz wanted to make something special for Jim to take but she didn't finally because she was afraid to ask Mrs. Smith for the eggs and flour and afraid if she bought them Mrs. Smith would catch her cooking. It would have been all right with Mrs. Smith but Liz was afraid.

All the time Jim was gone on the deer hunting trip Liz thought about him. It was awful while he was gone. She couldn't sleep well from thinking about him but she discovered it was fun to think about him too. If she let herself go it was better. The night before they were to come back she didn't sleep at all, that is she didn't think she slept because it was all mixed up in a dream about not sleeping and really not sleeping. When she saw the wagon coming down the road she felt weak and sick sort of inside. She couldn't wait till she saw Jim and it seemed as though everything would be all right when he came. The wagon stopped outside under the big elm and Mrs. Smith and Liz went out. All the men had beards and there were three deer in the back of the wagon, their thin legs sticking stiff over the edge of the wagon box. Mrs. Smith kissed Alonzo and he hugged her. Jim said "Hello, Liz," and grinned. Liz hadn't known just what would happen when Jim got back but she was sure it would be something. Nothing had happened. The men were just home, that was all. Jim pulled the burlap sacks off the deer and Liz looked at them. One was a big buck. It was stiff and hard to lift out of the wagon.

"Did you shoot it, Jim?" Liz asked.

"Yeah. Ain't it a beauty?" Jim got it onto his back to carry it to the smokehouse.

That night Charley Wyman stayed to supper at Smith's. It was too late to get back to Charlevoix. The men washed up and waited in the front room for supper.

"Ain't there something left in that crock, Jimmy?" A.J. Smith asked, and Jim went out to the wagon in the barn and fetched in the jug of whiskey the men had taken hunting with them. It was a four-gallon jug and there was quite a little slopped back and forth in the bottom. Jim took a long pull on his way back to the house. It was hard to lift such a big jug up to drink out of it. Some of the whiskey ran down on his shirt front. The two men smiled when Jim came in with the jug. A.J. Smith sent for glasses and Liz brought them. A.J. poured out three big shots.

"Well, here's looking at you, A.J.," said Charley Wyman.

"That damn big buck Jimmy," said A.J.

"Here's all the ones we missed, A.J.," said Jim, and downed his liquor.

"Tastes good to a man."

"Nothing like it this time of year for what ails you."

"How about another, boys?"

"Here's how, A.J."

"Down the creek boys."

"Here's to next year."

Jim began to feel great. He loved the taste and the feel of whisky. He was glad to be back to a comfortable bed and warm food and the shop. He had another drink. The men came in to supper feeling hilarious but acting very respectable. Liz sat at the table after she put on the food and ate with the family. It was a good dinner. The men ate seriously. After supper they went into the front room again and Liz cleaned off with Mrs. Smith. Then Mrs. Smith went upstairs and pretty soon Smith came out and went upstairs too. Jim and Charley were still in the front room. Liz was sitting in the kitchen next to the stove pretending to read a book and thinking about Jim. She didn't want to go to bed yet because she knew Jim would be coming out and she wanted to see him as he went out so she could take the way he looked up to bed with her.

She was thinking about him hard and then Jim came out. His eyes were shining and his hair was a little rumpled. Liz looked down at her book. Jim came over back of her chair and stood there and she could feel him breathing and then he put his arms around her. Her breasts felt plump and firm and the nipples were erect under his hands. Liz was terribly frightened, no one had ever touched her, but she thought, "He's come to me finally. He's really come."

She held herself stiff because she was so frightened and did not know anything else to do and then Jim held her tight against the chair and kissed her. It was such a sharp, aching, hurting feeling that she thought she couldn't stand it. She felt Jim right through the back of the chair and she couldn't stand it and then something clicked inside of her and the feeling was warmer and softer. Jim held her tight hard against the chair and she wanted it now and Jim whispered, "Come on for a walk."

Liz took her coat off the peg on the kitchen wall and they went out the door. Jim had his arm around her and every little way they stopped and pressed against each other and Jim kissed her. There was no moon and they walked ankle deep in the sandy road through the trees down to the dock and the warehouse on the bay. The water was lapping in the piles and the point was dark across the bay. It was cold but Liz was hot all over from being with

Jim. They sat down in the shelter of the warehouse and Jim pulled Liz close to him. She was frightened. One of Jim's hands went inside her dress and stroked over her breast and the other hand was in her lap. She was very frightened and didn't know how he was going to go about things but she snuggled close to him. Then the hand that felt so big in her lap went away and was on her leg and started to move up it.

"Don't, Jim," Liz said. Jim slid the hand further up.

"You musn't, Jim. You musn't." Neither Jim nor Jim's big hand paid any attention to her.

The boards were hard. Jim had her dress up and was trying to do something to her. She was frightened but she wanted it. She had to have it but it frightened her.

"You musn't do it Jim. You musn't."

"I got to. I'm going to. You know we got to."

"No we haven't Jim. We ain't got to. Oh it isn't right. Oh it's so big and it hurts so. You can't. Oh Jim. Jim. Oh."

The hemlock planks of the dock were hard and splintery and cold and Jim was heavy on her and he had hurt her. Liz pushed him, she was so uncomfortable and cramped. Jim was asleep. He wouldn't move. She worked out from under him and sat up and straightened her skirt and coat and tried to do something with her hair. Jim was sleeping with his mouth a little open. Liz leaned over and kissed him on the cheek. He was still asleep. She lifted his head a little and shook it. He rolled his head over and swallowed. Liz started to cry. She walked over to the edge of the dock and looked down to the water. There was a mist coming up from the bay. She was cold and miserable and everything felt gone. She walked back to where Jim was lying and shook him once more to make sure. She was crying.

"Jim" she said. "Jim. Please Jim."

Jim stirred and curled a little tighter. Liz took off her coat and leaned over and covered him with it. She tucked it around him neatly and carefully. Then she walked across the dock and up the steep sandy road to go to bed. A cold mist was coming up through the woods from the bay.

Anishinabeg in the Cranberry Swamp

Janet Lewis

Autumn bows
The headed grass
With frost
And narrowed stem. Hoarfrost
Has rutted the swamp.

Their baskets fill
With berries green as water,
Their fingers cut
With searching the hard grass.

Boats gather
At the point of land,
Deep hulls
Beneath the swing
Of wide red sails.

They beg old quilts
And blankets,
Wake at morning
Frost from hip to shoulder
Like morning mist.

1922

The Wife of Manibozho Sings

Janet Lewis

He comes and goes;
There is no rest
While he is here
Or gone.

I cannot say
That his feet have pressed
The leaves
He was standing on.

He comes and goes
And the maple leaves
Lie still
Under the sun.

The Indians in the Woods

Janet Lewis

Ah, the woods, the woods
Where small things
Are distinct and visible,

The berry plant,
The berry leaf, remembered
Line for line.

There are three figures
Walking in the woods
Whose feet press down
Needle and leaf and vine.

1922

The Old Woman Alone

Janet Lewis

The Grandmother picks her way
Among the stones, the stones.
She passes deer.

Upon brown flanks
The balsam needles fall.

Ah, stranger than a deer
Caught in the open sunlight,
The old woman.

1923

Along with Youth

Ernest Hemingway

A porcupine skin,
Stiff with bad tanning,
It must have ended somewhere.
Stuffed horned owl
Pompous
Yellow eyed;
Chuck-wills-widow on a biassed twig
Sooted with dust.
Piles of old magazines,
Drawers of boy's letters
And the line of love
They must have ended somewhere.
Yesterday's Tribune is gone
Along with youth
And the canoe that went to pieces on the beach
The year of the big storm
When the hotel burned down
At Seney, Michigan.

1923

Chapter Heading

Ernest Hemingway

For we have thought the longer thoughts
 And gone the shorter way.
And we have danced to devils' tunes,
 Shivering home to pray;
To serve one master in the night,
 Another in the day.

Fireweed (excerpt)

Mildred Walker

THE TALL WHITE PINE, SMOOTH AND WHITE-FIBERED, FIRST BROUGHT men to that piece of Michigan that juts out into Lake Superior. It is a state in itself, that higher piece, divided from the greater part of the state by the Strait of Mackinac. Michigan sprawls on the map like a hand and the upper peninsula hangs above it, always a little out of reach.

It was still the west when the lumberjacks of Maine and New Hampshire shouldered their belongings and tramped towards it. They had heard of white pine for the taking, close to the rivers and lakes, forests of it, miles upon miles, in the virgin timber lands of upper Michigan. Since the Indian days, only the French Canadian had blazed trails through these green solitudes. Only a few fishermen had tried the shore. They had left their nets to dry on the bright, white sand; left them to rot with the years, sometimes, and gone to know the cruelty of the clear, blue lake.

It was called frontier when the tales of Paul Bunyan were in the making across the shanty stoves of the lumber camps. Men wrestled with the strength of the tall, green giants; sinews of flesh with sinews of timber. Men's hands were covered with pitch, and barked and calloused from shoving the logs along. All day, the resin ran from the trees like blood. The white fibers strained and twisted and gave. Each day's sun found a wider clearing in the forest's gloom. At night, the lumberjacks went back to their shacks hungry as the wolves that watched their camp fires. Dark came down in the woods and the silent snowflakes dropped, dropped, dropped. They had stumps to cover and green boughs heaped in funeral piles.

Lumber . . . more lumber, for the new towns of the west; for ships and trains and new saloons! The saws worked faster. The logs piled up. The sunny clearing in the forest grew. But there is an end to all things, even the riches of the north country. The white pine fell, tree after tree, acre after acre, in one great massacre. The logs slipped well over the deep packed snows to the river bank. Day after day of winter, the saws kept working, the logs piled up.

Winter came to an end in the country north of the straits. The ice cracked, the rivers flowed free, only to be clogged by that great avalanche of logs, bobbing, bumping, floating down to the mills in the great spring drives. Doughty men rode the logs down the river. The lumberjacks tramped in from the camps to the nearest center, hungry for whisky, for women, for spending. Millions were made by men who moved down to the populous places of the state, or on to the further west where there was still white pine for the taking. The lumberjacks followed wherever there was ready pay at the end of the long winter's run. The tales of Bunyan reached to Oregon and Washington.

A lull came over the upper peninsula, an intermission in the drama of the north country. The sound of the saws was stilled. The hardwoods grew taller. Ground pine and alders and jack pine covered over the scars of the forest. Then again came the cry: lumber, more lumber; hardwood now, for fashionable mansions and polished bars, for chairs and chiffoniers. Back came the lumberjacks, for the hardwoods after the pine. The saws were at work again, but their way was harder now; maple and hickory and oak are tougher than the soft pine fibers. The men had to sit down on the old pine stumps to get their breath. Sweat flowed freely even when the breath floated white in the winter air. Many a walking boss coming upon the stumps of the white pine, left by that greedy and wasteful generation, whistled enviously. The lumberjacks were back, but they were mostly foreigners now. Paul Bunyan had to hold his own with the giants of Swedish and German and Finnish lore. Cursing in strange dialects was heard through the woods as the saws grated against a knot in the timber's heart or the skidder logs were snagged on a root.

The trains took the great logs. The mills came closer to the woods in the piece of upper Michigan men called the sticks. Towns grew around the mills and only the crazy or those fresh from the old country worked out in the camps anymore. A sensible Swede who had been here awhile, or a good German who liked a garden, found him a wife and lived in the mill town now. A few of the old sort, Black Jack Morris and Oliver Adams, who lumbered the white pine off the same piece thirty years before, could still pull a saw with twice the skill of the greenhorn "furriners." The lumber camp was in their blood, but their generation had gone with the white pine and the blazes of the old trappers' trails.

These latter years, things are different in the north country. The walking boss drives out to the very beginning of the fresh cutting in a Ford car. There are engines and pulleys to lift the great logs. The radio blares the latest Broadway hit in the heart of the woods. The lumber shacks are freight cars run in on tracks. The hungry wolves gaze wondering at the holes men make and slink farther north. Only cold and danger and the smell of the woods and the fall of the white snow and the bound of a deer are the same.

Timber is growing scarce. But men have steel now for trains and skyscrapers and even for chiffoniers and chairs. The veins of iron in the country beyond the straits have done their share. The beehive furnaces have melted that iron to steel. The country of the sticks looks less majestic, shorn of so many of its tall trees; naked in places except for jack pine and alders and paper poplars. Bad fires have cut a wide swath, too. Rich men, up for the hunting, talk of buying up a hundred acres and plowing it under, but at the end of the hunting season, they drive back in their big cars, content with the country if a buck is strung along the side, and leave the burned-over land of the upper peninsula to squirrels and beavers and deer and fox, and, here and there, a town. Where the roots of the tall trees are charred into the earth, a wild weed springs up. A pretty weed, it is, with a spire of violet pink blossoms, fragile-looking but sturdy at the roots. One old lumberjack said he'd seen it on the roadsides in Maine; fireweed, they called it there.

Real towns have grown up; three, five—not big as towns are counted below the straits, but large enough to hold a lumber baron's fortune in their real estate or the railway station for the ore cars, headed south and west and east. Back in, or up along the lake edge, here and there, a mill still saws the logs the trains bring in; not sufficient in itself these days, but subsidized by some great industry. The towns still squat around the saw mill; Pointe Platte, Grand River and Sacuenay, surviving eighteen, twenty years, some of them.

Pointe Platte, as it was on the old maps, Flat Point now, lies close to Superior, there where the shore juts out in a wide curve and then swings in again to make a bay. It was a man's town, first, with only a mill and a bunk house. Then the camp cook brought his wife; a big Swede, Sven Svenson, brought a blue-eyed woman he called Hanna. The lumber company built a street of houses up from the mill. One day, a baby was born in the Point. Men came to work in the mill who had never worked in the woods: millwrights and saw-filers, men who knew trades. Good Swedish names, Henderson, Bernsen, and Findarson: good German names, Schmitz and Schultz and Heinrich, were carried on and intermingled. French Canadians and Finns came drifting in and families from older towns where the lumber was running thin. Another street spread up the hill with twenty box-like, flimsy houses.

Now, a second generation has grown up in this small town. The Hendersons have a daughter, Celie; Lin Linsen has a son, Joe. There is a school and a company hospital and a Catholic church. Life is different, shorn of its need for pioneers. It is neither so hard nor so bare, lived closer to the few large towns, connected by flivvers and radios to the current of things. The "giants of the earth," the tall trees, are almost run out. The new generation, like the fireweed, spreads over the country of the sticks in their place.

The life, lived here between the great lake and the thinning timber lands, so close to town and yet so far, is a curious passionate growth, an epic struggle, unseen, unsung. All summer, and through the fall, there comes the persistent low music of the wind and the lake going on above the noise of the town, never quite drowned out, yet altered by it, taking from it some human cadence of tragedy and courage. Winter comes, and the music of the wind rises until it shrieks above the town like an ancient curse, malevolent and unearthly. The town is blocked off from the world by snow except for a single plowed road. On the edge of the great lake, ice-blocks wall it around like a prison camp and the life around the mill is thrown in on itself.

But, today, the snow in Flat Point was melting. The high walls of snow that lined the board walks down the three streets of the town were streaked with dirt and rounded and humpy like stone walls. The walks were slippery. In places, the heavy gold-seal boots of the men on their way to the mill had tramped the snow bare to the boards.

Celie Henderson's high-heeled opera pumps dug soft little holes in the softer snow of the walks and left no trace where there was still ice to slide along. March is a bad month underfoot in the towns along Lake Superior. But still it was March, and Celie Henderson had kicked her galoshes off in the woodshed with the first mild weather and was not to be snared into wearing them unless fresh snow fell. Celie Henderson always wore opera pumps. When the lumberjacks went clumping past with three pairs of woolen socks in their shoe-packs, and Celie's mother, thrifty Mrs. Old Henderson, wore thick stockings of her own knitting, Celie pulled on chiffon hose that might be half or all rayon but still were sheer, and slipped into her opera pumps.

"You spend half the money you make on your shoes," Mrs. Henderson complained, but Celie would smooth the light braids around her head and laugh.

"Two ninety-five isn't so much. That's all these cost!" Celie would point her toe in its short-vamped patent leather pump and shiny black heel. It was a pretty foot.

This morning, Celie's patent leather pumps carried her swiftly down to the rambling barn of a company store shortly after seven-thirty. They trod lightly on the long board steps of the store stoop. Celie went eagerly enough. Her introduction to life was there in the barny room with its foodstuffs and merchandise. All the world of Flat Point traded there. Even those who sent large orders to "Sears and Monkey Wards" to beat the company's profit had, at least, bread and eggs and occasional pork chops to buy. Anyone might lean over the counter and smile into Celie's young face. Men from the city who came up to hunt at deer season stopped in to buy provisions and often paid Celie compliments. Someday, they might need an extra girl in the office next door, who knew? Pretty Celie Henderson was there to watch her chances.

Already, this morning, Baldy, the stoop-shouldered old Finn, was bringing out the boxes of potatoes and turnips. Mr. Simpson, who ran the store for the company, was unlocking the candy counter and bread case. Mrs. Munsen was flicking a feather duster carelessly over the yard goods and toilet articles on the other side of the store in a superior way. Celie was supposed to stay over by the canned goods and vegetables, but sometimes she wandered over to Mrs. Munsen's side. Anybody could tell that was more her line than cornmeal and malt and prunes.

"'Lo, Baldy . . . Mis' Munsen."

She hung her coat and hat out where the girls from the office hung theirs. There was a wavy surfaced mirror on the wall. Celie powdered her nose and fluffed the hair out under her braid. She looked critically at her face. She was always too sleepy to see much in her mirror at home. She did have a "Garbo" look. Funny Joe didn't like Greta in the movies. He couldn't see that they were anything alike, either. "Doesn't have half the looks you have, Celie," he always said.

Celie twitched her belt in a practiced way. She could give an air to a $1.98 model by a simple twitch of her belt and a shrug of her shoulders. Satisfied, she walked smartly out on her high-heeled pumps to spend the next ten hours reaching and weighing and tying and charging up accounts on the company's charge slips.

Celie Henderson was quick. Old Mr. Quinn, the butcher, from down at the end with the meats, liked to hear her sharp, quick footsteps flying up and down back of the long counter. He looked up sometimes to see her light hair braided round like the girls back home in Sweden. She called him "butch," like the others, but with such a way to her, the name was a jolly thing. His clear blue eyes twinkled to hear her.

Celie had blue eyes. Real Swede eyes, her father said. They could grow dark with pity when she waited on Mrs. Daily the day after her man was crushed to death by a log down at the pond, or anger when one of the traveling Jew salesmen, who brought their samples periodically, "got smart." Or they could turn light blue like a child's when a little edge of fear crept into them. Celie Henderson had pretty eyes.

She was seventeen and had her height, a straight five feet six of it, with only a slight curve at the breast and hip. She could reach for the cereals on the next to the top shelf with easy grace while Mrs. Munsen was off to get a pole to hook them down.

"Bad walkin'," said Mr. Simpson, clinking his keys officially, "hope you had your gold-seal boots on, Celie."

Celie laughed and the sound of Celie's laughter in the store made old Mr. Quinn forget the sharp pain in his heart when he hefted the half of a side of beef onto the block.

"And how!" She extended her slim high-heeled foot to view.

Mrs. Konski wanted rice and yellow soap and onions. Celie rattled a paper bag open and poured the rice. The morning rush had commenced. The mill whistle blew the lunch hour at eleven-thirty, and eight o'clock was late to shop if you planned to have a pot roast or an Irish stew on for your man's dinner.

At eleven, there was a lull. Celie walked out to the front window by the cash register. Buddy Hefflin ran it. He lost a leg down at the mill and the company gave him the job on the stool in the cramped little box. Buddy Hefflin didn't care with Celie Henderson to look at. He hoarded any bits of gossip that he picked up on his trips to the office with his money-till to have the chance of talking to her. He had a sober Finnish face, but when he hissed mysteriously, "Hi, Celie!" his left eye squinted comically.

"Yea, Buddy, what's the hot dope?" Celie answered, leaning over the corner of the cigarette and tobacco case.

"The big gun's nephew is coming here. Goin' to learn the ropes and keep an eye on things for his uncle, they say." Buddy's face cracked into a humorous leer. "Won't he have a sweet time, though?"

Celie was interested. Anyone from the world beyond the straits was interesting. Anyone who belonged to the big shot was exciting. The big shot was Mr. Farley, administrative head of the Lake Superior Lumber Co. His word was law in Flat Point. He determined alike whether to repair the roof on house number 20 or run a night-shift at the mill.

"Yeah, an' d'you wanta know more?"

"Wait a sec, Buddy, there's little Bobby Irwin with a slip of paper."

Celie took a kerosene can from the small boy who stood in front of the counter and went back to a gloomy supply room to fill it from the large tank. Celie did it in a rush. She was afraid of rats in there, and Mr. Simpson always told her when he caught one or brought it out by the tail to make her scream.

". . . and two loaves of bread, and a pound of cheese, Bobby." She read from the crumpled slip in the little boy's fist.

Little Bobby Irwin rubbed the back of his hand across his nose. He had a snuffly cold and the Irwins had no time or money for handkerchiefs. He wore a sweater of his sister's pinned together with a safety-pin, and his cap with eartabs was too large, but he was a proud figure in his own four-year-old eyes. He was going to carry a gallon of kerosene, and groceries besides, all the way up home by himself.

"C'mon, Ginger, hi! Blast you, get out of that meat market!" Bobby called to his hound dog. He made his voice loud like his big brother's. He picked up the can and trudged out of the store.

Celie came back to the end of the counter, near Buddy.

Buddy pretended absorption in "figgers."

Celie hit him neatly with a gumdrop from the candy counter.

Buddy popped it into his mouth and took up where he left off.

"What's more, the big shot's sending his nephew up here cause the fellow wants to be a musician and Mr. Farley wants he should go in the lumber business."

"A musician!" said Celie who knew no men who were able-bodied who made music, saving Sabonich, the Austrian, who played the accordion.

"Yeah, played the piano in a night club in Detroit till his uncle made him quit."

"Celie, Celie, there's Mrs. Larsen waitin'!" Mrs. Munsen called over rebukingly from the dry goods department. "I'm busy." She was showing Mrs. Henry the newest thing in baby nighties since her last baby was born two years ago.

"They get new things all the time," she assured Mrs. Henry just as though they both didn't know that the coming Henry baby would wear throughout the clothes of the last three Henry children.

Celie recommended the Sunset brand of sliced peaches to Mrs. Larsen and Jolly Boy peanut butter. She made out the slip and put it into the little container that carried it with a squeaky whine to Buddy's booth. Then she got out new crape paper to flute for the display table.

She ought to meet him when he came into the store, first off, the big shot's nephew. She would wear her bright red dress this afternoon and tomorrow, just in case.

Celie went home for lunch at quarter after so's to be back in time to arrange the vegetables and count the bread that came on the one and only noon train through Flat Point. Her high heels made new holes in the snow on the way back up the street. The snow was melting fast under the warm sun. The walls of snow grew dirtier and lower. The sound of dripping water came from every roof. Even the three-foot-long icicle on the edge of Pop Slichter's roof was dwindling, but still hung dagger-like and shining in the sun.

The Hendersons' house was no different from the Bernsens' on one side and the Melsingers' on the other, unless the white sash curtains in the Hendersons' windows were starched a little stiffer and cleaner than any others on the street. There was a red geranium in a coffee can on the sill.

Celie went around back to the storm shed. She knew before she opened the door the hot steamy smell that would meet her. Mrs. Henderson took in boarders: three young fellows in the mill who'd rather pay a dollar more a week and get clean Swedish cooking than eat at the company boarding house. Mrs. Henderson and Ole were quick to turn a penny when they could. Celie hated it, hated the pile of dishes she helped with at noon and in the evening, hated the heavy meals they had to have every day . . . meat and potatoes and pie and coffee, or meat and rice and cake and coffee, day after day.

At first glance, there was no resemblance between Celie and Mrs. Henderson. The older woman's skin was of a leathery texture, reddened to an even color where Celie's was pink and white and smooth. The line from cheekbone to jaw was sterner. Her iron gray hair was scanty now and brushed back to a firm knot in the back. There was no quick flash of expression save only in her eyes, and her mouth was a thin line that closed tightly. Her body was lean and bony and her dresses were as she had made them when she came from Sweden to another mill-town like Flat Point, twenty odd years ago.

Christina Henderson wasted few words. She only looked up a second as Celie came in. She was busy dishing up. Celie hung up her hat and coat and took the dishes on the table. She and Ole ate their dinner with the boarders. Christina was busy in the kitchen most of the time.

At eleven-thirty the mill whistle shrilled forth and the men came up the hill in a steady stream. Celie looked out of the window at them unseeingly. Somebody new was coming to Flat Point, a musician who had played in a night-club, like that one she'd seen in the film Bebe Daniels was in.

The three boarders came in together.

"'Lo, mornin', Mis' Henderson, Celie." They were three Swedes, tall, hungry fellows . . . a half peck of potatoes lasted only a day and a half at the Hendersons'. Two of them were blond, but one was black-haired. He was Joe. His mother was a French woman and he was only second generation Swede. He had blue eyes, though, that went at once for Celie and rested on her while he ate. Joe Linsen was in love with Celie Henderson.

Celie broke the large slice of home-made bread daintily in two before she buttered it, with a self-conscious glance around.

"Joe, Sam, he say you goin' to run the limey engine next month, yeah?" Hans Mottberg held his well-filled knife in the air to ask.

"I guess," said Joe, shortly, his eyes on Celie. He hadn't meant to tell her till evening when they went for a ride. She looked up quickly. Then she went on eating. Celie ate mostly in silence at her mother's table with the boarders. Mrs. Henderson had set ideas as to what was right and proper for her daughter.

"I don't want you makin' yourself common, Celie," she had ordered.

"Well, Joe," said Ole Henderson, "that isn't the mill game, but you like machines—I guess you got what you wanted." Ole Henderson worked on the pond. He worked on contract instead of day wages, and made more than most of the men in Flat Point. It was a dangerous job, and had to pay more.

"I don't like it, Ole," Christina Henderson had been saying for five years, now.

"It's all right, Christina, I do it awhile. We got the girl to bring up and something to lay by, then I be millwright again or maybe buy a little farm. Don't worry. I'm careful of my skin," Ole always answered.

Christina Henderson would go back to her work grimly. Whatever fears she had she shut her lips tightly upon, in the habit of a lifetime. What else to do?

Joe knew Celie was dainty. She liked the way movie fellows did things. Joe held them up to scorn when they went to the show together. "Look at 'em . . . cake-walkers, Celie, nothing but!"

"Oh, Joe, not Jack Gilbert, not him!"

But when Ole and the others got up from the table they always helped themselves liberally to toothpicks from the glass hat on the center of the table. Joe didn't. He had seen Celie's look of scorn once. She had fancy notions like that, but that was right, Joe thought to himself. He and Celie weren't always going to live in a mill-town.

"Can I walk down with you, Celie?" Joe took out a cigarette. Celie hated chewing tobacco.

"No, Joe, I got to change my dress."

"Well, s'long, then, see you tonight." His smile was broad. He had a handsome face, not carved of hardwood like Ole Henderson's or Stumpf's, the walking-boss, or old Pat Weil's who'd come out back in the white pine days, but handsome in a softwood way, cedar or poplar or spruce, maybe. He was tall, six feet two, and his plaid shirt bent back a little from his belt, and his long arms swung as he walked in a free sort of way.

Celie cleared the dishes off and stacked them, then she flew up the steep stairs to the backroom. Not many girls in Flat Point had a room to themselves, but Ole and Christina Henderson had only one child. They'd lost two before her. Maybe they pampered her a little. She slipped into her red silk.

"You won't have anything if you wear the best you've got to the store, Celie," Mrs. Henderson commented.

"Oh, well, I thought, then, I wouldn't have to bother tonight."

Christina Henderson like red herself. She said no more. Her own dress was a gray printed flannel. She wore it all day, but changed her apron in the afternoon.

At the store, the new shipments were in. Celie like arranging them on the shelves. Ten more cans of peas, two dozen boxes of dried codfish, a hundred and fifty loaves of bread. Celie flashed up and down behind the counter. Afternoons were busy in the store.

By two-thirty the mail was out. Housework in Flat Point was done. Women came drifting in with their babies. They stopped to talk to Celie and Mrs. Munsen. Flat Point had changed in the fifteen years the town had stood. In the old days, provisions came in by boat. Women baked their own bread and visited each other in the afternoons for coffee instead of collecting at the store. Now it was common gossip that Tad Norton's wife fed her family out of the can, and plenty more besides her. Only the old people baked their own bread. Times were different.

"Celie, the new Sears catalogue's out." Selma Lichtenberg was Celie's age and just married. She spread the new catalogue on the counter. "There's a purple silk in here for $3.98 I think I'll get and you oughta see the console table!"

Celie was excited, too. The new mail order catalogue was Vogue and Paris itself to the female portion of the Point. But all afternoon, Celie knew whenever the latch of the store door was jerked up. No one in city clothes drifted in. Maybe he'd come tomorrow. She could see him asking for cigarettes and herself waiting on him.

At five-thirty, Celie was sweeping out behind the counter. She hated to get the dust in her red dress. She swept down by Buddy Hefflin's cage.

"Say, what you all decked out for, Celie? You musta expected the big shot's nephew."

A tell-tale red flushed over Celie's face.

"If that isn't a joke, he ain't coming till next week."

"Oh, don't be so silly, Buddy. I'm going out with Joe," retorted Celie crossly. "You think you're so smart." She brushed lightly back down to the butcher's end and put the broom in the corner. That could do.

THE OLD FORD BOBBLED FROM RUT TO RUT AND SLID BETWEEN THE newly frozen holes the sun had thawed in the road that morning. Joe and Celie were driving into town, thirty-five miles from Flat Point.

"Think we better go all the way, Celie?"

"Why not? We can get there for the late show."

"All right. I thought, maybe we could just drive."

Celie was silent. She watched the road streaking ahead between the dark trees on either side. There were cleared places at intervals, places where you could see through to the lake in the day time. Halfway there was the town of Mead. Twenty-five years ago it had been just such a town as Flat Point, deserted now, but with the tumble-down old houses still standing, two streets of them along with the framework of a store and part of a mill. It always looked spooky in the moonlight. Tonight, the deserted buildings crouched together in the shadows.

Trees came down to the road again and stretches of low jack pines. There was the place where Crazy Bill lived, who everyone said was rich from selling moon to the lumberjacks. Ten miles from town where the road drew into the lake again, the hunting shacks and cottages of folks from Clarion began. Celie always looked at them curiously. Sometimes, there were lights in one or two and big cars out in front. She would like to have a cottage on the lake to come to, and live in town, really.

"What's the matter, Celie?" Joe pulled her over to him.

"Nothing, only, I guess I'm getting sick of the Point."

"Well, wait awhile, Celie, we'll be getting out of there one of these days. I was talking to a man who sells radios and he says there's a big field in the mechanical side. Might even get to a bigger place than Clarion, Celie, Milwaukee, maybe."

Celie squeezed his arm a little. Joe was a bright fellow. They'd get there.

They were almost into town now. Mamma thought it was awful to get back so late, with Joe getting up at five-thirty; but you couldn't stay at home all the time.

"Kiss me, Celie, 'fore we get way in?"

Celie kissed him.

"You were nice, Joe, to come in to a movie tonight."

"Aw, that's all right, Celie." Lord! she was a swell kid.

Joe bought two red hots when they came out of the movie at eleven-thirty. They got in the car and started back.

"Sleepy, Celie?"

"Sorta."

"Curl up and go to sleep so I can wake you up to drive when I get sleepy."

It was an old arrangement. Joe never waked her. He liked to feel her cuddled up against his shoulder. Sometimes, her hair blew against his face. That made up for feeling half-dead in the morning.

The dim headlights of the old Ford cut a path of light back over the dark road, flashing for a second on a pane of glass in the old store at Mead or gleaming on a white birch. Once they caught a deer, stationary for a second before it bounded off into the deeper darkness.

1940

The Loon Feather (excerpt)

Iola Fuller

Part One

It was fur that made our lives what they were. Fur, and the people who lived by it. The earliest memories of my life are of soft deerskin clothing and warm fur robes that kept me as comfortable in winter as the bear in his cave. In these days a fine fur coat costs a great deal of money, but in that time it was the most natural garment to have.

One never forgets the luster of heaps and bales of furs. The golden fleece of the north, Pierre used to call it, for he had sometimes a bookish way of talking, and there was truth in that word golden. He had seen it, that sheen, like all of the French from the early day of the Sieur de la Salle, and his companion Tonty of the iron arm, down to the time of my story when large fur companies had thousands of voyageurs combing the forests. Others had followed the French, and were still coming in such numbers that instead of the narrow trails of single hunters, marked by a moccasin print or a broken twig, it was almost as if a huge army had crashed through the woods.

Furs were the means of getting whatever the Indian and the white trapper wanted, for in those days they were the legal tender and there was little that prime beaver would not buy. Hunters and traders wintered in lonely outposts, and then came by hundreds in their bateaux and canoes to Mackinac in spring, to bring in their winter's catch and celebrate with enough zeal and abandon to drive away memories of the lonely months behind them. Dancing, drinking, fighting, gambling, spending in one month the earnings of the other eleven,

38

they never rested. Nor did anyone else on the island while the traders' tents were there, and the beach was full of Indian lodges.

To this day the sight of a black feather brings it all back to me. A crow's feather in his hat was the badge of the leader of a brigade, and it was coveted by every man who hadn't it. It wasn't easily come by, but was rather like the laurel wreath of the olden days, as Pierre said. To win it a man must be a better man than the rest—he must be able to fight better, walk longer distances, and carry more than the usual hundred pounds over the portages, if need be.

The island of Mackinac, the turtle, rises high and rounding from the water. As I remember it, tall white stone cliffs rose abruptly in some places, and in others trees and bushes climbed a gentle slope. The high center was densely wooded, and ever quiet when the village in the half-moon harbor was wild and noisy. Groves of spruce, pine, and cedar, and the fragrant fir and balsam opened their green depths to make room for little, close-huddling maples, and birch and straight-limbed beeches. So close they were that even where a footpath passed among them, the trees closed overhead so it was like walking always in a bower, and a squirrel could go for miles without touching foot to ground. Everywhere the fragrance of balsam lay like a cloud on the air, mixed at the proper seasons with the aroma of wild strawberries, the thorny roses, and the pink flowers called arbutus. In the darkest nooks was the damp delight of ferns and moss, and in the sunlight of a clearing I used to catch my breath at the great beds of daisies, the largest there ever were, spreading their solid masses of flat white and yellow blossoms.

And there was always the water, for Mackinac is where the lakes meet, in the straits flowing between Lakes Michigan, Huron, and Superior. Pierre read from a book once about "seas of sweet water," and that was what we had on every side and in every direction, pure, beautifully colored, yet transparent almost as the air itself. I spent many hours on the water, and gazing out over it, watching whitecaps fleeing from the east wind.

Striking deeper than thought, this memory sends me back to stand again on the western heights of the island, far above the lake, where my destiny spoke to me that night so long ago. The sun is going down, making the water red in its path. A quick twilight has come and is passing into darkness. Coasts of the mainland and of Point St. Ignace grow dim, letting Mackinac withdraw into itself. Like a star set in space it rides on the dark water. Untouched by the movements of the outside world, it is complete in itself, having a sufficiency of its own. Around me are huge boulders, dropped ages ago by the glaciers, inspiring the early red men first to marvel and then to worship. The wash of the waves on the pebbles is something that has always been and will always be. From the trees behind me comes a hymn to those ears that can hear it, as if the winds were playing a requiem for someone departed. Rather than fear, there comes a tremendous sense of personal security. It is right. It is the only way.

1950

[Let's play a game]

Lorine Niedecker

Let's play a game.
　　　Let's play Ask for a job.
What can you do?
　　　I can hammer and saw
　　　and feed a dog.
You'll do! Take this slip
to the department of song.
　　　You must ask me where I'm from.
Oh yes, you're from the country
called The Source.
　　　Will the nurse in your plant
　　　give me sweet pills?
No! We're not at war.
　　　One console-ation is:
　　　we can always play
　　　Ask for a job.

1957–2001

The second part of *And Here* drops readers into a scene that will likely feel familiar to those with a passing knowledge of the U.P. We land in a mining town. On Iron Street. Sidestepping "two dog fights and a street brawl" on our way to Long Jack's Saloon. This opening scene of *Laughing Whitefish* by Robert Traver ticks the boxes, scratches the itch, brushes in the images that run latent in the minds of those who imagine, and perhaps mythologize, the U.P. At the time of *Laughing Whitefish's* publication, the Mackinac Bridge had only recently joined Michigan's Upper and Lower Peninsulas, and, fittingly, we enter this section through the eyes of an outsider: newly minted lawyer William Poe. Civilization comes to the U.P. Law and order. Through Poe's point of view we take in the local color—characters as rugged and veined as the land, a dialect as thick as any Scottish brogue, an exotic "Indian" maiden, "aloof but strangely exciting." We step into this section of the anthology as pioneer into the frontier.

With each poem, story, and essay, however, the feeling of being a tourist in this foreign land begins to fade, and readers are treated to a deeper understanding of the varied lives, thoughts, and concerns of the writers and characters filling these pages. The landscape of the Upper Peninsula remains a hallmark of these pieces (as inescapable, hypnotic, and indelible as it is in life), but the local color that opens this part gives way to a more nuanced view of the relationship between landscape and people, and though harmony remains abundant (see Michael Delp's "What My Father Told Me"), the defining quality in these pages is tension.

The tension between people and the harshness of the landscape is easy to see in Gordon Lightfoot's "The Wreck of the *Edmund Fitzgerald*" (I challenge you to read it without singing), but it is perhaps even more poignant, and more pertinent, when presented on a smaller scale. We see this tension in Jim Harrison's image of "stump fences surround nothing / worth their tearing down." We can see it as Judith Minty returns to the old family cabin, lights the stove, and "all the flies of summer burst alive again" and leave her wondering how long she'll last. And we see this tension run throughout these pieces in the juxtaposition of ruin and beauty, as in Stephen Tudor's depiction of the town of De Tour with its "fallen docks, / Blasted workshed, junkfield, scurvy road's end— / And wildflowers, risen among the debris."

In this latter half of the twentieth century, however, the conflict of human versus nature is compounded by a third party—industry. In the U.P., industry and landscape are one, as the same rich waters that draw the seagulls to the coast draw the fishermen who toil there. The iron that reddens the earth also draws in the mines to extract and the tankers to haul. The thumbprint of industry is evident throughout the works in this part, but the dissonance of homage and lament is on full display in Jane Piirto's "The Company" and M. L. Liebler's "On the Scrap."

But, ah, that landscape, both the literal and figurative bedrock of these worlds. Its indifference to the fleeting conflicts of its inhabitants is palpable, and, as the twentieth century closes with these pages, its permanence feels assured.

—Vincent Reusch

Laughing Whitefish (excerpt)

Robert Traver

I TETHERED MY HORSE AND BUGGY IN FRONT OF THE BREITUNG HOUSE on the east end of Iron Street and started on my quest. Before I left Marquette I had been told that this was the shortest and busiest thoroughfare in the neighboring iron-mining town of Negaunee. I soon discovered it was also the booziest, certainly in the town if not in Michigan. I had already counted seventeen saloons and not yet come to the one I sought. Meanwhile I had encountered two dog fights and a street brawl and, while crossing an intersecting street, narrowly escaped getting run over by a team of runaway horses dragging a wildly careening dray. I paused on the other side to catch my breath. Doggedly pushing on I passed two more saloons, and was beginning to despair. The next one I came to was the one I sought. I sighed and stopped and mopped my brow.

"Long Jack's Saloon," read weathered twin signs painted on either window, executed with a fine if slightly faded Spencerian flourish. I pushed open the screen door—upon which hung long vertical strips of old newspaper, presumably to alert the waiting swarm of somnolent flies—and, entering the darkened boozy interior, walked up to the bar.

"'Owdy, partner," the tall silver-haired bartender greeted me pleasantly, "Lavly summer day we're after 'avin'. Wot can I do for you, young fella me lad?"

"I'm looking for the proprietor, Mr. John Tregembo," I said. "Might you be he?"

"Not only might I be 'e, but I blawdy well is 'e," he said. "Glad you didn't ast for no drink," he went on, "cos av the new law aour legislative giants 'as recent passed wot says us 'ardworking saloonkeepers can't serve young lads under twenty-one no more. Blawdy nurse maids an' bookkeepers they now makin' outn us. . . . Me, I figger if a lad's ol' enough to earn 'is livin' toilin' ten–'leven hours a day at 'ard labor 'e's blawdy well old enough to spend 'is money 'ow 'e likes. . . ."

"I'm William Poe, the new lawyer over in Marquette," I said, both charmed and a little overcome by the colorful headlong rush of this man's extravagant vocabulary, which was rather less conversation than a kind of spilt exuberance. "I represent a young woman called Charlotte Kawbawgam," I explained, "and she said you might be able to help out with a legal case I'm handling for her. She said you once knew her father and had befriended him."

"Charlotte Kawbawgam?" Jack Tregembo echoed, pursing his lips and blinking thoughtfully, swiftly adopting the role of the thinker searching the shrouded mists of memory. "I'm afeared I don't knaow this 'ere young lydy," he said finally. "Ol' Jack's 'ad lots av parched customers these past thirty-odd years an' 'e can't 'spec' to 'member all av they. Was 'er ol' man an iron miner, might 'e been? Name daon't saound 'zactly Cornish to me. I wanst knew a Treboggin but 'e wos kilt up yonder mine by a chunk av falling ore." He swiftly hooked his thumb up towards the Jackson Mine, west of town, clasping his head and reeling drunkenly in pantomime of a man staggering from a mortal blow.

"No, the name's not exactly Cornish," I agreed, trying not to smile at his wild gesticulations and asides. "Perhaps I should explain," I went on. "Charlotte Kawbawgam is a young Chippewa Indian woman. Her given name in Indian means Laughing Whitefish, after the river by that name. Her dead father's name was Marji Kawbawgam and I thought maybe you—"

"*Marji Kawbawgam!*" Jack broke in, slapping the bar top with the palm of his hand. "Did I know ol' Marji Kawbawgam! Put 'er there, young fella," he went on, extending his big hand and burying mine in his grip. "W'y di'n't thee say so right off? Of course I knew ol' Marji. 'Chief' I used to call 'im. Guess maybe p'r'aps I was 'is bes' frien'—certainly amongst the w'ite folks I wos. A close-mouthed one 'e wos but 'e offen tole me sad an' confidential 'baout 'is little Laughing Whitefish. Closest ever I come to seein' an Hindian cry. Apple av 'is eye, she wos. An' naow she's a growed up young lydy—'ow time do fly."

"She's a fine handsome young woman," I said, recalling her grace and beauty. "She's just turned twenty-one."

"Muss be all of eight–ten years since poor ol' Marji got 'is. Le's see, naow"—he released my hand to do his sums as I gratefully flexed my aching fingers—"hit's 1873 naow an' take 1859—w'en poor Marji passed—from 'e, leaves—w'y it's *fourteen* years! 'Ow the time *do* fly!"

"That's correct, Mr. Tregembo," I put in. "Marji Kawbawgam was killed just over fourteen years ago, early in July, 1859. His daughter is a fine young woman, you'll be glad to learn, and I'm trying to help her collect her just due. That's why I'm here, Mr. Tregembo."

"Don't keep Mister Tregembo-ing me," he ordered, deftly drawing a small beer for himself. "Everybody calls me Jack—that is, all but me ol' lydy, an' wot she 'urls at me ain't fit fer 'uman ears, hespecially for hinnocent young fellas like thee."

"All right, Jack," I said, eager to get on with my mission. "I do hope you can help her out."

Jack downed his beer in one neat gulp, wiping the ends of his flowing mustaches in a swift two-way movement, and confidentially lowered his voice.

"Ow kin I 'elp aout, young fella? Any frien' av Marji's is a frien' av ol' Jack—even iffen 'e's a blawdy lawyer feller to boot, no offense meant, partner. Wott'll you 'ave to drink on old Jack? Compliments av the 'aouse."

"Do you have cherry soda?" I ventured, longing instead to order whiskey to show my vast maturity, but fearful of the consequences—after all, there was work to be done.

"Cherry soda?" he repeated, staring and blinking for a moment but rallying swiftly. "Ah, yes, I do. Keep some for the *Mining Journal* boy. 'Ere you are, young fella. 'Ere's mud in your eye."

"I'm really twenty-six," I explained hastily, sipping my soda, not going into the dreary fact that my extremely youthful appearance had long been my secret cross. "I never drink spirits—never, that is, when I'm working on a case."

"Every man to 'is taste," Jack said, "as the Dutchman said w'en 'e put salt in 'is tay." He motioned to a round-topped wooden card table standing in the far corner, with little shelved cubicles underneath to hold the players' drinks. "Le's set daown over yonder an' 'ave our talk, young fella—ol' Jack's legs ain't wot they used to be. This 'ere wos ol' Marji's favorite table," he said, rubbing his hand over the worn top. "Ah, yes," he sighed, looking at me closely. "Naow I hexpect your case 'as somethin' to do with Marji's ol' claim against the Jackson Hore Company, somethin' 'bout that ol' paper them first Jackson fellas guv Marji years ago."

"Yes, Mister—" I began. "Yes, Jack," I went on, "it certainly does. And it's going to be a tough case, that I see already, but I'm going to give it a good try."

"Good boy," Jack said. "Give 'em blawdy blue 'ell, lad. Rollin' in money, they is, but nary a tuppence dud they 'ave for poor Marji wot shawed it all to um."

Somehow I trusted this man and spoke to him freely about the case, about my doubts as well as my hopes. I explained to him some of the handicaps I had to overcome: that my own client, Marji's daughter, knew very little about her dead father's past or his connection with the Jackson Mine or about the people who might be her witnesses. I told him I had already visited Philo P. Everett in Marquette—one of the original founders of the Jackson Mining Company and the man who had written and given the original paper to Marji—and that I had found a frail old man of failing memory and hearing.

I told him that while Mr. Everett seemed kindly disposed towards my client and the justice of her cause, I was fearful about his failing health and memory and concerned, most of all, whether he would survive until the trial, and be able to testify. I told him about my fears over the possible legal effects of Marji's various marriages, about which I still knew very little, of my apprehensions over the long lapse of time since the paper had first been given him—1845—before any action was being taken on it nearly thirty years later.

"But 'ow cud ol' Marji ever 'ave sued anybody?" Jack indignantly broke in. "'E wos too much av a man to get after the ol' Jackson crowd w'en they wos daown on their luck, an' w'en finely they lost aout, 'e was far too broke an' unheducated to sue the new outfit w'en they tuck over. Moreover the only lawyer fella in the hull caounty not tied up wan way or tother with these 'ere minin' folks wos an ol' whiskey-drinkin' peg-leg lawyer daown at Marquette—I forget 'is name—an' 'e didn't come to these parts 'till long after poor Marji wos gone. So 'ow in 'ell cud Marji av sued? Wot wud 'e av sued with?"

"That's precisely what I propose to argue, Jack," I said, somehow greatly buoyed that this uneducated but shrewd Cornish saloonkeeper should penetrate so swiftly to the heart of my case.

We talked along and he gave me the names of a number of potential witnesses I might see: among them McVannel, the livery-stable man, for whom Marji had occasionally worked; Benny Youren, the drayman; and especially old Captain Merry, now retired and a very old man but still "chipper as a chipmunk chasin' hacorns after an 'ail storm." He told me many other things and gave me other possible leads, all of which I gratefully wrote down in my notebook.

Just then I felt and heard a slow series of subterranean tremors, a sullen chain of booming earth thuds. The floor shook and the decanters on the back bar clinked merrily.

"*What's that?*" I asked in alarm, fearful that an earthquake had hit us.

"Oh that," Jack said airily, "that's only the day shift blastin' daown ore for the night shift up at Jackson Mine—'Old Rumbly' us locals calls it. Do it every evenin' 'baout quittin' time." He grinned at me. "First time's always a bit unnervin', Willy."

"Did Marji ever show you this old paper of his that Philo Everett gave him?" I asked when I was able to speak.

"Only wanst, Willy, a long time ago. Let me see naow, it wos right after 'e wos let go by they there new mine folks."

"Did he tell you what it was about?"

"That 'e did," Jack said with conviction. "An' 'ow 'e wos fired an' thrun aout of 'is cabin on yonder mountain an' I tole Marji, I did, I tole 'im 'e ought to go 'ire hisself a lawyer an' sue the bla'guards from 'ere to Ludgate 'Ill."

I put away my notes, thanked Jack, and prepared to leave. Suddenly the front screen door burst open and in piled all the waiting flies accompanied by a throng of freshly scrubbed iron miners just coming off the day shift at the Jackson Mine.

In they stampeded with their shining faces, alone and in twos and threes, shouting, swearing, jostling each other, clomping about in their mine-stained half-tied boots, hastily depositing their gleaming metal dinner buckets under the billiard table, on the weight-lifting machine, the penny scales, on the tall glass-covered music box, alongside the potted ferns in the half-curtained front windows, then shouldering up to the bar, ordering drinks, shouting insults, still mining ore....

While busily fixing drinks Jack still managed to call out their names to me, in a kind of confused mass introduction, and when he paused for breath I had the vague impression that at least half of them began with the common Cornish place-name prefix of *tre*. There were representatives, I recalled, of the Tregembos, the Tregonnings and the Trebilcocks; the Trembaths, Trevarrows and Trelawneys; the Treloars, Tresedders and Trewhellas; the Tregears, Tremethicks and Trewarthas; the Tremberths, Trevellyans and the Trenarys—

"Get a move on thee, Jack, an' stow the hintroductions," someone shouted. "You saound like a train conductor back in ol' country, and you're makin' me bad 'omesick bawlin' all them bloomin' nymes."

"Pour the blawdy drinks an' cut aout the palaver," another shouted, eyes staring, clutching wildly at his throat. "I've jest 'ad ten hours av savage hamusement muckin' dirt up at they there Jackson Recreation Pavilion an' I'd dearly love to surprise me arid gullet with a drink. Do you think the lad 'ere needs to be *tole* we're a bunch av parched Cousin Jacks?"

"'Old your 'orses, me 'earties!" Jack shouted back. "This 'ere's William Poe, the new lawyer—William, this is the thirstiest bunch av Cornishmen in Hamerican captivity—halso, I do believe, the world's best miners."

"'Ear, 'ear—lissen to ol' Jack spreadin' the salve, will you? 'E's 'appy as an 'ore lydy on payday—ever'thin' comin' in an' damn little guven aout!... Ah, 'ere comes me lavly boilermaker—daown the 'atch, Jack.... Naow 'ow 'baout fixin' 'nother for your ol' mate, 'Arry Penhale?"

I stood watching these men, fascinated by their swift pulsing talk and animal vitality. Cornishmen might also be Englishmen, I reflected, but there was a distinctly different quality in their lack of restraint, in the way they seemed compelled to act everything out. Hadn't I read somewhere that the Romans and Spaniards had long ago invaded Cornwall during their forays into Britain? Had not ancient Phoenician sailors once come in quest of tin from its mines? Had not the land once abounded with mystic Druid priests and still exposed their age-blunted burial stones? Might not all this account for the distinctly un-English dash and flavor of their talk and deportment? Even the act of drinking became a little solo drama: the anticipatory wetting and smacking of lips, the glass lifted reverently as a chalice, the long slow blissful tug—as at some vast celestial teat—the rumblings and gulpings and swallowings that accompanied it, the soulful "ah" which sprang unbidden from the inner man, followed by a calm beatific expression, with lidded half-closed eyes.

Even the idlest bit of conversation was apt to bring on a full-dress drama: eager noddings of the head, shruggings of the shoulders, Gallic wavings of the arms and thrustings of the hands, thumbs suddenly hooked this way or that to indicate someone or something an inch or a thousand miles away; assorted whinnies, leers, grins of triumph and delight, grimaces or sympathy and sudden pain, wistful pauses; tugs at the neck, sudden digs in the listener's ribs.... I felt not unlike an uneasy Frédéric Chopin who, once finding himself marooned among the Scottish gentry, later told of "watching them talk and listening to them drink."

In a curiously inoffensive way these men plainly assumed they were squarely at the center of their universe; everything flowed and revolved around and about this pulsing central core. Their frequent detached references to themselves in the third person was all part of it. I found myself envying them their sturdy truce with their world, their fatalistic optimism—or was it optimistic fatalism? I also longed to feel just a fraction as sure of my *own* world.

And endlessly, obsessively they talked about their work: mining ore, burrowing drifts, erecting log cribbing, pushing heavy trams—which they called buggies, or rather "boogies"—crimping dynamite caps, 'ammering drills, setting off massive earth-shaking blasts—all this accompanied by vehement arm-wavings and strident neck-corded shouts. The din was incredible. Through it all a toiling Jack Tregembo beamed benignly as the little bell rang merrily on the wooden cash drawer.

The man they called Matt Eddy suddenly emitted a profound belch, and when the reverberations had died away all of them were eagerly off and away. . . .

"Thar she blaws, mates! Steady the boat, lads, an' man the 'arpoon!"

"Jack must av pumped 'ot air 'stead av beer in me glass," Matt proudly declaimed, elaborately puffing out his cheeks. "Oney blawdy thing besides hinsults, an' gab a body ever gets araoun' 'ere fer free."

"Saounds like the afternoon blast at ol' Number Two 'ole," another judiciously commented. "All kinds of ruction but damn little pay dirt."

"Mates," Jack cried out during a lull, "like I wos s'yin', this 'ere's young William Poe, the new lawyer fella daown at Marquette—where all the mining swells lives—a young gent who's fixin' to 'elp Marji Kawbawgam's daughter collect Marji's ol' claim against they there Jackson Company."

At the mention of Marji's name a hush fell over the company; those who spoke seemed delegates at an impromptu memorial service; I had the impression of suddenly being in church rather than in a noisy workingman's saloon.

"There wos no 'arm in Marji," one of them solemnly said. "'E bothered nary a soul, that 'e didn't."

"Some says Hindians ain't no blawdy good," put in another, "but that Marji 'e wos true blue through an' through."

"For wanst you're right there, Matt Eddy," another said. "Poor ol' Marji wos 'is own worst enemy."

Others delivered their brief homely tributes and Long John Tregembo soberly added the final benediction. "Mates," he said, "effen more of us w'ites was 'alf as good a man as that there Chippeway Hindian Marji, this bloomin' ol' worl' wud be a better place for the hull of us." He raised his glass. "C'mon, partners, toss wan daown the main shaft for good ol' Marji Kawbawgam, may the Lard rest 'is wandrin' soul."

Before I could get away the proprietor had proposed still another toast, this time to "this 'ere William Poe, brave young lion av they legal profession!"

and I speculated whether he was moved rather less by the solemnity of the occasion than the chance to stimulate business. Probably both, I concluded, watching the declamatory fervor in his pale blue eyes. I also perceived with a pang that the intemperate consumption of cherry soda would never become a problem in my life. . . .

"Go get um, Willy!" someone shouted.

"Sue they blawdy boogers, Willy," shouted another, "an' make um pay through the nawse."

"Sue an' sue an' make um rue the day they met the likes av you, Willy boy!"

"Jan's a poet, Willy, but 'e daon't knaow it!"

"Willy" they were already calling me, I ruefully perceived. Already my secret was out, my disguise penetrated—was there never to be any escape?

Amidst all this jostling and shouting, during which I had uttered scarcely a word, these boisterous men had swiftly perceived that *this* William was a Willy. . . . Sipping my soda I marveled over the mass intuition by which the Willys of the world are spotted and recognized on sight; suddenly I saw that the essential chemistry of a man often spoke louder than actions or words. It was not a matter of goodness or badness or of strength or weakness, or yet of courage or moral stature or the lack of it, or of timidity or boldness or even impressiveness or modesty or physique. Rather there was a subtle emanation from the psyche, an invisible aura, that one wore always about him like a cloak. It unerringly marked the Willys from the Bills, and from its verdict there was no argument or appeal. I sighed and gulped the rest of my soda. Alas, the Bills were Bills and the Willys were Willys, and never the twain should meet.

"Twist their blawdy tails, Willy, an' give um an hextra turn for we!" I took my leave amidst their shouted goodbyes and good luck wishes and several hearty thumps on the back. As I walked up Iron Street to get my horse and rig to return to Marquette I found myself strangely moved by what I had just witnessed. Their eulogies of Marji had been trite and sentimental, yet it was plain they had sprung from the hearts of these simple hard-working iron miners. Or were they so simple? They had managed swiftly to penetrate their

Willy, hadn't they? And in their tributes to Marji, Lincoln himself could not have been more sober and solemn when he had delivered his Gettysburg Address. These men *cared* about this obscure Indian called Marji Kawbawgam. Could it be, I asked myself, that no man was truly dead while yet one person lived who treasured his memory?

It was one of those glorious Northern evenings I was learning to love, the tall reddish sky shot and aflame with great soaring rays and reflections from the dying sun. The Creation must have been something like this, I thought. As my rented horse plodded along the dusty ore-stained road I reflected about this elusive thing called success and material attainment. Who was ever to say with confidence that the Marjis of this world were failures? By and by I found myself thinking about the complex new legal situation in which I suddenly found myself—my first big case—thinking about it and all of its ramifications, thinking, too, about my new client, the withdrawn and aloof but strangely exciting young Indian woman, Laughing Whitefish.

1965

Northern Michigan

Jim Harrison

On this back road the land
has the juice taken out of it:

stump fences surround nothing
worth their tearing down

by a deserted filling station
a Veedol sign, the rusted hulk

of a Frazer, "live bait"
on battered tin.

    A barn
with half a tobacco ad
owns the greenness of a manure
pile

a half-moon on a privy door
a rope swinging from an elm. A

collapsed henhouse, a pump
with the handle up

the orchard with wild tangled branches.

In the far corner of the pasture,
in the shadow of the woodlot
a herd of twenty deer:
              three bucks

are showing off—
they jump in turn across the fence,
flanks arch and twist to get higher
in the twilight
as the last light filters
through the woods.

The Wreck of the *Edmund Fitzgerald*

Gordon Lightfoot

The legend lives on from the Chippewa on down
Of the big lake they call Gitche Gumee.
The lake, it is said, never gives up her dead
When the skies of November turn gloomy.
With a load of iron ore, twenty-six thousand tons more
Than the *Edmund Fitzgerald* weighed empty,
That good ship and true was a bone to be chewed
When the gales of November came early.

The ship was the pride of the American side
Coming back from some mill in Wisconsin.
As the big freighters go, it was bigger than most
With a crew and good captain well-seasoned.
Concluding some terms with a couple steel firms
When they left fully loaded for Cleveland,
And later that night when the ship's bell rang
Could it be the north wind they'd been feelin'?

The wind in the wires made the tattle-tale sound
And the wave broke over the railing.
And every man knew, as the captain did too
T'was the witch of November come stealin'.

The dawn came late and the breakfast had to wait
When the gales of November came slashin'.
When afternoon came, it was freezin' rain
In the face of a hurricane west wind.

When supper time came, the old cook came on deck, sayin',
"Fellas, it's too rough t'feed ya."
At seven P.M. a main hatchway caved in; he said,
"Fellas, it's been good to know ya."
The captain wired in he had water comin' in
And the good ship and crew was in peril.
And later that night when his lights went out of sight
Came the wreck of the *Edmund Fitzgerald*.

Does anyone know where the love of God goes
When the waves turn the minutes to hours?
The searchers all say they'd have made Whitefish Bay
If they'd put fifteen more miles behind 'er.
They might have split up or they might have capsized;
They may have broke deep and took water.
And all that remains is the faces and the names
Of the wives and the sons and the daughters.

Lake Huron rolls, Superior sings
In the rooms of her ice-water mansion.
Old Michigan steams like a young man's dreams;
The islands and bays are for sportsmen.
And farther below Lake Ontario
Takes in what Lake Erie can send her.
And the iron boats go as the mariners all know
With the gales of November remembered.

In a musty old hall in Detroit they prayed
In the Maritime Sailors' Cathedral.
The church bell chimed 'til it rang 29 times
For each man on the *Edmund Fitzgerald*.
The legend lives on from the Chippewa on down
Of the big lake they called Gitche Gumee.
Superior, they said, never gives up her dead
When the gales of November come early.

Yellow Dog Journal—Spring (excerpt)

Judith Minty

29

When I last dreamed the bear, he rose
from the earth, the trees
parted in his path, twigs snapping, cracking
from his weight, his flesh
swaying as he lumbered up the hill.

When I last dreamed the bear, he climbed
the stairs of my porch, the rough pads
of his feet brushed in whispers
on the wood: my eyes
sliding back into my head when I turned to face him.

When I last dreamed the bear, he laid
his black head on my thigh,
the bear-smell rising rank around us,
his coat bristling my skin,
the great weight of him leaning, leaning into me.

And though we never spoke,
I knew then that he loved me, and so began
to stroke his rough back, to pull him even closer.

Yellow Dog Journal—Fall (excerpt)

Judith Minty

> Go, my daughter, to discover
> Why the grey-brown dog is barking,
> And the long-eared dog is baying.
> —Runo XVIII, *Kalevala*

1.

400 miles into north land, driving hard
like a runaway, each town peeling away the woman skin,
turning me pale and soft, as if I
had never married, had not
been planted twenty years in the suburbs.

I come here as my father's child, back
down his rutted road, through a cave of sagging timber
to the clearing. Nothing changed.
His land, his shack leaning over the riverbank,
the Yellow Dog barking home to Superior.

2.

This cabin has not been lived in
since August. October now, and rain
crawls over trees, roof. It muddies the trail.

Bone cold, I light the stove. Damp
shrivels into seams of the walls
and all the flies of summer burst alive again.

They beat their wings against the windows.
They whine and bleat in a confusion of seasons,
then cling to shadows on the ceiling.

I swing at them with a newspaper, wonder
how long I'll last here.
Maple leaves dry yellow on my boots.

3.

My father's slippers, found
in a trunk, now mine to wear.
Too large, creases in the leather
barely touch the flesh.
I slide my toes to the end, along the old ridges.

His feet clump over linoleum floor
table to dishpan, woodbox to stove.
Only the scrap of rug by the door
muffles his presence.

4.

Night comes early in October.
I prop my feet up,
lean into the old rocker.
Rain flows over the roof.
Flames from the wood stove
spin off walls, ceiling,

circle the amber in my glass,
this shack a hive humming.

5.

Last night I drank too much and, almost
asleep, thought of old lovers.
Decided I would hike three miles
to a phone in the morning, call a friend. Ask him
to come north, drive nine hours into autumn.

Today the sky is clear, the trees on fire.
I tie a scarf around my head and walk
to the river for water.

6.

All day, I stay close to the cabin.
My ax rings the morning. And half the afternoon
I gather kindling, spread the sticks
to dry. I am menstruating and have heard
that bear are attracted to women when they bleed.

I haven't spoken in three days, have seen nothing
bigger than chipmunks and squirrels
at the woodpile. It is only beyond the perimeter
that black shapes hide, breath steaming,
low growls circling their throats.
When the branch falls, I swirl to the sound, ax raised.

The Company

Jane Piirto

I have felt a keen longing for my own lands.
—Runo 29, *Kalevala*

I.

Negaunee caves in.
They're moving Palmer.
Republic used to be a bluff.
Ishpeming has no tax revenues
now the undergrounds have closed.
Tilden Location is now a metropolis.
Cliff's Drive is blocked off
with open pit low grade iron pellets.

In 75 years
the largest gem in the world,
Jasper Knob,
of jaspillite and hematite
will be an open pit too,
but they don't call it
strip mining.

Here's to The Company!

Mr. Mather and his friends
explored and coveted,
they bought and litigated,
claimed from the Chippewa,
and the word went,
New England and Europe
to the famished of famine—
Cornish, Irish, French-Canadian,
Swedes, Norwegians,
Finns and Italians later.
Poor people,
second sons, unmarried daughters
sailed to Ellis, huddled.
Carriage, canal, and railroad
Boat, and hope
carried them to Ishpeming, Michigan,
where their cousins worked.

Housemaids and miners,
housemaids and lumberers,
housemaids and carpenters,
shoemakers, merchants, farmers,
barkeeps and miners
and miners' sons
sought respectability
in claimed cedar swamps,
bearing
babies and an ethic,
work and not welfare,
damp mines and falling chunks,
the ore to make the autos

to make America
what it is.

Compasses went crazy,
north pointed south
at this iron. Red
dust soiled the sheets,
hand-wrung, hung
on clotheslines frozen
stiff as walls
between workers and bosses,
ore
red mud covered sensible
boots tramping trails
in mosquito-owned woods.

Adventurers became family men,
housemaids housewives,
and there were children,
and hope for the children,
and the Lutheran church,
and the Catholic church,
and the Methodists,
and the streets of taverns,
and The Company,
tentacled.

II.

We are yours, Company.
You pollute with our blessing.
You own the land.
You hired our grandfathers,

our fathers,
brothers, husbands.

You gave us girls college
at Northern—
"teaching is a good job
for a woman"—
you own the land.

Our sons go to Northern too.
They live in Detroit now,
work for the auto companies,
or hamburger franchisers,
teach school,
if they don't work for you,
'cause The Company pays good
now there's unions,
and being a miner
is a respectable job,
and we work for you
whatever we do.

III.

My dad died of cancer.
He worked in your shops.
The noise made him deaf.
The Company paid the bills.

My mother is a widow
with a small pension,
now there's unions.

My husband worked the Empire Mine.
He spit taconite, black ooze on the pillow
for a year after he quit,

but he made good money,
saved up for college.
My cousin's your accountant.

We are yours, Company.
You showed us the land.
Your land
seduces us—
trout, deer, waterfalls,
clean water, pine woods—
you only pollute a little.
You sent our kids to college.
You helped us own our homes.
We had nothing
when we came.

You own the land
our homes stand on.
You hire us
to move our homes
when you wish
to dig a shaft,
a pit,
a strip.
You own the land,
and jobs
are more important
than land.

We are yours,
wrapped and fenced.
We are your
links in the chain.

Pass it on.

1983

Pasty

Jane Piirto

My friends told me they crossed the U.P.
and had some pay-sties
as in the costumes of strippers.
Past-ties? I said.
Past as in present, past, future?
The Cornish meat pie that is ubiquitous.
The miners' wives would put it into lunch buckets
All the miners' wives of whatever nationality
adopted it and some Finns even call it a Finnish dish.
Wrong. Just go to Cornwall in England and see
all the pasty shops, just like in the U.P.
No such thing in Finland.
The cuisine of working people.
"Let's stop and get a pasty and go to the Island for a picnic."
"The church picnic will serve pasties."
"Mom, can I have your pasty recipe?" our children say
remembering their childhoods.
Every Christmas potluck here in Ohio
I bring it to work.
"Are you bringing your pasty pie?
The men really love it."

"What is the recipe?"
Meat and potatoes and onions
Salt and pepper
Pie crust.

Mother Earth Father Sky (excerpt)

Sue Harrison

SHUGANAN WAS NOT SURE HOW HE KNEW. PERHAPS IT WAS THE WISDOM of old age. Perhaps the voices of his carvings spoke to his soul as they often seemed to do when sleep stilled his body and gave his spirit time to live without the interference of doing and making. Perhaps it was Tugix or some greater spirit. But whether by spirit or by wisdom, Shuganan knew.

He had begun carving the seal many days before. He had used a walrus tusk, old and yellowed, fine-grained but brittle with age. He had soaked it for a long time in oil, softening it so his knife could shave away the pieces necessary to reveal the spirit within.

He sharpened the point of the tusk until it was nearly as fine as the barb of a harpoon. That was the seal's nose. Then the body curved and widened into flippers. Shuganan smoothed the blunt end of the tusk into a ledge that fitted snugly against the heel of his hand.

He finished the seal, then asked Chagak for tanned skins and heather. Chagak had seemed puzzled when he laid Samiq out on a sealskin and, using long sinew strands, measured the boy's arms and legs, the length from his head to his fat, round toes. But she had not asked questions.

Shuganan used a woman's knife to cut the shape of a baby from the sealskin. He used the first shape as pattern for a second and sewed the two together, then stuffed them with heather.

FROM A WIDE CURVE OF DRIFTWOOD, BLEACHED TO WHITENESS BY THE sun and sea, he carved a mask, making nose and mouth and closed eyes. Then, drilling holes through the sides of the mask, he sewed it to the head of his sealskin baby.

And one evening when Chagak was busy setting out food, Shuganan had asked to hold Samiq. He had felt no threat to his manhood in this, seeing that Kayugh sat beside an oil lamp, holding his son. And when no one was watching, Shuganan cut a bit of hair from Samiq's head. Perhaps there might be some power toward reality in the hair, some strength that would turn a man's eyes to seeing what he thought he was seeing instead of what was truly there.

That night, in his sleeping place, Shuganan stitched the hair on top of his sealskin baby's head.

NOW IN THE EARLY MORNING, BEFORE THE WOMEN HAD RISEN TO TRIM wicks and carry out night wastes, Shuganan wrapped his baby in one of the sealskins Man-who-kills had given as Chagak's bride price.

He waited on the beach, the baby within his parka, the carved tusk inside his sleeve. He waited until he saw one of the women leave Big Teeth's ulaq, then he returned to his ulaq and pretended he had gone outside only to watch the sea for signs of seal.

The next morning he also went out and the morning after that. On the fourth day he woke in the night and, feeling the urging of some spirit, again went to the beach, taking his baby and the ivory seal.

He waited during the darkest part of the night, watching the sea, listening for noise within the waves that was not animal but man. When the sky had begun to lighten, he was sure he heard the dipping of a paddle, something that kept its own rhythm, not the rhythm of the sea.

Shuganan slipped the ivory seal down into his hand, felt the tip of the tusk, as sharp as a knife, caressed the ledge that he had carved for the heel of his hand, something to lend strength to his thrust. Then he tucked it inside his sleeve and wrapped his arms over the sealskin baby as though he were a mother carrying her husband's son.

Shuganan saw the ikyak and the hunter within. He smiled. Yes. It was Sees-far.

He watched as the man guided his ikyak through the rocks toward the shore, as he untied his hatch skirting and leaped from the craft, pulled his ikyak to the beach.

Sees-far grinned at Shuganan but made no greeting. And so Shuganan, too, gave no greeting but said only, "Man-who-kills told me you would be coming. I have waited these four mornings for you."

"I have come to teach Man-who-kills how to fight again," Sees-far said and laughed. "He has lived too easily over the winter. He must be ready to fight Whale Hunters. We go soon."

Sees-far scanned the beach. "And so where is he?" he asked. But Shuganan had made sure that the men's ikyan were not within sight, and so knew that Sees-far saw nothing but beach gravel and drying racks.

"He is in the ulaq. His wife is also in the ulaq," Shuganan said. "She has been a good wife to him. They have a son."

"A son!" Sees-far said and began to laugh. "Now that she has given Man-who-kills what he wants, maybe he will not be so reluctant to share her with me."

"I brought the baby for you to see," Shuganan said, keeping his eyes on Sees-far's face, hoping to know when the first doubt came into the man's mind, hoping to act before Sees-far knew the truth.

"So he makes you do woman's work," Sees-far said and laughed.

"I can no longer hunt." Shuganan said and held out his bent and stiffened left arm.

"And so you will show me this son?" Sees-far asked. And he pointed toward the bulge under Shuganan's parka.

"There is too much wind here. We should stand against the cliff where there is shelter."

But as soon as he said the words, Shuganan saw the doubt in Sees-far's eyes, saw the man look quickly to the top of the cliff. So Shuganan said, "But Man-who-kills' son is strong, perhaps he is old enough for the wind."

The doubt faded. Shuganan reached inside his parka and pulled the sealskin baby from its place against his chest.

Sees-far smiled and leaned down to see the child. Shuganan slipped the carved tusk along the inside of his arm and worked the point to the palm of his hand.

Shuganan held the baby out toward Sees-far, then pretended to stumble. He saw the surprise in Sees-far's eyes, the quick movement of the man's hands to catch the baby. As Sees-far clasped the sealskin bundle, Shuganan dropped his right arm so the walrus tusk fell into his hand.

Shuganan had killed many seals, many sea lions. He knew the place of the heart, the sheltered place beneath the breastbone, and so he knew the best way of killing a man, the blow to the heart from the unprotected side, up from the stomach. He thrust the sharp point of his carved tusk up and into Sees-far's heart. The tusk-knife cut deep even as Sees-far said, "But this is not a baby. . . ."

And the words, though they had begun in a strong voice, ended in a whisper.

Sees-far dropped to his knees, the sealskin baby still in his arms. Shuganan placed a hand on the man's chest. The heart had stopped, but Shuganan could still see the spirit peering from Sees-far's eyes.

Shuganan drew his flint knife from the scabbard he kept on his left arm and, grabbing Sees-far by the hair, sliced through the front of the man's neck.

1984

Under the Lidless Eye

John Woods

These are hunters.
In their season, they lurch down
from the camper through gray-crusted snow
to hunch ancestrally:
the shiver-and-shake of urination,
marking the clearing with steam.
They have license.

When trees rage and char,
when we fold silkskins into the camphor,
chewing dark fat, these men take down long bows,
the fowling pistols and skinning knives.
Some have painted on grease-smoked cave walls
and some pass Polaroids. Their necks rasp.
Their nails deepen to blue steel.
Hair springs out of their cheeks.

Then there is the war of the bumper stickers,
hatchbacks glaring at each other in parking lots.
Some say the over-and-under, the magnums
loosen the groin; that the women they have shrined
with dual accounts jackknife in their jibes:

wet notches, receiving chambers
for the oily rounds. They say that these men
are the barbers who, cable-necked,
bump chests at Little League. Evenings they clean
their weapons, easy in the kitchen liquidities,
men as they were. Later the children hear,
from their high beds, that there are traps
around the office water cooler, spear pits
beneath that strange, lurching animal, *family*.

Up near Houghton, the buck's head sharpens.
Grazers turn the long triangles of imagination
toward the camper radio. The song says
there is one clearing
where we always leave a little blood
because the weasel must eat, the owl must drift down
on the shrew, the deer swell with parasites.

Through this clearing and the next,
through the camper, the little recording booth
winding country truths, a music moves so slowly
even the oak can't hear it, even the oak
who gave up passion for time, through whose eye
the hunter's flesh seethes around
precise armatures. Blood without passion,
it tells. Death without processions.

Over this clearing, the moon rises,
once the Huntress in the youth of her praisers.
When her eye opens, all our fats and colors
fry out. She can see cells detonate
and the long carapaces of lake ice.

She sees the hunter lift his taut bow,

the buck raise his heavy rack.

She sees compasses bowing at consecrated text.

Yes, she can make one white stone

burn in the stream bed,

but she makes the shadows darker.

We do not know who watches the moon.

1988

Lunar Eclipse

Carol R. Hackenbruch

Facing south on the porch,
my son and I watch a shadow
ease over the moon.
Fire flies dot the branches
of surrounding evergreens.
At our whispers and chair creaks,
the goat snorts, disturbed.

When the moon is capped,
stained black and orange,
the stars waver,
move and sway in our waning attention.
After we enter sleep,
the moon will emerge,
collect all our small shadows.

1988

Eggs

Phil Legler

for Mrs. Chinn's 5th Grade Class,
Phelps School, Ishpeming, Michigan

It was delivered, all right,
like a secret message,
the way, when I was a boy,
the milkman arrived,
as if we had taken an oath
like the one I swore on
with Donald Stutson with a pin
when we sneaked out back
behind the garage, vowing we'd
run away. It was eight o'clock
and getting light out and my wife
said when she phoned me at work,
"You'll never believe it!"
So what could I do
but rush out the door
as if for the first time
seeing the snow melting.
And how could I shout it
feeling the wind off the lake

puffing my shirt out,
rattling the traffic signs.
It was kite weather.
And striding back home on Pine
I noticed the houses I passed
stood out in their roofs
with the snow off, the way
the lake rises when the ice
breaks up and you know the first
ore boat, the *Edward B. Green*,
will dock at the harbor.
Almost home, stepping home,
I was sure all the joggers
would nod or wave on their path.
I was sure the day would fill
with the sun and women
and clothes baskets.
Opening the front door,
leaving the front door open,
I ran back into the kitchen—
it was there on the table
next to the dishes, somebody's
miracle hurting my eyes,
like staring into the sun
to make myself sneeze.
The house was empty
and I was dreaming again,
cupping my hands.
But it was your card, P.S.
sending me hunting:
"In the three mixed colored ones
there is a note," you said,

as if you were smuggling
clues in like "Count ten paces
from the steps to the maple
tree." And I reached down
into the cellophane grass
to find a trinity of eggs
and lifted them out
and opened them up
and read your words
this one good Friday to cry
what I never cried as a boy.

1988

De Tour Village

Stephen Tudor

1. *BOSLEY'S BOAT YARD (519) 297-3471; gas,*
diesel; transient moorage, electricity, ice;
haul-out to 35 tons, launch ramp, CB chan 11
monitored; hull repairs, gen mech. on duty;
courtesy car; tug service; restaurant,
laundry, groceries nearby.

But the place is a ruin: fallen docks,
Blasted workshed, junkfield, scurvy road's end—
And wildflowers, risen among the debris,

Thanks for them. For the few of them I picked
Go in water in a tumbler I've placed
In the gimballed drink-holder aft the tiller.

The common daisy and the black-eyed susan.
Head-proud, at ease beside the road;
Fireweed, thimbleweed, day lily, primrose.

Though I forget to water they last days,
And when I come to dock in towns I want
All to take notice: white clover, lupine

Chickweed, buttercup, bushy aster,
Meadow violet. Though winter comes,
Still blazing they linger in our eyes.

2. *FRED'S BAR*

A "river room" next to the ferry slip—
Bar at back wall, a few tables, games.

Through the big window, the *P.R. Clark* upbound;
Drummond Dolomite on the other shore.

I call Detroit from phone near men's room.
The place depresses me. Bare, grimy, sad.

Wife says "don't talk so loud. They can hear you."
I'm whipped and filthy, myself. Comes the beer,

Barside, and there's this gaunt, toothless old guy,
Not quite drunk, and we talk about the lakes.

To see him you'd think he'd lived on the boats.
True, but just one year: 'forty-two to 'three.

A dock or loading cable crushed his leg.
That must have hurt like hell. *Naw. I passed out.*

Nine months with his leg up. He kept at me
About the mail boat: "What was that thing named?"

I couldn't remember, myself,
Starting to fly on the strength of one beer.

Then it came to him—the *O. F. Mook*,
Our only floating U.S. Post Office,

And after the *Mook*, the *J.W. Wescott*.
Shoots out below the Ambassador Bridge,

Runs up alongside ships, sticks bag
Into the sky basket, takes on new mail.

That's my poetry, and she's still going strong.
That's my metaphor, after all these years.

3. *THE VILLAGE INN*

*"The four saddest words
That were ever composed
Are these dismal sounds—*
THE BAR IS CLOSED.*"*

Still feeling punchy from the long, wet day,
I plunk down on the stool nearest the door.
It's supper time. The long bar's empty now
Except for a threesome at the far end:
The boss-lady, her waitress, a patron
Having a good laugh at someone's expense.
The place is dark, warm, gay with the lit speech
Of beer signs: blue green, red, softly obscene;
Medallions, teams of horses, waterfalls,
A comfort to the eye. "They sent me here . . ."
I venture. "From down below—don't I know,"
The old gal says. I order up. She pours.
My image in the mirror behind the bar

Stares back at me through a kind of glass waste:
Whiskey bottles, gin, vodka, schnapps, rum.
About the walls, words of advice: *today*
Is the first day of the rest of your life.
I know, I know, I promise to do better.
And now the young waitress brings my burger,
Thick, hot from the grill, oozing cheese,
Rank with onions, dripping with the red-brown
Slime of condiments and ground-round fat.
She's smoking. Runs her fingers through her hair.
Wants to know whether the food's o.k. "Great—
They don't have bars like this in Ontario."
None so vulgar. And none in such poor taste.
"Enjoy your meal," she tells me, wreathed in blue.
I wolf it down; I light one up myself.

Soo Locks

Jim Daniels

for my mother

You talk about the Soo Locks
and how you love to watch the water
go up and down, and the boats,
and I laugh, *The water goes up*
and down, big deal,
and grab the lunch you made me
and run out the door
and drive to the job
to stack steel
and I watch the press go up and down
and the more it goes up and down
the more steel I have to stack.
I understand this up and down of the factory,
it is simple and American, machines and steel,
and I eat the lunch you made me
and close my eyes
and try to picture
the water going up and down.

American Americans (excerpt)

Jim Northrup

FOND DU LAC FOLLIES BOATED ON THE BIG LAKE—LAKE SUPERIOR—
with Curt Gagne. He was the captain of a herring net-setting vessel. Captain
Curt was going to get food from the lake. We offered tobacco before we left.
The boat was a sixteen-foot aluminum skiff. It was wide and deep. It looked
lake-worthy. A ten-horse Johnson motor (never seen a Johnson worth ten
horses, my cousin would say) pushed and pulled us around the lake. The lake
was bumpy in places. It seemed like it was alive. At times the right combination
of waves and boat gave us a light spanking. The color of the lake was gray and
green and everything in between. It moved with a life force all its own. We
could see all the way to Michigan—Isle Royale. The water was cold, the air
was warm. There was no wind. The seagulls were talking in their language
as we rode on the lake we shared. Some were flying around and others were
bobbing on the lake, waiting for supper or something.

Captain Curt said we were in about 120 feet of water when we set the net.
The net was eight feet tall and three hundred feet long. It was nylon and the
mesh was 2⅞ inches square. The net had floats spaced about five feet apart and
the sinkers were the same distance. A recycled antifreeze jug marked one end
of the net. A rock anchor was on the other end. The dark gray rock looked like
it came from the north shore of Lake Superior. Captain Curt played out the
net from the stern of the boat. He stood with one foot braced on the gunwale.
The net was sliding over his leg. The floats made a *clunk-clunk* sound as they

hit against the net box. Captain Curt separated the floats and sinkers as the Johnson *putt-putted* along.

The sun was just going behind the trees when we finished setting the net. It was your standard beautiful Minnesota sunset. After we were done, Captain Curt made a side trip for the tourist in the boat. We looked at a cave on the lakeshore. He said there were stories associated with that spot. It felt like it should have stories. It was big enough to hold ten boats like the one we were riding in. As Captain Curt winched his boat out of the lake, I suggested a name for his boat. He could call it the USS *Enterprise*. The name just beamed into my head as we completed our trek on Lake Superior. The next morning Captain Curt brought in seventy pounds of food.

> QUESTION: *Why do you call it a rez instead of a reservation?*
> ANSWER: *'Cause the white man owns most of it.*

I am not Indian. I am Anishinaabe. For almost five hundred years my ancestors and I have been called something we're not. It started with Columbus, then continued with the Puritans and Cotton Mather. Along the way the United States government started using it. Hollywood and other forms of mass media have perpetuated the use of the word *Indian* to describe us. It has become so common we have internalized it. We have heard it so much we begin to think we are Indians. I'm not Indian, I'm Anishinaabe.

It has been almost five hundred years since Native people discovered Columbus wading ashore. Almost five hundred years of being identified by the wrong name. I have nothing to celebrate. Columbus was just the point man for the invasion of this hemisphere. A way of life that was ecologically sound was transformed into a poisoned, polluted existence. Christianity and the lust for gold replaced respect for the land, air, and water.

As my way of de-celebrating the Columbus event, the word *Indian* will not cross my lips for one year. Instead of saying the word, I will use silence. Instead of writing the word out, I will use dashes. I am banishing the word from my vocabulary for one year starting October 12, 1991.

According to the World Book encyclopedia, we are called —— because Columbus didn't know he had stumbled onto a new continent. He was originally looking for a short sea route to the Indies, at that time India and China. Thinking that he had made it to the Indies, he called the inhabitants ——. He liked these people so much, he took some back as slaves. He called his slaves ——.

We have been using the word —— so long we have overdone it. For example: *The Circle*, 24 pages, 333 times; *News from —— Country*, 32 pages, 342 times; *Ojibwe News*, 12 pages, 417 times; *Fond du Lac News*, 2 pages, 26 times; Fond du Lac Follies, 12 pages, 19 times.

Dropping the word —— might have some interesting thoughts associated with it. I would have to call that Hoosier state ——a, its capital would be known as ——apolis. When talking about the American —— Movement, I'd have to use silence or dashes in the middle. What about the Bureau of —— Affairs? There are enough examples to keep it interesting. The —— Health Service, the National —— Gaming Act, the Cleveland ——s baseball team. The road sign on the edge of the rez would read Fond du Lac —— Reservation. My kids could still play, only now they'll play cowboys and ——s.

Out of thousands of English words, I can afford to give one a short vacation. I realize —— is a permanent part of the language. Giving it up for one year will be just my form of silent protest. I will get a chance to de-celebrate Columbus almost every day for a year. I am not ——, I am Anishinaabe.

WE HAVE A GRANDSON AND I JUST HAVE TO BRAG. HIS NAME IS AARON and he can scream loud enough to wake the neighbors. He is sixteen months old and doesn't know how to pee standing up. We call him Air and Water and he is just discovering the world. It makes me young to see it through his eyes. Air and Water gets up early so he can old-man around with his grampa. He climbs the stairs and greets me open armed. He is still sleepy as he tries to climb in my lap. We usually just sit for a few minutes feeling each other's heartbeat. Together we look around the yard to see if night has changed anything. We watch the birds flying by. We hear the train going by in downtown Sawyer.

I am getting him now because I know he will turn into a teenager. Being a grandparent is special. Do you want to see pictures of my grandson?

ANISHINAABE WERE EXERCISING THEIR 1854 TREATY RIGHTS IN THE ceded territory of what is now called Minnesota. Fond du Lac hunters register their kills with the Reservation Conservation Department. So far the largest moose I have heard of has an antler spread of sixty inches. The moose we got was average sized. Shinnobs are going to eat moose all winter. The Reservation Business Committee should be commended for their support of the 1854 treaty rights.

QUESTION: How do you say "moose" in Ojibwe?
ANSWER: "Mooz."

Charlie "Tuna" Nahganub and Nappy Ross were finally found not guilty in tribal court. Judge Dee Fairbanks thought the prosecution failed to prove they were violating the FDL band conservation code for possessing a spear in a closed season. When the prosecutor tried to refer to the Minnesota state conservation code, he was informed that the state of Minnesota did not exist when the 1854 Treaty was signed. The two Shinnobs celebrated by going out spearing after the court hearing. They speared fish in one of the rivers that empties into Lake Superior. Four salmon went to the Elderly Nutrition Program (ENP) in Cloquet (rhymes with okay and bouquet). Two fish went to the ENP in Sawyer. Elders were eating fish because two Shinnobs were willing to use their 1854 treaty rights. This case proves that the tribal court is aware of the 1854 Treaty.

I am not ——, I am Anishinaabe. It has been harder that I thought it would be to banish the "I" word from my vocabulary. At least twice a week I catch myself still using the word ——. My kids have made a game out of it. They mark the kitchen calendar every time they hear me using the word. There are stories about tricking someone into using the word.

We are learning how powerful words and labels are. Since I banished the word from my language, I have become aware of how pervasive the word is in our daily lives. We were watching a movie on TV the other night. In the first ten minutes of the film, we heard the word —— five times. The word —— is official. It is used in the Declaration of Independence. It's used in the many treaties. Rez government makes daily use of the word ——. Washington, DC, is one of the hotbeds for use of the word ——. Public Law 102-123 is a recent example. Senate Joint Resolution 172 states that the months of November 1991 and 1992 are to be known as "National American —— Month." The joint resolution has some nice things to say about the natives of this continent. It is also a reminder of the overuse of the word ——. My copy of the joint resolution uses the word ten times in a little over a page.

We keep hearing the message that we are ——. It's everywhere, it's everywhere. If you call someone a name or label, pretty soon they think they are that name or label. I think it may take a year to completely banish the word from my vocabulary. By that time it will be time to start saying it again. The calendar will be all marked up by then. The exercise has raised my consciousness about labels. Just another reminder of the power of words. I am not ——, I am Anishinaabe.

The Wilderness State

Jack Driscoll

HELL IS *NOT* ROOM 101. I'D GLADLY COME EYEBALL TO EYEBALL WITH the goddamn rats. *Bring them on*, I thought, staring at a class of mine. *Bring the ugly bastards on!* But nobody will—*1984* is already old hat and the new hell is this latest stack of freshman essays.

The first one I read ends, *And this is what I think.* I want to write, *No shit*, and hand it back, but I don't. It's Weasel Conroy's essay on dying. He claims to have seen his father kill a man and dump the body in a bayou. Who knows, maybe he did. But it's unlikely, and if I were a priest instead of a teacher, someone more honest, and Weasel came to me for confession, I'd tell him that. Instead I write on the bottom of his last page, *Interesting*, one of the words I hate most in this garble of a world.

Weasel's from Louisiana. I haven't a clue what he's doing at a technical college in northern Michigan nor, for that matter, what I'm doing here either. Teaching, if you stretch the definition.

My department chairman handed me a petition a few days after I arrived. I signed, one of thousands, he told me, who supported the Upper Peninsula as our fifty-first state. "The Wilderness State," he said. "The U.P."

U.P., D.C., UPI—I didn't give two shits as long as no one could find me.

"Without the bridge," he said, "we're not even connected to Michigan." He said his wife, all the wives who city-shopped, shopped in Green Bay. He said, "At least honor the land-mass—let us be part of Wisconsin!"

I agreed. It's my first year and I'll say almost anything because God knows I need the money. Fifteen hours of comp per week, 119 students, and my department chairman tells me I beat out applicants from twelve states, including a woman with a Ph.D. from Alaska. Jesus, I think, how absolutely depressing.

The good students have all tested out of the comp program, and I'm stuck with Weasel Conroy and his girlfriend Marcia Savage, a townie who says I'll get to love it here—the lakes and rivers *and* the snow. She says she does. She's ended her essay this way: *And so on and so forth.* They've got to be yanking my chain with names like Weasel and Savage, studying sentence structure in the Wilderness State.

Henry Gage, the short and unattractive class intellectual, said to me first day when I called the roll, "Call me Hank."

"Like in Hank Aaron," I said and smiled and he said back, "Like in who?"

I think, *C'mon, I don't need this right off the bat.* I've always taken an immediate and permanent dislike toward people, especially guys, who claim to know jack shit about baseball, and I used to tell them that, but I don't anymore. I let it pass like I do a lot of things.

I said to Henry Gage, "Hank it is." But when he wrote, camouflaged in the middle of a sentence on last week's assignment, *Check here if you've read this far,* I jotted him a note in the margin. *Surprise surprise*, I said. *Here's your check, Henry*, and I made a big one with a red pen, and then I wrote, *And this is as far as I go.* Then I printed his grade—F. I'd love to fail his ass for the whole semester, but the creep takes severe notes and reads everything I pass out and never misses a class, so it won't be easy. If, even for one minute, I ever really believed I'd father a kid like Henry Gage, I'd swear I'd cut my pecker off.

I'd give twenty-five—no, make that an even fifty percent—of my take-home pay to anyone competent and willing to correct these essays, anyone. I asked Charles Waddell, my office mate and certain lifer, what he thinks and he says, "That's what we hired *you* for." So I carry the damn things home again in my briefcase and promise myself I'll read seventeen a day, seven days a week.

The department chairman checks to make sure the students are writing and getting their papers back each week, getting their lousy money's worth. He's of the NO-FREE-TIME-ON-OUR-HANDS SCHOOL.

Still, I buy in, sort of. I tell my students they should care about language, and I mean it. Weasel says after class, "We care, or I do anyway," and Marcia nods and I think, maybe Charlie's right, maybe there is something that surfaces from all of this. Not writers, certainly, but something.

It's not my first teaching job, I remind Charlie at least once a day, but he's been here since 1970, and though he's only a few years older, he likes to lecture me, the new kid on the block. He says, "In Detroit, you'd have to teach your classes wearing a bulletproof vest."

"Standard issue?" I ask him and he says, "Hey, that's no shit."

I lie. I say, "I survived two tours in Vietnam," which seems okay to say these days. "What's to fear?"

"You've got it good here, soldier," he says, but I don't look like a soldier in my civies—white shirt, open to the neck, thin tie, blue jeans. My M.A.'s from Yale and I've got Hopkins and Stevens and Williams on my shelves. Charlie has said to me more than once, "There are no scholars in this bunch," and I can see he's proud of that. Nuts-and-bolts curriculum.

They all teach comp, too. "Just like you do," Charlie says, "same as you." But I'm not one of them which is why I'm not well liked in this department of five men, a kind of sporting club. I lie to get a foothold, to keep an edge on these boneheads who gather in my office for meetings because Charlie's got a miniature basketball hoop attached to the wall. They like the name of Minnesota's expansion team—The Timberwolves. I tell them I played a little college hoop, another outrageous lie, and Charlie tosses me the Nerf ball and I step to the foul line they've chalked off behind his desk and, without ever taking a practice shot, I sink ten in a row. I'd love to get these candyasses on a real court, get Weasel, who I'm sure has never dribbled a B-ball, but who is lean and wiry and goes a good six-two, a leaper, to hustle down to the gym and the two of us would take off our shirts and we'd take on the four of them, all pot-bellied and tenured.

CHARLIE ENCOURAGES ME TO ENCOURAGE MY STUDENTS TO ENTER essay contests around the country—religious, political, literary. Instead I encourage them not to. *Play the lottery*, I want to tell them. *It's up to twelve million and all it takes is luck.*

But Charlie hands me yet another announcement in the hall between classes, a CALL FOR MANUSCRIPTS, and I stop right there and open my briefcase and say, "Take one, go on."

"Any one?" he asks and I say, "Read one and you've read them all," and he does take one from the middle of the stack and skims it and says he likes the simile, *a cloud like a giant nipple.*

"You've seen a nipple like that?" I ask him and he says, "If you think about it long enough," and I say, "Exactly," but as always he misses the point and walks away.

They love it here and it's more and more obvious every day that I don't, plus they know now that I taught creative writing at a university in Massachusetts for one year where almost nobody ice fishes, nobody I know. These guys spend most of every weekend in their shanties out on the bay, fishing smelt.

"Make *that* exciting," I challenged my classes one day, and Marian Montjoy did. She described, in great detail, how, when she fished alone some nights in her father's hut, she'd lock the door and take up the lines and stoke the stove until she started to sweat. Then she'd take off all her clothes and lower herself slowly through that hole into the icy water. Nothing apocalyptic, and certainly no flow to the prose, but she did hold my interest, so I gave her an A, the only one I'd given all year, and asked her to drop around during my office hours when I knew Charlie wouldn't be there. She did, and I said, holding and pointing to her essay, "You don't really do this," and she said, "No, no, I don't," but she went on to say how it resembled something else, how, during the big winter storms, she runs naked from her sauna and dives headfirst into the deepest drifts of snow. She's rich, this one. She's trouble.

"That's okay, isn't it? I mean, to make it up?"

I tell her I've been making it up all my life, that and drinking too much and falling too quickly in love, and I say to myself, *Uh-huh, don't do it*, but it's too late and I lean forward far enough to let Marian Montjoy know the next move is hers. I don't know, maybe subconsciously I want to get fired, get out here, though I have no place else in the world to go, which is what I tell her later, and I admit I'm thirty-seven and divorced, all this while sitting naked on the edge of my bed. I don't feel badly though, not really, nor does she. She's eighteen and still under the covers and she says, "Give me an A for the course and I won't tell."

"No deal," I say, and she smiles and spends the night anyway and I drive her back to the edge of campus next morning and don't hear from her again. I check at the registrar's office but she hasn't dropped the class. And I've heard nothing from the dean. Maybe she'll spill the beans when I fail her, which I will, for unexcused absences, but so far not a peep.

YOU CAN'T SURVIVE IN A SMALL TOWN BANGING THE CO-EDS. THAT'S what my ex-wife said to me when I first started hanging around the college bars back in Massachusetts, drinking draft beer with my poetry workshop and bullshitting about curing the world with our poems. It sounded stupid even then, still in my twenties. *A young writer of promise*, as one reviewer of my first and only book once said about me. *Watch for him down the road*, and my wife did, literally, sitting alone on the couch in the dark of our rented efficiency, night after night, waiting for me to come home.

"Which one is it?" she asked one morning at breakfast and I said, still staring hungover into my plate, "Guess," and she did and got it right on the first try.

For once I didn't lie. I said, "Yes."

She said, "Do you love her?" and I answered honestly again. I said, "No, I do not," which felt good when I said it but then didn't seem to matter. After a short pause she said, "I'm moving out," but it was me who left, carrying a single suitcase. As I walked away toward the university, she shouted at me from the bedroom window, "Resign or I'll blow the fucking whistle, so help me God I will." Then she called me a whore but I didn't turn around, and she screamed that whores had no place in education, fucking these kids over.

Which I know now is true and, although I haven't changed much, Weasel Conroy says he's going to sign-up for every course I ever teach. I tell him he'll have to fail then and retake comp because it's all they'll give me. "Professor," he says, "I do like you, but I don't like nobody *that* much." I smile and Marcia says if they ever get married, which they will, they want me to read a poem of mine at the wedding, and they want to name their first son after me. "Sure," I say, "great," and Weasel slaps me on the back, right there in the Student Union lobby where I'm buying the local newspaper. And Charlie Waddell, who has just gotten into the cafeteria line, gives thumbs-up while holding his tray. Even from this distance I can see his stack of essays is about the same as mine, some of them in those colored, see-through folders I tell my students never to use.

Weasel says, "How come when you teach us you always rock back and forth on your heels?"

"I don't, do I?"

"Yes," Marcia says, "you do, and you touch your upper lip a lot, like this, like someone with a mustache," and she shows me and of course I don't want to believe her, the way I don't want to believe that I'll grow to love the snow which, since leaving the Student Union, is coming down so hard everyone I pass is a blur.

In the middle of the quad the snow is almost blue in the half-light, blue like the color of smelt, the color of Marian Montjoy's eyes.

I drop my briefcase by my feet and I stand there, holding the collar of my sport coat as high as I can around my ears. I can make out my lighted office window, but I do not want to go inside, though I'm shaking now, and badly. I think, *The Wilderness State*—names like Weasel and Savage, lovers of rivers and Timberwolves, a place so cut-off that beautiful women throw themselves naked into the snow. I tell myself it's no fluke that we end up where we do, not kneeling at the hearth, but freezing and staring into the bluish night, and believing that moment *is* the moment when all the beasts we've ever been bow their heads and are rescued.

1994

Renewal

Jonathan Johnson

This empty Monarch stove and rotting birch aren't much excuse
for my stack of stinking beer bottles. But we do have the snow,

the cars on snowpacked pavement, exhaust in subsequent taillight,
and I want to crack open my fingers, hear nothing

of argument or image, as pure song spills out and fills the room.
Maybe February enters this town with the clarity

of a child's hands, and the lighthouse stands to its knees
in black waves, searching the last cloudbellies before the horizon,

scanning as if some lover might be sailing Superior home tonight,
after all these years. This much alone'd be a sight.

Still, a fine desolation refuses to mix our casualties
with the first blood of the Ironwood girl as she runs

from a barn into a field, twisted junk cars abandoned
like her father's lovers, in the wreckage of the corn.

And if we belong to the Midwest only as abstract
expressionists, it's all the same. We live here

with lake effect piling in our yards. The snow moves through us
without lights and blasts between suspension wires at night

above the Mackinac Bridge, sticking in hundred-foot-tall strands.
And the band covers Pure Prairie League every Thursday, nine to close.

Out at the empty county airport where all the flights are cancelled
blue points strobe in time up the landing strip just in case.

Up in this gable room, the greatest possible bravery
is a hairbrush of yellow spider-web at dawn.

We always toy with hopefulness, splatters
of yellow dot my dark wood floor like dandelions

above all the empty setting, the people living there
under a ceiling of expected snow. Without me,

they sleep. But a few old ones eye the night like crushed food
they still can chew. And shove it in their mouths.

1995

North of Paradise

Phillip Sterling

Whitefish Point, Michigan
—for Dorothy

One could learn to fly from a shore like this,
above a lake the size of Kansas,
where even in July winter is
a loon we can't see from the window,
a movement the eye rejects although
the ear admonishes it, like the last
yellow jacket of the season, perhaps,
or the yawn of a milkweed pod.

One could learn from timid sand how
even great lakes cower sometimes,
how anything is possible
when a multitude of waterfowl
takes wing from stubbles far from here,
launching into air (like souls)
shared songs of passage.

1996

Paradise, Michigan

William Olsen

True, astronauts can see the wakes ships leave
and just as true the birds can see the stars
and it is also true that stars and fireflies
are equiponderant to human sight;
both sink into our very torment, our very
love of the turmoil we are to each other,
but only stars sink upwards from Superior.
The stars are nothing to the fireflies.
Both are prehistoric, both require night
to turn them on, both appear and reappear,
both hold one sky in common as do the
living and the dead, both strafe this dark thing
that sleeps in us all day until the sun falls
and the towns that we sleep in seethe anew
—as when all the lights in the house are burning.
You let your fingers brush my face the way moths
bang the screen door of this bright motel room
all they want. They're all the same, all
white as the moon and all wings till the last
little finger of your touch is everywhere,
and we awake to look across a graveyard
which is no graveyard at all, but Whitefish Bay.

Below a corrugated iron pier twelve miles
from Paradise
300 plus corpses are out there under water;
all these ships went down too perfectly
and yet this planet's crowded as it is,
and we don't have a clue as to how to make
the world dance to our love, so we dream
far into another summer of consent.
We heard two hundred dollars puts your name
upon a star, we actually talk about it.
Need says whatever comes into our heads,
need invents a telephone book of stars,
holocausts a dial tone away.
We need motels, the numbered doors of sleep,
we need the slow cat of the water's lap and leer
to slush against no piers money can buy
a name for, we need money more and more,
we need our need to pay outside so far
it blinds us with the light of where we are.
Need is what we believe, and we believe it all,
we believe the bottom right hand of the moon
to be precise and ruthless to the very edge
of where precision ends, and where consent begins—
cars topping the sludge of Michigan's great dunes,
the glowworms of illuminated beech trunks,
and in the motel sleeping couples who
consent to private dreams, whereas the
waking consent to one world in common.
No two can see the same star even once
and so we dream of squandering two hundred dollars
to name one star, one strife so far away
distance seems a blinking toy.

This firefly upon your shirt is worth
a hundred billion stars named after us.
This firefly above the planet Mars
despises dying way up here or way down
there all the same, and if we stare at stars
to keep them distant or to bring them near
is all the same, and it is all the same
to sit out on a beach as it would be
to turn back to our motel room, its
tiny soaps and cheerfully logoed matchbooks.
If day and night are one, if Heraclitus,
guardian of the living and the dead,
has gone the way of light-years into night
and if it's death for soul to become water
and life for water to ascend to fire,
then if it's all the same I'll stare
a little longer as the good philosophers
weeping or laughing must have stared because
weeping or laughing all the same is fire,
the dead lucidity and the living ignorance,
the stars gone under without sinking us,
the love-drained bioluminescing fireflies
gone asleep in the grass. . . . The dunes step off
soundless behind us and eat the stars.
Brave little lights are snuffed out everywhere.

A Daughter-in-Law Watches the Old Man Hesitate

Elinor Benedict

From the kitchen window I watch Grandfather
outside, standing on top of the long wooden
stairway that leads to the lake. Bundled
in blue wool, zipped up for zero, he waits
for something to happen. But what on a day
like this, frozen from thistle to oak,
could the old man expect? Something

about the turn of his head, his leather cap's
earflaps lifted like wings, tells me he's listening
to ice. I know the sound from another December,
the day I stood on the stairs myself, watching
birches lean on each other, brittle, ready
to drop their branches on snow. I'd thought,
old bones breaking. But to Grandfather

it's probably a noise I wouldn't imagine:
Artillery. Blasting in quarries. Hunters
blamming their rifles. Or woodcutters felling
the last of the white pines. Or if his mood

is milder, maybe a beaver slapping his tail
on water, or a grouse drumming his wings
for a mate. Whatever the old man thinks,

if he really goes down to the lake, he'll
hear the creak of his elbows reaming out
inches of ice with an auger; knees, knotted
and stiff, snapping with weight as he bends
to the hole with his bucket and gear.
I look him over—bandaged, almost,
in coats and muffler, surely unable to lift

a struggling pike thorough a small, dark "o."
He hesitates, seems to forget where he is.
I shake my head. If he belonged to an Eskimo
family, they'd send him off on a floe. But just
as I watch him drift out to sea, he lowers
his earflaps, buckles his boots, and booms
down the steps one more time.

What My Father Told Me

Michael Delp

WHAT MY FATHER TOLD ME, HE MOSTLY TOLD ME WHEN WE WERE fishing. It didn't matter that we had skipped church for the hundredth time, or whether he had walked into my school and gotten me out of class. He wanted to tell me things, he said, and the best place, he felt, was on the river. He said the river was as close to time as you were going to get. No sense, he said, watching a clock to learn about time. It wouldn't even do you any good to study rock stratification or fossils, as some scientists believed.

What seemed to arrest my father's attention most was the fact that rivers were always full of water. He would often stand on the banks of our cabin on the North Branch and ask over and over where all that water was coming from. Of course, he knew. And one summer when it was over 90 for almost two weeks in a row, we sweated our way north of Lovells and found the source: a small fingerlet seeping out from under a hummock in a swamp. Another time we stopped along the mainstream and my father showed me what he called a sacred spot. There was an iron ring in the ground, and looking into it was like peering into the eye of a river god, my father whispered.

MY FATHER TAUGHT ME ABOUT PERFECTION, TOO. OFTEN I HEARD HIM say "perfect, everything is perfect" and when I asked what he meant, he'd always say, "Just look around." But I remember him telling me a story about perfection, just to illustrate that perfection wasn't always an absolute quality in his life. Once in Montana he had been fishing a section of the Madison when he stopped in mid-cast to admire what he considered to be absolute perfection: a clear, evening sky, five-pound rainbows rising to midges, alone and miles from any house. Suddenly he heard the sound of tires squealing, the crush of metal against the guardrail a hundred feet above him and a Ford Pinto flew over the exact spot where he was fishing, landed in the river and sank in front of him. The driver swam toward him, my father half cursing his bad luck, but marveling at his one chance to see a car fly.

He taught me about glaciers and about how glaciers literally carved out the bellies of rivers. Move this water out of here he'd say, and all you got is a meandering single track through the woods barely deep enough to spit in, but add water and you've got a living vein. My father never talked much about God or religion except to say that whatever made rivers had to be wild.

My father loved wildness. He loved the fact that you could stand only so long in the current of a river until your feet started to drop out from under you. And he often said, over his shoulder when we were fishing together, that you could take something out of your imagination you didn't like, just as you would out of your pocket and let it go into the river and it would never come back.

He told me that whenever he felt any sense of failure, he would go to the river and just let whatever was bothering him loose in the water. He said he felt wild when he drank from the river, or caught brook trout and ate them on the same day. Trout particles, he called them and he was sure they had lodged in his bloodstream over the years until, he said proudly, he was more brook trout than man.

When I was twelve he took me to the Upper Peninsula for a fishing trip on the Big Two-Hearted. He was careful to point out that the river wasn't the real river Hemingway was writing about, that was the Black, further east of the Two-Hearted. This was before the Mackinaw Bridge, when you had to take a ferry across the Straits. We holed up in the station wagon, listening to Ernie Harwell call a late Tigers game. I could smell the odor of wet canvas. Tents and fishing bags. Fishing tackle.

On our way into the river my father told me that of all the places he'd been, all the rivers he'd fished, this place we were going meant the most. In the

40's, he and Fred Lewis had fished this water for weeks at a time. Years later, when Fred went blind, his wife dropped him off and he fished by himself for two weeks.

I still have pictures of Fred Lewis in my albums at home. In one, he's wearing a red plaid wool shirt. My dad says those were the best shirts you could wear to fish in. He told me to always have a fishing shirt handy. Never wear it for anything else, he said. And never, never wash it. If you can, he said, the first time you wear it, you need to anoint it with the blood of a few night crawlers and brook trout.

That's what my father fished for most. Brook trout. He could sneak into the smallest, brushiest streams where you'd swear there wouldn't hardly be any water. He'd dangle a short rod over the bank and slip the worm in without making a ripple. Then he'd mutter a prayer to the fish gods, to keep them close, he'd say, and then he'd lift the tip of his rod so slowly you couldn't see. I remember brook trout coming out of the clear water, how they looked like miniature paintings vibrant and loose with color.

My father told me, sitting on the banks of the Two-Hearted, that the best way to cook brook trout was in the coals. Pack them in river clay, he said and put it in the fire. When the clay cracked, the fish was done.

We ate fish like that for a week. My father drinking small glasses of wine. Sometimes he'd let me sip some and we'd lean back against the trees, our faces hot from the flames. Coming through the fire, his voice sounded like the voice of a god. It sounded hollow and large, as if it were coming from somewhere under the earth.

My father told me that rivers weren't really natural phenomena at all. Rivers, he said came directly out of the veins of the gods themselves. To prove it, he said, try to follow one. When you tromp through a swamp for a day or two, following something that's getting smaller and smaller and then finally vanishes under a hummock in some swamp somewhere, he said, you'd need to go down under the earth to find the source.

The source was in wildness, he said. A wild god making a river come up out of the ground by opening up one of his veins and letting his divine blood sift upward toward blue sky. When I think about my father now, I think about gods under the earth and about blood, about how he baptized himself there on the Two-Hearted that summer.

I'd already been baptized twice. Once in church when I was a baby, he said. But he'd had second thoughts about what went on, about who was sanctifying what. And another time by my grandfather with a handful of lake water. Now, he told me, I needed to drink from the same river that he drank from.

We were standing knee deep just about the mouth. Lake Superior was crashing below us. He lifted a cupped hand to my mouth and I drank and then he drank. Blood, he whispered. Keep this wild blood in you for the rest of your life.

WHEN MY FATHER WASN'T WORKING OR FISHING, HIS OTHER GREAT joy was quoting short lines of poetry while we fished. When he wasn't talking about the connection between rivers and the spiritual territory he tended so seriously inside me, he was talking about the wildness he loved in poets he'd read. I always thought it odd that a man brought up around huge tool and die presses would come to something as seemingly fragile as poetry. He particularly loved an ancient Irish poem. "The Wild Man Comes to the Monastery." Some nights when he was a bend or two below me I could hear him calling back, "though you like the fat and meat which are eaten in the drinking halls, I like better to eat a head of clean watercress in a place without sorrow." At twelve, those lines meant little, but over the years, something seeped in and built up, an accumulation of images, he liked to say to me, would get me through the hard times when my life would go dark. To keep away the loneliness he'd say and then whisper another line from Machado, or Neruda. Keep these poets close to your heart, he would admonish me and so I fished for years listening to the great Spanish surrealists drifting upriver to me in the dark.

WEEKS LATER WE WERE DRIFTING ON TURK LAKE TROLLING FOR PIKE. It was almost dark and my father was looking back over the transom, watching his line. One word came out of his mouth. Storm. I looked into the western sky and saw huge clouds boiling in, black and inky, the curl of them like a huge wave. Keep fishing he said. Keep casting from the bow. The pike will feed just before it hits, keep casting, cast your heart out, he said.

From where I stood I could see a white belly slashing up toward my lure. I could see my father etched by lightning, his rod low, then him striking, both of us fighting fish under the darkening sky.

We lost both fish. The sky seemed to literally fall on us. My father told me later in the cabin, that we'd been lucky, foolish, but lucky he said. He told me that luck was when skill met necessity and that his lightning theory was worth proving. Besides, he said, we had fished in the wildness of a storm, and what better way to end a day than to be wringing the wildness out of your wet clothes, sucking the wild rain out of your cuff, thirsty for more.

WHAT WENT INTO A BOY, STAYED INSIDE. I HID IT AWAY, KEPT MY father's voice inside me, packed in close to my heart. Whatever my father told me I always regarded as the absolute truth. I believed in the river gods. Believed that river water came from their veins; that if there was one god, He must be made entirely of water. That was years ago. For years I kept lists and journals of what I remembered my father telling me. It was all good.

Take the river inside as you would a text he would tell me more than once. He knew that once inside you could memorize every pool and run, every rock in a stream and unless there was a winter of bad anchor ice, you could come back in the spring for opening day and look for every mark you'd imagined in the winter. Even better, he told me, was the ability to enter the river inside whenever you felt the need to. "I got to light out for the territory" he was fond of saying, a good part of him given over to the wildest parts of Huck Finn's personality. And always there was that dark, brooding sense of the surreal, the river looming up inside both of us as if it were alive and breathing through our skins.

But, what I remember most clearly now is the way his voice sounded on the day he died. He was barely coherent, wandering through the double stupor of morphine and the cancer in his head. He was almost dead, but you could tell his mind was still reeling with images. On this last day he was talking rivers, and trips he'd taken. I showed him a new reel and he launched himself into a beautiful story about fishing the Two-Hearted again. Then, he said he had been overtaken the night before by a dream that he had turned into something purely wild. He didn't know what it was, he said, but he knew he had moved with grace, and that he moved under the earth with great force. He said that when he woke up, he felt a part of him was missing and that he had some sense in the dream that he had been deposited somewhere. Surely, he said, he must have dreamed himself into a river. He knew, and I remember him telling me, that there were Sioux Indians who could turn themselves into rivers. He said he had seen one such man when he was a boy traveling through Nebraska with his father. The Sioux had simply lain down, begun singing in low tones, stretching himself out further and further until he literally flowed past his feet.

My father's last dream had taken him back to that day, back to that wondrous opportunity to see flesh transcend itself. Now my father, weak from disease, lay still in his bed, only his mouth moving. What he told me on that last day was to honor my promise to take him away, to take him back to the river.

I remember my father telling me he had scouted years for the spot. He was never one for fanfare, or ceremony, and the measure of a good day was calculated by hard work. A good spot had requirements he had said: shade most of the day, a gravel bottom and a mixture of currents, a mixing place. We visited only once. That afternoon he sat with me and talked mostly of dams. It was either a wing dam, he thought, or more probably a coffer dam.

In the sunlight that filtered through the trees he drew diagrams in the dirt. Head the river off gently, he said, or it would surge over everything. With leaves he made the wash of the river, traced it exactly over the spot where he wanted the grave. Mud he said, the trunks of trees jammed by the current against steel rods driven into the bed of the river to hold back the water. He was firm about this desire, and his firmness carried itself into the waking dreams I had of the dam, the daily visions I had of myself felling trees, driving the steel rods, packing mud like a beaver.

AFTER HE DIED I SIMPLY CARRIED HIM OFF FROM THE FUNERAL PARLOR, out the back door and into the truck. His friends buried the coffin in the cemetery on the hill and I drove his body to the river.

I worked most of the first day cutting. The trees came down on the bank and I moved over their limbs as if the saw were a scythe. He lay up higher on the bank, his head on a rock as if he were sleeping. I drove the stakes in two feet of water, then rolled the trees in, guiding their huge trunks against the stakes.

That night I worked against the river, my hands digging up river stones, mud, clay from the banks. I looked often at him lying up above me, his face barely visible in the cast of light from the lantern. I had made the cuts like he had instructed. Like putting a log cabin together, he had motioned in the dirt that day, one log grooved, the other mortised. The seam of the logs joining together was barely a scar against my hands.

I slept off and on, working, sleeping. Packing mud and clay, repacking small spots where the water wanted to get in. When I finished, I was standing in something that looked like a wooden arm growing out of the bank and angling back against the flow of the river. At the lip of the dam I held my hand against the water, then turned back to look at the moist bottom of the river below me, open to daylight.

I drug down below grade, through rocks and smaller rocks, into the clay that cradled the river, the water seeping into the grave.

No mumbo-jumbo he had said, no remorse, just let me go back. I laid him face up at first, then rolled him to his side so one ear might be toward the river, the other toward the sky. I packed him in, tight he had said, wedged into the bottom of the river and then I covered him, first with clay and heavy stones, then with lighter rocks and pebbles.

I waited until early evening, lit the lantern and then began dismantling the dam, only enough to let the water in, letting two logs drift away in the darkening current. The water sluiced over the dam, now inches under water, over the stones, and sifted down, I am sure into my father's lips. I wanted to speak something to him in the dark, but couldn't. He had wanted silence; wanted the sound of the river all around us.

Now, in summer, I drift over his spot. The remnants of the dam still hold. I imagine my father has gone back completely by now, and only his bones are held in the belly of the river. I think of him often, how he carried me far beyond the years he could. How his life merged and moved with mine and then swept in another direction. I think of him alive and casting, examining and selecting flies like a surgeon, his love of poems and wildness fused together and fueled by his desire to take in all of the world in front of him. I think of how his life comes back to me each time I fish, each time I step into the current. Mostly, I think of how both of us are carried by rivers, how his memory sifts through me like the current where only his bones are left to tell the story.

1997

Suspension Bridge

Kenneth Pobo

We slap and slap
black flies. I remove
rust-reddened sneakers.
You snap

pictures. Water bruises
our feet: we walk on
cold sky, roomy,
imagine miners who worked

in towns that sprawled
and fell,
head off in

different directions.
Later I warm
swollen feet
as you drive us
to a river
cutting into the Lake.

We walk over
a suspension bridge—

how familiar,
you and I on
a trembling bridge,
death flowing
beneath us,

Superior's purple star
calling us to come
get it.

A Cold Day in Paradise (excerpt)

Steve Hamilton

THERE IS A BULLET IN MY CHEST, LESS THAN A CENTIMETER FROM MY heart. I don't think about it much anymore. It's just a part of me now. But every once in a while, on a certain kind of night, I remember that bullet. I can feel the weight of it inside me. I can feel its metallic hardness. And even though that bullet has been warming inside my body for fourteen years, on a night like this when it is dark enough and the wind is blowing, that bullet feels as cold as the night itself.

It was a Halloween night, which always makes me think about my days on the force. There's nothing like being a policeman in Detroit on Halloween night. The kids wear masks, but instead of trick-or-treating they burn down houses. The next day there might be forty or fifty houses reduced to black skeletons, still smoking. Every cop is out on the streets, looking for kids with gasoline cans and calling in the fires before they rage out of control. The only thing worse than being a Detroit policeman on Halloween night is being a Detroit fireman.

But that was a long time ago. Fourteen years since I took that bullet, fourteen years and a good three-hundred miles away, due south. It might as well have been on another planet, in another lifetime.

Paradise, Michigan, is a little town in the Upper Peninsula, on the shores of Lake Superior, across Whitefish Bay from Sault Ste. Marie, or "the Soo," as the locals call it. On a Halloween night in Paradise, you might see a few paper ghosts in the trees, whipped by the wind off the lake. Or you might see a car filled with costumed children on its way to a party, witches and pirates looking out the back window at you as you wait at the one blinking red light in the center of town. Maybe Jackie will be standing behind the bar wearing his gorilla mask when you step into the place. The running joke is that you wait until he takes the mask off to scream.

Aside from that, a Halloween night doesn't look much different from any other October night in Paradise. It's mostly just pine trees, and clouds, and the first hint of snow in the air. And the largest, coldest, deepest lake in the world, waiting to turn into a November monster.

I pulled the truck into the Glasgow Inn parking lot. All the regulars would already be there, I was sure. It was poker night. I was a good two hours late, so I was sure they had started without me. I had spent the entire evening in a trailer park over in Rosedale, knocking on doors. A local contractor had been setting a new mobile home when it tipped over and crushed the legs of one of the workers. He wasn't in the hospital more than an hour before Mister Lane Uttley, Esquire was at his side, offering the best legal services that a fifty percent cut could buy. It would probably be a quick out of court settlement, he told me on the phone, but it was always nice to have a witness just in case they try to beat the suit. Somebody to testify that no, the guy wasn't stone drunk and he wasn't showing off by trying to balance five tons of mobile home on his nose.

I started at the scene of the accident. It was a strange sight, the mobile home still tipped over, one corner crumpled into the ground. I worked my way down the line as the sun set behind the trees. I wasn't having much luck, just a few doors slammed in my face and one dog who took a nice sample of fabric out of my pant leg. I'd been giving the private investigator thing a try for about three months. It wasn't working out too well.

Finally, I found one woman who would admit to seeing what happened. After she described what she had seen, she asked me if there might be a few bucks in it for her. I told her she would have to take up that matter with Mister Uttley. I left her his card. "Lane Uttley, Attorney at Law, specializing in personal injury, workers' compensation, automobile accidents, slip and fall, medical malpractice, defective products, alcohol-related accidents, criminal defense." With his address and phone number in the Soo. She squinted at the tiny letters, all those words on one little business card. "I'll call him first thing in the morning," she said. I didn't feel like driving all the way back to his office to drop off my report, so she'd probably call him before he even knew who she was. Which would confuse the hell out of him, but I was cold and tired, much in need of a drink, and already late for my poker game.

The Glasgow Inn is supposed to have a touch of Scotland to it. So instead of sitting on a stool and staring at your own face in the mirror behind the bar, you sit in an overstuffed chair in front of the fireplace. If that's the way it works in Scotland, I'd like to move there after I retire. For now, I'll take the Glasgow Inn. It was like a second home to me.

When I walked into the place, the guys were at the table and already into the game, like I figured. Jackie, the owner of the place, was in his usual chair with his feet by the fire. He nodded at me and then at the bar. There stood Leon Prudell, one hand on the bar, the other wrapped around a shot glass. From the looks of him, it was not his first.

"Well, well," he said. "If it isn't Mister Alex McNight." Prudell was a big man, two-fifty at least. But he carried most of it around his middle. His hair was bright red and was always sticking out in some direction. One look at the guy, with the plaid flannel shirt and the hundred-dollar hunting boots, you knew he had lived in the Upper Peninsula all his life.

The five men at the poker table stopped in midhand to watch us.

"Mister McNight, Private Eye," he said. "Mister Bigshot, himself, ay?" With that distinctive "yooper" twang, that little rise in his voice that made him sound almost Canadian.

There might have been a dozen other men in the place, besides the players at the table. The room fell silent as they all turned one by one to look at us, like we were a couple of gunslingers ready to draw.

"What brings you all the way out to Paradise, Prudell?" I asked.

He looked at me for a long moment. A log on the fire gave a sudden pop like a gunshot. He drained the rest of his glass and then put it on the bar. "Why don't we discuss this outside?" he said.

"Prudell," I said. "It's cold outside. I've had a long day."

"I really think we need to discuss this matter outside, McKnight."

"Let me buy you a drink, okay?" I said. "Can I just buy you a drink and we can talk about it here?"

"Oh sure," he said. "You can buy me a drink. You can buy me two drinks. You can get behind the bar and mix 'em yourself."

"For God's sake." This I did not need. Not tonight.

"That's the least you can do for a man after you take his job away."

"Prudell, come on."

"Here," he said. He stuffed one of his big paws into his pockets and pulled out his car keys. "You forgot to take these, too."

"Prudell . . ."

I didn't expect the keys to come at me so quickly, and with such deadly aim. They caught me right above the left eye before I could even flinch.

All five men rose at once from their table. "No need, boys," I said. "Have a seat." I bent over to pick up the keys, feeling a trickle of blood in the corner of my eye. "Prudell, I didn't know you had such a good arm. We could have used you back when I was playing ball in Columbus." I tossed his keys back to him. "Of course, I got to wear a mask then." I wiped at the blood with the back of my hand.

"Outside," he said.

"After you," I said.

We went out into the parking lot and stood facing each other in the cheap light. We were alone. The pine trees swayed all around us as the wind picked up. The air was heavy with moisture off the lake. He took a couple swings at me without connecting.

"Prudell, aren't we a little too old for this?"

"Shut up and fight," he said. He swung at me with everything he had. The man didn't know how to fight, but he could still hurt me if I wasn't careful. And unfortunately, he probably wasn't quite as drunk as I hoped he was.

"Prudell, you aren't even coming close," I said. "Maybe you should stick to throwing your keys." Get him mad, I thought. Don't let him settle down and start finding his range.

"I've got a wife and two kids, you know." He kept throwing big round-house punches with his right hand. "My wife isn't going to get her new car now. And my kids won't be going to Disney World like I promised them."

I ducked a right, then another right, then another. Let's see a left, I thought. I want a nice lazy drunken left hand, Prudell.

"I had a guy working for me, helping me out when I was on a job," he said. "I swear to God, McKnight. That was the only thing keeping him together. If something happens to him now, it's all on your head."

He tried a couple more right-hand haymakers before the idea of a left-hand jab bubbled up through all the rage and whiskey in his brain. When it came, it was as long and slow as a mudslide. I stepped into him and threw a right hook to the point of his chin, turning the punch slightly downward at the end, just like my old third base coach had taught me. Prudell went down hard and stayed down.

I stood there watching him while I rubbed my right shoulder. "Get up, Prudell," I said. "I didn't hit you that hard."

I was just about to get worried when he finally pulled himself up from the gravel. "McKnight, I will get you," he said. "I promise you that right now."

"I'm here most Friday nights," I said. "Hell, most nights period. You know where to find me."

"Count on it," he said. He stumbled around the parking lot for a full minute until he remembered what his car looked like. In the distance I could hear the waves dying on the rocks.

I went back into the bar. The men looked at me, then at the door. They reached their own conclusions and went on with the poker hand. It was the usual crew, the kind of guys you didn't even have to say hello to, even if you hadn't seen them in a week. You just sat down and looked at your cards. I held a napkin over my eye to stop the bleeding.

"That clown must have stood there for two hours waiting for you," Jackie said. "What was *his* beef?"

"Thinks I took his job," I said. "He used to do some work for Uttley."

"A private investigator? Him?"

"He likes to think so."

"I wouldn't pay him two cents to find his own dick."

"Why would you pay a man to find his own dick?" a man named Rudy asked.

"I wouldn't," Jackie said. "It's just an expression."

"It's not an expression," Rudy said. "If it was an expression, I would have heard it before."

"It's an expression," Jackie said. "Tell him it's an expression, Alex."

"Just deal the cards," I said.

I played some poker and had a few slow beers. Jackie went over the bridge every week to get good beer from Canada, just one more reason to love the place. I forgot all about trailer parks and pissed-off ex-private eyes for a while. I figured that was enough drama for one night. I figured I was allowed to relax a little bit and maybe even start to feel human again.

But the night had other plans for me. Because that's when Edwin Fulton had to come into the place. Excuse me, Edwin J. Fulton the Third. And his wife, Sylvia. They just had to pick this night to drop by.

They had obviously just been to some sort of soiree. God knows where you'd even *find* a soiree in the whole Upper Peninsula, but leave it to Edwin. He was decked out in his best gray suit, a charcoal overcoat, and a red scarf wrapped around his collar just right. The suit was obviously tailored to make him look taller, but it could only do so much. He was still a good six inches shorter than his wife.

Sylvia was wearing a full-length fur coat. Fox, I would have guessed. It must have taken about twenty of them to make that coat. She had her dark hair pinned up, and when she took off her coat, we all got to see a little black number that showed off her legs and her perfect shoulders. God damn it, that woman had shoulders. And even on a cold night she had to go and wear something like that. She knew that every man in the place was looking at her, but I had a sick feeling that she wouldn't have taken her coat off at all if I hadn't been there. She slipped me a quick look that hurt me more than Prudell's keys.

Edwin gave me a little wave while he ordered up a couple quick drinks.

He had that look on his face, that deadpan look he always wore when he was out in public with his wife.

"Tell me something," Jackie said to nobody in particular. "How does a woman like that end up with a horse's ass like Edwin Fulton?"

"I think it has something to do with having a lot of money," Rudy said.

"You mean if I had a million dollars she'd be sitting over here on my lap instead?"

"I don't know about that," Rudy said. "Guy as ugly as you, you'd probably need five million."

They didn't stay long. One drink and they were gone, just a quick stop to dazzle the locals and then be on their way. She gave me one more glance as Edwin helped her into her coat. Whatever point she had hoped to make had apparently been made.

I kept thinking about her while I played poker. It didn't help me concentrate on the cards and it didn't help my mood any, either. Outside the wind really started to pick up. We could hear it rattling the windows.

"November winds are here early," Jackie said.

"It's after midnight," Rudy said. "It's November First. They're right on time."

"I stand corrected."

About an hour later, Edwin came back into the place. He was alone this time. He stood at the bar for a while, wearing his hangdog expression this time, hoping I'd notice him. I was glad he didn't try to come over to our table. He had actually played with us once before, and had lost his money as fast as a man can lose money playing low-stakes poker. But it's just no fun taking money from a guy when you know it doesn't mean anything to him. That and the way he kept yammering on like he was suddenly one of the boys. He never got asked to play again.

On most nights, I would have at least gone over to him for a minute to see how he was doing. I don't know if I just felt sorry for the guy, or if I felt guilty because of the business with Sylvia. Or maybe I really liked the guy. Maybe I considered him my friend despite all the obvious reasons not to. But for some reason I just didn't feel up to it on this night. I let him stand there by the bar until he finally gave up and left.

I felt bad as soon as the door shut behind him. "I'm gonna call it a night, guys," I said. I was hoping I could catch him in the parking lot, but when I got outside he was already gone.

On the ride home, there's a stretch on the main road where the trees open up and you get a great look at the lake. There wasn't much moonlight coming through the clouds, but there was enough to see that the waves were getting bigger, maybe four or five feet. I could feel the truck rocking in the wind as I drove. Somewhere out there, a good thousand feet under the waves, there were twenty-nine men still sleeping, twenty years after the *Edmund Fitzgerald* went down. I bet that night felt just like this one.

The wind followed me all the way home, and even when I was inside the cabin, I could feel it coming through the cracks. I turned off every light and crawled under my thickest comforter. In the total darkness I could hear the night whispering to me.

I slept. I don't know how long. Then a noise. The phone.

It rang a few times before I got to it. When I picked it up, a voice said, "Alex."

"Hello?"

"Alex, it's me, Edwin."

"Edwin? God, what time is it?"

"I don't know," he said. "I think it's about two in the morning."

"Two in the . . . For God's sake, Edwin, what is it?"

"Um, I've got a little problem here, Alex."

"What kind of problem?"

"Alex, I know it's real late, but is there any chance of you coming out here?"

"Where? Your house?"

"No. I'm in the Soo."

"What? I just saw you at the bar."

"Yeah, I know. I was on my way out here."

"Edwin, what the hell's going on?"

I stood there shivering for a long moment, listening to the wind outside and to a distant hum on the phone line. "Alex, please," he finally said. His voice started to break. "Please come out here. I think he's dead."

"Who's dead? What are you talking about?"

"I really think he's dead, Alex. I mean, the blood . . ."

"Edwin, where are you?"

"The blood, Alex." I could barely hear him. "I've never seen so much blood."

The World's Largest Living Thing

Laura Kasischke

The world's largest living thing is a
37-acre fungus in Michigan's Upper Peninsula.

We have waited all our lives
to taste it, waited

through hate & rain, licking
the wind, spooning through the fog, while it

spread in all directions, rolled

through the forests, across the fertilized lawns. Call

it mildew, mushroom, smut. What

is it if it's not
the world's moldy heart, the god

who gobbles up

young girls in bunches? Blood-surge, sweet meat, sleep. It is a gorgeous sprawling brain, dreaming

you & me.

2000

On the Nature of Human Romantic Interaction

Karl Iagnemma

WHEN STUDENTS HERE CAN'T STAND ANOTHER MINUTE, THEY GET drunk and hurl themselves off the top floor of the Gehring building, the shortest building on campus. The windows were tamper-proofed in August, so the last student forced open the roof access door and screamed *Fuck!* and dove spread-eagled into the night sky. From the TechInfo office I watched his body rip a silent trace through the immense snow dunes that ring the Gehring building. A moment later he poked his head from a dune, dazed and grinning, and his four nervous frat brothers whooped and dusted him off and carried him on their shoulders to O'Dooley's, where they bought him shots of Jägermeister until he was so drunk he slid off his stool and cracked his teeth against the stained oak bar.

In May, a freshwoman named Deborah Dailey heaved a chair through a plate-glass window on the fifth floor of the Gray building, then followed the chair down to the snowless parking lot, shattering both ankles and fracturing her skull. Later we learned—unsurprisingly—that her act had something to do with love: false love, failed love, mistimed or misunderstood or miscarried love. For no one here, I'm convinced, is truly happy in love. This is the Institute: a windswept quadrangle edged by charm-proofed concrete buildings. The sun disappears in October, and temperatures drop low enough to flash-freeze saliva; spit crackles against the pavement like hail. In January, whiteouts shut down the highways, and the outside world takes on a quality very much like oxygen: we know it exists all around us, but we can't see it. It's a disturbing thing to be part of. My ex-Ph.D. adviser, who's been here longer than any of us, claims that the dormitory walls are abuzz with frustration, and if you press your ear against the heating ducts at night you can hear the jangling bedsprings and desperate whimpers of masturbators. Some nights my ex-adviser wanders the subbasement hallways of the Gray building, and screams obscenities until he feels refreshed and relatively tranquil.

I used to be a Ph.D. student, but now my job is to sit all night at a government-issue desk in the TechInfo office, staring at a red TechHotline telephone. The TechHotline rings at three and four A.M., and I listen to distraught graduate students stammer about corrupted file allocation tables and SCSI controller failures. I tell them to close their eyes and take a deep breath; I tell them everything will be all right. The TechInfo office looks onto the quadrangle, and just before dawn, when the sky has mellowed to the color of a deep bruise, the Institute looks almost peaceful. At those rare moments I love my job and I love this town and I love this Institute. This is an indisputable fact: there are many, many people around here who love things that will never love them back.

A Venn diagram of my love for Alexandra looks like this:

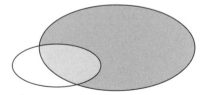

My inventory of love is almost completely consumed by Alexandra, while hers is shared by myself and others (or, more precisely: $|J| > |M|$; $\exists\, x$ s.t. $x \in (J \cap M)$; $\exists\, y$ s.t. $y \in J, y \notin M$; $\exists\, z$ s.t. $z \notin J, z \in M$). We live in a cabin next to the Owahee River and the Institute's research-grade nuclear power plant. Steam curls off the hyperboloidal cooling tower and settles in an icy mist on our roof, and some nights I swear I can see the reactor building glowing.

Alexandra has hair the color of maple syrup, and she is sixteen years younger than me; she is twenty-five. She sips tea every morning in the front room of our cabin, and when I turn into the driveway and see her hair through the window I feel a deep, troubling urge.

Alexandra is the daughter of my ex-adviser, who has never claimed to be happy in love. On Wednesdays at noon, he meets a sophomore named Larissa in the Applied Optics Laboratory and scoots her onto the vibration isolation table and bangs her until the air pistons sigh. Every morning my ex-adviser straps on snowshoes and clomps past our cabin on his way to the Institute, gliding atop the frozen crust like a Nordic vision of Jesus. I have given Alexandra an ultimatum: she has until commencement day to decide if she wants to marry me. If she does not want to marry me, I will pack my textbooks and electronic diagnostic equipment and move to Huntsville, Alabama.

When students jump off the Gehring building, they curse and scream as though their hands are on fire. I can't say I blame them. This is the set of words I use when I talk about the Institute: *hunger, numbness, fatigue, yearning, anger.* Old photographs of this town show a cathedral of pines standing in place of the bare quadrangle, and a sawmill on the Owahee in place of the nuclear plant. People in the pictures stare at the camera with an unmistakable air of melancholy, and looking at them I wonder if there was ever a happy season on this peninsula.

Alexandra tells me I'm ungenerous toward the Institute; she tells me the cold has freeze-dried my kindness. Here is a fact I cannot refute: on nights when the TechHotline is quiet and snow is settling in swells around the Gehring building, the silence is pure enough to make you want to weep. Windows in the Walsh Residence Hall blink off, one by one, until the quadrangle is lit only by moonlight. Icicles the size of children work loose and disappear into snowdrifts. Bark-colored hares hop lazily toward the Owahee. In the early-morning dark, before the sun climbs over the Gray building and the Institute begins to stretch, you can wade into a drift and lie back like an angel and let snow sift down onto you, and the only sound you hear is the slow churn of your own unwilling heart.

SLANEY IS THE NAME OF THIS TOWN: A FEW THOUSAND HOUSES AND shops crushed up against the Institute like groupies. Slaney has a short but tragic history: founded in 1906 by a Swede as a company town for the Michigan Land and Lumber Company; within a year there were four hundred inhabitants, six boarding houses, two general stores, a meat market, an ice-house, a whorehouse, seven saloons. The Swede, his heart full to bursting with pride, felled the tallest white pine in the county and propped it in the middle of Slaney's main drag as a monument to the town's greatness. By 1925 there was nothing left around Slaney except birch and tamarack and scrub poplar, and if tumbleweeds existed up here they'd have blown through the abandoned streets with a lonely rustle. The monumental white pine was dragged off to the sawmill in the middle of the night by timber thieves. The Swede drank himself into a stupor in Dan Gunn's empty saloon, then passed out during the twelve-block walk to his house and nearly froze to death.

That spring the hills hiccuped with dynamite blasts from prospectors looking for iron ore, and the state legislature chose Slaney as the location for the brand-new Michigan Engineering Institute. Every year in Slaney someone loses grip and commits an unspeakably self-destructive act. Here is something my ex-adviser does not think I know: seven years ago, when his ex-wife still lived in Slaney, he followed her to her house on Huron Street for eleven straight days, and one night as he crouched outside her kitchen window he was knocked unconscious by a blow from a policeman's nightstick. When he woke he was shackled to a stainless-steel toilet. Ontonagon County, I've heard, has the toughest antistalking laws in the state.

On Friday nights the TechHotline is quiet. Dormitory windows are dark as graves, and the quadrangle echoes with shouts of horny undergraduates. I lock the TechInfo office, and Alexandra meets me on Mill Street outside the Caribou Lounge, where a six-piece band called Chicken Little plays Benny Goodman and Cab Calloway and Nat King Cole. Twenty-one-year-olds wearing circle skirts and two-tone shoes jam the dance floor and Charleston like they're scaring off demons. Rusty, the bandleader, wears a white silk suit and by eleven is drenched in sweat. I lindy until my knees ache, but Alexandra's just getting started: she climbs onto the stage and whispers into Rusty's ear. He says, *We're gonna do one for the spitfire in the pretty pink blouse.* I sit at the bar and watch Alexandra press up against strange men, and remind myself how miserable it was to be alone.

On Saturday nights students throng to the Newett Ice Arena to watch the hockey team lose to future NHLers from Houghton and Escanaba. Bartenders on Middle Street stockpile pint glasses and rub their hands together, waiting for the postgame crush. My ex-adviser locks his office door and drinks a half-bottle of sherry, then calls his ex-wife in Sturgeon Falls. He waits until she says *Hello? Who is this? John, please*—then hangs up. Afterward he dials the TechHotline, stammering, and I tell him to close his eyes and take a deep breath; I tell him everything will be all right. He says, *I'm sorry, Joseph, good Christ,* and begins to sniffle. Snow ambles down outside the TechInfo window. One Saturday, drunk, my ex-adviser called and managed to say, *Listen, I'm not going to repeat this: my daughter can be somewhat difficult, and I frankly don't know if you're up to the challenge.*

The Swede kept a leather-bound journal detailing the events of his life from the day he arrived in Slaney until the day he died, and I read a Xeroxed copy of it when the TechHotline is quiet. *Town has grown faster than even my most incautious estimates,* he wrote in 1911. *Andrew Street now one-quarter mile long. Irish, Finns, Cousin Jacks have come, and for some reason a band of Sicilians. No chicken for eight months.* When Slaney was booming in the 1910s, lumberjacks from as far as Bruce Crossing would descend on the town on weekends and get knee-walking drunk on Yellow Dog whiskey, then smash pub stools to splinters with their peaveys. Their steel-calked boots punched holes in Slaney's plank sidewalks. A tenderloin sprang up along the eastern edge of town, and the Swede met a young prostitute named Lotta Scott at Hugh Grogan's place on Thomas Street; she charged him two dollars. *Disarmingly frank,* he wrote. *Eyes dark as bituminous coal. Slim ankles. Short patience.*

Before I leave for the TechInfo office in the evening, Alexandra walks from room to room shedding her prim librarian's turtleneck and knee-length skirt and woolen tights, then lies back on the kitchen table, naked, ravenous. Her eyes follow my hands, nervous as squirrels, as I unbuckle myself. She tugs at the seam of my jeans. Outside, snow movers pound down the ice-packed street, their carbon-steel blades gouging the curb. Alexandra smells archival—glue and musty paper and indelible ink—and she loves sex as much as a snowman loves cold. This is what I do: I say a small prayer just before I begin, even though I am not religious. By her own count, Alexandra has had sex with more than thirty-five men.

Alexandra called the TechHotline one night and said, *Sometimes I wish you'd cool it a little bit, Joseph. I mean, I love you, I love all the nerdy things you do, I just don't understand why you feel the need to control me. We can love each other and still lead normal, semi-independent lives.* I could hear the soft rush of her breathing, a sound that made me dizzy. Alexandra is stingy with love; she is afraid of ending up like her parents, who squandered their love like drunks at a craps table. *I don't want to control you,* I explained, *I'm just a little uncomfortable with the idea of you having sex with strange men.*

The Swede in his journal described the deep silence of the woods, which seemed to him a cruel and beautiful sound. *Streets filled with sweet smell of pitch. Pine as far as I can see. Have fallen in love with that dissolute woman, Lotta Scott. Consumed by thoughts of her.* His spindly hand filled the journal pages. On May third he recorded the purchase of a new frock coat, for four dollars, tailored by *a clever Polander from Detroit,* and a set of linen *of surpassing quality.* Then on the tenth of May, 1919, the Swede in deliriously shaky script wrote that he and Lotta Scott were married in Burke's saloon by the justice of the peace with forty-four witnesses present. *I feel as the French explorers must have felt,* he wrote, *when they gazed for the first time upon the vast forests of this wondrous peninsula. Glorious, glorious chicken.*

I have tried to convince myself that Alexandra is not a tramp, that she simply suffers from too much love—that she loves too much for her own good. My ex-adviser knocks on the TechInfo door when he's too lonely to go home. One Saturday night, his shirt unbuttoned and a styrofoam cup of sherry balanced on his knee, he told me that I am too particular when it comes to love, that I should accept love no matter how it appears and be grateful. He sipped sherry in a languid, pensive manner. *There's a certain kind of imperfection that acts as a reference point, that gives a sense of perspective. Understand? The pockmark on the perfect cheek. The small, tragic flaw, like a beauty mark, but deeper.* He squinted out at the forlorn quadrangle. *I don't trust perfection. Alexandra's mother was so wonderfully, perfectly imperfect.* I once snuck into an auditorium in the Gray building and watched my ex-adviser deliver a Physics 125 lecture on kinetic and potential energy. As he lectured, he smiled at a pair of sleepy-eyed sophomore girls, showing his artificially whitened teeth.

The harder I pull Alexandra toward me the harder she pushes away. It's heartbreaking. Every third Saturday in February the people of Slaney hold Winter Carnival, where they flood the Kmart parking lot and ice-skate under a mosaic of stars. Teenaged boys in Red Wings jerseys skate backward and play crack-the-whip to show off. My ex-adviser dons a black beret and circles the rink in long, fluid strides. Last February Alexandra and I skated couples, and in the chilly night her skin was as smooth and luminous as a glass of milk. *What a world!* I found myself thinking, *where a failed engineer with a crooked nose can skate couples with a syrup-haired woman who smells archival.* On Andrew Street we ate elephant ears and watched a muscular young townie lift people in his arms to guess their weight. Alexandra gave him a dollar, and he hoisted her up with one meaty arm and hugged her to his chest. Alexandra shouted *Whoa, hey! Wow!* and kicked her legs girlishly. When the townie put her down, she kissed him on the cheek, and when she came back and saw my face she said, *Oh, for God's sake, Joseph. Grow up.*

That night at three A.M. I turned on the bedroom light and knelt over Alexandra and asked her to be my wife. I felt tearful, exultant; I felt as vast and weightless as a raft of clouds; I felt all of Lake Superior welled inside my bursting chest. Sweat seeped from my trembling hands and dampened Alexandra's nightdress. *Joseph,* she said, *Joseph, Joseph, Joseph. Oh God.* She kissed my cheek, the same way she'd kissed the townie. *I just don't know, honey. I just don't know.*

THIS TOWN: EVERYWHERE I LOOK I SEE EQUATIONS. ICE FLOES TUM-bling in the Owahee, snowflakes skidding past the TechInfo window: everywhere I look I see fractals and tensors and nonlinear differential equations. Some mornings when my TechInfo shift is over I stand in front of the Bradford Student Center and hand out pamphlets entitled "Proof of God's Existence by Series Expansion," and "The Combinatorics of Ancient Roman Orgies." Undergraduates walk broad circles around me. They're bundled in scarves and wool hats; only their eyes show. Alexandra tells me I make people uneasy, that not everything can be described by mathematics, and I tell her she's probably wrong.

I have considered admitting to Alexandra that I hate dancing but worry that she'll find another partner. One night at the Caribou Lounge I ducked out for fresh air, and on a whim wandered into the meager woods; there were no lights in sight, but the moonlit snow glowed bright enough to count change by. I lay down and stared up at the muddy streak of our galaxy. I thought—how to explain?—about the nature of imperfection. My ex-adviser every September stands before his Physics 125 class with his arms spread wide, like a preacher, and says, *Listen sharp, this is important: Nature. Hates. Perfection.* Alexandra says I sometimes remind her of her father, and this bothers her more than she can say.

In 1919 Slaney sent three million board-feet of pine down the Owahee, and the sawmill howled from morning to dusk. Lumberjacks, tired of two-dollar whores on Thomas Street, sent agonized letters to *Heart and Hand* matrimonial newspaper and convinced scared young women to pack their lives into trunks and board the train north. The Swede on May seventeenth—one week after his wedding—walked deep into the thinning woods and realized the pine would not last forever, that in four or five years it would be *cut out*, and Slaney would be *all caught up. Lumbermen will move westward, toward Ontonagon and Silver City,* he wrote. *Saloons will empty, sawmill will fall idle. Lotta departed for Hurley this morning at dawn to visit her mother. Declined my offer to accompany her.* Lotta Scott, before she left, borrowed two hundred dollars and a gold-plated pocket watch from the Swede.

I like my ex-adviser but worry that he cares too much about the wrong things. Larissa, the sophomore he bangs on Wednesdays in the Applied Optics Laboratory, has told him he'd better stop worrying about ancient history and start focusing on the here and now. *For Christ's sake,* my ex-adviser said, *she's nineteen years old—a child—telling me this. I love Larissa, but it's not the kind of love she thinks it is.* Alexandra does not remember the names of some of the men she has slept with. It was just sex, she explains, it wasn't a huge colossal thing. After the first time we made love, she stroked my hair and explained that I was not supposed to cry, that it was not supposed to be that way.

The tombstones in Slaney's cemetery have Finnish and Polish and Swedish names; they say COOPER and SAWYER and LUMBERMAN. Women who came to town, it seems, took a dismayed look around then headed back south. The lumberjacks died alone. The Swede, two weeks after Lotta left for Hurley, wrote, *Met a man Masters from Sault Ste. Marie, who claims the entire eastern half of the peninsula is cut out, not a stick of white pine standing. Martinville, Maynard, Bartlow he claims are empty, the houses deserted and mill torn down for scrap. Queer fellow. Says land looks "naked and embarrassed" without the pine. No word from Lotta.*

The tenderloin was razed in a fit of prohibition righteousness in 1931 and lay vacant and weed-choked for twenty years. A Methodist church now stands where Dan Gunn's saloon used to be. Hugh Grogan's whorehouse has been replaced by an electronics store called Circuit Shack. The Swede wrote nothing in his journal for two weeks, then, *Took train to Hurley to find no trace of Lotta. Walked all up and down the dusty streets. Back in Slaney, heard from John Davidson that Lotta was seen on the Sault Ste. Marie train as far along as Allouez. Davidson was drunk and perhaps not being truthful. Nevertheless I fear she is gone completely.* This is a fact: I live with a woman with syrup-colored hair who loves me in a hard, unknowable way. My ex-adviser one Sunday in the TechInfo office, his feet propped on my desk and a cup of sherry balanced on his knee, smiled cryptically and said, *I believe I can solve your problem with my daughter. I have an idea. A theory.*

ALEXANDRA LEFT TO VISIT HER MOTHER IN STURGEON FALLS TWO weeks after Winter Carnival. At the station I blinked back a swell of longing as her train dragged slowly north. Alexandra leaned out the window and blew me a kiss, then tossed a small white bundle into the snow. She was supposed to stay one week in Sturgeon Falls; she was supposed to tell me *yes* or *no* when she returned. I searched for almost two hours but never did find the bundle she threw out the window.

My ex-adviser that night, sprawled in front of the TechInfo radiator like a housecat, told me I cannot expect to understand Alexandra with mathematics alone, and that my view of love is analytical whereas his is romantic. My ex-adviser as he thawed smelled stale, like cooked cabbage. I set my mug of Seagram's down and on a wrinkled envelope wrote:

$$\frac{dJ}{dt} = aJ - bJA$$

$$\frac{dA}{dt} = cJA - dA$$

Where J is my love, A is Alexandra's. The predator-prey equations—very elegant. My words were cold clouds of Canadian whiskey. I rattled the ice cubes in my glass like dice. *You should trust mathematics,* I told him. *Nothing is too complex to describe with mathematics.* Alexandra called the next morning to tell me she'd decided to stay an extra week in Sturgeon Falls. I closed my eyes and listened to her syrup-colored voice. *I'm going to sit in my mother's sauna and think about everything. Have you ever been in a sauna, honey? It's incredible. First you feel like you're going to die, then you pass a certain point and feel like you're going to live forever.* She sighed. *And I'm helping my mother plan her wedding—she's getting re-married. Don't tell my father.*

I can build you a sauna. I can build it in the backyard, next to the big poplar.

His name is Harold. He breeds minks. There's hundreds of minks running around up here, honey. Her voice dropped to a whisper. *It makes me horny, in a weird way.*

I didn't say anything.

Joseph, I have never cheated on you, she said suddenly. Her voice held an edge of desperation. *I want you to understand that.* Alexandra, before she hung up, said that the bundle she threw out the train window contained a peach pit, nothing more.

My dissertation, which I never finished, was entitled, *Nonlinear Control of Biomimetic Systems.* The first chapter, which I finished, was entitled "On the Nature of Human Romantic Interaction." It begins: *Consider a third-order system with three states corresponding to three distinct people, a, b, and c. a is attracted to both b and c. b and c are both attracted to a but not to each other. We would like to describe the behavior of this system over time.*

One night while Alexandra was in Sturgeon Falls, I sat staring into the darkened quadrangle for a long time. Finally I called her and said, *I can't wait forever. I can give you until commencement day, but then I'm moving to Huntsville, Alabama.* Alexandra was stunned, silent. *I don't know what else to do.* My ex-adviser convinced me to give Alexandra the Huntsville ultimatum. I had four handwritten pages of equations contradicting his advice, but he took the pencil from my hand and said, *Joseph, my friend, it's extremely simple: the only reason my daughter will not marry you is if she does not, in fact, love you.* Huntsville, Alabama. I chose Huntsville randomly off the map; I don't know what I'd do in a January without snow.

In my dissertation I proved analytically that it's possible to design a control system such that a's attraction to b grows exponentially, while a's attraction to c diminishes exponentially. In the concluding paragraph, however, there is a caveat: *In practice the coupling factors are highly nonlinear and difficult to predict, and depend on phenomena such as shyness, boredom, desire, desperation, and self-knowledge, as well as numerous local conditions: the feeling of self-confidence gained from wearing a favorite pair of socks, the unexpected sorrow of seeing the season's first flock of geese flying south, etc.*

Alexandra returned from Sturgeon Falls five weeks before commencement day wearing a white muff, a gift from her mother's mink-breeder fiancé. She walked from the front door to the bedroom and dropped her suitcase on the bed, then walked back into the kitchen and gripped my shoulders and said, *Listen to me, Joseph: I love you. I love the shit out of you. But I'll never belong to you.*

That night I waited until Alexandra was asleep, then pulled on boots and a parka and walked the half-mile to the Institute. The Gehring building was quiet except for a dull chorus of electronic devices. The TechInfo office was silent as a prayer. Suddenly I had an idea: I ran across the quadrangle to the Olssen building, the tallest building on campus, and sprinted from classroom to empty classroom, turning on lights. I formed a four-story lit-up A, then an L, then an E, then part of an X—then I ran out of classrooms. The Olssen building wasn't wide enough. Back in the TechInfo office, I threw open the window, breathless, and looked out across the quadrangle. ALE. The lights spelled ALE. A group of fraternity brothers had gathered, and when I appeared as a silhouette in the TechInfo window, they shouted, *Yo, hotline man! Ale! Fuckin' A!*

I closed the office door and turned off the lights, picked up the telephone and dialed. The phone rang three times, four times, five—and then Alexandra answered. Her voice was husky and irritable, the voice of a confident young woman disturbed from sleep. She said, *Hello? Who the hell is this—Joseph?*

I hung up.

THEY FOUND ORE IN THE HILLS AROUND SLANEY IN 1926—NOT THE glittery hematite they were seeing in Ishpeming, but a muddy blue sludge that assayed at sixty percent iron. Overnight, Slaney was reborn: the front glass of Dan Gunn's saloon was replaced and the floor replanked, Hugh Grogan's place on Thomas Street was scrubbed down and reopened. The Swede awoke from a month-long bender, his handwriting looser and less optimistic. *Strange to see trains unloading again. Excitement even at the meat market; ore, they say, is everywhere. No chicken for nine months.* My ex-adviser, one chilly April Sunday in the TechInfo office, explained that his ex-wife had taken out a restraining order, and if he called her one more time, he would be arrested. It took me two months to realize that *chicken* was the Swede's code word for intercourse.

Alexandra's mother, my ex-adviser said, *has the sort of posture you see in Victorian portraiture. Ivory skin, fingers that are almost impossibly delicate, yet strong. Beautifully strong, and that noble Victorian posture.* He stroked his stubbled chin and nodded, agreeing with himself. *And I treated her like shit on a heel.* My ex-adviser, one month before commencement day, somehow learned about his ex-wife's impending wedding, and he wandered into the quadrangle and slumped down in the dingy snow and refused to budge.

Alexandra was asked by her mother to be maid of honor. She sipped tea in the front room of our cabin, tearing pages from *Bride* magazine and acting like everything was okay. Alexandra does not understand the urgency that grips you at thirty; she does not understand the desperation that settles in at forty. I began staying late at work, wandering the Gehring building's damp subbasement tunnels. Down in the tunnels, I walked for hours without seeing a hint of the morning sky, and I felt how I imagined the old ore miners must have felt. One morning I told Alexandra that if she marries me, she does not necessarily have to stop seeing other men, and she looked at me with confusion and deep pity and slapped my face.

The Institute graduated its first class of engineers in 1930, but the residents of Slaney had no use for book-taught miners. The Swede, caught up in the excitement, paid thirty dollars for a claim on fifteen acres he'd never seen, and his first week out found a nugget of what he thought was solid gold. He squatted in the snow outside his lean-to and threw his head back and shouted at the moon. He was sixty-two years old. *As much as I can haul out*, he wrote. *Nuggets size of fists. Rapture.*

The Slaney Mountain was a wet hole of a mine with a safety record that made the sawmill look like a nursery. A 1931 cave-in sent pressurized air pounding through the shaft, and thirteen miners were punched off their feet then flung down, uninjured. A moment later the creaking support timbers fell silent, and a blanket of rock crushed the breath from their lungs. All thirteen died. In 1932 an Italian accidentally stubbed his cigar into a tub of freshly thawed dynamite, and the blast rattled windows as far away as Andrew Street. The Swede on March 13, 1933, convinced he'd hit a mother lode, sold his house and hocked his gold family ring for three hundred acres and a pair of mules. He sat all night atop his tiny hill, staring at the forest draped in darkness and dreaming of Pierce-Arrow automobiles and English leather gloves, and when the sun broke over the frozen valley he began to dig.

Two weeks before commencement day I woke to find Alexandra sitting at the foot of the bed, teary-eyed. *Bride* magazine lay tattered on her lap. She climbed beneath the comforter, sniffling, and said, *I wish you'd just quit what you're doing. I wish you'd let things keep going the way they're going.* It's crushing to remember the years before Alexandra: ordinary differential equations, cold beef pasties, the smell of melting solder and the heartless glow of a fluorescent lamp. I pulled Alexandra close and told her to close her eyes and take a deep breath, I told her everything would be all right, and she leaned her forehead against my chest and said *Cut it out.*

The Swede stockpiled gold for five months, then one morning hitched his mules to a rented sledge and paraded his mound of nuggets down Slaney's main drag. Old broken prospectors with hematite in their hair and an alcoholic's tremble stared out through Dan Gunn's front window and muttered softly at the sight. *Celebrated with sirloin steak and Yellow Dog whiskey, then strolled over to Thomas Street. Feasted on chicken.*

One week before commencement day the snow in the quadrangle began to shrink, then as if by sleight-of-hand the sun appeared where there had been only clouds. Physical plant workers tucked geraniums into planter boxes, and for the first time in months students unwrapped their scarves and looked around. One night I stayed sixteen hours at the TechInfo office. When I got home, I packed my books into milk crates and stacked them next to the door; Alexandra waited until I was asleep then unpacked them and placed them neatly back on the bookshelf. The nuggets the Swede had spent everything to pull from the ground were not pure gold, he discovered, but copper spiked with fatty veins of pyrite. The rock he'd spent five months hauling from his plot was worth nine dollars and sixty-three cents.

The morning before commencement day I purchased a nonrefundable ticket to Huntsville. I had not showered, and the TechInfo office reflected what must be my own human smell: lemon and sour milk and powdered cumin. That night, his feet resting on the TechInfo desk, my ex-adviser said, *You should not let yourself go like this, Joseph. It's undignified.* After he left, two Slaney policemen knocked on the door. Their furry snow hats were pulled low on their foreheads. They were looking for my ex-adviser. When I asked what they wanted, the smaller policeman pursed his lips and said, *We can't divulge that information.* When I asked if my ex-adviser was in trouble, he said, *We can't divulge that information.*

The police, I learned eventually, were searching for a man who'd climbed into the heating ducts of the Benson dormitory and watched an unnamed freshwoman apply lotion to her calves. The police had swept the Gray building and sat for hours watching the student center, but no one had seen my ex-adviser. I told them I had no idea where he was. I told them it's not easy to hide in a town this small.

The ore around Slaney, it turned out, was not a single wide vein but pockety and impossible to follow. The D & C, Silver Lake, and Petersen mines stopped drilling in 1937. The Slaney Mountain mine—the first mine—stayed stubbornly open, and in 1939 engineers thought they'd hit a million-ton ore body. But two months later the ore was gone. The Mountain shut down. The last miners boarded the train west, for Houghton or Ishpeming. Dan Gunn nailed planks across the front window of his saloon and left Slaney for good. The Swede, penniless and without a home, took a bottle of Yellow Dog whiskey into the cut-out woods and sat down in the snow and put a .45 pistol in his mouth and pulled the trigger.

The pine around Slaney is gone. The ore is gone. The shaft house stands crumbling and windowless a half-mile from the Institute, and on Friday nights high-schoolers sneak inside and drink Boone's Farm Strawberry Hill and grope one another. My ex-adviser says that men never dig for iron or copper or coal; secretly, in their heart's heart, they're digging for gold. The Swede before he shot himself in 1940 wrote: *Heard from a man Jonsson that Lotta is in Grand Rapids and married to a furniture magnate. Said he saw them two months ago in church, Lotta dressed in silk and singing a beautiful soprano. Not certain Jonsson was being truthful; told of Lotta only after securing a loan of thirty dollars. So be it. Wherever Lotta is I wish her happiness. I write these words without regret.*

ON THE MORNING OF COMMENCEMENT DAY THE AIR SMELLED SALTY, like trouble, and from nowhere a milk-gray sheet fell over the sky and the temperature dropped twenty degrees in twenty minutes. By eight A.M. snow was swirling in the late May breeze, and by nine there were four inches on the highway and the radio was saying it looked like we were going to get socked but good. Alexandra and I stayed in bed. I rolled her into a position we called the log drive, and she told me—she shouted—that she loves me, goddammit, *yes*, and wants to be with me forever. I stopped. Outside, the wind sobbed. Alexandra, her face flushed the color of ripe rhubarb, stumbled from the bedroom and closed the door. Forty minutes later, when it was clear she wasn't coming back, I bundled myself in a parka and thermal snow pants and set off for the Institute.

From outside the TechInfo office I heard a floorboard creak, then a moist sniffle. I opened the door: Alexandra was sitting in the TechHotline chair in front of the window, staring into the quadrangle. She looked at me; she looked back out the window; she shrugged awkwardly and said, *So, this is it. The famous office.*

In the quadrangle a stage had been erected near the Gray building, and on the lawn an assembly of crimson-gowned seniors squirmed and hooted in the driving snow. Behind them underdressed parents shivered in their seats, wondering what kind of people could live in a place like this. At the edge of the quadrangle the Caribou Brass Band sent up a frozen-lipped Sousa march. I drew the window shade, momentarily nostalgic at the sight of so much unbridled optimism, and as I did the crowd quieted and the provost took the podium and cleared her throat. *Students, parents, distinguished guests, fellow alumni and alumnae: welcome. Today is a joyous day.*

Alexandra took the telephone from my desk and placed it on the bookshelf. She scooted onto the desk, her snow-booted feet not touching the floor, and pulled me down to her. *Just lie here,* she said. *Don't get funny.* Her breathing was loud in my ear: a seashore, a multitude. I kissed her smooth neck, and let myself believe for a moment that we were two strangers pressed together, shivering with possibility. Alexandra stroked my back, but when I began to stir she gripped my shoulders with heartbreaking finality. *Just don't,* she said. *Okay? Please. Just stay.*

From the quadrangle the voice of the Institute's first female graduate drifted into the office. *I remember a bedroom was made up for me in the infirmary, and boys would stand outside arguing over who would walk me to chemistry class. I remember walking to class wondering how in the world a girl like myself ended up at a place with so many wonderful, wonderful boys.* Alexandra shifted beneath me. Suddenly there was a ripple of applause, and the microphone reverberated as if it had been dropped, then the tinny, shouted voice of my ex-adviser announced that he was having an immoral relationship with an undergraduate.

Alexandra struggled to her feet. The crowd hushed. Alexandra shoved aside the window shade and said, *Jesus Christ, fuck, dad*—then grabbed her parka and threw open the TechInfo door and clattered down the Gehring building stairs.

Outside, the crowd had fractured into a jumble of bewildered voices. The provost stood at the podium with her arms raised, saying, *Okay, let's just be calm, people*—then a woman screamed and two people stood and pointed: I followed their gaze to the roof of the Gray building, where my ex-adviser stood in full academic regalia, looking like an Arthurian pimp. His arms were hugged against his chest in a way that struck me as tremendously fragile. He shifted his weight from foot to foot, his crimson robes billowing in the snowy breeze; then I spotted Alexandra, a red-jacketed streak across the quadrangle. She sprinted past the confused brass band, past the podium, and burst through the Gray building's tall front doors.

I threw open the window, half-expecting the TechHotline to ring, as a distant wail went up from the Slaney firehouse. Atop the Gray building my ex-adviser was a blot against the chalky sky, a singularity. He tugged off his eight-cornered hat and tossed it limply over the edge. It fluttered down, down,

down, then landed on the sidewalk, flopped once, and lay flat. An anxious moan rose from the crowd. He climbed the safety railing and leaned over the roof edge, his wispy hair whipping in the breeze, and the provost over the loudspeaker said, *Okay, okay, wait: Jesus God.*

Then Alexandra appeared behind her father. She approached him slowly. He turned to her and spread his arms wide, his face a mask of nervous relief, then seemed to slip on the icy roof: he took a quick step backward and froze, arms thrown up to heaven, and then he was airborne. Down he went, his crimson robes rippling as he bicycled in the frozen air then disappeared without a sound into a steep bank of snow.

A chorus of screams rose up, and the provost whispered *Sweet Jesus* into the microphone and turned away from the roof and covered her face. Alexandra rushed to the roof edge. A quartet of Slaney firemen jogged into the courtyard with a folded-up safety net and looked around, confused. I made a quick calculation: a 180-pound man, falling thirty feet under an acceleration of 32.2 feet per second squared—I drew the shade and turned away from the window and closed my eyes.

Wind howled past the TechInfo window. A baby broke into a restless wail. After what seemed like a long time I heard a hopeful shout, and I peeked around the shade: my ex-adviser was struggling from the snowbank, clutching his left shoulder, surrounded by shocked firemen. I closed my eyes. I looked again: Alexandra, red parka gone and hair whipped into a cloud, rushed hip-deep into the snowbank and threw her arms around her father's neck. She touched his cheek, as if to make sure he was real and not some snow-blown mirage. My ex-adviser, his eyes squeezed shut with pain, slumped down in the drifting snow and hugged his daughter with his good arm and began to weep.

The Detroit train left at eleven-thirteen P.M., and from there it was two connections and twenty-one hours to Huntsville. I sat in the TechInfo office until it was time to leave for the station, and when the TechHotline rang, I didn't pick up. The CALL light threw jagged shadows against the dark office walls. I knew there were equations describing the contour of the shadows, the luminescent intensity of the CALL light, the heat distribution in my hands as I clasped them together, the stress distribution in my eyelids as I pressed my eyes shut. In the quadrangle, snow drifted down with perfect indifferent randomness. In thousands of dormitory bedrooms, young men and women were asleep and dreaming of numbers.

I would begin a new line of research in Alabama, I decided. I would throw away my textbooks and Institute notepads and start fresh. What effect does geography have on love? What effect does weather have on love? There are events in nature, I've noticed, that cannot be explained or reproduced, that simply *are*. It's enough to give a person hope.

2000

On the Scrap

M. L. Liebler

> come take a little trip with me in 1913
> to Calumet, Michigan, in the copper country.
> —Woody Guthrie, "1913 Massacre"

In a small, big town 1913
    At the northernmost reaches
Of America—sticking out
        Into the cold, deep waters
        Of Lake Superior—beautiful
        Body of lake and fresh earth
        Packed heavy with whitefish and copper
    Land, veins mined by immigrants:
Croatia, Hungry, Finland, England.

American multiculturalism
    Long before the academy labeled people
        Through their longitudinal studies and statistics.
        Here, in Michigan, the working class
        Once again defined the country's future by building
        A firm foundation: Keweenaw County—just another place
        Where labor awakened to confront business
    Owners who were determined

To keep workers enslaved, endangered, and under

Control. When the first cry of "union" sprung
    From the workers' wintry lips as they stood upon the frozen—
        cold streets, the mine owners' mantra was loud and clear
        The managers' chant of
        "We'll let the grass grow on your streets
        Before we concede to the uncivilized
    Working class," was an offense to the few who

Understood English. Those words were met with
    A reckoning response from labor everywhere.
        Fortunately for the mining men of Calumet
        There was a strong-willed woman
        Who refused to let injustice trample
        Her community down to ash in the name of
"Business as usual!"

During the Great Mining Strike of 1913, Big Annie
        Clemec of Calumet stood up to be counted,
        And she took on the mine owners by challenging
        them to "Kill me! Run your bayonets and sabers
        Through this flag and kill me! For I will not
    Be moved. If this American flag will not
Protect me, then I will die holding it."

Sweet Annie Clemec, Eastern European angel of the mines—
    Tall, beautiful Upper Peninsula woman of integrity,
        Who marched daily through
        The copper-rich streets of Calumet with her American
        Flag raised, stars, red, blue, and white,
        High above her flowing brown hair,

Encouraging other men, women, and children to stand
Together for union and for their fair share.

Big Annie—Lady of Calumet—marched
    Head on into the Federal Militia who watched her
        From horsebacks with their silver sabers drawn
        Are ready to knock her flag of freedom from her
        Steady hand, but Annie marched forward, always,
        Spitting on the yellow-bellied soldiers who dared
    To take the working man's birthright of fair
        Pay for an honest day.

The miners wanted to work
        A little less and spend a little more time
        With their families—The miners wanted
        To be safer in the dark dungeon
    Mines webbed with the evil sound of the widow-maker drill;

In the end, the company won the Strike of 1913
        In Copper County, Michigan. They broke the back
        Of labor in their typical, hurtful, murdering way
        When they planted a scab-snitch
in the old Italian Hall on Main Street—

December 24th at Big Annie's Christmas party
        For the penniless children
        And the families of the striking men. As gifts
        Of oranges, handmade dolls, clothes, and such
        Were passed to the children from Santa on the stage,
A loud cry of "Fire! Fire!" rose up over the heads of the children
And the frantic strikers. A cloud of panic hung like a noose.

Over the people who scrambled toward the one and only door.
A human stampede where body after body piled up on the stairway out.
    When calm was restored,
            74 people, mostly children, lay buried in a twisted heap
            Of bones, blood, skin, and hair. A Working-Class
            Nightmare in the Home of the Brave. All
            Brought on by another nameless company snitch
    Who yelled "fire" from his stool-pigeon perch,
And was never seen again in Calumet City.
    So—Big Annie picked up

Her flag, one more time, to bury the dead children in the frozen land—
    December 28, 1913. She led the funeral procession
        To their snow-covered graves.
        The Calumet newspapers reported that miners won
        Nothing of significance during the Great Strike.
        They went back to work without their babies,
    Without a raise, without better working conditions, and without
    Recognition for their union. All of that was buried
            In 1913 in the cold Michigan earth.

2001–2017

In the summer, I keep a wooden rowboat stashed on a hidden beach on an upper Michigan harbor. Occasionally, I go down to the boat at night, row out through silhouettes of sailboats in the mooring fields toward the breakwall beacon and the moonrise, and lift my oars. The town toward which the breeze off Lake Superior drifts me back is a string of little lights. Down shore, the lights thin until the land is a long, dark horizon.

The little lights of town and the dark woods toward which my boat's drift returns me are home. Home in the usual sense and home of my imagination. In every light and in the dark shore itself are poems and stories. As arguably the best literary cartographer of the U.P., editor Ron Riekki has given us our most current map of these poems and stories by including in the following part works written in the twenty-first century.

The new U.P. writing here is rich in familiar natural sensuality. The forest-fire smell in Keith Taylor's cabin is timeless, as is the death Eric Torgersen imagines in Lake Superior at night, "carried off by some huge wave." The sensual here has always been transformative, as in Hannah Baker-Siroty's Ovidian bee-swam/human-body metamorphosis and Alex Vartan Gubbins's ritual efforts to restore lost sensation. There is timelessness in the journeys here too, in Gordon Henry's Hiawatha woman "with no destination"; in the migrations of L. E. Kimball's couple, like a pair of sandhill cranes; in Bonnie Jo Campbell's odyssey of a man's subterranean descent in search of love. But now we also learn the U.P. as part of a wider world's geography. Tom Bissell's Donk carries his nickname from the Porcupine Mountains all the way to Afghanistan; Jillena Rose's missionary teaches his daughter "a reverence for water" in Saigon; Ingrid Hill's family of blended Chinese and Finnish ancestry travels the perilous Keweenaw woods; and Jeff Vande Zande's night-driving father is about to lose his twelve-year-old to Paris.

Thankfully, the U.P.'s character endures. Sally Brunk grieves the loss of Ojibwa culture but calls on her people to fight for what's left. As if in reply, Margaret Noodin says, "This place speaks to us" in the language of its waves and Native people. Yes, it's still a hard place. Austin Hummell is right—"Whole months pass without sun"—and Russell Thorburn articulates the economic cruelties perfectly—"there was nowhere / for a father to stand / without being poor." As Kathleen Heideman laments, tulips bloom too soon in the harsh spring, and Corey Marks's lighthouse keeper's son is forced to live in "a cage set in the wind." Wild death comes to Julie Brooks Barbour's patio. The ghost of a brutal secret haunts Justin Machnik's woods. Lisa Fay Coutley bears unflinching witness to domestic abuse. Threat braids through Eric Gadzinski's tenderness.

But the U.P. also remains a place of solace and grace. John Smolens finds one thing to keep—a lost wife's gathered stones—in his exquisite widower's soliloquy. April Lindala evokes generations of Native people, while Shirley Brozzo finds humor in a tribal center visit for free food. Russell Brakefield gives the U.P. its surfer's love song, and M. Bartley Seigel knows this place can dull the sharp edges of pain like beach glass. "Snow is coming," Cameron Witbeck says, but as Jennifer Yeatts instructs us, we can wake from the blizzard to "love / the dumb, early dark harder than ever." "We are drift," Ander Monson says so eloquently of upper Michiganders, and Cynie Cory's lover's lament ends, "I drift north." Whoever you are, reader, from whatever lights you have come, drift in with me toward the poems and stories of this shore.

—Jonathan Johnson

Death Defier

Tom Bissell

GRAVES HAD BEEN SICK FOR THREE DAYS WHEN, ON THE LONG STRAIGHT highway between Mazar and Kunduz, a dark blue truck coming toward them shed its rear wheel in a spray of orange-yellow sparks. The wheel, as though excited by its sudden liberty, bounced twice not very high and once very high and hit their windshield with a damp crack. "Christ!" Donk called out from the backseat. The driver, much too late, wrenched on the steering wheel, and they fishtailed and then spun out into the dunes alongside the road. Against one of the higher sandbanks the Corolla slammed to a dusty halt. Sand as soft and pale as flour poured into the partially opened windows. The shattered but still intact windshield sagged like netting. After a moment Donk touched his forehead, his eyebrow bristles as tender as split stitches. Thin watery blood streaked down his fingers.

From the front passenger seat Graves asked if the other three men—Donk, Hassan, the driver—were all right. No one spoke. Graves sighed. "Glad to hear it." He gave his dune-pinned door two small impotent outward pushes, then spent the next few moments staring out the splintery windshield. The air-freshener canister that had been suckered to the windshield lay quietly frothing lilac-scented foam in Graves's lap. The spun-around Corolla now faced Kunduz, the city they had been trying to escape. "I'm glad I'm not a superstitious man," Graves said at last. The driver's hands were still gripped around the steering wheel.

Donk climbed out on the Corolla's open side, cupping his throbbing eye socket and leaning forward, watching his blood patter onto the sand in perfect red globules. He did not have the faintest idea what he had struck his head against until Hassan, wincing and rubbing his shoulder, muscled his way out of the car behind him. Hassan looked at Donk and shrug-smiled, his eyes rimmed with such a fine black line they looked as if they had been Maybellined. His solid belly filled the stretched sack of his maroon cardigan sweater, and his powder-blue *shalwar khameez*—the billowy national pants of Afghanistan, draped front and back with a flap of cloth that resembled an untied apron—were splattered with Donk's blood. The whole effect gave Hassan an emergency-room air. Donk did not return Hassan's smile. The night before, in Kunduz, after having a bite of Spam and stale Brie in the rented compound of an Agence France Presse correspondent, Donk and Graves found their hotel room had been robbed. Graves had lost many personal items, a few hundred dollars, and his laptop, while Donk had parted with virtually all of his photographic equipment, including an irreplaceably good wide-lens he had purchased in London on the way over. Hassan, charged with watching the room while they were out, claimed to have abandoned his sentry duties only once, for five minutes, to go the bathroom. He had been greatly depressed since the robbery. Donk was fairly certain Hassan had robbed them.

Donk fastened around his head the white scarf he had picked up in Kunduz's bazaar. Afghan men tended to wear their scarves atop their heads in vaguely muffin-shaped bundles or around their necks with aviator flair. Afghanistan's troublous Arab guests, on the other hand, were said to tie the scarves around their skulls with baldness-mimicking tightness, the hem just millimeters above their eyes while the scarf's tasseled remainder trailed down their spines. This was called *terrorist style*, and Donk adopted it now. It was the only way he could think to keep blood from his eyes. He also sort of liked how it looked.

"Hassan," Graves snapped, as he climbed out of the Corolla. It was an order, and Graves—a tall, thin Brit with an illusionless, razor-burned face—had a voice seemingly engineered to give orders. He had thick brown hair and the ruined teeth of a man who had spent a large amount of time in the unfluoridated parts of the world. His hands were as filthy as the long sleeves of his white thermal underwear top, though his big fingernails seemed white as shells. Graves made his way to the truck, twenty yards down the road and askew on its three remaining wheels. He glanced down at the tire, innocently at rest in the middle of the highway, that had shattered the Corolla's windshield. Donk noted that Graves looked as stately as was imaginable for a sick man wearing one of those silly war-reporter khaki vests and red Chuck Taylor All-Stars. Hassan rushed to catch up to him, as Graves had not waited.

This left Donk and the driver, a kind of bear-man miracle with moist brown eyes and a beard it was hard to imagine he had not been born with, to have a look under the Corolla and assess the damage. Monoglots each, they could do little better than exchange artfully inflected grunts. Nothing seemed visibly wrong. The axel, for instance, was not bent, which had been Donk's greatest fear. But the steering wheel refused to budge and the ignition responded to the driver's twist with a click.

"Hmn," Donk consoled him.

"Mmn," the driver agreed.

Donk looked over at Graves, who was speaking through Hassan to the truck's stranded driver. Graves was nodding with exquisitely false patience as the curly-haired boy, who looked no older than twenty, grasped his head with both hands and then waved his arms around at the desert in huge gestures of innocence. Bursts of dune-skimmed sand whistled across the three of them. The bed of the boy's truck was piled ten deep with white bags of internationally donated wheat. His truck, Donk noticed, was not marked with any aid group's peaceable ideogram.

It had been a strange morning, even by Donk's standards. A few hours ago some "nasties," as Graves called them, had appeared on the outskirts of Kunduz, though they were supposed to have been driven out of the area a week ago. In fact, they were supposed to have been surrendering. Graves and Donk had jumped out of bed and rushed downstairs into the still-dark morning autumn air to see what they could see, hopping around barefoot on the frigid concrete. The battle was still far away, the small faint pops of gunfire sounding as dry as firecrackers. It appeared that, after some desultory return fire, Kunduz's commander called in an American air strike. The great birds appeared with vengeful instantaneousness and screamed across the city sky. The sound was terrific, atmosphere-shredding, and then they were gone. The horizon, a few moments later, burped up great dust bulbs. But within the hour the gunfire had moved closer. The well-armed defenders of Kunduz had been scrambling everywhere as Donk and Graves packed up what little remained of their gear into this hastily arranged taxi and sped out of town to the more securely liberated city of Mazar.

"Bloody fool," Graves said now, when he walked back over to Donk. He was speaking of the curly-haired boy.

"Call him a wog if it makes you feel better," Donk said. "I don't mind."

Graves cast a quick look back at the boy, now squatting beside his hobbled truck and chatting with Hassan. "He's stolen that wheat, you know."

"Where was he going?"

"He won't say."

"What's he doing now?"

"He's going to wait here, he says. I told him there were nasties about. Bloody fool." He looked at Donk, his face softened by sudden concern. "How's that eye, then?"

"Bleeding."

Graves leaned into him optometristically, trying to inspect the messy wound through the do-rag. "Nasty," he said finally, pulling away. "How many wars did you say you've covered?"

"Like war wars? Shooting wars? Or just wars?"

Graves nodded. "Shooting wars."

"Not counting this one, three. But I've never been shot at until today." While they were leaving Kunduz their Corolla had been hit with a short burst of Kalashnikov fire, though it was not clear whether the bullets were intended for them. The driver had used the strafe—it sounded and felt like a flurry of ball-peen hammers strikes—to establish a median traveling speed of 125 kilometers per hour. They had very nearly plowed over a little boy and his pony just before the city's strangely empty westernmost checkpoint.

"And how did you find it?" Graves asked, as though genuinely curious.

"I found it like getting shot at."

"That was rather how I found it." Graves's face pinched with fresh discomfort. He sighed, then seemed to go paler. His eyelids were sweaty. Graves stepped toward the Corolla searchingly, arms out, and lowered himself onto the bumper. "Think I need a rest." The driver fetched a straw-covered red blanket from the Corolla and wrapped it around Graves's shoulders.

They had been in Kunduz for two days when Donk noticed Graves tenderly hugging himself no matter the heat thrown off by their hotel room's oil-burning stove. His pallor grayed by the day, and soon he was having trouble seeing. Initially Graves had not been concerned. They went about their business of covering the war, Donk snapping Kunduz's ragtag liberators and the dead-eyed prisoners locked up in one of the city's old granaries, Graves reading ten hours' worth of CNN updates a day on his laptop and worrying over his past, present, and future need to "file." But his fever worsened, and he took a day's bed rest while Donk toured Kunduz on foot with the city's local commander, a happily brutal man who twice tried selling Donk a horse. When Donk returned to the hotel a few minutes before curfew that evening he found Graves twisted up in his vomit-stained sheets, his pillow lying in a sad crumple across the room. "Deborah," Graves had mumbled when Donk stirred him. "Listen. Turn the toaster? Please turn the toaster?"

Donk did not know Graves well. He had met him only ten days ago in Pyanj, Tajikistan, where many of the journalists were dovetailing stories by day and playing poker with worthless Tajik rubles by night. All were waiting for official clearance before venturing into Afghanistan. Graves—with an impatience typical of print journalists, their eyewitness being more perishable—elected to cast a few pearly incentives at the feet of the swinish border guards and asked Donk if he wanted to tag along. Donk, dispatched here by a British newsweekly, was under no real pressure to get in. His mandate was not one of breaking news but chronicling the country's demotic wartime realities. He did not even have a return flight booked. But he agreed.

Donk did not regret following Graves, even as he forced mefloquine hydrochloride tablets into his mouth, crusty with stomach ejecta, and splashed in some canteen water to chase them. Graves, Donk was certain, had malaria, even though it was late November, a season at the outer edge of probability for contracting the disease, and even though he knew Graves had been taking mefloquine since October. The next day Donk convinced one of Kunduz's aid workers—a grim black Belgian—to give him a small cache of chloroquine phosphate pills, as mefloquine was useful mostly as a malaria preventative. The chloroquine seemed to help, and Graves, still as shivery as a foundling, had recommenced with his worries about filing a story. Graves was rather picky with his stories, seeking only narratives that presented this war in its least inspiring light. Unfortunately, Kunduz seemed fairly secure and the people weirdly grateful. Indeed, despite predictions of a long, bloody, province-by-province conflict, 60 percent of the country had fallen to American-led forces in this, the war's fourth week.

After they were robbed Graves noted that his chloroquine pills were among the missing items. As the regrouped nasties waged this morning's hopeless surprise counterattack, neither Donk nor Graves had the presence of mind to beg more pills before they left, though Donk was fairly certain the aid workers would have pulled out of Kunduz too. That one could simply leave a firefight and come back a bit later was one of the odder things about this shadowy war. Roads were safe one day, suicide the next. Warlords thought to be relatively trustworthy one week were reported to have personally overseen the meticulous looting of an aid-group warehouse the next. All of this seemed designed to prevent anyone from actually fighting. From the little Donk had seen and heard, gun battles here seemed founded upon one's ability to spray bullets blindly around rocks and walls and then beat a quick, spectacular retreat.

"How do you feel?" Donk asked Graves now.

Graves, still sitting on the bumper, flashed his ruined teeth. The dirty wind had given his eyes a teary under-rim. "How do I look?"

"Fading. We need to get you somewhere."

Graves looked down, angrily blinking away his eyes' moisture. "Where are we, anyway?"

"About an hour outside Kunduz."

"That's another hour from Mazar?"

"Roughly."

Graves glanced around but the dunes were too high to see anything but the road and the road was too straight to reveal anything but the dunes. "Not far enough, I imagine."

"Probably not."

"We could hitch. Someone is bound to be along."

"Someone is. *Who* is the problem."

"You don't think the poor devils would use *roads*, for God's sake, do you? This far north? They'd be bombed within minutes."

"I have no idea."

With shiatsu delicacy Graves massaged his face with his fingertips. A bright bracelet of untanned flesh encircled his wrist. Graves's watch, too, had been stolen. His hands fell into his lap, then, and he sighed. "I hope you're not worried, Duncan."

Donk decided not to remind Graves, for what would have been the fortieth time, that he preferred to be called Donk. The nickname—a diminutive form of *donkey*—dated to one of the boyhood camping trips he and his father and older brother Jason used to take every year in the Porcupine Mountains of Michigan's Upper Peninsula. If he had never especially liked the name, he had come to understand himself through its drab prism. DONK ST. PIERRE was stamped in raised black type upon his ivory business card; it was the name above which his photographs were published. People often mistook his work for that of some Flemish eccentric. When colleagues first met him, something Donk called The Moment inescapably came to pass. Faced not with a tall, spectral, chain-smoking European but a short, overweight Midwesterner with frizzy black hair and childishly small hands, their smiles faded, their eyes crumpled, and a discreet little sound died just past their glottis. "I'm not worried," Donk said. "I'll be even less worried when we figure out where we're going."

Graves stared at Donk as though weighing him in some crucial balance. "You seemed rather jittery in Pyanj. Wasn't sure you'd be up to this."

When Donk said nothing Graves stood, listing momentarily before he steadied himself against the Corolla with one hand. Hassan loped back over to them, grinning beneath the pressure of one of his patented "discoveries," always uncanny in their relative uselessness. "My friends, I have discovered that nearby there is village. Good village, the driver says. Safe, friendly village. We will be welcome there. He told for me the way. Seven, eight kilometers."

Although this was much better information than Hassan was usually able to manage, Graves's expression was sour. Sweat dripped off his nose, and he was breathing hard. Merely standing had wiped him out. "Did he tell you that, or did you ask him?"

Hassan seemed puzzled. "I ask-ed him. Why?"

"Because, Hassan, information is only as reliable as the question that creates it."

"Mister Graves, I am not understanding you."

"He's saying," Donk said, "that our wheat-stealing friend may be telling us to go somewhere we shouldn't."

Hassan looked at them both in horror. "My friends, *no*. This is not possible. He is good man. And we are gracious, hospitable people here. We would never—"

Graves, cruelly, was ignoring this. "How's the car?"

Donk shook his head. "Wheel won't turn, engine won't start. Back wheels are buried in sand. And there's the windshield issue. Other than that, it's ready to go."

Graves walked out into the middle of the highway, drawing the blanket up over his head. Each end of the road streaked off into a troubling desert nothingness and appeared to tunnel into the horizon itself. It was before noon in northern Afghanistan, and the country felt as empty and skull-white as a moon. Not our familiar moon but another, harder, stranger moon. Above, the clouds were like little white bubbles of soap that had been incompletely sponged off the hard slate of the blue morning sky. Donk was compelled to wonder if nothingness and trouble were not, in fact, indistinguishable. Graves marched back over to the Corolla and savagely yanked his duffle from the front seat. "We walk to this village, then."

When it became apparent to the driver that they were leaving he spoke up, clearly agitated. Hassan translated. "He says he won't leave his car."

"I don't blame him," Graves said, and peeled off three twenties to pay the man.

AFTER LEAVING THE MAIN HIGHWAY THEY WALKED ALONG A SCARRED, inattentively paved road toward the village Hassan had promised was only six or seven or was it eleven kilometers away. Human Conflict, Donk thought, rather abstractly. It was one of his lively but undisciplined mind's fascinations. It differed from land to land, as faces differed. But the basic elements (ears, nose, mouth; aid workers, chaos, exhilaration) were always the same. It was the one thing that survived every era, every philosophy, the one legacy each civilization surrendered to the next. For Donk, Human Conflict was curiously life affirming, based as it was on avoiding death—indeed, on inflicting death preemptively on others. He loved Human Conflict not as an ideal but as a milieu, a state of mind one absorbed but was not absorbed by, the crucial difference between combatants and non-. His love of Human Conflict was as unapologetic as it was without nuance. He simply *enjoyed* it. "Duncan," a therapist had once asked him, "have you ever heard of the term 'chronic habitual suicide'?" Donk never saw that therapist, or any other, again.

He kicked from his path a billiard-ball-sized chunk of concrete. How was it that these people, the Afghans, could, for two hundred years, hold off or successfully evade several of the world's most go-getting empires and not find it within themselves to pave a fucking road? And yet somehow Afghanistan was, at least for the time being, the world's most significant place. Human Conflict had a way of doing that too. He remembered a press conference two weeks ago in the Presidential Palace in Tashkent, the capital of neighboring

Uzbekistan, where the fragrant, rested-looking journalists who had arrived with the American secretary of state had surrounded him. Donk had taken his establishing shots of the secretary—looking determined and unusually Vulcan behind his press-conference podium—and quickly withdrawn. In one of the palace's uninhabited corners he found a splendid globe as large as an underwater mine, all of its countries' names in Cyrillic. Central Asia was turned out toward the room; North America faced the wall. Seeing the planet displayed from that strange side had seemed to Donk as mistaken as an upside-down letter. But it was not wrong. That globe was in fact perfectly accurate.

Up ahead Graves was walking more slowly now, almost shuffling. Donk was allowing Graves the lead largely because Graves needed the lead. He was one of those rare people one did not actually mind seeing take charge. But Graves, wrapped in his red blanket, looked little better than a confused pensioner. The sun momentarily withdrew behind one of the bigger bubbly cloud formations. The temperature dropped with shocking immediacy, the air suddenly as sharp as angel hair. Donk watched Graves's bootlaces come slowly and then floppily untied. For some reason Donk was too embarrassed for Graves to say anything.

"Mister Donk," Hassan said quietly, drawing beside him. "Is Mister Graves all right?"

Donk managed a weak, testy smile. "Mister Graves is fine."

Hassan nodded. "May I, Mister Donk, ask you questions?"

"You may."

"Where were you born in America?"

"Near the Sea of Tranquility."

"I ask, what is your favorite food?"

"Blueberry filling."

"American women are very beautiful, they say. They say too they have much love."

"That's mostly true. One should only sleep with beautiful women, even though they have the least love. Write that down. With women it's all confidence, Hassan. Write that down too. You might look at me and think, But this is a fat man! And it's true. But I grow on people. You're not writing."

"I hear that American women make many demands. Not like Afghan women."

"Did you steal my cameras?"

"Mister Donk! No!"

"That's not nice, you know," Graves said suddenly, glancing back. "Teasing the boy like that."

"I was wondering when I'd get your attention."

"Leave the boy alone, Duncan. He's dealt with enough bad information to last his entire lifetime."

"I am not a boy," Hassan said suddenly.

"Don't listen to him," Graves said to Hassan. "War's made Mister Duncan barmy."

"How are you feeling?" Donk asked Graves. "Any better?"

Graves dropped his eyes to his open palm. "I was just checking my cell phone again. Nothing." Some enigma of telecommunications had prevented his Nokia from functioning the moment they crossed into Afghanistan. He tried absently to put away the phone but missed his pocket. Graves stopped and stared at the Nokia, a plastic purple amethyst half buried in the sand. Donk scooped it up and handed it back to Graves, who nodded distantly. Suddenly the sky filled with a deep, nearly divine roar. Their three heads simultaneously tipped back. Nothing. American F/A-18s and F-14s were somewhere cutting through that high blue, releasing satellite- and laser-guided bombs or returning from dropping bombs or looking for new places to drop bombs. Graves shook his head, quick and hard, as though struggling to believe that these jets really existed. Only after the roar faded did they push on, all of them now walking Wizard-of-Oz abreast. Graves still seemed angry. "Sometimes," he said, "I wonder if all the oil companies and the American military purposefully create these fucking crises to justify launching all those pretty missiles and dropping all these dreadful, expensive bombs. Air Force. Error Farce is more like it."

"Coalition troops," Donk reminded him. "Those could be British jets."

"Somehow, Duncan, I doubt that."

Donk swigged from his canteen and wiped his mouth with his forearm. Talking politics with Graves was like being handed an armful of eels and then being asked to pretend that they were bunnies. He did not typically mind arguing, certainly not with a European, especially about the relative merits of the Land of the Red, White, and Blue. But Graves did not seem up to it. Donk settled on what he hoped was a slightly less divisive topic. "I wonder if they caught him yet."

"They're not going to catch him. The first private from Iowa to find him is going to push him up against a cave wall and blow a hole in his skull." Graves seemed unable to take his eyes off his feet.

"Well," Donk said, "let's hope so."

Graves looked over at him with lucid, gaunt-faced disappointment. He snorted and returned his gaze to his All-Stars, their red fabric so dusty they now appeared pink. "I can't believe someone as educated as you would think that's appropriate."

"I'm not that educated." Donk noted that Graves was practically panting, his mouth open and his tongue peeking over the fence post of his lower front teeth. Donk touched him on the shoulder. "Graves, hey. You really look like you need to rest again."

Graves's reaction was to nod, stop, and collapse into a rough squat, his legs folding beneath him at an ugly, painful-looking angle. Donk handed Graves his canteen while Hassan, standing nearby, mashed some raisins into his mouth. Graves watched a chewing Hassan watch him for a while, then closed his eyes. "My head," he said. "Suddenly it's splitting."

"Malaria," Donk said, kneeling next to him. "The symptoms are cyclical. Headaches. Fever. Chills. The sweats."

"Yes," Graves said heavily. "I know. Until the little buggers have clogged my blood vessels. Goodbye, vital organs."

"Malaria isn't fatal," Donk said.

Graves shook his head. It occurred to Donk that Graves's face, which tapered slightly at his temples and swelled again at his jawline, was shaped rather like a foot. "Untreated malaria is often fatal."

Donk looked at him evenly. Graves's thermal underwear top had soaked through. The sharp curlicues of grayish hair that swirled in the hollow of

Graves's throat sparkled with sweat. His skin was shinier than his eyes by quite a lot.

"Tell me something," Graves said suddenly. "Why were you so nervous-seeming in Pyanj?"

Donk sighed. "Because nothing was happening. When nothing is happening I get jumpy."

Graves nodded quickly. "I heard that about you."

"You did?"

"That was a splendid shot, you know. The dead Tajik woman in Dushanbe. Brains still leaking from her head. You were there—what—three minutes after she was shot? I wonder, though. Do you see her when you sleep, Duncan?"

It was probably Donk's most famous photo, and his first real photo. The woman had been gunned down by Russian soldiers in the Tajik capital during an early ugly paroxysm of street fighting. The Russians were in Tajikistan as peacekeepers after the Soviet collapse. Her death had been an accident, cross fire. She had known people were fighting on that street, but she walked down it anyway. You saw a lot of that in urban warfare. Chronic habitual suicide. In the photo her groceries were scattered beside her. One of her shoes was missing. A bit of her brain in the snow—just a bit, as though it were some glistening red fruit that had been spooned onto a bed of sugar—the rest shining wetly in a dark black gash just above her ear. Her mouth was open. The photo had run on the wires all over the world and, from what he had heard, infuriated the Russian authorities, which explained the difficulty he always had getting into Russia. "I guess I'm not a very haunted person," Donk said finally.

Graves was still smiling in a manner Donk recognized for its casual hopelessness. It was a war-zone look. He had seen it on aid workers' faces and correspondents' faces but most often on soldiers' faces. He had witnessed it, too, on the bearded faces of the POWs in Kunduz's granary. Hassan had stopped eating his raisins and now watched the two men. He saw the look too—perhaps because, Donk thought, it was his own default expression.

"But you love death, though, Duncan, yes?" Graves asked. "You have to. We all do. That's why we do this, isn't it?"

Donk began to pat himself down in search of something. He did not know what. He disliked such emotional nudism. He stopped pawing himself, then, and, feeling not a little caught out, traced his finger around in the sand. He made a peace sign, an easy shape to make. "Graves, I have learned not to generalize much about people in our line of work. The best combat photographer I ever knew was the mother of two children."

"Russian?"

"Israeli."

Graves leaned forward slightly. "Do you know what Montaigne says?"

Donk neither moved nor breathed nor blinked. He heard *Montaigne* as *Montane*. "Can we walk again now?"

"Montaigne believed that death was easiest for those who thought about it the most. That way it was possible for a man die to resigned. 'The utility of living consists not in the length of days'—Montaigne said this—'but in the use of time.'" Graves smiled again.

Donk decided to switch tacks. "Your Royal Illness," he said cheerfully, getting to his feet, "I bid you, rise and walk."

Graves merely sat there, shivering. His khaki vest looked two sizes too large for him, his hair no longer so thick-looking now that it was soaked to his skull, his snowy scalp showing through. Graves seemed reduced, as unsightly as a wet rodent. "Isn't it strange," he asked, "that in the midst of all this a man can die from a mosquito bite?"

Donk's voice hardened: "*A*, Graves, give me a break. *B*, You're not going to die."

He laughed, lightly. "Today, no. Probably not."

Donk had a thought. *Deborah. Turn the toaster.* This Deborah had to be Graves's girlfriend or common-law wife. The man did not seem traditional husband material, somehow. "Graves, you need to walk. For Deborah."

Graves's puzzled face lifted up, and for a moment he looked his imperious self again. "Who the devil is Deborah?"

"Mister Donk—" Hassan said urgently, all but pulling on Donk's sleeve.

"Graves," Donk said, "I *need* you to get *up*."

Graves lay back, alone in his pain, his skull finding the pillow of his duffel bag. "It's my head, Duncan. I can't bloody *think*."

"Mister Donk!" Hassan said, but it was too late. The jeep was approaching in a cloud of dust.

THE OWNER OF THE JEEP WAS A THIRTYISH MAN NAMED AHKTAR. HE wore blue jeans and a thin gray windbreaker and, as it happened, was only lightly armed, outwardly friendly, and claimed to live in the village they were headed toward. It was his "delight," he said, to give them a ride. He spoke a little English. "My father," he explained once they were moving along, "is chief of my village. I go to school in Mazar city, where I learn English at the English Club."

"You're a student now?" Donk asked, surprised. He found he could not stop looking at Ahktar's thick mustache and toupee-shaped hair, both as impossibly black as photocopier ink.

He laughed. "No. Many years ago."

Hassan and Donk bounced around on the jeep's stiff backseat as Ahktar took them momentarily off-road, avoiding a dune that had drifted out into the highway. Jumper cables and needle-nose pliers jangled around at Donk's feet. Graves was seat-belted in the shotgun position next to Ahktar, jostling in the inert manner of a crash-test dummy. Donk had yet to find the proper moment to ask why in Afghanistan the steering wheels were found on the right side of the car when everyone drove on the right side of the road. He thought he had found that moment now but, before he could ask, Ahktar hit a bump and Donk bashed his head against the vehicle's metal roof. "Your jeep," Donk said, rubbing his head through his terrorist-style do-rag.

"Good jeep!" Ahktar said.

"It's a little . . . military-seeming."

Ahktar looked at him in the rearview and shook his head. He had not heard him.

Donk leaned forward. "Military!" he shouted over the jeep's gruff lawn-mowerish engine. "It looks like you got it from the military!"

"Yes, yes," Ahktar said, clearly humoring Donk. "I do!"

Donk leaned back. "This *is* a military jeep, isn't it?" he asked Hassan.

"His father maybe is warlord," Hassan offered. "A good warlord!"

"Where are you from?" Ahktar asked Donk. "America?"

"That's right," Donk said.

"You know Lieutenant Marty?" Ahktar asked.

"Lieutenant Marty? No, I'm sorry. I don't."

Ahktar seemed disappointed. "Captain Herb?"

"No. Why do you ask?"

Ahktar reached into the side pocket of his gray coat and handed back to Donk a slip of paper with the names *Captain Herb* and *Lieutenant Marty* written on it, above what looked to be a pi-length satellite phone number. "Who are they?" Donk asked, handing the paper back.

"American soldiers," he said happily. "We are friends now because I help them with some problems."

"Is there a phone in your village? We could call them."

"Sorry, no," Ahktar apologized. "We have radios in my village but nearest phone is Kunduz. I think today I will not go to Kunduz. They are having problems there." He motioned toward Graves, who seemed to be napping. "From where in America is your friend?"

"I'm not an American," Graves muttered with as much force as Donk had heard him manage all day. "I'm *English*."

"What?" Ahktar asked, leaning toward him.

Graves's eyes cracked open, dim and sticky like a newborn's. "I'm *English*. From England. The people your countrymen butchered by the thousand a hundred and fifty years ago."

"Yes," Ahktar said soberly, downshifting as they came to a hill. Something in the jeep's heater was rattling like a playing card in bicycle spokes. The waves of air surging from its vents went from warm, to hot, to freezing, to hot again. Ahktar drew up in his seat. "Here is village."

As they plunged down the highway, hazy purple mountains materialized along the horizon. From the road's rise, Ahktar's village appeared as an oblong smear of homes and buildings located just before a flattened area where the mountain range's foothills began. Now came a new low-ground terrain covered with scrabbly, drought-ruined grass. Along the road were dozens of wireless and long-knocked-over telephone poles. The jeep rolled through the village's outer checkpoint. Set back off the highway, every fifty yards, were some small stone bubble-domed homes, their chimneys smoking. They looked to Donk like prehistoric arboretums. None of it was like anything Donk had ever before seen in Central Asia. The virus of Soviet architecture—with its ballpark right angles, frail plaster, and monstrous frescoes—had not spread here. In the remoter villages of Tajikistan he had seen poverty to rival northern Afghanistan's, but there the Soviet center had always held. In these never-mastered lands south of the former Soviet border, everything appeared old and shot up and grievously unattended. These discrepancies reminded Donk of what borders really meant, and what, for better or worse, they protected.

The road narrowed. The houses grew tighter, bigger, and slightly taller. The smoky air thickened, and soon they were rolling through Ahktar's village proper. He saw a few shops crammed with junk—ammunition and foodstuffs and Aladdin's lamp for all he knew—their window displays tiered backward like auditorium seating. Black curly-haired goats hoofed at the dirt. Dogs slunk from doorway to doorway. Dark hawk-nosed men wearing shirts with huge floppy sleeves waved at Ahktar. Most looked Tajik, and Donk cursed his laziness for not learning at least how to count in Tajik during all the months he had spent in Tajikistan. Walking roadside were beehive-shaped figures whose bedspread-white and sky-blue garments managed to hide even the basest suggestion of human form. These were women. Around their facial areas Donk noted narrow, tightly latticed eye slots. Children ran happily beside the jeep, many holding pieces of taut string. "Kites," Graves observed weakly. "They're flying kites."

Ahktar's face turned prideful. "Now we are free, you see." He pointed at the sky. Donk turned his head sideways and peered up out the window.

Floating above the low buildings of Ahktar's village were, indeed, scores of kites. Some were boxes, others quadrangular; some swooped and weaved like osprey, others hung eerily suspended.

Hassan looked up also. "We could not fly kites before," he said quietly.

"Yes," Donk said. "I know. Let freedom ring."

"When they leave our village," Ahktar—a bit of a present-tense addict, it seemed—went on, "we see many changes, such as shaving of the beards. The men used to grow big beards, of course very long, and they checked!"

Donk smiled. "So you had a long beard?"

"Of course I have. I show you my pictures. It was a very long beard! Now everybody is free to shave or grow as their own choice."

It seemed impious to point out that virtually every man momentarily centered within the frame of Donk's murky plastic window had a griffin's nest growing off his chin.

"When did they leave?" Donk asked. "Was it recently?"

"Oh, yes," Ahktar said. "Very recently!" He cut the engine and rolled them down a rough dirt path through a part of the village that seemed a stone labyrinth. Sack-burdened peasants struggled past plain mud homes. Kunduz suddenly seemed a thriving desert metropolis in comparison. A high-walled compound guarded by two robed young men cradling Kalashnikovs stood where the path dwindled into a driveway. Inches before the compound's metal gate the jeep rolled to a soft stop. Ahktar climbed out of the vehicle, and Donk followed.

"What's this?" Donk asked.

"My father's house. I think you are in trouble. If so, he is the man you are wanting to talk to now."

"We're not in trouble," Donk said. "My friend is sick. We just need to get him some medicine. We're not in any trouble. Our car broke down."

Ahktar lifted his hands, as though to ease Donk. "Yes, yes." He moved toward the compound's gate. "Come. Follow."

"What about my friend?" But Donk turned to see that the guards were helping Graves from the jeep and leading him toward Ahktar's father's compound. Surprisingly, Graves did not spurn their assistance or call them bloody Hindoos, but simply nodded and allowed his arms to find their way around each guard's neck. They dragged him along, Graves's legs serving as occasional, steadying kickstands. Hassan followed behind them, again nervously eating the raisins he kept in his pocket.

The large courtyard, its trees stripped naked by autumn, was patrolled by a dozen more men holding Kalashnikovs. They were decked out in the same crossbred battle dress as the soldiers Donk had seen loitering around Kunduz: camouflage pants so recently issued by the American military they still held their crease, shiny black boots, *pakuls* (the floppy national hat of Afghanistan), rather grandmotherly shawls, and shiny leather bandoliers. While most of the bandoliers were empty, a few of these irregulars had hung upon them three or four small bulblike grenades. They looked a little like explosive human Christmas trees.

"Wait one moment, please," Ahktar said, strolling across the courtyard and ducking into one of the many dark doorless portals at its northern edge. The guards deposited Graves at a wooden table, and a minute later he was brought a pot of tea. Donk and Hassan, exchanging glances, walked over to Graves's table and sat down in the cold dark light. The soldiers on the compound's periphery had yet to acknowledge them. They simply walked back and forth, back and forth, along the walls. Something about their manner, simultaneously alert and robotic, led Donk to guess that their weapons' safeties were off—if Kalashnikovs even *had* safeties, which, come to think of it, he was fairly sure they did not.

"Nothing quite like a safe, friendly village," Graves said in a thin voice. He sipped his tea, holding the round handleless cup with both hands.

"How do you feel, Mister Graves?" Hassan asked eagerly.

"Hassan, I feel dreadful."

"I'm sorry to hear this, Mister Graves."

Graves set down the teacup and frowned. He looked at Hassan. "Be a lad and see if you can't scare up some sugar for me, would you?"

Hassan stared at him, empty-faced.

Graves chuckled at the moment he seemed to recognize that the joke had not been funny. "I'm joking, Hassan." He poured them both a cup of tea, and with a dramatic shiver quickly returned his arm to the warm protective folds of his blanket. "Bloody freezing, isn't it?"

"It's actually a little warmer," Donk said, turning from his untouched tea to see Ahktar and an older gentleman walking over to join them. Ahktar's father was a towering man with a great, napkin-shaped cinnamon beard. He wore long clean white-yellow robes and a leather belt as thick as a cummerbund. Stuffed into this belt was what looked to be a .45. He was almost certainly Tajik, and had large crazed eyes and a nose that looked as hard as a sharp growth of bark. But he was smiling—something he did not do well, possibly for lack of practice. When he was close he threw open his arms and proclaimed something with an air of highly impersonal sympathy.

"My father says you are welcome," Ahktar said. He did not much resemble his father, being smaller and darker-skinned. Doubtless Ahktar had a Pashtun mother around here somewhere. Donk could almost assemble her features. His father said something else, then nudged Ahktar to translate. "He says too that you are his great and protected guests." His father spoke again, still with his effortful smile. "He says he is grateful for American soldiers and grateful for you American journalists, who care only of the truth."

"English," Graves said quietly.

"Whatever trouble you are in my father will help you. It is his delight."

"Ahktar," Donk stepped in gently, "I told you. We're not in any trouble. My friend here is very sick. Our car broke down. We were trying to go to Mazar. It's very simple." Ahktar said nothing. "Well," Donk asked, "are you going to tell your father that?"

"I tell him that already."

"Then can we go to Mazar from here?"

The muscles of Ahktar's face tightened with regret. "Unfortunately, that is problem. No one is going to Mazar today." He seemed suddenly to wish that he were not standing beside his father, who of course asked what had just been said. Ahktar quietly back-translated for him, obviously hoping that his pea of an answer would be smothered beneath the mattress of translation.

"Why can't we go to Mazar?" Donk pressed.

At this mention of Mazar his father spoke again, angrily now. Ahktar nodded obediently. "My father wishes you to know you are safe here. Mazar is maybe not so safe."

"But Mazar's perfectly safe. It's been safe for days. I have friends there."

"My father is friendly with American soldiers in Mazar. Very friendly. And now we are helping them with some problems they are having in this region. We have authority for this. Unfortunately, Mazar's Uzbek commander and my father are not very friendly, and there my father has no authority. Therefore it would be good for you to stay."

After a pause, Donk spoke: "Who, may I ask, is your father?"

"My father is General Ismail Mohammed. He was very important part of United National Islamic Front for the Salvation of Afghanistan, which fought against—"

"But Mazar's commander was part of that same front."

"Yes," Ahktar said sadly. "Here is problem."

Donk had met a suspiciously large number of generals during his time in Afghanistan, and was not sure how to judge General Mohammed's significance. Warlord? Ally? Both? He let it drop. "Do you have medicine here?"

Again Ahktar shrugged. "Some. But unfortunately it is with my father's soldiers now. They are out taking care of some problems for Lieutenant Marty."

"Is Lieutenant Marty with them?"

"Oh, no. Lieutenant Marty is in Mazar."

"Where we can't go."

"Yes."

There really were, Donk had often thought, and thought again now, two kinds of people in the world: Chaos People and Order People. For Donk this was not a bit of cynical Kipling wisdom to be doled out among fellow journalists in barren Inter-Continental barrooms. It was not meant in a condescending way. No judgment; it was a purely empirical matter. Chaos People, Order People. Anyone who doubted this had never tried to wait in line, board a plane, or get off a bus among Chaos People. The next necessary division of the world's people took place along the lines of whether they actually knew what they were. The Japanese were Order People and knew it. Americans and English were Chaos People who thought they were Order People. The French were the worst thing to be: Order People who thought they were Chaos People. But Afghans, like Africans and Russians and the Irish, were Chaos People who knew they were Chaos People, and while this lent them a good amount of charm, it made their countries berserk, insane. Countries did indeed go insane. Sometimes they went insane and stayed insane. Chaos Peoples' countries particularly tended to stay insane. Donk miserably pulled off his do-rag, the bloody glue that held the fabric to his skin tearing from his ruined eyebrow so painfully that he had to work to keep the tears from his eyes. "So tell me, Ahktar. What are we supposed to do here?"

Before anyone could answer, Graves had a seizure.

A FEW HOURS LATER, DONK WAS SITTING OUTSIDE THE ROOM IN WHICH Graves had been all but quarantined. He was petting a stray, wolfish mongrel with filaments of silver hair threaded through its black coat, waiting for the village medicine man to emerge from Graves's room. This man had claimed he was a doctor and offered up to Donk a large pouch of herbs as evidence. Donk did not have the heart to argue. The compound was quiet, except for some small animals fighting or playing along the eaves just above Donk's head and the occasional overhead roar of a jet. Hassan, sitting a few feet away, watched Donk stroke the dog's head in revulsion.

"Why," he asked finally, "do you do that?"

Donk had always taken pity on Central Asian dogs, especially after learning that one could fend off a possible attack by miming the act of picking up a stone, at which the dogs usually turned and ran away. He lowered his lips to the creature's head and planted upon it a chaste kiss. The dog smelled of oily musk. "Because it's lonely," Donk said.

"That is a filthy animal," Hassan told him. "You should not touch such a filthy animal, Mister Donk."

Donk chose not to point out that Hassan was, if anything, far dirtier. The boy had spent a night with Donk and Graves in Kunduz. His body odor had been so potent, so overwhelmingly cheesy, that Donk had not been able to sleep. Misplaced Muslim piety, he thought with uncharacteristic bitterness.

"You're right," Donk said at last. "The dog's filthy. But so am I. So there we are."

Hassan *hmph*ed.

During the seizure Donk had stuffed his bloody do-rag in Graves's mouth to keep him from biting off his tongue, even though he knew convulsive people rarely, if ever, bit off their own tongues. It was one of those largely ceremonial things people did in emergencies. Donk had pushed Graves up on the table and held him down. Graves shuddered for a few moments, his eyes filled with awful awareness, his chest heaving like the gills of a suffocating fish. Then, mercifully, he went unconscious. Donk used the rest of his iodined water to try to rehydrate Graves, but he quickly vomited it up. At this General Mohammed had sent for his medicine man.

Donk knew there were at least two kinds of malaria. The less serious strain was stubborn and hard to kill—flulike symptoms could recur as long as five decades after the initial infection—but it was rarely lethal. The more serious strain quickly turned life threatening if untreated. He was no longer wondering which strain Graves had contracted. Graves was conscious now— Donk could hear him attempting to reason with the village doctor—but his voice was haggard and dazed.

Donk looked around. Thirty or forty yards away a small group of General Mohammed's soldiers watched him, their Kalashnikovs slung over their shoulders. They looked beaten, bullied, violent. Hair-trigger men. Their faces were like shadows. And these were the *winners*. Donk found himself, suddenly, missing women. Seeing them, staring at them, smelling them. Afghanistan had mailed into Donk's brain a series of crushingly similar mental postcards: men, men, desert, men, men, men, guns, men, guns, guns, desert, guns, men. One might think that life without women would lead to a simpler, less fraught existence. No worries about hair or odor. Saying whatever you wanted. But one's eye tired of men as one's nerves certainly tired of guns.

It was not just women, however. Donk missed sex even more. He needed, he admitted, an inordinate amount of sex. Heavy people needed things—hence their heaviness. Sex was a large part of the reason he had been reluctant to leave Chicago to come to Afghanistan. He was having a Guinness Book amount of it with Tina, who was maybe his girlfriend, his first in a long time. As luck would have it, Tina was menstruating the night before he left. They had had sex anyway, in her bathroom, and left bloody foot- and handprints all over the white tile. They Windexed away the blood together. It had not been freaky. It had almost been beautiful, and he loved her. But for him distance was permission, and newness arousal itself. Plane tickets and hotel rooms were like lingerie. He had already slept with an AP reporter in Tashkent. He did not regret it, exactly, because he had every intention of lying about it later. It occurred to him that he had also lied to Graves, about not being haunted. Strangely, he felt bad about that lie. It seemed like something Graves should have known. But Donk had not known where to begin.

A decade ago Donk worked as a staff photographer for a dozen family newspapers peppered throughout central Wisconsin, all somehow owned by the same unmarried Republican. His life then had been sitting through school-board meetings and upping the wattage of the smiles of local luminaries, drinking three-dollar pitchers of Bud after work, and suffering polite rejection from strangers he misjudged as unattractive enough to want to speak to him. That life began to end when the last of five sudden strokes stripped Donk's father of his mind and sent him off into dementia. Donk was the only one of his siblings who lived within a thousand miles of Milwaukee, where his father was hospitalized; his mother had long refused to speak to the man. So, alone, Donk set up camp beside his father's deathbed.

Death was a peculiar thing. Some people endured unenviable amounts of firsthand death without its one clearest implication ever occurring to them. Donk had never much thought about his own death before. The prospect had always felt to him like a television show he knew was on channel 11 at eight o'clock but had never watched and never planned to. Donk stared at the monitors, listened to the hiss of his father's bed's mattress as the nurses pistoned it up and down, timed the steady beep whose provenance he did not care to isolate. It was all he could do to keep from thinking that everything was assembled to provide the man a few last deprived moments of life. Donk realized that even if he were beside his father at the moment his final journey began, the man would still die alone, as Donk would die alone, as we all die alone. Horribly, doubly alone, for just as no one went with us, no one greeted us when it was over.

Nurses found him weeping in the hospital's cafeteria. When his father's doctor brought some final forms for Donk to fill out, she slipped into his catatonic hand a small packet of diazepam. The nervous breakdown, Donk expected. The estrangement from his surviving family—who could not understand his "sudden obsession" with dying—he expected. Quitting his job and investing his small inheritance, he expected; becoming a freelance combat photographer, he did not. People who were not correspondents laughed when Donk told the story, which he often did. It sounded so unbelievable. But people are not born combat photographers any more than they are born lawyers. One day you were waiting tables; the next you were in law school. One day you were heartbroken and megalomaniacal, the next you were fax-ing visa requests to embassies using stolen letterhead. Only Tajikistan's had answered him. If Tajikistan's embassy wondered why the *Waukesha Freeman* felt it needed a photographer in Dushanbe, it did not share that curiosity with Donk. He was awarded his first visa to his first war, a genuine hot war, a civil war. He told everyone he met in Dushanbe that he was "stringing," even though he was not sure what that word really entailed. In Tajikistan he saw his first gunshot wound, his first dead baby. He learned that combat photographers either spooked or did not. To his surprise, Donk did not. At least, he spooked no more than on the afternoon he watched his father burp, sigh, and stop breathing. The photo of the gunned-down old woman, taken after five months and $3,000 of squandered savings, led to Donk's covering the reconciliation trials in Rwanda for one of India's biggest dailies. There he learned that he no longer had much patience for American minorities' claims of oppression. Rwanda led to Jerusalem, shortly after the intifada. There he leaned of the subterranean connections world media outlets had expertly tunneled beneath continents of human misery, and how often you passed the same faces when traveling through them. Jerusalem led to Dagestan, where he spent a day with a Tatar Muslim warlord whose nom de guerre was Hitler and who made an awkward pass at Donk when they were alone. He learned that, of all the countries in the world, America was most hesitant to publish graphic "bang-bang" photos. He learned that arms and cocaine were the world's second and third most profitable exports, after human sex slaves. He learned how to shop for a Kevlar vest. He learned how to take a good picture while running. He learned, when all else failed, to follow refugees. And he learned that the worse and more ugly the reality around him, and the more impervious to it and better he felt, the more he forgot his father. He learned that the only thing that truly frightened him was quiet, because he knew death was quiet—the longest quiet. He learned that the persona that came with this strange fearlessness was able to win, if only for a night, a certain kind of troubled heart belonging to a certain kind of woman more worldly than Donk had any previous right to expect, and he learned that he was the type of man to abuse this ability.

His brother and sister called him a fear addict, a desperate idiot on a danger bender; they claimed he had never "dealt" with their father's death. Donk's brother Jason was a first-team whiskey addict (three interventions and counting: "What, this again?" he had asked, after the most recent). His sister, Marie, lived in Anchorage, too far away to provide Donk with any idea of what, exactly, she was into. Judging from her insensate three A.M. phone calls, it was high-impact. Who were they to speak of fear, of "dealing the natural process of death"? Death was actually the least natural thing Donk could imagine, involving, as it did, not living. Death's stature as a physiological event did not mean it was natural. The trapped mink does not accept its own death; it chews off its leg. No, death was something else, uncategorized and dreadful, something to be fought off, defied, spat upon. Human Conflict, he thought. Death was the unappeasable aggressor. And he stroked the dog's small head.

The medicine man stepped from Graves's room. Without consulting him, Donk rushed inside. It was a little past ten in the morning now, the light in

Graves's room brighter than he expected. Graves was supine on a thick mass of blankets with another, thinner blanket mostly covering him. He seemed very still. His eyes were dry. Though he did not look at Donk, he raised his hand in brief acknowledgment. Donk crouched next to Graves's makeshift bed and said nothing. Then, on an impulse, he took Graves's hand and held it crossways in his own, as though hoping to offer him some mysterious transfer of strength.

"Did you once think," Graves asked, "about how dirty dying is? I'm lying here in my own shit. You can smell it, can't you? I should really do something about this." He shifted positions, and Donk did smell Graves's shit, thin and sour and soupy. In response he squeezed Graves's hand. "In England," Graves went on, wincing briefly, "I think something like eighty percent of all deaths now take place in hospitals. I watched my mother and my father die in hospitals. They went quietly. It was lovely, in its way. But fifty years ago only forty percent of the English population died in hospitals. We sequester the dying, you see. Because it *is* ugly, it *is* dirty. I think we don't want to know that. We want to keep that little truth hidden away. But think a moment about how most people have died, Duncan. They've died in places just like this. So if I'm going to die here I'm joining legions. For some reason this makes me happy." Graves's head rolled an inch on its pillow, and, for the first time, he looked at Donk.

Donk stared back at Graves, the connection allowing him to locate the voice, as faraway as a quasar, in his mind. "You're not going to die."

Graves smiled. "Old men have to die. The world grows moldy, otherwise."

Graves, Donk knew, was forty. His sympathy left him in one brash gust. "What did the doctor say?"

"Oh, you mean St. John's Wort, M.D.? Hell if I know. He all but sprinkled me with voodoo dust. Duncan, calm down. I'm either going to make it through this or I won't. I'm not upset. I just have to wait." He closed his eyes. "'Of all the wonders that I yet have heard, / It seems to me most strange that men should fear; / Seeing that death, a necessary end, / Will come when it will come.' That's Shakespeare. Preternatural, isn't it? Any occasion one can think of, and there he is."

Donk knew he could barely quote Shakespeare if he were spotted "To be" and "not to be." In a low voice he said, "You *are* going to die, Graves, if you've already convinced yourself you're going to die."

"A puzzle."

Donk let go of his hand. "It's not a fucking puzzle."

"Getting upset, Duncan, isn't going to help me."

"Then what *is* going to help you?"

"Medicine. Medicine they don't have here."

"Where?" Donk asked. "Where do I go?"

Graves looked at him again. Suddenly Donk saw the fear just below the flat blue composure of Graves's eyes, a stern, dignified terror barricaded so completely inside of him it barely recognized itself. Graves's lips were shaking. "Jesus, Duncan. I—you—you could rent that chap Ahktar's jeep. You could—"

With that Donk rushed out, collared Hassan, and went to find General Mohammed and Ahktar. Seven hundred dollars was hidden beneath the insole of Donk's boot. This would be enough, he hoped, for a safety deposit on the jeep. He would drive to Mazar with Hassan. He would walk into UNICEF's office or Doctors Without Borders or find Lieutenant Marty and he would come back here. Graves was too sick to travel, and if they broke down again or were stopped—it was too complicated. That was the one truly upsetting thing about Human Conflict: It made everything far too complicated.

Donk found General Mohammed alone in his quarters. He was wearing glasses, surprisingly enough, sitting at a plain wooden desk, reading a book in Persian. His .45 was flat on the tabletop. Behind the general, on the wall, hung a green-and-black flag last used in Afghanistan during the reign of its deposed king, thirty years ago. Without knocking, Donk announced he was renting Ahktar's jeep and going to Mazar. Without looking up, General Mohammed informed him that Ahktar had, only an hour before, left in his jeep to take care of a few more problems. He would be back sometime tomorrow, perhaps maybe. Donk stood silently in the general's doorjamb, feeling himself growing smaller. *Perhaps maybe.* The national motto of Afghanistan.

"He says," Hassan translated for General Mohammed, "that Mister Graves is very sick. He says he has spoken to his doctor."

"Yes," Donk said, looking at the general. "He's going to die."

General Mohammed frowned and spoke again. The man's face, Donk thought, was 70 percent nose. Hassan translated. "His doctor says there is one thing that can help him."

"What's that?" Donk asked, the second word cracking as it left his mouth. He was still looking at the general.

"There is a grass that grows in a valley in the mountains. A special grass. Medicine grass?"

"Medicinal grass."

"Yes. This grass his doctor can boil for Mister Graves, he says. Then Mister Graves can drink the broth." General Mohammed spoke again, nodded, and returned to his book. "He says Mister Graves will get better." Hassan shrugged.

"He has malaria," Donk told Hassan numbly. "Grass won't help malaria. He needs antibiotics." Donk had not meant for Hassan to translate this, but he did.

"Yes," General Mohammed said, through Hassan. As the general went on Hassan began to shift and nod. "Okay, now he says once he suffered this himself. Six years ago, in the summer?" General Mohammed kept talking. "And many of his men as well. They were all very ill, he says, just like Mister Graves. He says they have seen much of Mister Graves's sickness here. But they drank the boiled grass and a day later they were well."

"Do they have any of the grass here?"

"No. He says it is in a valley in the mountains beyond the village." Hassan listened. "He is saying now he can tell for you how to find the grass and give you two of his men. Together, he says, you can go get the grass. Then, Mister Graves will be well." Hassan smiled.

"I need a vehicle," Donk said. He did not intend to find the grass. He would simply drive to Mazar. If General Mohammed's shadow-faced men did not care for this, they could shoot him. They could give Donk his own shadow face.

The General was reading again. When Hassan translated Donk's request, he breathed in deeply and turned a page. He spoke. Hassan: "It is not a far walk, he says. His men will show you."

"Tell him I need a vehicle."

General Mohammed peered at Donk over the top edge of his glasses and spoke, it was clear, for the last time. Hassan shook his head: "He says he is sorry, Mister Donk, but they have too many problems today to spare any vehicles to go to Mazar."

When Donk returned to Graves's room he found him asleep, his white face and reddish-purple cheeks agleam with perspiration, his forehead creased and dented. He was holding his purple Nokia. NO SIGNAL, its LCD read. Again Donk sat next to Graves's bed. Getting close to Graves was now like entering a force field of heat. He could smell Graves's bad breath, which smelled like shit, and his shit, which smelled like bad breath. Donk's did not now and never had much believed in God, or in human goodness. He did not think that people had a "time" they "had to go," or even that this special mountain grass would do fuck-all for Graves. He believed in and tried to think about very little. He believed in photography, which he loved, and death, which he hated. He thought about how he had been using one to deny the other. He thought about how clearly he felt death in Graves's bright room, the same greedy cool-edged core of heat that a decade ago he had felt zeroing in on his father. He refused to abandon Graves to it. Of course, this was just more ceremony. Graves was dying as he looked at him. But death, too, was ceremony, the one sacrament that, in time, singed every tongue.

Donk touched his own lips, absently. They were cold. No signal.

HASSAN DISAGREED THAT HELPING DONK FIND MEDICINAL GRASS WAS an implied part of his duties. He had no wish to leave the relative safety of this village. He seemed surprised, in fact, that Donk even wanted him along. Donk began to wonder if robbing them was not Hassan's polite if highly indirect way of attempting to end their association. The two soldiers General Mohammed lent Donk most clearly did not want to go find the grass either. The only person who wished less than they to go out and find this grass was Donk.

General Mohammed assured them that leaving by 1 P.M. would afford them plenty of time to find the valley, fill a satchel with grass, and return by the evening. Before they left, one of General Mohammed's wives fed them all a pile of meatless pilau that they chased down with gallons of cherry compote.

Just outside the village, Donk watched as the two loaner soldiers loaded a small donkey with canvas pouches and plastic bags emblazoned with the Marlboro logo.

"Why," Donk asked Hassan, "are they bringing a goddamned donkey? We're only going to be gone for a few hours."

Hassan asked them, but the soldiers did not respond and kept loading the donkey with plastic bags. "I am thinking," Hassan hazarded, "that this donkey belongs to one of them. Like pet? Maybe they want it to receive its exercise today."

That these were not General Mohammed's ablest men was evident in several ways. They had been lucky enough to receive the American camouflage uniforms, but in place of the boots Donk saw on proud display among the general's other soldiers these men were wearing what he realized only incrementally were tire treads held to their feet by twine.

"I have a rule," Donk told Hassan to tell the soldiers, neither of whose names he had any interest in learning. "I'm going to call it Rule One. Rule One is: No talking. Unless it's an emergency, or unless they see the grass. Otherwise I don't want to hear any talking. Okay?"

Hassan looked troubled. "Mister Donk, why this rule?"

"Because I'm sick of talking, I'm sick of languages I don't understand, and I'm sick of words in general. I just want to walk."

"Can I talk if I talk English?"

Donk looked at him. "Did you steal my cameras?"

"Mister Donk! Why would I steal your cameras? Where would I put them?"

"You can talk in English. A little. But ask me first."

Hassan shook his head, lamely mouthed Donk's edict to the soldiers, then walked away a few feet and moped defeatedly. The soldiers had scarcely listened, their limited attention still fully commandeered by the donkey. The donkey was a youngish creature with a rust-and-toffee coat and teeth the size of shot glasses. Once it was loaded up, one of the soldiers smacked the donkey with proprietary cruelty on its bulbous muscular hindquarters. The donkey trundled forward a few steps, then stopped and shook its head, its long ears flapping. The first soldier, whose angular and almost handsome face was nearly hidden behind a bushy black beard that began growing just below his eyes, laughed. The second soldier, a smaller man whose beard was redder and less ambitious, walked over to the donkey and whipped it with a switch. This time the donkey walked and did not stop. Donk stared at the animal with dejected, secret confederacy, then followed after it.

They hiked for an hour without talking, saw no one, and reached the range's first serious hill just after two. They cleared it easily, and though another, steeper hill lay just ahead, Donk was pleased. These foothills were not very challenging. Even this range's highest faraway peaks were snowless. In Tajikistan he had trekked over far more punishing country. The trails were well worn and dusty, and the wind was low. The sun was bright; beneath it Afghanistan looked like a blizzard of gray and brown. A nature hike, minus the nature.

Donk thought back to the Porcupines in Upper Michigan, family trips his brother, Jason, now referred to as "hurt-feelings competitions." But Donk did not remember them this way. Donk was always deputized to carry the party's RV-sized tent, as well as anything that related to the inevitable screaming match that doubled as the tent's assembly. Donk had been a shortish, overweight boy, a puffing congenital sweater. On one trip, Jason had likened his younger brother's hunched appearance under thirty pounds of fatly wrapped weatherproofed nylon to that of a donkey. The word's homophonic closeness to Duncan or, worse, Dunc, his family nickname, did not immediately occur to Jason, and for the remainder of the trip Duncan inured himself to being known as "Donkey Boy." On their last night in the Porcupines—traditionally, the one time their father let the boys drink beer before they headed back to Milwaukee—Duncan had plunged his hand into their cooler's watery lukewarm dregs in search of a can of Miller Lite. "Hey, Donk," Jason called over, distracted with the fire, "Grab me one too?" Donk knew, even before Jason and his father had exchanged looks of revelation, that he had just been rechristened. The nickname spread as though it were a plot. His mother was the longest holdout, but after six months he was Donk even to her. He thought that nothing could have ever happened to him out there. That was what the trips now meant to him. They were pre-danger. Pre-death. Once, after he had had too much to drink during one of his infrequent visits back to the Midwest, Jason had unkindly disclosed that the trips' whole purpose had been their father's attempt to rid Donk of what the man always called "that goddamn baby fat." This had hurt Donk, a little.

"Mister Donk," Hassan said, apprehensive to be violating Rule One, "you are well?"

"Fine," Donk said. "Some dirt in my eye."

Hassan almost smiled. "Both eyes?"

Hassan was smarter than Donk realized. Everyone, Donk thought, was smarter than you realized. "Yes, Hassan. Both eyes."

Hassan fretted with the front flap of his *shalwar khameez*. "Mister Donk, I have maybe an emergency."

"Oh?"

"I think perhaps General Mohammed's soldiers are not pleased."

"What makes you say that?"

Hassan was quiet a moment, listening to the soldiers. They were ten feet back, softly chatting, their rifles' thin black straps cutting across their chests and their tire-tread sandals slapping against the hard soil. Their language sounded to Donk, strangely, like yodeling. Hassan edged closer to Donk and whispered, "They are talking about leaving us."

"Fuck them, then. I have a compass. I can find our way back. We don't need them."

"But what of the grass?"

Donk had completely forgotten about the grass.

"I am thinking," Hassan said, looking straight ahead, "that these are bad men."

THE SECOND HILL TOOK LONGER TO CLIMB. IT WAS STEEPER, THE PATH more friable. The sun's warmth had opened Donk's eyebrow, and sweat soaked into the wound lividly. The donkey, especially, was having trouble, its hard little hooves slipping in the thick gray gravel. Red Beard decided the best way to hasten the donkey's ascent was to whip it across the face with his switch. The donkey hissed at him, its huge rotten teeth bared, its eyes rolling wildly in its sockets. Red Beard whipped it again, this time across the nose. Black Beard observed all this with nodding satisfaction. Hassan shook his head wretchedly, turned away, and kept walking. As the beating went on, it gathered a terrible energy, as crying does, as pain does, and Donk took a seat on a pathside stone and watched. As bad as he felt for the animal he was not about to step between it and Red Beard, whose streak of ferruginous cruelty was certain to run deeper than Donk could even begin to imagine. Thus he was cheered when the donkey, rearing bronco-style on its hind legs, its huge testicles bouncing, cunningly maneuvered its position in such a way to deliver into Red Beard's chest a quick and astonishingly forceful double-barreled kick. Red Beard managed, somehow, to stay on his feet. After a few moments of absorption, however, his expression loosened, opened to a hundred new possibilities of pain. He dropped his stick and—gently—sat down. He rolled onto his side and rocked back and forth in the dirt. Donk noticed, remotely, that Red Beard was barefoot. The donkey had kicked him right out of his tire-tread sandals. With equal remoteness, Donk watched Black Beard calmly level his Kalashnikov at the donkey and squeeze off three quick rounds into its hindquarters. The donkey kicked blindly a few more times and then galumphed down the path, back toward the village, screaming. That was, Donk thought, really the only word for the sound he was now hearing: screaming. It did not get far. With the Kalashnikov's stock tucked snugly into his shoulder, Black Beard tracked the donkey and fired twice. The donkey's head kicked up, the reports' echoes saturating the afternoon air. The donkey staggered ahead for a few steps more, tried to turn around, then dropped onto its side. Its legs were still moving at different speeds and in different directions. In the meantime, Red Beard had struggled to his feet. With one arm wrapped around his cracked rib cage he limped over to Donk and spoke.

Hassan was shaking with terror; his voice broke register as he translated. "Mister Donk, he says he is injured and requests that we go back."

Donk nodded at Red Beard thoughtfully, his hands tucked away in his hooded sweatshirt's front pockets to hide the fact that they were trembling. "Tell him, Hassan, that when we have the grass we can go back."

"He says he is injured very badly."

"Tell him this is his own stupid fucking fault."

"You tell him this!" Hassan cried.

Black Beard, his Kalashnikov now slung over his shoulder, was pulling the pouches and Marlboro bags off the donkey. Donk was about to speak when he noticed Black Beard stand quickly and look off warily to the east, instinctively reaching around for his rifle but not unshouldering it. Before Donk had even turned his head he heard the hollow patter of an approaching horse, then a low snorty sound. Upon the horse was a soldier. He rode in slowly, stopping at the midpoint between Donk and Black Beard, whose hand was still frozen in midreach for his rifle. The soldier looked to Donk, then to the dead donkey. Finally he rode over and circled the donkey's corpse, looking over at Black Beard only after he had made a complete orbit.

"Salaam," the soldier said, his horse's ears smoothed back, clear evidence of its distress at the sight of its murdered cousin.

"Salaam," Black Beard returned, his hand lowering.

The soldier was an American. His fatigues were lightly camouflaged, a few blobby splashes of faint green and wavy brown upon a dirty tan background. His backpack's two olive-green straps ran vertically down his chest. Another, thicker strap corseted his waist, and two more cinched around his thigh, where a 9mm pistol was sheathed in a camouflaged holster. Affixed upon his shoulder was the bulky black control pad for his air-to-ground radio, its CB hooked to his waist. Somewhat ostentatiously, Donk felt, he was wearing a floppy Afghan *pakul*, and around his neck was the same make of white scarf Donk had bought in Kunduz. He galloped over to Donk, young and triumphantly blue-eyed, his nose snout-like and his chin weak. A southerner, Donk guessed. Obviously he was one of the commandos Donk had only heard about, Special Forces boys leading on horseback whole garrisons of guerillas, shining lasers into the nasties' mountain hidey-holes for the F/A-18s' laser-guided bombs, and vacuuming up customs and language as they went. Some of these guys, it was rumored, had been here as early as September 14.

It was against SF doctrine to travel alone, and Donk imagined that right about now he was zooming up in the digital viewfinder of the binoculars that belonged to this commando's partner, who was no doubt watching from a hill or was perhaps even hidden in some impossibly nearby rocks.

"Sir," the commando said to Donk. "You're an American?"

Donk pulled his hands from his sweatshirt's pockets and stood. "I am."

The commando, squinting, gazed down at Donk from his mount. He threw off the hard, unapproachable aura of sunlight on sheet metal. "Are you wounded?"

"What?"

The soldier tapped himself above the eye.

"No," Donk said, touching himself there and, with a flinch, regretting it. "It's nothing. A car accident."

"Sir, I've been following you. And I have to ask what you're doing out here, for one, and for two, why are your men discharging their weapons in a hostile area?"

"They executed our donkey," Donk said. "I'm not sure why. And they're not my men. They're General Ismail Mohammed's."

The horse footed back a few steps, its huge stone-smooth muscles sliding around one another beneath a dark-brown coat as shiny as chocolate pudding. The commando, with the steadiness of a centaur, had not taken his eyes off Donk. "That leaves what you're doing out here."

"I'm a journalist. My friend is back in General Mohammed's village, like I said. He's very sick. I'm out here looking for grass."

The commando stared at him. "Pardon me, sir, but the stuff practically falls out of the trees here. There's no need to be out this—"

"Not marijuana. Grass. A special kind of grass."

"Ho-kay," he said.

"Look, forget that. Can you help me?"

"Sir, I don't really have any guidance."

"Any what?"

"Guidance, sir. I can't talk to the media."

Donk always admired military men, young military men in particular, for their peculiarly unsullied minds. "I'm not looking for an interview. My friend has malaria. He's back in General Mohammed's village. He's dying."

"Sir, be advised that these mountains are not safe for civilians. They're crawling with hostiles. And I don't mean to sound like a hard-ass, but I'm not really authorized to use this radio for anything other than ordering air strikes. We're doing pest control, sir, and I strongly recommend you get back to that village."

"Where's your commanding officer?"

"He's in Mazar-i-Sharif, sir."

"Lieutenant Marty, right?"

The commando paused. "I'm not at liberty to say, sir."

"Look, do you have any malaria medicine? Antibiotics? Anything you have. Believe me when I say it's an emergency."

The commando pulled back on the reins. The horse turned with the finicky heaviness particular to its species, and the commando started off.

Donk was not surprised. "This is all about reporters fucking you guys over in Vietnam, isn't it?" he called after him. "Well you should know I was about six when Saigon fell. Were you even born?"

The commando stopped and turned back to him. "Leave this area, sir. Now."

Donk saluted the commando, who politely returned the salute and ya'd his horse to a full gallop. The cool thin dust swallowed them both just before they would have vanished over the nearest hill's lip. Donk asked Hassan to inform Black Beard and Red Beard that his mission was now under the protection of the American military, owners of fearsome fighter planes, magical horseback summoners of aerial bombs, benevolent providers of PX-surplus camouflage. Neither Red Beard nor Black Beard had much of anything to say after that.

SHORTLY AFTER FOUR P.M. THEY FOUND THE VALLEY WHERE THE GRASS was supposed to grow, a large scooped-out gouge of grayish sand and brown rocky soil amid a ragged perimeter of half a dozen steep hills. A long twisty road wended through the valley and disappeared into an identically shady pass at each end. The hill they were now atop had provided them the least hospitable, most distinctly mountainous trek yet. Its top ridge was cold, windy, and dustless. As they stood in the sunlight looking down into the valley, Donk saw why the commando had wanted him to return to General Mohammed's village. Along the valley's road was a smudged line of charcoal-colored transport trucks and pickups. Black Beard withdrew from one of his satchels a pair of binoculars. After having a look he handed the binoculars without comment to Donk. They were, Donk saw, cheap enough to have been pulled from a cereal box. Nonetheless, they helped him discern that the smudges were blast marks; the dark charcoal color could be credited to the fact that each vehicle had been incinerated from the outside in. It took them another twenty minutes to climb down into the valley, and they walked along the road's wreckage as warily and silent as animals. The bombing had not happened terribly recently. Not a single piece of hardware was smoking, and the truck husks had the brittle, crumbly look of a scorched old log one cleared from a well-trafficked campsite's pit before building a new fire. The wreckage looked picked over, and the shrapnel was in careful little piles. Black Beard and Red Beard muttered to themselves.

"What are they saying?" Donk asked Hassan.

Hassan shook his head. "Their prayers for the dead."

"But these men were their enemies."

"Of course," Hassan said, looking at Donk hatefully.

Donk approached the bombed convoy's lead vehicle. Its tires had melted and its doors were gone. The empty cab and bed were both largely intact, though they had been parted from each other after sustaining what looked like a direct hit. There were no craters, Donk knew, because this campaign's bombs were designed to explode a few feet above their targets. Donk walked further down the blasted line. He did not see any bodies at all until the penultimate vehicle, a nearly vaporized Datsun pickup so skeletal it looked like a blackened blueprint of a Datsun pickup. The charred driver was barely distinguishable from the wreckage around him. He was just a crispy torso of shrunken unrealness. His face and hair had been burned off, his head a featureless black oval. Donk reached for the camera he did not have and stepped closer, discovering that the reason no one had moved his body was because it was melted to its seat. His stomach gurgled and turned. Something in him clenched. He did not have his camera. The image would never swim up at him from the bottom of a plastic platter filled with developing fluid. It would stay exactly this way . . . Donk forced the thought away.

"Mister Donk!" Hassan called over to him.

He turned, rubbing his beating heart through his chest. "Yes, Hassan. What is it?"

He pointed at the Beards. "They say the grass is nearby."

Donk took in this information. He felt the same mild surprise he remembered experiencing when he had learned, thanks to a concert Tina had taken him to, that people were still writing symphonic music. Surprise that he would be so surprised. The grass actually existed. How unaccountable. "Where?"

Hassan pointed across the valley. "They say over there."

Donk looked. At the far side of the valley stood a sparse stand of trees, the first trees he had seen all day. They made him feel better, somehow. Around the trees was a long squarish field of desiccated grass the color of wheat. The road this annihilated convoy had been traveling along would have taken them right past that field. They walked, Black Beard and Red Beard having now unshouldered their weapons. Walking across this valley felt to Donk like standing in the middle of an abandoned coliseum. Above, the sky was getting darker. The day was silent. Donk noticed, as they grew closer to the trees, that they had not yet completely shed their leaves, little pompoms of bright orange and yellow still tipping their branches. The setting sun was pulling a long curtained shadow across this valley. He realized, then, that even if they pushed themselves they were not going to make it back to the village before nightfall. He hurried himself ahead, and Hassan and the Beards jogged to keep pace with him. He did not care to learn who or what ruled these hills at night.

"Mister Donk," Hassan said, "please slow!"

"Fuck off," he called back. Donk's thoughts suddenly felt to him alien and disfigured, exalted by fear, disconnected from the internal key that transformed them into language. He veered off the road and sprinted toward the trees through the grass abruptly growing all around him. His boots were scything up great cheerful swaths of the stuff. He did not know why he was not gathering up any of it. He was not certain what might make one kind of grass more restorative than another. He had a quiet, appalled thought at all the things he did not know. He then remembered to believe that the grass was not going to help Graves. Not at all.

"Mister Donk!" Hassan called again. Donk turned to see Hassan following him across the field of grass in an unsteady, not-quite-running way. "They say we must be careful here! Mister *Donk!*" Black Beard, now shouting something himself, endured a moment of visible decision-making, then left the road and followed after Hassan.

Donk's head swiveled forward. He was almost to the trees. The grass just under the trees looked especially boilable, thick and tussocky. Then, oddly, Donk seemed to be looking at the trees and the grass from much higher up. His horizon lifted, then turned over. Donk had heard nothing, but when he landed he smelled something like cooked meat, cordite, loam. He lay there in the grass, blinking. With his fingers he pulled up a thick handful of grass, then let it go. He looked over. Hassan was beside him, ten feet away, screaming, though still Donk could hear nothing. Hassan's mouth was bloody and his cardigan sweater was gone but for some shreds, and what Donk initially believed to be large, fat red leaches were crawling all over his stomach and chest. On the other side of him Black Beard was creeping away on all fours, shaking his head in dazed way. After a few feet he stopped and lay down. Donk thought that he, Donk, was okay. But for some reason he could not sit up. His legs felt funny, as did his back. He did not panic and lifted his left leg to watch the tendons and veins and muscles fall away from it as though it were a piece of chicken that had been boiled too long. Then he was bleeding. The blood did not come out of him in a glug but in a steady silent gush. There was so much of it. He lowered his leg and from his prone position saw broken-ribbed Red Beard struggling down the road. Yes, he thought, that's right. Go get help. Donk thought he was going to be all right. It did not hurt yet. Oh wait yes it did. Suddenly it hurt very, very much. Donk always believed that you learned a lot about a place by the first thing you heard said there. In Chechnya it was: "It doesn't work." In Rwanda: "I don't know." In Afghanistan: "Why are you here?" He had not stepped on a mine. Slowly, he knew that. No reason to waste an expensive mine in such a remote place. He had stepped instead on a bomblet, a small and festively yellow cluster of ordnance that had not detonated above the eradicated convoy but rather bounced away free and clear and landed here in the grass. Hassan was no longer screaming but simply lying there and looking up at the sky. He, too, was mechanically blinking. Hassan needed help. Donk did not care if he stole his cameras. Donk could help him. Donk, suddenly, loved him. But first he had to rest. He could not think about all this until he had some fucking rest. Could he get some rest? He had to help Graves because if he did not Graves would die. He thought of his father, how he had looked in the end. God, Donk thought, I do not want to die. But he did not much care for old age either. A problem there. "Dad!" Donk yelled out suddenly. He did not know why; something in him unclenched. Or maybe he had not said anything at all. It was hard to tell, and it was getting dark. So: rest. Rest here one minute and off we go. Red Beard could use the company. Use the help. Ho-kay. He was all right. He just needed to figure this out.

2003

Vacationland

Ander Monson

This place, this bearer of the chilly winter burst,
the white-out everywhere and flurry,
the not-in-the-terms-of-Dairy-Queen,
this blizzard with a lowercase *b*,
far from commercial in its constancy,
its threat, impact, and our recovery:
always from it. We are always re-shoveling
out the driveways and panking down the snow
or breaking up the ice with handmade iron spears
or spokes wrested from bikes that have succumbed
at last to rust. This is my vacationland, my very own
Misery Bay, my drudge, my lighthouses, my vanishing
animal tracks in snow. Everyone who is not from here
is *not from here*, and that is all there is to say.
Everyone from here is still from here
regardless of where they are or where they end.

White light filters through snow like dust.
There is always light coming down
like a donation from God—a little perk
to get us through the winter. This light

lights up our faces, lights up the faces
of the frozen dead as seen on TV from Canada.

This vacationland, this motel open year-round,
is now a Best Western and that is good, I guess.
This vacationland, this Michigan,
my Michigan, is no destination, no getaway
for us, those who are always *from*.
We have no destinations. We have no way
to get away from her, from here, to get away
from romantic winter getaways and those
who've come to get away from their dull bombs of city lives.
We cannot get away from *from* and from the doldrum
winter silent burn. We might as well be stone—agates,
mottled trifles, appearing periodically on the beach
to be taken home, to be put with other pretty rocks
and bits of lake glass in jars. We are meant for your mantel
and for the light that will find us there.

We might as well be the kind of rock
that passes for rock on the radio up here,
meaning Foreigner and Journey and nothing
that could be ever meaningful again
because it has been subsumed by soft-rock
crap-rock, classic-rock, by radio, by frequency—
by modulated energy in air, by the tyranny
of awful playlists and shitty DJs
and no hope of getting a decent song
played for us to be indifferent to at prom.

We are what is left. We are drift.
I guess this is a sort of manifesto.

2004

God's Early Church

Austin Hummell

Whole months pass without sun. February
all coffee and the stink of iron. Once,
a girl from Carolina left me
for dead. Something about ambition
and the ropy vein in the bend of my arm.
I lanced them both with flowers from another
country. You should have seen it.

Years of that until the windows were full
of a juice called methadone designed I guess
to sweep the streets of me. I weighed myself down
with coats of it. I unplugged the voices of my friends.
The world? Fuck. I can't get enough of it.

2004

Nothing He Can Put a Finger On

L. E. Kimball

1. Sticks and Stones

Until two weeks ago, Davis couldn't have told you the last time he'd looked inside the '55 Willy's Wagon. But now he looks every day. His stiff fingers grip the door frame as he lowers rack-like shoulders into the car, eases his aching body onto the ragged leather seats that burn the backs of his thighs. He's careful of that trick left knee, not a Korean War wound as most people assume, but the result of a childhood fall out of a tree. He stretches the leg straight once he's seated. And then he takes stock.

The first thing he'd noticed wasn't a *thing* at all. Not the smell of someone, not physical evidence of someone. Nothing he can put a finger on. More significant than the sense of trespass: An altered perception. As if he no longer sees the inside of the old automobile through his own eyes.

The Jeep had been twenty years old in 1975 when he restored it to better-than-mint condition: vinyl seats for leather, vertical front grill and headlights replaced, the engine overhauled. But now nearly thirty years have passed. Sell it, Lenore had said once. No, better yet, sell the Jaguar. Shit, no, he'd told her, he'd be damned if he'd sell either one. He'd imagined himself taking up hunting or fishing, using the Jeep in that capacity, but instead it carries Irish Whiskey and Bombay Gin (or Lenore's grocery list) from the Canadian Soo. Not to say that he wouldn't hunt or fish someday. You got to have *possibles*, he tells himself. But to please her he keeps the wagon parked across the road in a metal pole barn with the left-over wood scraps and garden tools.

It's hard to say how many days have passed without it actually registering inside his head, but now it does. The McNally Road Atlas, curled and soiled at the edges, has been moved from the dashboard onto the backseat. And when exactly did he become aware that it's served, rather poorly, as a headrest, a pillow of sorts? Whoever has sat inside his car probably assumes no one will notice something so inconsequential, but Davis is a man who notices much: Drops of glue on the edges of repaired plastic or along the edges of window casings; asymmetry: on faces or buildings; weakness: of joints, mechanical or human, of cloud cover, of emotion. An article in the *Drummond Island Digest* sticking out from under the atlas catches his eye. About a Pecan Nut Fundraiser, the proceeds to be used to fund a university reading room at Saginaw Valley. That's what I need, he thinks. A *nut* fundraiser.

He checks the glove compartment: A flashlight with batteries long burned out. A pair of binoculars he'd lost track of. An odd assortment of loose screws. A faded yellow car registration from 1974 but no current one. Shit, he thinks. Where has that gotten to? There's a pair of dime store reading glasses, folded but caseless, with scratches and smudges in a vertical pattern down the lenses. His? He isn't sure. He exchanges the glasses for the ones on his face, and is aware of only the slightest improvement in the newspaper's fine print.

He looks carefully at the odometer. It's turned over at least once, that he knows. It registers 12,623 miles now. Isn't that a hundred miles more then he remembers? A few loose wires dangle from below the dashboard and swing slightly from the impact of his knees. Has it been hotwired? He is convinced not only that someone has been squatting in his car, but that the wagon has been covering ground without him.

He feels his stomach lurch. Nerves? Or is it those damned runny eggs he'd fixed himself for breakfast, Lenore having worked until all hours again on one of those bleak sculptures of hers? Another jutting, post-modern rendering in stone to be placed against the cracked concrete walls she had poured in place fifteen years ago. Concrete walls and floor, post and beam open-framed construction. Her ideas of simplicity. A reduction, she would say, of the psychic distance between people and things. Regardless, concrete seems cold to him and nothing short of ridiculous in this frigid climate. Today, in this ninety-degree heat, concrete is a blessing.

Though Davis notices much, remembering is another story. Did the eggs upset his stomach or did he even *eat* eggs? He isn't sure. When he does remember, he's never sure how or when things happened. Hundreds of stray details lurk inside his head, not linked in any contiguous order, forming for him a jumbled and disordered present. Was it this morning he'd watched Lenore sleep? Or is it every morning he watches her slight chest rise and fall? Counting breaths as if each will be her last. Not because she is in ill health, but because, like always, despite his notion about the possibles, he simply can't imagine a future for himself; consequently, he can't imagine one for her, either. Sometimes she opens a tentative eye in a face like white alabaster. He prays every time he sees her face that it will crack finally, split from ear to ear. Then she'd see how unconditionally he loves her.

She might open her eyes. "Are we there yet?" she might ask, her running joke with him.

"No," he always answers her. "We're not there yet."

"Thank God," she'd say. Then, perhaps, he'd rest a hand on one of her breasts and she'd close her eyes again. She has never once moved his hand.

He climbs out of the wagon, and though this is the first time it has occurred to him to check, he searches for fresh tire tracks, but last night's rain has washed away any sign of them, or any sign of a footprint. He sticks his head back inside the wagon. It's nearly imperceptible, but Davis is more certain each day that he can divine the essence of an odor where he hadn't been aware of one initially. He's pretty sure what the odor is: Tobacco. Not cigarette smoke, but *tobacco*. And there's something more, but he's having trouble putting his finger on it.

Something makes a rodent-like rustle in the corner of the pole barn. He strains to lift his head, but isn't fast enough to catch a glimpse. It's so fucking hot, he thinks. Even for me, a person whose blood is barely pumping. He figures it's maybe noon, and he knows he needs a drink of water, but instead he walks down to the end of the long drive, in search of what he's not sure. A sign of anything out of the ordinary. Before he knows it, he is at the edges of the Maxton Plains.

The Plains look like sheets of crumbled concrete, shimmering white in the choking heat, vegetation-like neglected weeds erupting between the cracks. Something that appears like chalk dust hovers a few feet from the ground. He looks east and then west across the treeless expanse, expecting to see nothing less than divine judgment written across the horizon. But there's nothing in any direction but pitiless blue sky. He looks down and sees the cairn fields in front of him, and has a dim recollection of Lenore all those years ago, pregnant, forcing him to gather rocks with her by the hundreds. Or did he dream it? How she'd laid them around a house they'd owned back then, one by one, each rock touching the next in a linear progression that connected one to another, yet seemed to lead nowhere.

He's never believed in rocks, and despite the fact he knows he isn't supposed to, he picks up as many now as he can carry, and as he walks through the dried Alvar grasses, a blast of musty-sweet air hits him in the face. Butterflies float into his face and into each other, and as he walks back into the line of trees, he puts up a ruffed grouse. It whirrs away sounding like a small engine in need of repair. He makes thirteen trips carrying the rocks, sweat dripping down his face, along the sides of his stooped back, sand chafing raw cracks on his hot, gloveless hands. It occurs to him, finally, to use the wheelbarrow and then he makes another twenty trips. A song from a forgotten childhood runs through his head. *I've been working on the railroad.*

It's twenty degrees hotter inside the pole barn than it is outside, the late morning air silty and hideously orange due to the translucent red metal roof overhead. He transfers every load into the back of the wagon, throwing each rock with as much fury as his weak shoulders can muster.

He hasn't seen her in years. Can he picture Sally Crow closing her eyes, resting her head against the seat bottom, long black hair streaming onto the floor? Sort of. He can picture her *sort of.* He continues to carry rocks of all shapes and sizes, and as he heaves them into the cargo body of the Willys, he tries to picture that black head, not just as it might appear now, but how it might possibly look ten years from now, and fails. He finds there is no future to be imagined for *her*, either.

He's been counting, and as he drops load thirty-three into the back end, as the rocks knock one into another like a pile of discarded days, he dismisses the future and tries for the past. It exists, but in random flashes, like black and white film negatives of someone else's life. But then, as one old tire blows (that will fucking show her), and then two others, one memory crowds his mind like phantom pain from a missing limb. He remembers clearly what he'd said to her.

"Get the hell out of my car."

2. GRAVEL

"Get the hell out of my car."

It's September, 1980, and he has just walked out of The Northwoods Bar, and found her in the front seat of his '55 Willy's Wagon. It's still light out. Maybe six P.M., and the car is parked right in front of Sune's Grocery. Will Jansen has just stumbled out of the bar as well. Davis knows sure as hell that Will, pompous bastard that he is, won't believe he doesn't know the woman from Adam. She's asleep, but she moves her head, and her long black hair sweeps across the driver's seat, a maple leaf stuck in the silky strands. He smells something sweet and moldy, like old beer as he leans over and shakes her by a meaty shoulder. She props herself up in the passenger seat in a kind of daze.

"I just want a ride home," she keeps saying to his repeated attempts to get her out of the car.

"You're an Indian, aren't you?"

She smiles at him, and he sees what looks like a tiny piece of lettuce or some kind of herb stuck between gleaming, healthy-looking teeth. She's wearing blue jean cut-offs and a red-and-white striped peasant top gathered at the neckline. She's maybe mid-twenties, average sized, breasty, and there's an open hole under the string tie that reveals a dewy cleavage. She seems to read his mind about the lettuce and her tongue searches her front teeth and when she smiles the next time, it's gone.

"Look, I'm hungry, and I need to get some dinner. I'm not driving you home."

But then Davis thinks what dinner will be if he goes home to Lenore. Since they've moved to Drummond two years ago, she's taken up power cooking. Soups, shoulder ham, capons, salmon, quail, confit of duck, assorted breads and pies, even a cold timbale of woodcock, all cooked in one day on either the woodstove or over a fire pit, refrigerated or sometimes frozen. A week's worth of food that she might or might not sit down with him to eat. The meals taste remarkably good warmed up, but it's the lack of ceremony, the lack of celebration of a day well spent, that he misses. He imagines that in some way having a week's food prepared ahead of time anchors her to survival—of at least that many days. Or does it free her from them instead? He isn't sure. But cooking day is the only exception to the informality, when she cooks lamb or thick steaks on the wood fire. They'd sit down across from one another; beef tongue and jars of mincemeat would fight them for elbow room on those days. The mountain of food filled his mind with gluttonous thoughts of excess which tended to make him lose his appetite. But cooking days hold out the only hope for him, with just the table between them. So he'd sit there swilling gin, watching her fork hearty portions of red meat into her mouth, while he wished for pastry or confections. Of any kind.

"I'll wait while you eat, then you can drive me home," Sally Crow says now. "I'll pay for it."

Take what you want, Davis's father always said (purportedly quoting God), *but pay for it*. Davis believes in that. It's the creed he lives by. Some people would say he doesn't know the meaning of the words, but that isn't true; he knows what it means to pay for things.

"God dammit, get out of the God dammed car."

But he's afraid someone else will see him sitting with this woman and since he can't feature dragging her out by the hair, he drives to Chuck's Place for dinner. They don't talk on the way. The Andrews Sisters sing "Boogie Woogie Bugle Boy" on the Jeep radio, part of Stage Door Canteen. Sally Crow moves a crossed foot in time to the music. It's dusk now and Davis drives carefully, watching for deer alongside the road. Wind gusts blow Sally's hair around inside the car like a black funnel cloud, and he leans slightly left to keep it from obstructing his vision. A strand catches in the crease of his neck and he leaves it there. Though he doesn't ask, Sally Crow tells him she lives with her uncle on the south side of the island, in a house with no plumbing and no electricity. Ever since her parents died of food poisoning, that is, and they had buried them in the back yard, which, yes, she realizes, is against the law.

"What do you want?" he asks her, indicating Chuck's Place as he pulls into the parking lot. She looks hungry but says, "Nothing."

After grabbing a burger to go, Davis stops across the street at Johnson's and gets a six pack. Then he drives out Johnswood Road to the southeast side of the island. Wordlessly, he hands her a beer. Then he passes her the burger and she takes a big bite, her tongue sliding out to catch the grease which nevertheless runs down her chin. As she hands it back, a slice of onion falls between her legs. He watches Sally Crow wipe mustard from the inside of each bare thigh and considers. He listens to the wheels slip against the gravel, each stone slightly diminished from the friction of his tires. He can hear the stones becoming *less*.

"My people believe there are spirits in everything, even stones," Sally Crow says.

She must be watching the stones, too. Then, he thinks: stones that blanch powdery-white under his headlights, moments before his tires roll over them.

He sleeps with Sally Crow in the end, not because she owes him anything, and not because he has a burning desire to, but because it makes no difference to anything. He tries to imagine the *price*, the implications of a future that will tie this night to the next, but try as he might, he can't picture a day when he'll be loading the Willys full of rocks, hauling his ass across the Maxton Plains. He can't project to the rock heaps he'll gather in the future. Neither can he summon the past, a past far *enough* in the past, to jog a familiar chord of youthful optimism. And if he could, it still wouldn't matter.

Sally Crow smells like tobacco, and he sees she has unrolled a pouch of it along with some herbs. "Are you a medicine woman?" he asks her.

"Holes," she says. 'I heal holes."

"You better be careful then," he tells her. "That could ruin not only your sex life, but your records won't play very well." She laughs and her voice reminds him of blues harmonica, the way it seems to travel in pitch and emotion, sliding around, not staying put.

"That's what you wanted to hear, though, wasn't it? That I heal people?"

"I don't know."

She takes his hand and moves it to her left breast. He keeps it there, moving a tentative finger for a long minute, then lets it drop. They don't say anything for a while and then she starts talking again.

"There was a neighbor lady once who got me into Girl Scouts," she says. "I used to believe in Brownies, fairies who come and do all your work while you sleep. For cookies and a bowl of milk. Then I found out it was *me* who was supposed to be the Brownie."

He sees a stack of magazines in her lap he hasn't noticed before. "Isn't that a catalogue for Superior State you've got there?"

"Maybe."

He drives on and the stones spurt out behind the car, leaving rolls of dust hanging in his rear view mirror. As he drives, he tries to imagine a future with this woman, their bodies joined, the taste of her smoky lips ripened with age to them, and though it all will certainly happen, he fails to form any tangible picture of it. Nor can he picture her feet gracing a college campus, or see her enrolling in the inevitable accounting classes. Or maybe he's wrong about her altogether and it would be pre-med classes? What would she look like working at one of the casinos? Or summoning Great Spirits to heal holes in lonely white men in her Uncle's rundown shack on the southern part of the island? He peers through the dusty windshield, as though it's a window through time, hoping to see how it all might happen. How Sally Crow would, in fact, do all of the above and more. But it's impossible. He's not sure he can visualize even the next half hour, in spite of how hard he's grown watching her. So he tries again for the past. He'd like to remember being a child, the *feelings* of being a child, but once again *that* past eludes him.

He pulls off the road onto an overgrown two-track. A mixture of pine and hardwood branches reach into the open windows, familiar figures with almost-recognizable features that tap them each on a shoulder. They hunker in closer, and pretty soon the two-track ends at an enormous granite boulder. Another road block. As the grill of the wagon comes to rest against it, as Davis sees Sally Crow pull off the red-and-white peasant top, he struggles to picture even the next thirty seconds in which surely his hand will touch that olive skin. But he can't. Can't imagine even that, and the Maxton Plains flash inside his head instead, those 2,000 acres of grasslands and cairn fields. And he remembers just what he'd said his first trip there.

"What the hell could you possibly want with all these rocks?"

3. ROLLING STONES

"What the hell could you possibly want with all these rocks?"

1954. He looks around him. *Pon-ta-gan-igy,* A View of Beautiful Islands, is what the Indians called Drummond Island. Glacier revealed, it is a silent land of limestone bedrock surrounded by water, much of the island forested evergreen and hardwood. The edge of Potagannissing Bay, where Davis will one day live with his wife, is forested as well. But not the Plains, of course. The Plains consist of 2,000 acres of Alvar Grasslands, lying atop the *Niagra cuesta,* a resistant landform of dolomite and shale, a landform found only here, a few places in Canada, and the Baltic Sea coasts of Scandinavia. The thin soil atop the bedrock accounts for soggy conditions in spring and early summer, searing heat and drought conditions later in the year, supporting vegetation unique in that it consists of both arctic and desert-loving plants; a land of extremes.

"I want them," Lenore tells him, a rock in each hand.

The Plains remind him of Alaska, where he'd been stationed for the last three years during the Korean War. He watches Lenore standing on top of a stacked pile of rocks, arms spread wide like a soaring eagle or hawk, in some ritualistic, sacrificial sort of posture. The soon-to-be endangered Prairie Smoke gathers at his knees, pink cotton candy in the approaching dusk. He wonders what the cairns mean, if they are Indian memorials, or some kind of direction markers. Years later, he'll ask that question and be told that they have no meaning at all, that it's just a "monkey-see-monkey-do" kind of phenomenon, and that will seem jarringly ironic as well.

"There's a whole beach here comprised of fossil rock, did you know that?" she asks him. "Why so many in one spot do you suppose?"

Davis has no idea, and can't imagine living on this island. What did he have in common with people like these, he wonders? The Island will draw a few influential people, but for the most part the inhabitants will seem largely unremarkable. Yet frighteningly impervious. The kind who, years ago, had actually bussed their children over the frozen ice to school in Detour. What kind of people do something like that? He will think every time he crosses on the ferry how interesting it is that they made you pay to ride over, but they let you *off* for free.

Yet he'll come. Soon he'll belong to the Lions Club, golf on occasion with a few of the other retirees, join the snowmobile club. Though he'll never quite understand the cold metal, the whine of the engine screaming its misplaced frozen horsepower. He'll feel like some kind of mechanical cowboy one shadowy night when he and rest of the club race around great herds of deer the sportsmen feed on the south beach in winter. It will be an absurd and ghostly round-up, the deer fanning out in random groups of panic, some forced out onto the ice, heading, seemingly, toward mainland, others breaking wildly inland, hooves clattering in a thunderous crescendo, the moon a chunk of gleaming ice overhead. "Refracted terror," is how Sally Crow will describe the event when he tells her about it.

"Are you happy here?" Sally will ask him.

"Lenore is," he'll answer.

And he'll walk that fossil beach Lenore talked about one day in the future, only with Sally Crow, his feet crunching over the echoes of remaining life forms. He'll think about mistakes and wonder, when it's all said and done, if they could ever be viewed so simply. What hope would he have, after all, without them?

"Do you believe in a defining moment?" he'll ask Sally, pointing at a stone he'll hold in slippery fingers. "A moment that hardens your life into an impression like that forever?"

"Maybe," she'll answer. "But then, it would necessitate standing still, wouldn't it. For a very long time?"

But these thoughts of indentation and immutability come much later. For now, and for the next five years, they will be merely visitors, he and Lenore, and each time, she'll abscond with at least thirty pieces of stone. Stone that has nothing whatever to do with the mediums she'll later work in. No thought yet of carving and shaping it; she has not yet learned "how to walk" as the sculptors say. She knows only about dreaming so far. She appears so light and ethereal, he is sure that at any moment the wind will lift her from her perch on the rock. He has the odd notion that for Lenore, the rocks serve as emotional paperweights, a grounding that even the eight months of her advancing pregnancy cannot afford her.

"I want them," she says again, because it's still 1954 and for now he's still suspended in this cairn field.

"For God's sake," he answers. "Don't you think I can get you all the rocks you could possibly ever want?" And then he says, "You married me for my rocks, and now they're not good enough for you, is that it?" He's kidding and he smiles, but he sees a guilty, sideways look cross her face.

"As long as your rocks are good enough for *you*, I guess that's what matters," she says, and now she's smiling back at him. He holds her and lowers his face, sandwiches it between her breasts and the protrusion of her abdomen. Keeps his head there, but turns and looks out across the Plains. It's almost dark now, early June, but off in the distance he can just see the heads of sandhill cranes bobbing slightly above the grasses. In the autumn of years to come, he'll watch them fly overhead in groups like hovering pterodactyls. But tonight, in a matter of moments, they'll disappear into the depths of the Alvar fields and into the night.

"Are there bears out here?" she asks.

"Well, if there are, you'd see them coming from a long way, that's for sure . . . well, at least during the daytime."

"I look like a bear," she says. He wonders if his face looks guilty now, though he's not sure why it should. They've been married only six months, but what mattered, what was *important,* was that he'd asked her *before* she became pregnant, before they'd even made love, for Christ's sake. That's what matters.

"I love you," he says. "Do you know that?"

Her face is hard to see in the evening light. He's glad he can't see into her eyes as he says these words. Not because he doesn't mean them, but because he just doesn't want to see her eyes.

"If there ever *is* someone, you should go for it," she says.

"What?"

"What possible point could there be in me stopping you from anything you want to do."

He grabs her shoulders, off balance at her words, off balance like he feels most days with her now. "So you don't give a shit if I go to bed with anyone I want to? What kind of marriage is that?"

"What possible meaning could there be in a relationship between you and me, if I am standing in the way of your desires."

"Well, for Christ's sake, why did you marry me then?"

She smiles. "For your rocks, of course."

His rocks. He pulls her to him, and tries to picture himself sitting at the desk of Associated Aggregates ten years down the road, and he fails. He can't picture himself with a child, or even with a wife five years down the road, despite the fact that he has one and is about to have the other. Did he feel like this during the war? He doesn't think so, but he isn't sure. Was he capable of imagining the future back then? What about the past? He remembers it, of course; he isn't fucking crazy. But it seems to belong to someone else, like a story he'd read once.

But the fact is, he *will* inherit that desk in Oxford, Michigan, once his father dies of that coronary embolism that has loomed over him for years. His mother has been dead since Davis was five, a rare form of bone cancer, so that will leave only him. He'll sit there after his father is gone, at the great mahogany desk covered with glass and wonder why the desk makes him so uncomfortable. Lenore will tell him one day, it's the psychic distance of the glass between himself and the texture of the wood, that it is even separating him from his father and from himself, and she's right in a way, but what he hates most is that he can see his own reflection in it. Despite this, he'll never remove the glass. He'll take it as long as he can, approximately five years, and then he'll hand the reins over to his Vice President, Leonard Kranston, the man who runs nearly everything anyway, and move to Drummond Island, where Lenore has long wanted to be. But before he does, for those five years, he'll sign purchase orders and pay checks and memoranda until noon each day, the mahogany desk hard and cold beneath his hands. And at least once a week during that time, he'll drive down the road to a small gravel pit owned by a friend of his, Jerry Shaw.

Jerry is older than Davis, and had once worked for Davis's father. The first time Davis saw him, he was seated on a boulder, eating a pastrami sandwich, the crack in his rear end showing above soil-covered jeans. Davis would complain about his father to Jerry, and Jerry would shrug, and say, "He's fuckin' aces to me, man."

Jerry's bad eye had kept him out of the war, so he'd purchased his forty acres with a small inheritance, and taken to mining it all by himself. He had no employees and delivered his loads of gravel in a rusty old Peterbilt dump truck. Jerry had an excavator, a loader, and a backhoe, and Davis would sit and watch him load yards of oversize into the Austin Western jaw-crusher. Or some days he'd just run the roll crusher on the smaller material and rely on the grizzly to separate out the slightly bigger rocks. There was a shaker, a harp screen and the sand classifier #1, like a giant strainer lifted from a child's sandbox: One-inch stone and smaller is used for basements; 10-A pea stone is used for septic stone in drain fields; potato stone (the size of potatoes or bigger), is bought by landscapers. Piles of redi-mix concrete sand and yards of mason sand, like small Egyptian pyramids, surround the pit.

On rainy days, Jerry makes road gravel since that is the only thing he can do on wet days; winter he does mechanical work on the trucks and designs new equipment. Business is carried out from Jerry's home, a mile down the road.

Jerry travels only the distance from the yard to his house, sends his wife on necessary errands. For years, he'll run the yellow excavator in the pit, displacing the dirt, the layers of clay, much of which is simply discarded, eventually uncovering valuable veins of sandstone and granite.

Now and then Davis will watch him do his pit run with the big excavator. He'll sit at the top and listen to the crusher grinding and scraping, listen to the engine stutter. And then when Jerry is done, he'll offer him a beer, or sometimes a shot of whiskey. Jerry will wipe the grime off his face, and smile. Talk about how there are all kinds of dirt in this world, and he prefers the kind he can see.

"I've been working the front twenty for the last eighteen years," he'll say to Davis one summer day, the day Davis turns thirty-nine. "In another two I'll move to the west ten, then ten years after that, if one of these goddamn walls doesn't come down on me, I'll do the south ten."

"How can you fucking *do this*?" Davis will ask him, though something about it fascinates him, "And then what?"

Jerry smiles. "Then, I'll dig myself my own goddamn grave."

At this point, Jerry's years are all in front of him in designated slices of earth. He'll raise his children in the front twenty, bury his wife in the next twelve. Jerry had been able to afford only limited test-core drilling on the site, so before he can finish the last eight, the vein, like his life, will disappear on him. Layers of ground are called horizons and Jerry's "sky" just dissolves one day into useless overburden. Eventually he'll sell the pit to prospective golf club developers. He'll lose his leg to diabetes, and die in a leather chair there in his front room. A chair he bought used the same day he bought the pit. "Ya takes your chances," Jerry will say to him.

And it will turn out that Davis's rocks are indeed not good enough for Lenore. At least not exclusively. After she takes up sculpting, she will occasionally buy a chunk of dolomite from the limestone quarry on Drummond Island, but more often, she buys exotic material that must be imported. Sandstone from Spain, Travertine or Alabaster from Italy. All white or cream colored stone. Davis will watch Lenore create figures out of clay, watch her use a da Vinci-like pointing machine later to copy the figure into stone. Lenore's days will take on the same planned-out quality as Jerry's. Her future is full of mallets and chisels and drill sanders and rasps. Ten years of vessels followed by approximately the same number of years in wall sculpture. Another ten talisman-type years; ten years of headless human torsos. The thing Lenore will work on last just looks to Davis like a big chunk of rock. A rock turned into another rock, which, amazingly, only looks larger. And this is the part that will always get him, something he will never understand or be comfortable with, in sculpture or otherwise: the requisite process of removing mass, things becoming *less* to create something *more*.

But for now, only one thing has gone missing. They are standing in this Cairn field in 1954, and Davis's face is enveloped in the contours of Lenore's body. Davis is aware only that he's pushed her into a future she has not envisioned for herself, and that something small yet significant has been lost, something he can't quite put his finger on. The rest eludes him. And will continue to: He will fail to recognize how Lenore will simply envision for herself a new future.

Davis pushes away from her body and lights a cigarette. Sits on one of the rocks and tries to imagine it, the rock, sitting in front of the new tri-level they have just bought downstate. Moves it in his mind to different locations. Next to the light pole, out by the edge of the drive, off by the west corner in a flower bed sitting next to a tree. But the rock seems out of place everywhere, or rather, can't be two places at once. It's under his ass, after all.

4. GATHERS NO MOSS

1953. His body glistens wet from the dip in his father's quarry pit. He's reclining on a huge boulder that has retained the day's heat, his body temperature cooler against the warm rock. He's looking at the stars and the moon, thinking how there was no such thing as a summer "night" in Alaska. He'd spent the last three years at Shemya Air Force Base at the western tip of the Aleutian Islands. "The Black Pearl," or "The Rock" as they called it, an ideal refueling stop on the Great Circle Route during the Korean War. Most of them who fueled there were "Pole-vaulters," the name they gave for the Reconnaissance

Squadron stationed at Eielson, south of Fairbanks, a squadron who flew frequent missions over the north pole. The pilots told him tales of earthquakes through the mainland, and Davis had sworn he could feel the tremors all the way out at Shemya, feel the land tip sideways, threaten to dump him into the sea. For three years, airplane landing lights descended upon him like falling stars in what was certainly an endless night, then lifted off again like great birds running for air speed, the island little more than a momentary touch-down. All of it leaving him rootless, groundless, like the island itself. Three years of keeping fuel logs, occasional trips to Fairbanks or Juneau, endless nights passing into endless days.

He rolls over, pulls Lenore's wet body toward his and remembers the first time he saw her. Lenore's father worked for the Road Commission, and had been murdered by a disgruntled employee and Davis's father had insisted they all attend the funeral. Lenore's mother, originally from the Isle of Hope, south of Savannah, stood next to the grave at the interment, wearing a straw bonnet, looking graceful and wilted and flower-like. Lenore had stood back, slightly, behind a massive stone memorial, like some unwelcome illegitimate daughter surreptitiously watching her father laid to rest. She had been staring off when their eyes had connected over the stone, and he'd felt that rush of reciprocated lust between them, a feeling like sticking his head out a car window, a car traveling at great speed.

Now, his engagement ring sparkles on Lenore's left hand, the rock glimmering in the dark like those landing lights he is used to in Alaska. He pulls her, feels her resistance.

"I want to wait," she tells him.

"Wait for what?" he answers. "What difference will it make—a few more weeks mean nothing. All we really have is this moment, you know. That's all that really belongs to us. If we let it go, it'll be gone."

She smiles at him. She isn't sure about what belongs to her, she tells him, whether a moment lost is lost or simply preserved. She does know her love for him has nothing to do with time one way or another. Her smile is tender, and she puts her mouth against his, her breasts showing full against the soaking t-shirt. "I like the future and the past because they make the present stay put, right where it belongs."

Her reluctance, he will find, has nothing to do with the past, the present or the future. Or with whether or not she loves him. Or any romantic sense of saving herself, as he assumes. In fact, there is nothing extenuating or complicated about it. Nothing that fills her mind with dire repercussions. He will understand soon that she simply prefers to wait, like she likes the color red over the color green, or apricots over oranges.

He pulls her wet shorts and panties off, his hand between her clenched thighs.

"I just want to wait," she says again, giving him one more chance at it.

"You're everything I could ever want," he tells her. And then he doesn't talk anymore. He doesn't have to because he feels her body relax under his hands. He starts to pull her off the rock onto the soft ground, but she says no, it has to be here, and he puts his hands under her hips in an effort to shield her body from the hardness of the rock, the knuckles on his hands and his knees scraping raw with the motion of his body. She moves his hands from beneath her thighs and he tries again to move her into the sand, but she holds to the sides of the rock, clings to it, her back arched. Their bodies fit together despite the rock, her body compliant somehow, not rigid as he expects. He has the odd thought that she's protecting him from the rock, but only partially. He thinks he hears her whisper that she loves him, and when he comes, it seems nothing compared to the exquisite pain of the rock shredding the tissue of his bloody knees. And then he stops moving, Lenore as still as death beneath the weight of his body. And for some inexplicable reason he thinks of the future, gets a glimpse of it for a moment, an image like old movies flipping through a projector. He sees flashes of limestone bedrocks, and cairn fields and sculptures and fossils. And then it's gone, his future, as if he had never had one. As if this is the last moment of his life. And so he does the next thing, a thing he will become used to doing through the years. He searches for the past. What was it Lenore had said to him a few moments before? There was something.

He struggles, overturning rocks in his mind but under each is an empty hole. He looks up into the moonlight, expecting to see Lenore's face turned from him, but it isn't. Instead the moon shines full across her countenance. What is it he sees there? Disappointment, resignation, validation, love, pity? Something he can't put a finger on. And his mind races on in a blur. He knows there is something of significance that has just happened to him, some chance he might have taken, some suggestion he might have heeded, some impression of himself he'd had that is already missing. Who had he been ten minutes ago? He looks again into Lenore's eyes, which reflect bits of stony light and he feels his body flush. There is a stirring of recollection, a hint of familiar ground he'd once covered, an echo of the past, some memory of a past when he still possessed a future.

Isn't there?

There must be something there, he's sure. But for the life of him, he can't put his finger on it.

Iceberg

Cynie Cory

I can't swallow the distance
it has traveled without a jar. Nervous and glass-like,
it clinks without sophistication,
pulses to the slow tempo of night
like an afterthought grown cold, lingering,
half-surfaced, a swollen witness.

I cannot budge the iceberg. It is locked inside my skull
like a form of etiquette.

2004

The Smell of Snow

Cynie Cory

The eyelash moon returns to the black above this city where I don't recognize the sound of my favorite song. In a desert you carry me across broken waves. I am dying, loving you like this. My heart is a cave burdened by distance. But in this movie we tear each other open, we devour flesh as though we are harnessed by nothing. I own the impossibility of you. I own the shape of your shoulders, the pulse of your neck. I lose my breath under stars I have tried to rearrange.

We are on this journey fueled by night. Because I have given myself to work I lose sight of you. I call for you repeatedly. I wait among the turnstiles in the subterranean dark. You appear with a memory coded by afterthoughts. I try to crack it, to penetrate your deliverance. There is so much at stake, we have lost the will to speak. — You are so far from here, walking in tall grass, rhyming your verbs. I drift north.

Ursula, Under (excerpt)

Ingrid Hill

ON A CRYSTALLINE, PERFECTLY BLUE MORNING IN JUNE, AFTER A DAY OF angry pewter skies and of sheeting, driving rain, we enter our story. Clouds pile themselves picturesquely, theatrically, like plump odalisques, against the blue, clear-edged and astonishing. The forest all around is a palette of greens. Wild chokecherry trees are in raucous bloom. It is as if this were the first morning of the world, perfect. Even the garter snakes slithering under the roots, over rocks, over roots, through the grass seem a part of the day's jubilance. Dew on fat ferns catches the sunlight in bursts and disperses it, starlike.

We are just miles inland from the tip of the Keweenaw Peninsula of Michigan, which juts out into Lake Superior, the arrival point for the earliest hardy wide-eyed settlers arriving from the East on lake packet boats to stake claims and seek copper, well before the Civil War. Lifting off from a branch overhead, a red-winged blackbird calls out clearly something that sounds much like *kee'-we-naw*, the native word for "portage." Many things here that are not called Keweenaw are called its English equivalent, Portage, almost as if life were much like a brief transit across a wee stretch of land.

It is Monday, June 9, 2003. Our story itself began long before, if we believe that all back story is also story, that the underside of the iceberg explains what we see above: all those wind-sculpted shapes that, looking for all the world like praying hands, came to be called, by fanciful meteorologists, *nieves penitents*, or penitents sculpted of snow. Still, a painful and highly unusual event happens this glorious morning, and it is through this tiny aperture that we enter our narrative.

We are at the moment seeing through the eyes of Ursula Wong, a child with dark Asian eyes, café-au-lait complexion, and a thick blond braid down her back that seems frankly too much hair for a two-and-a-half-year-old to have had time to grow. Ursula has had her second birthday on November 19. She is a child small in stature, five pounds nine ounces at birth and now just over twenty-seven pounds, as of her spring checkup. She wears denim bib overalls with a purple T-shirt beneath; in the cool of the morning she has insisted on putting on her purple hooded jacket for the weather. Snow mittens are clipped to the sleeve ends. Yes, they are purple too. It is perfect and cool in the sixties.

Her mother, Annie, says, "Honey, you don't need a coat. It's June." Her father, Justin, says to Annie, "She'll figure it out pretty quick. She'll take it off herself and think it was her own idea."

In a clearing a couple of hundred feet down an untraveled dirt track into the forest, a glade carpeted by short grass kept low by odd gravel-shot soil, Ursula is crouched on her haunches examining tiny white blooms on wild strawberry plants in the grass. Each tiny bloom is a star. Ursula is transfixed.

Ursula and her young parents have traveled almost five hours west and north from their home in Sault Sainte Marie, Michigan. They have spent the night at a Super 8 Motel in Houghton, a town that houses the state's mining college now more diversified as mine after mine has shut down. The motel faces Portage Lake, and Justin, who is an installer of vinyl siding and gutters, has paid the five dollars extra for a room with a view of the lake and the opposite shore. They rarely leave home, and this overnight away is a treat.

Ursula has splashed in the pool and run around on the motel's wooden deck, puddled from the day's rain. She has giggled delightedly as with the heel of her hand she pounded buttons in the lobby vending machine to make foil packets of chocolate-chip cookies fall, *klunk*, to the bottom of the machine. Ursula has suggested in a business-like way that they might live here. Justin has reminded her that Grandma Mindy is back home, and her purple carpet in her bedroom and all her stuffed animals. "Oh," Ursula has said. "That's true." Sober as a church mouse, clear-spoken as a valedictorian.

The Wongs have come here because Annie, a librarian, has gotten a bee in her bonnet of late: she wants to know more about her great-grandfather's death in a 1926 mine collapse, and then more about his life. Seems dumb, she has said, to live so geographically close to it all and know nothing much about our roots.

So the previous fall they had gone to a commemoration of the disaster at the iron mine where her great-grandfather died, and now, several months later, in weather as lovely as Eden's, they have come to search out the site of the copper-mining camp where the family lived when her father's grandfather was a blond barefoot boy new to Michigan, new to America. Her father is foggy about family history, does not remember being told much; he is beer-sodden most of the time anyway.

Annie has spent the previous afternoon in the archives of the Finnish college across the lake, reading accounts of the 1926 tragedy an hour and a half south, in Rovaniemi, Michigan, while Justin and Ursula first nap and then dry-roast in the sauna until they glow. Ursula loves the sauna. She sits with a sober expression, for only a few minutes, nonetheless, and then says perkily, "I'm done," ready to move on to the next thing. She is after all two years old. "I'm not," says Justin lugubriously, peering out at her from under the wet towel draped over his head and then retreating back under. He takes sauna seriously.

So Ursula sits and waits, rolling her eyes in the way she has seen little Olivia do on old *Cosby Show* reruns, precocious, in charge but obedient. Ursula's swimsuit is purple, like her bedroom carpet and her coat and everything else in which she has a say, and she sits on the hot cedar bench on a small purple towel. She draws the line at the television dinosaur called Barney. "Get outta here," she says, when anyone mentions him, with an exaggerated wave of her tiny hands, dismissive, parodying someone else—maybe from Brooklyn—she's seen on TV.

Ursula's even having come to be—considering Annie's injuries (a fractured pelvis from a hit-and-run accident at age ten which also broke both her legs) and all the doctors' attendant warnings—is a miracle in everyone's eyes. It has occurred to Annie that the birth of any of us, our coming to birth at all, in light of all the hazards every ancestor faced, is pretty much a miracle too, and she has been chewing on this thought for several months.

While Justin and Annie are awed and protective toward Ursula, they also believe that she needs to learn to make choices from early on. So she gets to make choices. She is, as a result, a bright, perky child, astonishing everyone.

That evening, taking Ursula for a final packet of cookies, Justin hears the roar of the crowd on the lobby TV and plunks himself down between a tool salesman from Ironwood and a grandfather from Escanaba who is en route to see his little granddaughter Ursula's age, in Bay Mills, and has stopped here to visit the shrine of a sainted priest-missionary for his wife, who has cancer. They are all watching the Stanley Cup playoffs. There is a television in the Wongs' room upstairs, of course, but the lure of the lobby and all of these hockey fans is irresistible to Justin. He drops into a chair and starts roaring with the rest of the men.

Out through the glass door of the lobby, in the twilight, the surface of the lake sparkles. Ursula stands waving her silver packet of cookies with a defeated look but also with flashes of a tiny anger. She makes an exasperated face at the desk attendant, as if to say, *Men*. The attendant laughs heartily. The New Jersey Devils are playing the Anaheim Ducks, and the Devils are on their way to shutting out the Ducks.

Justin does not know that two defensemen, one on each team, playing against each other, are actually related, at not so great a distance back in time, to his wife, Annie, who is here after all seeking out her ancestry, and neither he nor Annie will *ever* know it. On the Devils, Oleg Tverdovsky, from Donetsk, in Ukraine, is descended from an ancestor who migrated east; on the Ducks, Fredrik Olausson, of Dädesjö, Sweden, has hands shaped like those of Annie's great-grandfather dead in the mine, passed down from a shared great-grandfather of their own. The degrees of separation are considerable—the connections go back to the beginning of the nineteenth century—and no one is asking the question, anyway. Justin's high-school team in Sault Sainte Marie was called the Blue Devils, and he is rooting for the Devils.

The lady at the desk has a name tag that says EILEEN. She looks down at Ursula standing rolling her eyes, waving her packet of Mrs. Fields cookies, waiting for Justin. "Who do you want to win, honey?" she asks.

"Well, who's playing?" says Ursula perkily, her eyebrows lifted.

The attendant is surprised at the response. What did she expect? "The Devils and the Ducks," says Eileen.

"I like ducks," says Ursula. "I hate devils. Devils are ba-a-ad."

The attendant laughs heartily. "They're not *real* devils," she says.

"I don't care," Ursula says. "I like ducks."

Justin and the tool salesman and the grandfather hear none of this. There is a great deal of roaring from the onscreen crowd as well. Pucks fly, ice shivers up in fine flurries, blood flows. All is adrenaline joy.

The attendant helps Ursula open the cookies and gets her some milk from the breakfast room, checking with Justin first in pantomime. Justin nods yes, but this is after all hockey he's watching: she might have asked him anything and he'd agree.

The Devils win, three-aught. Annie comes down in the elevator, using her cane, looking for them. She and Ursula and Eileen have a good laugh at the hockey fans. "She likes ducks," Eileen says to Annie, reporting the remark. "But she doesn't like devils." Eileen crouches to Ursula's eye height and high-fives her. "Gal after my own heart," she says, slapping palms.

They are driving today to the site of a settlement where Annie's great-grandfather had lived in his childhood, soon after he came over from Finland, the now overgrown location of an abandoned copper-mining community out toward the point.

On their way north from Houghton this morning they have stopped in Calumet to take a couple of pictures of Ursula sitting on the lap of the oversized statue of Alexander Agassiz, Harvard naturalist, copper baron, and aristocrat, otherness incarnate and no friend to the hoi polloi. Still, his sculpted bronze robes are cool, and Ursula poses sitting on his knee as if he were a dear, loving uncle.

The plan is to have a picnic here—the glade looked inviting, and time is abundant—and to spend the rest of the day seeking out where the camp would have been. Camp Grit. *Its name must surely have been a joke*, Annie thinks—*or maybe no*? Nature has taken over again at the site of the camp, perseverant, triumphing over all humans' intents. The land had been leveled, entirely, but, the historian at the college has told Annie, the forest has reasserted itself and is as thick as if it were first growth. The cabins will be gone, even the traces of their foundations, he says, as well as all traces of the two churches that came later on, whose bells were transported inland for two other churches, both Lutheran, one Finnish, one Norwegian. Finns and Norwegians did not worship together, even if both were Lutherans.

Perhaps, Annie thinks, all *traces of human habitation will be gone*, but still she wants to see where her great-grandfather lived as a child. To set her feet on the earth there and know it directly. Justin is less curious about his own heritage.

Annie's father, Garrett Maki, spends most of his days and nights drunk since her mother's death, eighteen years before, while Annie was in the hospital recovering from the crash that crippled her. Garrett is on disability now, as a Vietnam veteran, but no one is certain just what his disability is. Annie suspects—no, believes—that her father was responsible for her mother's death: there had been a great deal of abuse, and Liz Maki died of a head injury the night of an outburst on Garrett's part. There were no witnesses, there were no charges. Domestic violence was not a thing people were comfortable talking about then. The eighties are as distant as the glaciers.

Annie walks with difficulty, always with that cane, and invariably wears long skirts to cover her scars and her atrophied muscles. Justin is able-bodied and hearty, half Chinese. He is known to local hockey fans as Wild Man Wong. Annie and Justin are fiercely in love.

BECAUSE URSULA IS CLAMORING FOR LUNCH, THEY HAVE PULLED THE truck over onto a graveled apron of the road, then meandering through a patch of woods, and are wandering peacefully in an odd clearing a short distance into the woods. They have no idea that this clearing once held the boiler house of an old mine. The grass grows up through a layer of finest ashy pea-gravel, a relic of the long-vanished brick structure. When the mine was operating, the land was scalped clean: no trees anywhere. The forest is thick again.

The fragrance of lilacs hovers in the air: there are wild lilac bushes to either side of the clearing. Lupines with their intense tiny indigo blooms poke up here and there. Clumps of wild lavender tuck themselves everywhere. Something else—a bush?—smells like licorice. Justin has set down the picnic basket in the grass. A tiny brown-speckled bird lands on its arched handle. Ursula chortles in delight and leaps to grab it.

"Nope," says Justin. "Birds are to fly." The bird, as if to demonstrate, lifts off. Ursula claps her hands in delight. Then she crouches again and tries to pick one of the tiny white blossoms. "Let it be," Annie says. "It will make a strawberry." Ursula rises to standing, her full height of two feet plus, plunks her fists onto her hips, elbows akimbo, and scowls in frustration: Here we are out in all this great sweet stuff and I can't do *anything.*

At the edge of the denser forest at the back of the clearing, there is a rustling sound. Papery, slight, but distinct in the silence. Ursula's head turns. A flash of white: a deer, venturing tentatively out of the forest, has spotted them, and turns tail to run. It is perhaps a dozen feet away. Ursula runs after it, squealing. The deer, of course, will not be caught, and there is nothing to say except "Let it go." Annie and Justin smile at each other, a moment too quick in its passing to run to the truck for the camera.

Ursula tiptoes dramatically, thinking perhaps of Olivia again—she watches those *Cosby Show* reruns, mesmerized, over and over night after night and can recite people's lines along with them. She cranes back over her shoulder at Justin and Annie to make sure they see her. They beam at her. She puts her finger to her lips: *Shhh.* Her back is to them. The blond braid down her back shines like silk floss in the sunlight, against the plum violet quilt of the coat. The deer is still in sight, a few feet into the leafy green shade of the forest. She is determined to catch it. The delight in her eyes is unmistakable.

She gives them a sign in mime: Watch me. Ursula's every gesture seems meant for the comedic stage. She is a natural. She tiptoes toward the tree line. The deer disappears deeper into the forest, as silent as breath. Ursula puts on a burst of speed, silent herself, looking back at Justin and Annie, steps into the trees, and disappears from sight. The only sound is an astonishing tiny intake of breath from Ursula as she goes down, like a penny into the slot of a bank, disappeared, gone.

Annie looks terror at Justin, trips on the long skirt that covers her scars, lurches forward, and falls awkwardly onto her bare elbows. They sting and ooze blood. Justin is already at the spot where Ursula disappeared. "Oh, God, Annie," he says. His voice is barely audible.

Annie raises herself on her cane and stumbles toward him. They stand transfixed, staring down. The opening into which Ursula has fallen is amazingly small, and they can see nothing but darkness. They certainly cannot see Ursula herself.

Neither of them wants to call out to her, unconsciously afraid their voices will echo back at them from too deep an emptiness. Both of them think: *What is this? How deep?* and *Dear God, no.* Both of them think: *A mine shaft?* Neither says the word.

Annie had tried to imagine the shaft into which her grandfather descended one August day three-quarters of a century ago and from which he did not come out alive: fifteen hundred feet deep. No one could survive such a fall . . . but is this such a shaft? Annie is telling herself, no, it must be something else. Too small for a mine shaft, surely. Way too small. Then it must be a well. She heaves a half-sigh of imaginary relief. But what would a well be doing out here in the forest? The answer would be: The same thing as a mine shaft, serving a different landscape, a different time. And why in the name of anything would a well seem a relief? Her breath clutches up again.

Rough old timbers are laid across an opening in the ground six or seven or eight feet square. It is too early in the summer for much foliage to have sprung up yet, but each year it has grown up and died off, and grown up and died off, so the timbers remain exposed. One of those years, perhaps forty years ago when Justin and Annie's parents were in high school—and no one much has been here since, wandering into this forest which is after all nowhere—a tiny shoot grew up between the first and second timbers. As it grew, it pushed them apart, and it has become a tall solid tree, growing from inside the hole, through the timbers set into a collar to seal this shaft. As it happens, this is indeed a mine shaft, an air shaft, meant only for ventilation of the long since abandoned passages below.

Annie kneels painfully, all her weight on her cane, and calls into the darkness: *Ursula.* She can't tell anything about the depth of the hole. She calls again: *Ursula,* and then sobs. She looks up at Justin. It has been a providence that Ursula was so close and they both had their eyes on her, or they might fall into blaming themselves or each other in their grief. Neither even considers that.

Justin's eyes dart wildly but his mind is clear. "How far would you say it was since we saw civilization?" he says. "Thirty miles?" He stops. "*Three* miles?" It could be either.

"The cell!" Annie says. "In the truck?"

Justin runs to the truck, his work boots seeming to shake the ground. The cell phone lies on the front seat, tiny and useless amid a scattering of animal crackers. In crisis the mind focuses on minutiae: he thinks, *Now is that cookie a rhinoceros or a hippopotamus?* He picks up the phone. No signal. *Of course, no signal: there are no towers out here in the wilderness.*

He tries to remember how many cars they saw on the road. All he can remember is the fat, furry rear end of a black bear cub shambling off into the trees near a river, and Annie trying to take a snapshot. He follows that rabbit trail into his mind and recalls the bright topaz eyes of what must have been a cougar just off the road as they drove up in the dark in the rain, the night before. But of course a car coming along the road now, Justin thinks, would be no help at all: none of *their* phones work either. A rusty dark red Subaru zooms by, heading north. The road is once again empty and silent, the sunlight bright and impassive.

Justin remembers a time as a teenager when his first car, a beater the color of pea soup, had stopped dead just west of Sault Sainte Marie at twilight. A passing car had offered to send help, then didn't. He recalls walking alongside the road in the dark, kicking stones, mumbling "goddamn fucker" again and again. Can't chance that kind of thing now. Trust no one. Justin has not trusted many folks in his life anyway. He carries a grudge about his father's having abandoned the family when he was three, not much older than Ursula is now.

Justin calculates the distance back to the last town they passed, Eagle River, and then estimates mileage forward to Eagle Harbor, next on the map. Forward seems best. He runs back to Annie.

She sits silent on the ground, her legs out painfully straight before her, her eyes filled with tears. Justin's attention is drawn to the pattern of the fabric of her skirt: a pattern of tiny blueberries and green leaves. His mind is recording that to keep from attending to what has just happened. *Blueberries*, he thinks. *I never noticed that those were blueberries.*

The silence from the gap between the timbers is deafening, the darkness there impenetrable and magnetic as a black hole. They can see only a few inches into the opening: the leaf cover overhead is thick and the shade almost palpable. In the silence, the birds' twittering seems obscene, out of place.

Annie seems in a trance. She is not. This is just slow to register. Justin, however, is functioning in hockey mode: alert, aggressive, all nerve ends ready. "No phone," he says to Annie. "No towers." He sees the look of dismay in her eyes: lost, disbelieving. "I'm going to drive on to Eagle Harbor," he says. "I'll get help." He feels as if he will throw up his innards. "You can do this. Ursula will be okay." He sounds calmer than he feels. Annie just stares at him as if dumbfounded by his composure. "Look," he says, half-angrily. "Was she a miracle or *what*? So would God just let her *go* this way?" Annie can't believe he's talking this way. He can't stand for her to mention anything in the *vicinity* of God, shuts her down when she tries. All of a sudden he's preaching?

And of course Ursula is in no danger. Of course. This will all be explained in a moment. We're on an old *Candid Camera* show. No, *America's Funniest Home Videos*, that's it.

"Okay," Annie says, her voice belying her pounding heart. "Go then. I'll wait." She tries to think of something important to say about logistics, what he must not forget to do, but she can think of nothing at all. So she just repeats herself. "I'll wait." The tone is as if she were waiting her turn at the butcher's or the photo counter at Wal-Mart.

"Yeah, right," Justin says, his eyes wide with terror. He leans and kisses Annie on the top of her head. Her hair is warm. The pale skin of her part looks so vulnerable. He focuses on anything but that hole in the ground. "We'll get our miracle," he says.

"Hurry," she says, the audible quavering of her own voice this time scaring her. She squeezes his hand, and he's gone, the truck spraying up gravel.

IT WILL BE SEVEN HOURS FROM NOW—MONDAY NIGHT—A NEWS TEAM on the TV will be helicoptered up from Marquette to broadcast nationally what is not this morning known to anyone else, what has not quite even registered in Annie's consciousness—before the remark is made. A woman her parents' age back in Sault Sainte Marie will be lounging alone in the newly remodeled high-ceilinged living room of the home she inherited from her parents, passed down from her grandfather the judge. Fried and sour after two gins, she will grumble at the TV screen, "Why are they wasting all that money and energy on a goddamn half-breed trailer-trash kid?"

Annie's mind is pulling up, as from a well, the tacit answer to that as yet unasked question. Annie cannot think of Ursula down that hole, so she thinks: *So many generations, back into history and then prehistory, all concentrated into this one little girl.*

This is the answer to the as yet unasked question, in backward format: this little girl carries with her the inheritance of generations uncounted, precious, induplicable. She is priceless, not only to Annie and Justin, but to the planet, the whole big fat blue-green ball hurtling through space.

As Annie's mind drops as far as it can conceive, down the dark hole of her own lack of knowledge about her own and Justin's families' past, an unfocused image of someone Chinese—male or female she cannot see, an older person, to judge from the posture and shuffling step; likely a male now, to judge from the shoulders and slight baldness, wearing a green gown—flits past her consciousness like a resurfacing memory of something she never knew to begin with.

She cannot flesh it out into focus so instead she begins trying to name the trees that surround her, to keep her mind off that hole and its darkness, and she cannot remember the names of the trees either. Her eyes fill with tears and, just for a brief second, overflow. The birdsong is deafening.

Justin heads north on the winding road, taking the curves too fast, hearing himself saying out loud to the empty cab, "Christ," again and again, and then "Crap," and then "Christ," and then silence.

2006

Water Mission

Jillena Rose

My father is a missionary
in Saigon, and every day
he sits or stands
in his white cotton shirt
and talks to servicemen
and the Vietnamese about Jesus.
While my mother rests
through the heat of the day,
I walk behind him
to Buddha's temple. There,
in a small public pump house,
open on four sides and draped
in flowers, he chooses one
of the dozen brass water spouts
under the pagoda-shaped
roof and fills our collapsible
plastic vessels with water purified
through filters and blessed by the priests.
After seven months,
we will send the sponsors slides.
Report from the Field:
my father behind a podium

in a crowded upstairs room;
my father in the park
near the elephant exhibit;
my father in a flak jacket
in a jeep headed for Da Nang.
This is the prayer he left for me:
women in white silk
laughing, letting water run
over their fingers, and my father
kneeling hatless in the flower-scented
air, learning another sound
for praise, teaching his daughter
a reverence for water.

Upper Peninsula Fires

Keith Taylor

A hundred miles north the forest is burning.
Smoke drifts down this far at night and just at dawn
I smell something like wet charcoal in my cabin.
Sunsets glow deeper red and spectacular
the longer the fire burns, the more the peat,
cracked and brittle, and those cedars in their dry swamps
smolder into the autumn of a parched year.

2007

Jazz Tune for a Hiawatha Woman

Gordon Henry

You know where I'm coming

from:

On the same street past the tracks

where last august

we drained a few predawn

quarts made promises against

a mural of imperial oppression

on the wall of the workers

of the world bookstore

(later closed up and reopened later

as a Hollywood Video.)

Now

a few tripped out

two-spirit women skins

verbally fuck with

a panhandling Devils Lake

wino in a Viking shirt

outside the currency exchange.

As I make my way toward

you over the bridge nicknamed

"Two Suicides" (with a graffiti lightbulb

launch point on the railing

and sprayed fluorescent sketches
          Of pornographic body parts, rubbing
    up against dollar signs

on the concrete stanchions
            underneath.)

          Try not to blame me that
the pow wow windigo kahn got
            your cell number from
               the table at the city park
where I carved the digits
      with a leatherman before I put
the last number down
in blood I drew with
        broken glass and mixed
   with a pinch of ash
          from my menthol
camel.
      (He wrote it all backwards
under his ANISHINABE name
        on his fist)
    Just tell him when he calls
         you love it when he calls.
            He'll go back to dancing
while reading the news in the
        Circle just like he did
     behind the middle-aged
        jingle dress matrons,
dangling their moccasin
        matching bags with limp wrists,
glaring under the beady flora

of woodland tiaras,

knowing and not liking

the clown mocking their

steps behind them

at the upper Midwest gathering.

I heard from Spotted Eagle

at the halfway   house

after he ticked off conditions for my

release from three freezing

moons of treatment:

(No drugs No pot No speed No black cadillacs No more shooting your
grandfather's IHS painkiller prescriptions No drinking No driving No
parties No bad influences AA twice a week ay You go to meetings at our
Lady of Whatyacall or you can go Tuesdays at the Indian center just give
in to a higher power and keep up the sober interior monologues).

your Ma's still hanging on

to that Big Knife bricklayer

who ate the leftovers

I brought from Hard Times Café

for you

the day I walked all the way

back here

In clothes I found in a garbage

bag in the back of a dodge

pickup parked in the drive

at Uncle Salem's

only to find you'd gone north

for a funeral.

Could it be more complicated?

At 10 I tracked deer with my

Aunt and waited by a tree
in falling snow, shot
my last round into the air
just to let her know
where I was before it got
too late to search for me.

Nine years later, at the U
I took classes, studied philosophy,
European history and social
linguistics, chemical tables
world religions and I still managed
to remember my name and
the names of relatives and places.

I've lived and traveled
with no destination to speak of.
I even stopped myself in the
middle of dreams just to wake up
So I would remember faces
conversations, the speakers
And the voices, the mists and animals
the roads and enclosures,
the running, the flying and
the fear dreaming of immobility brings.

Still,
as I make my way back
to you, stand before another door
I know that inside there is
No one, as your having left
remains the hand of another
door of my arrival.

Disappearances

Jeff Vande Zande

DAD'S HANDS MADE SMALL MOVEMENTS ON THE STEERING WHEEL. IN my side vision, in the glow of the dashboard, his outline was ghostly. He hadn't said anything since we crossed the bridge.

"You can sleep," he said, "if you want."

I told him I wasn't tired.

A few seconds passed. "Are you scared?" he asked, turning toward me for a moment and then back to the road.

I wasn't sure what he meant. "No," I said.

"It's just that your mother doesn't like to drive at night."

I thought about it. It didn't make sense. "She drives at night, now," I said. "She drives to Houghton sometimes after work. John works at the Houghton hospital once a month, and they meet at a restaurant when he gets done."

Mom was with John now—over in Paris trying to find us a place to live. John was offered a job to be a doctor in France. He's some kind of specialist.

"That's fine," Dad said. "It's just that she used to be scared." He didn't say anything for a moment. "You want me to tell you Rip Van Winkle?"

It's about some guy who falls asleep for a long time and then wakes up and nothing is the same. It was the story Dad told me all the time when I was little. I didn't feel like I was little anymore. Twelve isn't little. "No, thanks," I said. I closed my eyes. The van was warm and hummed with the passing of the road.

"Grayling," Dad said, waking me.

I opened my eyes, sat up, and looked around. Lights glowed along the edges of the highway. I could see buildings. A McDonald's. "What?" I asked.

"Sorry," he said. "It's just a town. Grayling. Named after a fish."

"Grayling?" The lights were becoming more scattered.

He nodded towards the darkness outside his window. "The Au Sable River's out there. It used to be full of these fish. Grayling. Kinda like trout."

I stared into the darkness as though I might see the river.

Dad told me that over-fishing killed the grayling. "They have old fishing journals from the turn of the century. Guys writing about catching fifty or sixty grayling a day. Keeping 'em. They didn't appreciate what they had."

I didn't like that the fish wouldn't come back. "There aren't any grayling in the river? How do they know?"

He told me they know. They do tests on the river. He told me they can shock the river and make fish float to the surface. "They haven't found grayling in a long time."

The road was dark again. I thought about the fish. I wanted to see a grayling, and it made me mad that I couldn't. The wolverines bothered me too. I hated stories about animals that were no longer in Michigan. I told Dad that I didn't like to see things disappear, and he said that he didn't either.

"It doesn't make sense, Dad. The town is called Grayling, but there aren't any grayling? They should change the name. It doesn't even make sense."

Dad squinted into the darkness out beyond the headlights. "Sometimes things don't make sense. Sometimes it forces your hand and you have to make your own sense."

I looked at him. "What do you mean?"

"Nothing."

We drove on.

"Roscommon," Dad said later. "Another town."

I looked but there were no lights. "Where?"

He told me it was a few miles off the interstate. He told me about the south branch of the Au Sable River too and about some auto executive named George Mason who bought up land around the river to protect it. "He gave the land to the state under the condition that it could never be developed. That was a guy who did what needed to be done."

I couldn't really listen to him. My eyes kept closing.

"We'll gas up in West Branch," he said.

"Where are we going to sleep?"

"We really can stay anywhere. You're mine, right?"

"For two weeks," I said. "We got two weeks."

He nodded. "Yeah. Two weeks."

I looked for lights out in the darkness. "Why didn't we just camp by the Mackinac Bridge like you told Mom we would?"

His hands squeezed the steering wheel. "I just think we should do something bigger, something better."

"Because it might be awhile before we see each other again?" I asked.

He nodded slowly.

"Where are we going to sleep tonight? I'm getting tired."

He rubbed his hand over his face. "You want to listen to the radio?" He turned it on. He reached over and squeezed my knee. "You listen to the radio, kiddo," he said. He turned it up. "I'm just going to drive."

I rested my head against the window. It was cold. I stared into the darkness. Then, I thought of something. "Mom said that you can fly to Paris. She said that there are times in the year when it's not so expensive. You can come see me."

He turned up the radio a little more. "Just go to sleep," he said, not turning from the windshield. "I feel like I could drive for a long time yet."

2008

Rent

Russell Thorburn

We felt for a way to disappear
without ever leaving

the house, hide in rooms
without speaking to each other.

Every month we struggled
to find the rent and pretend

it didn't matter. We listened
outside the bathroom

to our children laughing
and knew we were safe

as long as they splashed
that milky water.

Sometimes we raked for hours,
visible to the landlord

who expected a check
by morning.

We raked until our arms hurt
to show the children

we were unafraid
and scuffed our feet

as if the friction through leaves
could carry us somewhere else.

Even the word rent
didn't matter

as we said it to the night
stooping over us,

who with its red-backed spiders
cornered us, dangling their finery

at the metal mailbox
outside our front door.

The landlord heard us
above in his duplex, his face

appearing at the window
lit by unspeakable lies,

for we didn't have the rent,
and the yard with the whole tree

told the truth, then silence:
the wind burying even that

as it grew louder
and there was nowhere

for a father to stand
without being poor.

2008

Come Sunday, the dog of his thoughts will bury something unspeakable in your muddy garden

Kathleen M. Heideman

That corpse you planted last year in your garden,
Has it begun to sprout?

—T. S. Eliot

Dearest Christ, how's the new job coming
—administrative assistant, you said?
did my last postcard mention how the tulips
are poking up their ruddy erections from
every corner of the yard? so many, I forgot
the humus held so many! though it's too soon
for bloom—cruel spring—that rose which
should have graced my back gate eternally,
Paul's Everblooming Scarlet, "winter-hardy to zone 3,"
—the one I mail-ordered from Gurney's? It froze.
But then a seed catalogue is a list of the deceased
and not a bible. (Or a bible too, you think?)
Bless me, but I get confused.

2009

I Will Die in Lake Superior

Eric Torgersen

I will die in Lake Superior on an August night,
naked because it is dark
and I ran out of the sauna, all rosy and wrinkly
in the candlelight of the cabin,
though in the dark outside no one will see,
not even I in my last moments;
thin moon, stars all blazing and boiling
like I'm Vincent van Gogh,
but I will have left my glasses in the bathroom.

I'll feel that first chill grip as I hit the water,
and think, "My heart is pounding,
as it should be"; then I'll dive in and go under,
once, again, and a third time
as the pounding grows, as if something really
large means to be let in.
I'll turn to go back, but the dim light of the cabin
will get farther and farther away,
as if I were carried off by some huge wave.

2010

Watching

Julie Brooks Barbour

It was a haunting, a shadow:
a hawk making a meal of crow
on my patio. I watched
the hawk pick his prey clean,
gulping strips of flesh.
Then he vanished.
I craned my neck to see what was left:
a skeleton, perfectly intact—
a museum piece
reflecting the late-afternoon light.
On the other side of the patio,
my young daughter stood at the door,
palms pressed against the glass.
Neither she nor I stirred.
It was a moment left to itself,
a vision I woke from in the morning
and kept glancing back toward
with a mother's attentive eye
that could only watch.

Cripple

Cameron Witbeck

I saw someone walk the way you walk
and I thought you were leaving—
you've been dreaming of wolves again.

Snow is coming.
You can feel it in your knee.

I stand in the kitchen cutting:
potatoes, onions, mushrooms.
I can think of nothing but the snow and your knee.

You come home. You insist on walking.

I scrape my knife clean; and leave it in the sink.

You speak with your hands
of a man you met, who lost two brothers this fall.
You tell me that the wolves in your dreams
are asking you to leave for the winter.

You want to go. You want to run again,
feel tendons push bone beneath skin.

As you talk, I look out the window
and pray for snow to come and lock your knee,
for it to fall and fall and fall and never leave.

To Dance Is to Pray

April E. Lindala

I. Grand Entry

A gathering of ages begins
Beaded moccasins dusty, eager. You step aside,
between,
in front of,
behind
other Indians.

Beaded earrings glitter
glass seeds of spirit
appear, disappear
morning lights dance atop blue waves of thin air.
Beads of sweat moisten your brow,
you beam, grateful for the sun's appearance,
its countenance.

You step some more. Watching you
are keen eyes
wrinkled with wisdom.
Braids, soaked in bear grease,
wrapped tightly, thick with

story. White plumes, *miigzii migwaan*,
partner with the afternoon breeze.

Tailored colors ripe with boldness
satin ribbon on satin shirts, satin skirts.
Silver bracelets,
copper bells,
quill barrettes,
turquoise rings,
furs . . . shawls . . . shells . . .
you step some more.

A porky roach atop the *ogitchidaa*,
a crown of Indigenous rights. Veteran. Warrior.
His arm bears a tattoo, *Native Pride*.
Bones drape his chest; warrior's armor.
Leather straps tight around his jowled face.
His black eyes meet yours. He extends his hand.
You shake it.

You keep moving, searching for your place. A mother inhales
a Marlboro cigarette. It stands at attention
between her fingers.
She smiles at you.
You return the gift, then nod
and tiptoe behind her,
behind her daughters,
behind their daughters,
securing your place in line.

You stand patient, shawl hanging stately. You swallow in a breath

of late summer air and taste
snapshot memories of pow wows past. Your toes
wiggle, ready. Your fingertips
tender with anticipation
caress the eagle feathers
of your fan. Thousands of Indians,
dancers, mothers, uncles, nephews, granddaughters
all of their moccasins tied tight.
Thousands of Indians, yet
you stand solo
in prayer.
Strength—fragility
     Wisdom—humility
Your blood pumps with purpose,
in rhythm. Thunderous chills climb,
your spine—spirit passengers riding your bones
ascending, spirits of those yet to be born. Spirits of those
who have passed on, spirits of those
who lie alone, awake
dying.
The heartbeat sounds. The lead singer on the
host drum cries to the open sky. At the base of hundreds
of pines
a thousand footsteps
erupt in time.
Grand Entry begins.

II. Sneak-Up

A bouquet of *miigzii miigwaang,*
eagle feathers,
form a bustle on his back.

Copper bells on tanned ankles
clang for attention.
Drumbeats call him to attention—
the hunt begins.

He leans over, searching, searching
his father's dancing stick in his
right hand, his eagle feather fan in his left.
He bows towards Mother Earth
once and then again.
His eyes lift to the clouds
seeking, searching.
He bows again to his steps not yet taken
to track his spirit
prey
within the forest
of his troubled heart.
His black eyes hidden in red face paint, his face hidden in
dance, his footsteps hidden in lightening, his sorrow
hidden in pursuit, his hunger hidden in pride.
The final drumbeat. Stillness.
He greets his kill.

III. Feast Time

My wooden bowl filled
hominy soup overflowing
I start by sucking bits of sizzling salt pork.
Sautéed venison with bits of bacon.
Hand harvested wild rice, *manoomin*
Lightly danced upon by the young man
who carved his spirit name
in his cedar ricing sticks

Manoomin mixed with cranberries and cashews.
The light, flaky fry bread gives me
moist kissable lips from fry bread grease.
Black coffee
        too much sugar
savor a swig or two of that coffee.

Lake Superior whitefish
        caught this morning,
        breaded this afternoon,
            fried in front of us in the feast line.
A thick slice of juicy moose meatloaf
that juicy, juicy, greasy, greasy meatloaf
that grease
that spilled
inside oven #2
caught fire and almost
burned down the tiny kitchen   with all of us   in it.
Miigwech for resurrected moose meatloaf.

Potato salad, fruit salad, leafy salad, pasta salad,
tuna salad and that surprise Jell-O salad
that turned out orange
when we all think it should have been   *red*.

Spaghetti noodles, penne noodles, green beans, pork and beans
more coffee
damn, that's good coffee.

Commodity peanut butter cookies, spicy pumpkin bars with
melting whip cream, chocolate cake with white frosting, a giant
bite of gushing summer watermelon

that drips
down
my
chin.

While managing my mouth
full of laughter
I thank the Creator with each spoonful that I am here
among my relations
savoring the
flavors of feast time.

IV. Two-Step
"Ladies' choice two-step,"
announces the emcee. " . . . swing and sway the
Anishinaabe way."

You've never known a two-step to not be ladies' choice.
You sit back in your maroon-colored
folding lawn chair and
fold the fringe
of your hide dress in your lap
and then you fold your chilled hands.
You inspect the mother-of-pearl stone ring
on your wedding ring finger and ponder your choice
to marry a white man.

"Ladies," the emcee continues.
"If he turns ya' down. He'll owe ya,
a fry bread taco and a Pepsi Cola."

You have known men to turn you

down and you have returned to your seat
thirsty and hungry. Starving
for your own man's touch
between your lonely
fingers.

You inhale the coolness, evening
air ripe with lustful apprehension,
as couples wrap their arms around each other
and step closely in time
the scent of your lover
absent.

You wiggle the ring you wear
on your wedding ring finger
to remind you that the sweethearts, lovers,
married couples—no longer lovers,
cousins, siblings—all of them,
all of them dancing in the long, steady line—
in tonight's two-step
will eventually
go back
to their seats
too.

V. Healing Song

Silver metal cones, beads, shells and dripping summer sunbeams
a sparkling wave
illumination
in the dance arena.
The audience stands out of respect
for the sacredness of these

jingle dresses,
the sacrifice these women make
when they dance
for our people.
The metal cones crash gently
a vigorous rain
for cleansing, for healing—
it is the sound of my dress
that I miss most.

I look down at my feet.
The rip in my moccasin is under my big toe. I pick up my foot
to check the electrical tape holding
my moccasin together.
In secret I wish that one   only one
    of those dancers is praying for my right foot
holding in place an injured ankle.
I secretly wish that one   only one
    of those ladies is praying for my spirit.

Beads of sweat fill my back. My hide dress
shrink wrapped
around me in the summer heat. I hang my head
aware of each selfish thought. My traditional dress
like the white electrical tape on the
bottom of my sole—is a bandage doing its
best to keep me together.
The song ends.
It only I didn't feel the enormous tear within my spirit.

VI. Hand Drum Contest
Five guys, tall. All of them

their hair tied back
in a pony tail
hanging black silkiness. All of them
in their white sneakers and white hats
in time
in beat
in voice
singing sweetly
to their sweethearts
about the night sky, the moon's light, the
magic stars and their eternal hunger
for
fry bread.

VII. Giveaway
Blankets make the best gifts.
Soft woven
colorful threads of warmth
wrapped around you and your lover
you stand on your tiptoes to greet him
to kiss him. He kisses you back
wraps his arms around you
lifts your body to meet his.
The blanket still wrapped around the two of you,
holding your devotion within,
together
in concert.

You cling to each other
tighter
on Sunday night
after being apart

after being in
your own
individual worlds.

Your foreheads meet
bodies tired after fulfilling weekends—exhausted
still you look down and inward
into each other's soul
thankful that you are safe   within embrace.
His heart sounds
against your chest   the presence of heat
rises from within the colorful threads.

You breathe deeply
gratifying desire   inhaling
the perfume of his body
the scent of his hair
—his whole being.

"Where did you get this blanket?" he whispers.
"The giveaway."
His cheek,
patches of sharp stubble,
rubs against the smoothness
of my face.
Our lips
dance.

Lake Surfing at Whitefish Point

Russell Brakefield

This is Polynesia in the mitten, hidden past the trailers
    where iron sky meets iron water.
We tread beaches like two lovers tread the bedroom, moving
    slowly toward a point we both know.
Some days all I want is to press my hands against your chest,
    lie against you as against the thin water.
Past the second break, my hands sink like shallow cups into
    the calm blue.
We spread across the lake, two hawks perching on different
    branches of the same tree.
I want to tell you the difference between tooth and skin or me
    and wolf: I crave to lay my hands along your thighs,
    under some open sky, out here along the shore, with the
    gravel and headlights.

At night my skin burns for the coastline, the wind, dawn's
    rising orange billiard, the current knocking holes in the
    sandbar.
I lie awake and rack my brain for that wet smell, that far off
    ring of riggings on the flagpoles, for low howls, or ghosts,
    for the logging ships cold pressed and caught for air, for

your movement on the board, your rush of tyranny over
the water.

With you, out here on this wind-burnt tunicate of earth, my
    tongue is caught, a sunken vertebrate, some cast-off gull-
    torn carcass.
I know that beneath your suit is a body so warm and smooth
    it should still this water further with every inch of you
    that moves into it.
I know there are few bodies I could love more than those
    shoulders, hard rock arched around Lake Superior.
I know these things are persistent and mutually exclusive.

Along these old lines, my stomach rolls on and on.
    The highway cries behind us.

Goin' for Commods

Shirley Brozzo

You never know when just a simple ride can turn into a real journey 'round here. It was the first Thursday of the month, so it was time to go for commods again. Maggie, my good friend of several years, offered to take her car, cuz she had a full tank of gas. Maggie was a dear for offering, but I wasn't sure that all of our combined food subsidies and the both of us would fit into her dark blue Toyota with the red front fender. But she assured me that we could all fit, just fine.

She crawled in behind the wheel. I climbed into my seat, and tried to pull the door shut. It didn't close. So I pushed it open again and slammed it shut again.

"Wait," Maggie shouted. "You got to just pull it shut, then hook that bungee cord up under the dash to hold it."

I just looked at her, then tried to hook the cord onto something solid to keep the door from flying open. "So how long you been doing this?" I pointed with my lips.

"Ah, just since last week. The door froze shut in last week's ice storm. So Bobby kicked it to try to get it open. Well. It opened all right. But now it won't close. So just use the cord, okay?"

The drive down the highway to Wetmore passed without event. The trees along the side of the road hadn't changed much since the ice storm. All of the animals listened to their instincts and didn't try to cross the road in front of our car. Creator has even seen fit to give us good weather and sunshine to travel in.

259

The 50 or so miles we needed to travel to collect our free food seemed to fly by, covered by good conversation between friends. At last we reached the Tribal Center, drove round and round the parking lot to find an open space to leave the Toyota, parked her, and walked toward the building, past the chorus of "*Boozhoo*," "*Aanii*," and "Hello." By the time we had entered, all the good seats, the ones with cushions at the back of the room, were taken and we had to wait for the office lady to pull out and set up more of the hard metal folding chairs that nobody wanted to sit on. While we waited we signed in, noting that we were numbers 50 and 51. Then we sat down to wait. You could never tell how long it would be before the commodity truck would show up from the Soo. Sometimes it was only 15 minutes late. More often than not it was an hour and 15 minutes late. Maggie and I continued our earlier conversations about our writing and our kids, but also joined in with those around us. We were all a loosely knit family, coming together monthly for our traditional rights of hunting and gathering—hunting for the letter saying we were qualified for the commods then gathering together to pick up our bounty.

A small dark-haired boy dressed in tattered tennis shoes, ragged jeans and a blue, red and green striped polo shirt came running in yelling, "Momma, Momma, the truck is here. The truck is here." His jacket wasn't zipped up, but he didn't look cold at all. People who had gone out to smoke came piling back in. If they missed hearing their number being called, they had to go to the end of the list. No one wanted that. The whole idea of coming early was to avoid being the last one.

After the truck stopped, the warehouse workers who drove it opened the back of the 18-wheeler and prepared to parcel out the packages. Meanwhile, the nutritionist and office assistant entered the building to get set up. Their first stop was the bathroom. Then the nutritionist started passing out samples of foods made from many of our commodities. Today's samples were oatmeal muffins and corn bread. There was also unsweetened apple or orange juice to wash them down. The nutritionist stated, "To make the corn bread, all you have to do is:

Mix together	*Cut in*
1 cup corn meal	¼ cup shortening
1 cup flour	
¼ cup sugar	*Blend in*
4 teaspoons baking powder	1 cup milk
½ teaspoon salt	1 egg

Bake in a greased 8" × 8" pan at 425° for 20–25 minutes or until golden brown or grease a muffin pan and use that."

The samples she handed out were little more than teasers, but were supposed to get us to try new recipes to use all the food. The office assistant began barking out numbers and people lined up to give her their requests for foods like juices, peas, butter, cheese, dry milk, etc. After waiting another hour it was finally time for me and Maggie to place our requests. Maggie showed her letter and placed her order. As I moved forward to place mine, Maggie said to me, "I'll go get the car. Come out when you're done."

I told the office assistant:

1 case corn	1 case pears	1 bag oatmeal
12 cans peas	1 case peaches	1 bag of corn meal
12 cans carrots	25 pounds flour	6 cans beets
6 pounds butter	4 cans beef	2 cans chicken
4 cans pork	6 cans asparagus	2 bottles corn syrup
2 bricks cheese	1 bottle honey	1 case apple juice
2 cans shortening	2 cans tuna	2 cans salmon
6 cans pineapple juice	1 case grape juice	1 case apple sauce
12 bags powdered eggs	2 cases evaporated milk	
3 boxes powdered milk		

At last my order was finished and I went to join Maggie. She was nearly done loading her order, roughly the same size as mine, and I could see that there wasn't much room left for my commods. I shot her a concerned look.

"Plenty of room," she said. "Just go get your stuff."

So I did. The boxes kept coming and coming. Soon the back seat and trunk were stuffed. But there was one more case to fit in. After enough pushing and shoving, the box ended up on the floor in the front seat, beneath my feet. As Maggie and I climbed back in, I could feel the car sinking lower still. I was afraid it was going to scrape the road, or refuse to budge at all. But she took off, slowly. The bungee cord was securely holding my door shut, but I felt like it was going to be a long ride home. We hadn't gone very far when Maggie looked at me, and I looked at her and she said, "Want to stop for a burger?"

We burst out laughing at the irony of having a car full of food, yet we still had to go out and eat! We stopped at the local A&W, ordered a burger basket and large frosty mugs, and enjoyed. As we finished our last bites, the waitress brought our bill:

White's A&W

M 28 East

Munising, MI

---

2 burger baskets

2 lg RB $9.89

There we were with a carload of free commodity foods from the Sault tribe and a $10 restaurant bill from White's! It was just too much. We laughed about it all the way home.

2011

Dominos

Ron Riekki

He smelled like shed,
his clothing as colorless as hospital walls.
His hair screamed for paramedics,
a sad head. He was my boss
at the pizza shop. Him, 53. Me, 44.
We'd sunk into these jobs like corpses
with weights tied to torsos.
He told me he was anti-war,
now, said this aggressively,
that he'd spent time in Africa
as a mercenary ten years ago,
when he was my age, roughly,
that I should be out doing something
like that, not here. Houghton,
Michigan. The job was killing
my car.

I told him the bread sticks
were getting cold. He said don't worry about it,
you see, I worry too much. The phone rang.
I went outside and stared at sky.

The clouds were the color of bones.
I wondered what made people leave families.
I wondered what it would be like if your bones
felt like clouds.

2011

Waboos

Eric Gadzinski

If you were a rabbit
I'd shot,
I'd put the cold muzzle
of the barrel
under your soft chin,
your dark eyes wide,
to end your struggling
quickly,

but this is no bullet
from no one's gun
that makes a hot hole
under your heart,

and the white winter light
bends down
where you lie
to watch.

2011

Beach Glass

M. Bartley Seigel

SHIVERING IN THE MORNING LIGHT, WE GATHER LIKE CIGARETTE butts at the water's edge, our thousand naked bodies in a long chain bent from burden and burnt to the filter. What we've learned. Scars are replaced with more scars. Hair grows up from scorched earth. Once, we would have cut ourselves with broken glass, that the wind might rush through the breach to line us with fallen limbs and leaves. But beach sand has since worn dull the sharper edges of that pain. Stomachs now empty and growling, we've come at last to these shores copper wired, gear and pulley. All coiled spring and iron will, our words tin typed on our tongues, we clasp arms and dive in together, electric and beautiful. We disappear beneath the lake's surface for what seems a grateful eternity, knowing somewhere ahead, out beyond the tree line's reflection, there is a sandbar.

2012

Self-Portrait as Blizzard

Jennifer Yeatts

If enough of us could land among the rest.
If this reflected gleam—drift, waft, sullen
wind—would wait for the next gust
before leaning headlong into the heap
that used to be the garden,
we'd join with each slush & flake, melt
into pools that tomorrow'd be a perfect glare
ice union for run-&-slide, slip-&-fly.
                              If figure skates.
If mittens. March would crunch dry
under tracks, sell its subzero Midwestern truth
for a late-model carol. And when the squall
forgets its origin (so long since anything
but frozen kaleidoscopes),
when schools run out of snow
days, we'll hit you stiff, calamity of whiteout
thicker than a sky full of marshmallows,
storm within a storm, & you'll sleep
one more night with your boots on,
shiver yourself warm under polarfleece
& patchwork, breathe in quick
through your numb nose, & you'll love
the dumb, early dark harder than ever.

2012

And Winter

Corey Marks

Au Sable Point Lighthouse, Lake Superior, 1879

I.

When Father opens the door, the storm
is with him, it rushes the dark rooms, flushes
dust from the backs of books and unused chairs.
Down the shore a ship has run aground;
Father's seen it from the tower, a row of lanterns
threading toward us through the rain.
                              Ready yourself,
he calls, *light the rooms* . . . The gale raves
over his words with its two mouths—wind
and water. Beyond him, the lake rends
its new scars.
                              No home now but this,
Father said in the summer calm
when we arrived, though this is no home.
It is a cage set in the wind.

2.

We have our tasks. Father shrinks into the black
frame of the storm, below the beam
from the hive-shaped lens flailing
the exaggerated night. What choice do we have?
The shipwrecked read a promise in our light
we do not mean.

                      I thought we'd taken residence
at the heart of a refusal that sends the coming world away.
Isn't *that* the vocation he chose for us? Carry the oil
up the narrowing spiral, fill the lamp,
wipe the lens, trim the wick,
set blazing its obstinate *No*?
Autumn arrives with its own commandments.
And winter, which won't stay away—isn't
that the arrival the storm prepares? The edges
seize and the bays close hard
and there is no need to tell anyone not to come
where promise shuts
                    its sky-dark door.

2012

Beekeeper outside Escanaba, Michigan

Hannah Baker-Siroty

In the Upper Peninsula some bees
made a connection with a body.
The story is 2nd hand, from a friend
of a friend. It's not important
to be there, exactly, outside Escanaba,
to know how she took her dress off.
It was loose, light fabric, and bees were under it.
A swarm began, so she removed the only
layer, slowly, until, naked, she
scraped honey from the comb

2013

Possession(s)

John Smolens

WHEN YOUR WIFE DIES YOU FIND MUSIC TASTES DIFFERENT AND FOOD sounds the same. You don't walk, you creep. Some days you crawl. Others, best just to lie still. The closets are full of ghosts. Blouses she wore when she was twenty-six. A denim skirt. Killer dresses. Shoes—heels, pumps, a pair of Capezio tap shoes—entombed in boxes. When you open the closet door her coats hold still, suspecting they're gonners. Threads of memory. She wore this one there, that one here. Every garment a chapter. The clothes of the dead have no future. You could burn them. You could leave them be, decades of sartorial history hanging from a pole sagging with the weight of remembrance. You could cross-dress with a vengeance. *Everything Must Go.* Not discarded, donated. To the Women's Shelter, cartons and paper bags and piles of clothes, until the woman behind the counter says they're overstocked. You're tempted to take them all back. Who denies the donation of a dead woman's clothes? The rest to St. Vincent DePaul's, and there her cottons and linens and rayon blends are added to bins heaped with corduroy and polyester. (But for one satin nightgown that will not be donated.) Until the closets seem empty. Your clothes don't count—they aren't you, but just neglected shirts, pants, and jackets. As summer wanes, you open a drawer and find sweaters, scarves, wool hats and gloves. Gear for a woman who understood winter. You send sweaters and shawls and silk scarves to the women and girls in her family. They respond with photographs of ten-year-old daughters wrapped in blue for the fifth grade's Colonial Day. Still you are possessed by possessions. Even after you dispossess yourself, they turn up in the kitchen drawers and cabinets, where she kept jars of dry goods, beans and grains, future meals. And there, in the freezer, plastic containers: soups, tomato sauce, chili. Nutritional messages from the afterlife. Hoard them. Defrost only as a last resort. Yet through the winter the freezer becomes as spacious and cold as your heart. By the time you open the last tub, labeled *Black Bean Chili 3/14/10*, food no longer has any meaning. It's no longer an act of love, a gesture of kindness. There is no intimacy in tuna salad or in marinating chicken thighs. It's embarrassing to recall how often you ate by candlelight; it's like the satin nightgown tucked away in a drawer you never open. Instead just heat and serve. Just nuke it. Just eat. Overcooked sustenance. When you eat dinner right out of the skillet or pot, the temptation is to glance over your shoulder in shame. No one is watching, except the cookbooks. Shelves of cookbooks, back issues of *Gourmet* and *Bon Appétit*, and a three-ring binder stuffed with recipes, a culinary legacy handed down from grandmother to mother to daughter. Recipes written in her shorthand, scrolls and waves and loops fetching across the page with an occasional word, a white cap of English. Instructions for future meals, for candlelight dinners, for guests. There are no recipes now, there are no guests; no need for the wedding china, the good tablecloth. Don't forget *Widower's Rule #1: Never turn down a dinner invitation.* You're the guest now. And after dinner you walk about the house, speaking to the dark. *Go ahead, come back and haunt me. Move the book on the table. Slam the bedroom door. Anything, I'm ready. Go ahead, I dare you. Scare me to death. I am ready.* The reply is the deepest silence. Yet sometimes you feel her in the silence: nothing moves, no hinges creak, no lights flicker. Just her silence. Fuck you, Steven Spielberg; death has no special effects. There is no possession, just possessions. To break the silence you play music. CDs in horizontal stacks; vertical rows of plastic jewel boxes, never properly alphabetized (as she so often suggested). Songs with melodies, lyrics, choruses, verses, movements, codas. Songs you can't live without. Songs you'll never listen to again. Songs you know by heart. Songs you want to forget. Songs you can't forget. Songs for dinner, for reading, for dancing, for killing a bottle of wine, for making love. Songs to break the silence. Songs against eternal darkness. But one day (maybe) you'll make a deal with the silence. You'll sit in her grandparents' chair and it will only be a chair. Or you could give it away. All of it. Everything. Everything except the stones. She was forever (or so it seemed) gathering beach stones. She'd return from a beach with her coat pockets sagging, doing her best Virginia Woolf. Round stones, egg-shaped stones, disk-shaped stones, stones ground smooth by water and time. Stones from England, Scotland, Ireland, Italy, Turkey, Cape Cod. Stones stored in shoe boxes, in plastic bags, in bowls; clusters of stones distributed about the house like incense. She liked the look of them, the feel of them, rattling in her palm. You could get rid of it all, but not the stones. You could walk on them, sleep on them, sit on them, eat off of them. Your house would be silent, filled with stones. You would have solitude. You would not be alone. You would have the stones.

2013

Marquette

Justin Machnik

I AIN'T SURE I KILLED HIM, IF THAT'S WHAT YOU'RE LOOKING TO FIND OUT.

Eighty-six was a bad year for us all. The rest of the country was growing but we were near enough Canada, up in the U.P. that we didn't see none of that. Hutch had rolled his Nissan pickup that year off 553 before he finished payments on it. I told him, "That's what you get for driving with a head full of whiskey," and he told me, "That's what I get for not buying American." He used a roll of duct tape to keep the doors from swinging open now and we had to climb through the windows if we was going anywhere. Hell, at least he had a car.

That morning, we had drove up the skidder roads, the old two track logging roads so narrow we folded the mirrors in so the trees wouldn't knock them off. Hutch liked to drive these dirt trails fast, mean as he could and really put those tires to work. The gun cases slid across the bed of the truck and hit the walls as Hutch took the corners sharp and I could see Gene getting pissed, but he kept his jaw tight, took a pull from the bottle and passed it back to me, and then I passed it back to Hutch. Gene had a thirty-ought-six back there that he put more love into than his girl. We had to get Gene drunk before he's let us use that gun. I had a little twenty-two revolver that my Daddy had given me a long time ago that I kept in my pocket. It was only October, and snow was coming down through the tall pines and resting on the hood of the car. Winter always came a couple of months early in Marquette, and thinking back on it now I wonder why anyone would live there. We pulled into a muddy spot, under an electrical pole, and already my head was light and I was strong drunk. We were high up on a slope in the Tahquamenon forest, where pines pointed their burr tips at the thick steel sky. The buzzing of the electrical wires overhead seemed almost natural. Here, there was a bare strip of land that went down the face of the mountain all the way to Superior. A big open space cut out of the moss old trees. Giant steel towers carrying the weight of the electrical wires lined the clearing, bringing power down to Marquette. Out on the bluff you could see the shine of the city next to the black water of the great lake. This was a place that we came to pretty often to shoot. Hutch took another long pull from the bottle and the stupid ass was already hollering, barely out of the window with a little pistol in his hand, shooting up in the sky. The shots sounded like a clap of thunder over the open space. Hutch had these sparkle crazy blue eyes and his hair was messy. He always looked dirty, a thick line of black under his nails, and thin blonde mustache. Gene was taking his time, pulling out his rifle and checking to make sure everything was all right. I would go as far as to say he would have kicked our heads in if something hadn't been right, but he never got pushed to that. Gene wasn't much of a talker. Didn't smile much neither, but he was tough and loyal. We passed around Gene's rifle, shooting at rocks and trees, and then the iron legs of the buzzing electrical structures, listening for the loud pang and betting drinks on who could hit the ones most far off. And when the bottle ran dry, we started throwing it up in the air, and taking potshots at it. The bottle twirled in the sky where the faint sun was fogged by the snow clouds, making a light that cast no shadows.

"You just don't know how to use a gun this fine," Gene said, shouldering his rifle, firing and missing the bottle as it landed in the frosty grass.

"I'll put twenty I hit it before you." Hutch took his turn and missed.

"You ain't got no money." I missed too, and the shot jolted my body and sobered my eyes. I hadn't really been aiming.

Then I threw up the bottle, high as I could just to show I could, and it blew apart when Gene pulled the trigger, with bits of glass showering down. We all hollered and listened to the echo of our own voices.

"You owe me twenty." Gene said.

"Never shook on it."

"Figures you God damned Indian giver."

"The hell is that?" I said, pointing to a black ribbon of smoke a long ways down our shot path. It was rising from the coast, by the dark rocks where the water was crashing soundless from this distance.

"The hell *is* that?" Gene repeated getting a scope out of his gun case. He looked through it and there was a stillness about it, the way his breath came out like cloud in the cold air. He didn't say anything. I noticed how the trees had started to gather dry snow while we had been there. "I don't know—" he said in a way that made me think that he did.

"Give me that," Hutch took a turn, moving the scope closer and further from his eye impatiently. "What the hell's someone camping in this weather for?"

I took it and looked. Through the glass everything seemed to be flat with no depth and the edges faded to black. The image trembled with the pulse of my hands, shaking blurry. I followed the smoke down to a campfire and there was a little camouflage tent by it, still pretty small through the lens.

"Jesus, we was just shooting—" And I felt them mad at me for saying it out loud. "Well we was! Should we go—"

"No way we shot by it. There's too much space, no way nothing went by it." Hutch's voice was almost quiet for the first time. "I'm sure of that, might have spooked the guy, but we would have known. Probably out fishing anyway. You trust me, nothing went near there."

There wasn't more to say, but we stood there for a while, and looked down the slope between the electrical lines over the cleared strip of land where the grass had grown tall and where pines had once stood. Down the slope where the trees narrowed to a point and the gray water mirrored a grey sky and a little wisp of smoke rose. Further on up the shore, the black ghost of the city hugged the banks of Superior and at a point further on you couldn't tell the difference between the waves and the sky.

NOW I HAVE TO TELL YOU, WE REALLY DIDN'T PUT MUCH MORE THOUGHT into it. We didn't think much more of that tent. Hutch was right, it would have been damn near impossible for our shots to wander just that way, just right. But maybe not. It was a few weeks before we thought about it again and I ain't sure who heard first about Jimmy. We wasn't about to bring it up. Marquette's a small place and there's not many people dying aside from their own hands. So it was big news, all over the paper and TV. Jimmy Tyler had been a student at the university, nineteen and a year younger than me, but there wasn't nothing similar about us. He was a college boy, and a smart boy too. That's what a girl on the news said in an interview. She was a friend, or maybe a classmate of Jimmy's and her cheeks were red with cold and shining. She had blonde hair, permed, and a blue eyeliner on. She was crying, the way she was talking about him, just crying into the microphone and I turned off the set. He was shot dead, found in his tent in the Tahquamenon woods. No one knew why he was up there, least of all me. And I thought to myself, I thought, that's just stupid thinking you had anything to do with this. Just stupid. Could have been twenty other people in line to shoot that bastard. Maybe he did it himself. Just a bad place to be, that's all. I didn't read the papers, but I started saving them. I didn't want to know more than I already did. I went out of my way to pick up a copy of the press on the way home from work, but never to read it. Though I would look at the picture of Jimmy, stare at the photo of him on the front page. There was a picture of a twisted piece of metal, too, lying next to a ruler. The caption said, *The 30.06 round removed from Tyler's body.* He didn't look like a dead person. He didn't look dead at all. His eyes weren't dead, even in black and white. He gave a big smile. Maybe a school picture of him. He was clean and looked like the kind of person I wouldn't get along with. But not hate, I never hated nobody. I would stare at the picture for hours moving it closer until it stopped being a face at all and was just black dots on white a different ways apart. When I looked closer I could see how each dot bled into the paper, not dots at all but splashes.

That weekend Hutch and Gene and me met up at the Black Rocks to the south of town. We used to come here as kids to a little peninsula of rock, worn smooth and shiny from waves, and jump into the lake. It was so high we thought the fall would kill us, but we always did it again, digging our fingers into the cracks of the rock-face and pulling ourselves up for another go. When we got there the moon was up and the stars filled the sky, white dots on black a different ways apart, and I wondered if I could move the sky back would they make a picture? We climbed out of the windows smoking cigs and drinking our beers. There was a little dirt trail that worked its way through the spruces to the rocks where the waves hit with a force and the spray hissed like flame. We hadn't said a word to each other, not that night or any another time, we hadn't said nothing about Jimmy Tyler. Gene had brought his thirty-ought-six with him, held it standing up between his legs on the ride over. On the rock the wind pushed me back and Gene yelled out, "You think I can hit that from here," and pointed at the moon. I thought it was a damn strange thing to say and he caught me off guard when he started shooting, and this close to the city. Nothing happed and the moon stay still in the sky, purple clouds starting to cover its face while the wind screamed past. "You'd be amazed—" he said, and that's all he said. I wondered what it meant, but I thought I knew. Then he grabbed the butt of the rifle with one hand and threw it as far as he could until it hit the surface of Superior and came to rest at the bottom where so many ships have sunk before it. I couldn't hear the splash through the wave crash and the wind buzzing my ears. Then, following its lead, Hutch jumped off that rock, clothes and all. His arms circled, wind-milling as he fell and then disappeared into the coal black waves. White swill came up like cracked veins to the surface, rocking in the tide, and then Hutch came up. Gene jumped next, cigarette still in his mouth, and before his head popped up I was in the air too. Falling for what seemed like too long to do anything. The water was so cold it stopped my heart and pushed the air right out of my lungs. When I came up I could feel the little bits of ice licking my face as the waves pushed by. We didn't climb out. We just lay there, the three of us, letting the water throw us side to side, until through the cold, we couldn't feel ourselves or anything much more.

A LOT OF YEARS WENT BY, BLACK YEARS WHERE I FELT A SICK PUNCH IN my stomach every morning and wondered if I was going to make it out alive. I thought about Jimmy almost every day for a while, and then he started to slide back, started sinking to a part so far back I wondered if it really happened at all, or if it was just a dream I had when I was younger. I moved west to Wisconsin, to a little town called Bayfield where I got work on a press. Gene and Hutch stayed. I met a girl there, Mandy. She was a small thing, a little over five foot, and I didn't care much for the way she dressed, but she made me forget about things for a while, and that was good enough reason to keep her around. We spent three or four years together before I asked her to marry. Mandy had been pushing the idea for a while, but I wasn't much for it. Maybe I ran out of reasons not to.

It was August and the season was already turning. Those August nights are the lonesome ones, when the fireflies have died and the crickets and mosquitoes are gone for the winter. Those nights are dark and silent. We were driving back from the rehearsal and Mandy stared out at nothing, shivering with her arms crossed. I had my window down and was trying to sober up.

"Could you put that up, I'm freezing." She wasn't happy with me tonight.

"I'm hot."

"God damn it Ross—" It sounded like she had more to say, but then she stopped and turned back to the window, staring at nothing.

The cracked road passed in the headlights. My eyes were heavy and it was hard to see the lines that had mostly rubbed off with time.

"Maybe I should drive, you look drunk." She said after a while.

I kept driving.

"Did you hear what I said?"

I drifted a little into the gravel shoulder, then overcorrected and my back tires fishtailed a little when I pulled back onto the road. That's all that happened, I didn't even lose control.

"For Christ's sake, Ross, let me drive, you're going to *kill* someone!"

I stopped the car and slapped her across the face as hard as I could. She didn't cry, but just looked back at me with those green eyes, cold as Superior.

I hit her again. The next day, we were married. She covered up what I did with makeup and put too much on, she didn't look very pretty in the photos.

THEN I HEARD ABOUT HUTCH. GENE TOLD ME HE WAS DRIVING AROUND heavy drunk and lost control. He never really had control. This was a couple years after the wedding, when Mandy and me just had Nathan. I guess Hutch had taken his old pick-up out to the skidder-roads, and drove around those turns too fast, the way he did when he was young. He had a new truck but for some reason he took the old one, the one we used to ride in, now ribbed with rust, and managed to wrap it around a tree. I know what you're thinking, and I can't tell you for certain. I'm not sure if he meant for it to be that way. This happened a few days after Christmas and blue and green lights showed through Gene's front window, turning the snow those colors when I drove up. He was letting me stay over for the funeral. Gene had himself a wife now too, and two kids by her, but they didn't look much like Gene. I had known the girl in high school and from what I knew, it was pretty obvious those kids weren't his.

We had drinks that night, by the fireplace until both our palms and heads were warm. Gene had a good setter that lay next to the fire panting. I can't remember that dog's name now. The walls were wooden and glowed gold in the flicker light and a couple of deer heads stared glassy eyed down at us. Dead black eyes. The whole place smelled like the forest, wood and pine and animal.

"I can't believe we have kids now," that's what Gene kept saying all night. "I just can't believe that, Ross. Ross? Can you believe that? Can you believe we have kids now?"

I shook my head but didn't say anything until I felt stupid drunk.

"You think Hutch pulled the trigger?" I gave Gene a smile.

Gene looked something fierce, and then checked the dark hallway behind him even though he knew his girl and kids were in bed.

"You think that's why he drove himself into the trees? You think he knew it was him?"

"Cut the shit Ross—"

"Or maybe he had no idea, maybe that's what did it to him, maybe he would have rather known." I looked at the Christmas tree that Gene had turned off earlier. "Trees have their own glow to them in the woods, but once you cut them out you have to run lights through them. Otherwise they just look dark, you have to force the light into them, because once you cut them out of the ground, it's gone forever."

"Now I'm warning you Ross, you keep your voice down." The light of the fire licked his teeth and the shine of his eyes. I could see that same shine in the deer heads, mounted on the wall. Snow blew past the window, caught in the light only long enough to disappear into darkness.

"You think it was Jimmy Tyler's ghost who steered Hutch into the Tahquamenon forest?"

"I don't know no Jimmy Tyler," Gene's face had lost its color and he stood up knocking over his chair when he did. Down the hallway a baby started crying.

"Jimmy was the name of the boy we killed—"

"Get the hell out!" Gene yelled. He went to the kitchen and I heard a drawer turn over and silverware scatter across the floor. Down the hall a baby was screaming and his setter woke up and started barking loudly.

"Gene, what the shit's going on?" His wife came down the hallway in a nightgown.

Gene came back with a knife as long as my arm and pointed at the door.

"Get the hell out of my house!"

I picked up my coat and opened the door. "Yeah, I do."

Gene lowered the knife a little.

"I do think it's crazy that we have kids now," I said, and I walked out into the snow and when I put my keys in the ignition I saw that Gene had re-lit the Christmas tree.

I STARTED PULLING OUT THE NEWSPAPERS FROM '86 THAT I KEPT IN A box in the basement. The paper had grown yellow, and I looked at the picture of the boy on the cover. He looked younger than I remember. A boy, that's what he was. Just a boy. I started reading the articles. One of the top students of his class, he was a basketball player. On October 19th, of 1986 a couple of hikers in Tahquamenon had found Jimmy's body half crawled out of his tent. He had been dead a couple of days and a fox or something had chewed away a good part of him. A 30.06 round had hit him in the shoulder and spun down into his spine. He bled out quick. Jimmy Tyler was six foot two, a tall kid, and had green eyes. I could never tell from the picture. My son has green eyes, same as Mandy, his mother. Jimmy grew up in Marquette, son of Jonathan and Ann Tyler. He had a kid sister too. I went back to Marquette on the weekend. I told Mandy that Gene was having a rough time with Hutch being dead and needed a friend nearby, but I never went to see him. In the motel I found a Jonathan Tyler in the yellow pages and decided to drive by the house. It was in a nice neighborhood that overlooked the water. I could tell it was an old house that had been redone, painted blue with a white frame. In the driveway there was space for a basketball court and a pole that rose out of the ground, but the board had been taken down. The windows were black, dark like the glass eyes of a deer.

I told Mandy the boss had me working Saturdays now, and spent the day driving across the border, into Michigan just to drive by the Tyler's house, just to look into those empty windows and wonder what it was like on the other side of black glass. I wondered if you didn't notice because everything outside was so bright, or if that brightness never reached you there, if a place like that always stays dark. In spring, when Nathan was just learning to walk, I drove by the Tyler's house and there was a man in the front yard, digging up dirt and pushing flower bulbs into the ground. It wasn't sunny, but the weather had been turning nice and I was wearing a t-shirt with the windows down. I pulled into the drive and he walked over to the car. He was a tall man; white hair combed back and sturdy looking arms for his age. He had green eyes.

"Can I help you with something?" He rested his hands on the roof of the car and looked in through the window. He smelled like the spring, like a warm place, like something I hadn't smelled since I was a boy. I needed to know what it had done to him.

"Yeah, hi. Sorry to bother you—"

"No bother, what can I do for you?" He smiled.

"It's just I'm new to the area, I seem to have gotten a bit turned around. I was trying to find my way to the Tahquamenon Reserve," I paused to watch his smile lesson. "Heard the trails are beautiful out there, you ever go there?"

"No," he shook his head, his face like a Christmas tree going dark, "no, I'm sorry I don't go out there. If you just back out and follow this road about a quarter mile and take a right on 553, you'll find the trails, it'll be marked."

"Thanks, just moved to the area for my son, heard it's a safe place to raise a kid, is that right?" I wasn't doing it to hurt the man. I was doing it so I could see what we had done, see what *I* had done to him.

"I wouldn't know." He said and walked away, he didn't look like anything more than an old man.

I started on my way home and pulled off to the side of the road to shake and spit.

THAT NIGHT WHEN MANDY WENT TO SLEEP I WENT DOWN TO THE basement and pulled out that little twenty-two revolver my daddy had given me. I thought about Jimmy's father and slid a bullet into the cylinder. I thought about his mother and his sister, and slid another bullet in. And then I thought about Jimmy. I thought about that bullet working its way into his meat and the way he must have known he was going to die. What he must have thought right before he died. I slid a third bullet into the cylinder and then lifted the muzzle to my arm and pulled the hammer back. What did it feel like? What did he think of right before he died? How easy it was? Dying was the easy part. I thought about Jimmy's father and walked up stairs. He was the one left, replaying that bullet ripping its way through his son's skin, tearing tendons and arteries. I walked over to Nathan's crib and pushed the cold barrel against my baby's chest as it rose and fell. He woke up and looked at me half asleep with those green eyes. I put my finger on the trigger and thought about pulling it back, just a little and the spray of my child filling the crib. His blood, my blood. My boy. I pressed the gun harder into his side and he started crying. I pushed harder. I thought about if it was me that pulled the trigger that killed

Jimmy Tyler, if it was any of us, and I thought about yellow guts spilling out of my boy. Mandy came in and screamed when she turned on the light. Then she scooped up Nathan and ran out of the house with him. I still remember the way his arms and head swung as she scrambled to unlock the door, scared as hell. That was the last time I ever saw my son. I thought, it wasn't fair, I deserved worse than that.

I TOOK MY CAR OUT EAST TO MARQUETTE. DROVE OVER THE STATE LINE and through the Ottawa National Forest and the Porcupine Mountains. The Mountains backs rounded, quills of evergreens poking at the sky. The sun was going down and the sky was purple in the rear view like a bruised face. I drove along the coast of Superior, the great lake where ice still rolled in the waves crashing on the shore. I have heard that those waves have stolen the life out of many men, filled their lungs with the cold whisper of the dead and drown them in the great northern waters. Froze their very souls and pulled them down where there can be only stillness under the moving water. Only inches really. The lake is a monster and it only takes a couple of inches to drown a man. I know a thing or two about drowning, drowning without ever getting your feet wet. Only a couple of inches. A couple of inches and Jimmy Tyler would be alive. A couple of inches and that bullet would have just spun on by him and he would have stopped and said, "I could have died, but I didn't." A couple of inches or a strong breath from Superior. A big gust could have pushed that bullet out of the way. And Jimmy would still be alive. But it had to be, just like that, those couple inches, right there; it had to be like that. "You'd be amazed—" Gene had said to me once. And I am.

I drove down the two-track logging roads until my car got stuck in the mud. Then I walked to a space under a giant metal tower that held up electrical wires that powered the city. The grass has grown tall. Once, twelve years ago, there was a boy that was shot here. Then I loaded my handgun and walked up the mountainside, up a path where the trees had been cleared out to make way for the electrical wires. Toward where some boys I used to know shot guns. And I shot. I fired into the sky, again and again and then when my hammer fell silent, I reloaded. I shot and wondered who my bullets would fall down on. Shot at the electrical wire and watched them hiss with explosions, blue lightning and sparks, and the thunder of my gunshots. I kept shooting, trying not to miss a single one. I could see the black coast rise up where Marquette lay and I watched the lights go out.

Researchers Find Mice Pass on Trauma to Subsequent Generations

Lisa Fay Coutley

Even before I was born, before my father
took my mother's head in his hands,
her black curls like sprockets

sprung from his palms, & held her face
under the lukewarm water of our tub,
her belly a heavy globe—my only

armor—pressed against that bright white
porcelain, before I took my first breath
two months after my father failed

to cinch it, her, I mastered a palpable fear
of choking. It's all a mind game, Dad
would say, shoving another M&M

in my mouth: swallow. Pseudodysphagia—
even before I learned the word I knew
the shame that came from fearing

fear rooted in the fiction of my mind—hers
& hers & hers & hers.

2014

Arm

Ron Riekki

IN SOUTHERN SPAIN, IN THE MILITARY, IN DECEMBER, I ONCE DANCED in a field of sunflowers. Or not danced, so much as sang. Or not sang, so much as listened to a helianthus symphony where a Sunday of Gods and witches were painted a noon-light yellow so bright that I felt like I was a non-denominational church myself. In full dress blue uniform with the first Gulf War so distant and the happiness that no one I knew had died or was hurt terribly. Below, a pool at my feet that looked filled with vodka was really a carnival of rain, a mirror for clouds, a pond of hope and youth.

2014

When the Lake Lost Its Sound

Alex Vartan Gubbins

I did my best to get it back.
I cracked fire-sticks
over beaver bones,
fed flies unraveled gut,
aligned rain-stones
to point the way
the snowman travels.

Maybe, I'd have to do
like lake-lovers: divide
a heart for ice and fish.
The current would pump
the aorta, the beach
thump, like how a crane
calls after building a nest,
sees its emptiness.

ELF INCANTATION

Ander Monson

```
OUR ELF WAS BIG AND SKY

AND AIR AND SEA AND ALL

OUR ARC WAS FAR AND WON THE WAR


OUR ELF WAS HUM      OUR SUB WAS HID

OUR FOE WAS TOO      SUB EYE SUB ICE

OUR ARM WAS AWE      BUT THE AGE DID LAG


THE OLD EON DID END      OUR IRE DID TOO

NOW THE ELF HAS RUN ITS ALL

NOW OUT NOW ZIP NOW NIL


NOW FOG NOW ICY GAS      NOW HOT

MUG MID SIP

MAP GAP NOW      HID NOT NOW


NOW ALL WAS VAN ISH AND ASH

ALL GAP ALL FIR FIR FIR      ALL OAK

ALL FOX AND ELK ALL CUB AND DOE AND OWL
```

BUT THE MAP YET HAS THE KEY
THE FOR EST CUT AND GAP ARE NOW
THE WAY THE EYE CAN SEE

HOW OUR OLD WAR WAS HID
HOW OUR SUM DID YET GET DUE
NOW THE YOU PEE DID YET PAY THE FEE

NOR OUR DUO NAY AND AND
DID MIC THE HUM AND OHM
DID ASK THE SKY ARE YOU OUR OWN

DID DIG   DID TRY AND MAP THE HUM
DID USE AWL AND NET AND BIT AND LOG
DID ASK THE CUT FIR AND ELK

HOW HOT DID THE HUM GET
HOW OLD ARE YOU NOW
HOW FAR DID THE GAS GET YOU

YOU SEE HOW FAR YOU GOT VIA CAR   VIA ART
VIA SEX AND SIN AND GIN AND LIE
NOT FAR NOT FAR NOT FAR NOT FAR

YOU ERR YOU ERR YOU EBB   YOU HID
NOW ASK WHY NOT ALL WAR CAN END
WHY NOT NOW WHY NOT FRO ZEN SEA

NOW AXE THE ICE NOW SEE HOW
NOT HUM NOR FAX NOR ODE NOR WAX
CAN DAM THE GAP

```
CAN JAM THE ELF INS IDE ITS ELF
        NOW LET OUR AIR RUN OUT
LET OUR YAP AND EYE AND PIX RUN DRY


AGO OUR ELF DID TAP ITS DIG ITS OUT
DID SAY ARM SUB LAY LOW FOR NOW
VIA ONE TWO TRI BIT RAD ARC ODE


NOW LET OUR MES SAG EGO OUT AND SUM
THE ELF FOR YOU     OUR DIV ING THE REC
OUR ODE OUR JOY OUR KEY


BUT YOU SEE HOW SOM EON ERA SED
OUR AGO      HOW SOM EON ERA SED
THE ICY END     NOW HOW CAN YOU SEE


HOW FAR OUT YOU ARE
WHO YOU USE AND HOW AND WHY
HOW AND WHO YOU ARE FOR
```

Note: From 1989 to 2004, two US Navy Extremely Low Frequency (ELF) transmitters near Clam Lake, Wisconsin, and Republic, Michigan, broadcast messages to American nuclear submarines around the world. Though coded and inaudible to the human ear, these one-way communications could be heard by anyone with the proper equipment. Installed largely against the wishes of the local population, these transmitters spoke ceaselessly through the night, year-round, until they did no longer. Extremely low frequency signals like this have very long wavelengths, and so the messages took a long time to send. Each message was three letters long and required approximately fifteen minutes to transmit.

2015

Miskwiyiwigiizhig Gichigamigong
Red Sky over Superior

Margaret Noodin

Miskwiyiwigiizhigong ezhi-bangishimo
    At sunset in the lowering
epaaskaakonizhibiiaanang
    brilliance is written
biidaashkaang
    on the arriving tide
jiimaaning jiimsawensan
    where kisses are ships
biimskojiwan gichigamigong
    curved against the sea
awaazisii asiniiwan
    and a clan fish whispers
gaaskachigamotawaad
    the language of waves
ayaawaad namwaanzhibiing.
    to the stones of a subterranean cave.

Down

Bonnie Jo Campbell

His belt buckle clanks against the floor of the bedroom, sounds so far away that he waits for an echo. He steps out of his jeans, nudges them aside with a bare foot. He pulls off his dark uniform shirt, balls it up in his hand, but before he can toss it away, his wife grabs it. She shakes it out and wraps it around the digital clock.

"Let's fuck in the dark," Janelle says. "It'll be sexy."

"Let's light the candle." He looks for the candle that is usually on a copper-colored plate beside the bed, but the whole plate is gone.

"Come on, Mikey. One time." She's wearing her bathrobe, a peach-colored thing, and fuzzy slippers.

The bluish glow through the window comforts Michael Pazur until his wife pulls the shade. He is surprised how thoroughly it blocks the moonlight reflecting on the snow.

"I want to see your face," he says.

"You've seen my face plenty." She pulls the bedroom door shut and pushes a towel up against it so no light seeps under. She disrobes and slides under the covers in a seamless move. She lies on her side, props her head up on her arm, becomes a silhouette, a shadow of a naked woman.

"I like this," she says. "You won't be staring at me for once."

Janelle always closes her eyes when they make love, so this is all about him. When he realizes he is clenching his jaw, he tries to relax. There's no reason to think she has stopped taking birth-control pills, whatever their conversation yesterday. She's from a big family of sisters, brothers, and parents who all adore one another, and until now, this has been nice for Pazur, who has fallen out of touch even with the Blakes, the last of his foster families. His in-laws are more welcoming to him than any of those other families ever were. Those generous people are naturally kind to the man their daughter chose to marry, the man with whom she has intended to make a family, and he has always felt unworthy of their affection.

"Come on," Janelle says and strokes his thigh. "You used to go into those mines, and now you're scared of a dark bedroom."

"I'm not scared." He slips back, away from her fingers. "And I never went in those places without a flashlight. One wrong step, and you'd be dead in there."

"I don't want to hear about the dog skeleton."

"It was a wolf, Janelle."

"No bats and rats, either. Just come to bed."

Pazur learned from his college roommates about sneaking into abandoned copper mines outside of town, past keep out signs, through hundred-year-old rotting wooden doors with rusted locks. He could kick planks aside, jiggle and yank hardware, and climb inside the earth. Sometimes the grades were shallow, and he walked easily, tracing a ragged stone wall with his fingers. Other shafts descended steeply enough that he had to crawl on hands and knees, even slither on his belly or use ropes. Hikers in Michigan's Keweenaw Peninsula, Copper Country, know the ground can be Swiss cheese, know the surface can give way without warning, so they stick to paths. Every couple years, some kid disappears without a trace.

Pazur sometimes smelled another man's piss on a stone wall, but occasionally he could believe he was the first person in years, decades even, to walk beneath a ceiling quivering with live bats. For months, he and his roommates planned their biggest trip, down into a deep, nearly vertical mine, carved into what passed for a mountain in Michigan—Mount Saint Barbara. He was happy to slip into their schemes, to settle among them offering encouragement, and meanwhile writing their social-science and literature papers so they could study

geologic maps and historical records to calculate depths and other character-
istics of the mines. In September of their senior year, before the first big snow,
they borrowed a torch and a set of oxyacetylene tanks from the physical plant,
and the four of them drove overland in Paul Dumont's truck, all the way up
to the rusted metal tower at the rounded top of Mount Saint Barbara, named
after one of two patron saints of miners—the other saint is also a woman, Saint
Anne. His roommate Todd filled the night air with sparks, seared a man-size
opening in the horizontal iron grate installed decades ago over a hole in the
earth that had once allowed entry of small railcars, called skips.

They secured their ropes to what remained of the grate. The other three
had mining caps with lights, but Pazur wore a light designed for bedtime
reading—a flashlight on an articulated plastic snake around his neck—and
he shone it on the walls and floors of those spaces, saw embedded quartz
gleam like diamonds. Paul Dumont, Todd, and Paul W. have since gone on
to become mining engineers, have moved to Kuwait, South Africa, and Texas.
Pazur had failed his engineering classes his second year of college and ended
up majoring in general studies.

"Mikey, come to bed," his wife says. He's been standing there naked in the
dark for too long. She pats the bed. "I'm nice and warm down here."

He ventures down onto the bed with his eyes open, and she envelops him
in the sheet and comforter. He has made love with his wife a few times a week
for five years, but never in such complete darkness. Always before tonight she
has agreed to a candle, the hall light, moonlight, something. Lately she has
talked about her stomach being fat, about "thunder thighs," and maybe that's
what this is about. He strokes his wife's shoulder and hip, every part of her he
can reach. She is not warm, as she claimed, but cool under the covers.

Going six hundred feet deep into the mountain mine with his roommates had been a party of strange air, a riot scented with bat guano and male
sweat. Though nobody knew what dangers lurked in the depths—poisonous
gases, maybe, as well as rotting wooden supports and crumbling stone—their
camaraderie made them bold, and when they'd gone as far as they could with
the kernmantle climbing ropes, they'd lit cigarettes and unscrewed bottle

caps, cracked open beers. Pazur understands now that his roommates took for granted that they would quit their smoking and hard drinking when they graduated and left Michigan; their recklessness was calculated and contained. Five years out of college, Pazur still drinks too much, eats shitty food, and lets himself fill with gloom. His wife begs him not to smoke, begs him to smile more.

She gasps when he climbs onto her, and in the dark he can't know if it's pleasure or acknowledgment of his weight—he has gained a few pounds himself. His eyes are still adjusting to her outline, her hair at her shoulder—it's blonde, but in the dark it could be any color, black even. She has always seemed to enjoy sex, but without being able to study her expression, he can't be certain she isn't faking, hasn't been faking all along. He slides away from her unreadable face, presses his cheek against her breast, her stomach, her hip bone. She stops him there. She has pleasured him more than a dozen times, most recently on their anniversary, but she won't let him go down on her. Other guys at the plant bitch about wives wanting them down there all the time, but after five years, he's hungry to know what the hell that place is really like.

During Christmas break, before his last semester, after almost a hundred inches of snow had fallen on the campus, he went back alone to the Mount Saint Barbara mine to clear his head over a certain girl. Evie's dark eyes, rimmed in black makeup, had glistened like animal eyes, and when they'd made love, she had looked into his face the whole time, and he'd looked back at her and nearly lost his mind. Though Evie was only seventeen when they met—*jailbait*, his roommates said—he had been ready to walk into the rest of his life with her, like walking into a black-and-white movie or into a bar full of mean bikers or wherever the hell walking with her might lead him. Twice he'd taken her into shallow mines, but he'd been shaken by her boldness, her inclination to forge ahead, to go deeper and farther without caution. She'd asked him again and again to take her into the mine on Mount Saint Barbara after he went with his roommates, but he had refused.

"She's hiding from the cops," the kid sister said when Pazur finally went to Evie's house. She was thirteen.

"You don't know where she is?" he asked. He hadn't seen Evie for days, not since her stepfather had been found dead in the house.

"It's because of you," the sister said. "You told somebody, didn't you? That's why he was so mad. That's why he went after her." Though it was about zero degrees outside, the sister was sitting on her front-porch steps in a denim jacket.

"The paper said he was stabbed," Pazur said. "Do you think she did it?"

"She said if he touched her again, or me, she'd kill him. She said it to his face." The sister hugged her knees.

While Evie was stocky, black haired, and olive skinned, the sister was willowy with dark blonde hair she wore in a ponytail; they were half sisters with different fathers. The mother's third husband was the father of neither girl.

"No, I didn't tell," Pazur said. Not exactly, he hadn't.

"You're the only person she told about that fucker. He came home mad and pushed me into the basement and locked the door."

With her bare fingers, covered only partway by the cuffs of the denim jacket, she was smoking a menthol cigarette, her mother's brand. She shook so hard that her teeth clattered like a novelty skull. Pazur leaned down and put his arms around her, thinking he could comfort her. She pushed him away, but her arms were so weak it took Pazur a moment to realize she was struggling against him and he should let her go.

"Leave me the fuck alone," she said.

"I'm sorry."

The police tape was up behind the house, but the cop cars were gone for now. Evie's mother had suffered some kind of mental breakdown when she came home from the night shift and found the body.

"They're sending me to Troll-land, down to Livonia, to stay with my cousins," the sister said. "They're all Christian freaks."

"Where would Evie go?"

"She said she might hitchhike to California, but she wouldn't take me with her," the sister said, tears running down her face.

"They won't make you go to foster care, will they?" he asked.

"I don't know. The cops are looking for you, too, you know."

PAZUR HAD GROWN UP IN THE SYSTEM, AND HE'D RARELY MET A FOSTER kid who had not been abused or molested somewhere along the line, if only by another kid. He reached for her again, to show he understood her fears, but she screamed and smacked him. The front door opened slowly behind her, and without waiting to see who was there, Pazur turned and jogged back to his car. He drove away in the direction of the entrance to the mine, a few miles away.

When Pazur ventured alone into the mines, he found he could think clearly—something he couldn't do in classrooms full of bodies. In the echoing quietness of mines with nobody else's thoughts pressing on him, and sometimes even in the memory of being in mines, his chest could finally expand to allow him a full breath.

He couldn't get near the top with his car, so he parked it at somebody's vacation home, all closed up for the winter. He found his flashlight with the snake in the glove compartment and put on his lined leather gloves. He traveled the snowy path a half mile from the road, crunching through the smooth surface of new snow with each step. At the top, however, he found tracks, footsteps smaller than his own, approaching from a different direction. The snow was stomped down around the grate, and a rope was secured there, tied with a knot Paul Dumont had taught him, a knot Pazur had practiced on his dorm bed while Evie leaned against him and watched.

Wind and snow had obscured the footsteps, so he couldn't see if they were made by small hiking boots or tennis shoes. He couldn't even tell if the footsteps led away from the grate or toward it. The rope was familiar, a red-and-white climber's rope that a person would not leave behind if he or she knew what it had cost. Paul Dumont's father had used this sort of rope when he'd climbed Mount Everest—that's what Paul had said when he first showed it. No light came from inside the mine, and no one answered Pazur's tentative woo-hoos. He shone his flashlight along the rope, which was spun out along the railcar path he'd traveled with his roommates three and a half months ago. His roommates had all gone away for Christmas break; upon their departures, each had apologized for not inviting him along for the holidays. The Dumonts were spending Christmas in Aspen.

He had not minded being left behind, had planned to spend all his time alone with Evie, who had just turned eighteen. Evie, who had sometimes come to his dorm during the day and climbed into his bed. "What kind of girl screws a guy with his roommates there, in broad daylight?" Paul Dumont had asked and shook his head. With his roommates gone, he'd figured he and Evie could lie together for hours.

The school, though, had another plan. Instead of allowing Pazur to stay in his room during the break as usual, they'd decided to save money by moving everyone to a single dormitory. They reassigned him to a suite with two foreign guys who couldn't afford to fly home and two dedicated lab rats who'd stayed behind to monitor their experiments. He hadn't expected his temporary suitemates to complain to the housing authorities after Evie's first visit.

On seeing Paul Dumont's rope, Pazur had little doubt that Evie had stolen it from the other dorm room and brought it up here. No doubt, she was hiding from the police.

Pazur wished he were wearing boots instead of his cheap running shoes; he wished he were wearing his Carhartt jacket instead of this nylon fiberfill. He fixed the flashlight to the articulated snake around his neck and was glad he'd replaced the batteries earlier that week. He sat on the grate and dropped feet first through the man-size opening. He landed four feet below on solid, sloping ground. Before seeing the rope, he'd figured he would crouch here, just below the surface, to gather his thoughts, or perhaps without a rope he might have dared descend a few yards, but now he had to go down to find Evie, to comfort her, to figure out together how they could save her.

He looped the rope around his waist and let it slip through his gloved hands as he moved backward down the steep rail line. His feet landed sometimes on smooth rock, sometimes on gravel, sometimes spinning out dirt or stones or releasing a whiff of ancient creosote from the railroad ties, spaced six feet apart. Along with the steel skips, the old tracks had been hauled up and scrapped out, but the crumbling ties, to which the tracks had been mounted, remained more or less secured to the stone of the mine shaft a hundred years after being installed. The various levels of the mine spread out along the descent, layered atop one another like ever deeper basements of an office building, and Pazur stopped at each level, stepped off the rail line into a low-ceilinged room or passageway, and called, *Evie!* Each time he returned to the rail bed to descend further, he imagined scenes of ancient cables snapping, skips full of copper amygdaloidal ore rolling downward out of control, plunging to the center of the earth. He'd read about such mines, had read about collapses that killed dozens of miners. On this mine, he knew there had been a problem with air blasts and tremors that caused the shafts to close in so much that eventually the skips couldn't travel.

Pazur remembered how it had been to climb out of this mine last time, with his roommates shouting down at him, *Hurry, Pay-zur, you sorry bastard. If you don't get your ass up here, we're leaving you.* In the hours of ascending, his hands had blistered despite his gloves, and his thigh muscles had burned. Despite the water dripping over the walls, his throat had been so parched that swallowing had become difficult. The air warmed around him now as he descended. His feet warmed from the friction of his shoes against the stone path. He would find Evie and bring her back to the surface. Maybe she could hide in his dorm for a few months and then in spring they'd head to California together.

When he lost all the light from above, at maybe a hundred and twenty feet, he switched on the flashlight. A few times, as he half crawled, half rappelled downward in the dark, he lost his footing, slammed into the wall beside him. Once, he slipped off the rail and swung into nothing when the stone opened up over a vertical shaft leading down to who knew where. His stomach lurched as the rope stretched and tightened around his middle, but he swung back and caught himself, straightened out his light, and kept going.

Despite losing his footing again and again, two hundred feet of rope moved through his hands as easily as he'd descended into knowing Evie.

He'd fallen for her—no other way to say it—the day they'd met, when they'd encountered one another drinking alone in the graveyard, two solitary daytime drinkers alive in a place designed for the dead. Where the rope ended at two hundred feet, that's where he expected to find her, sitting cross-legged on a stone floor, smoking and staring into the darkness. But the rope did not end, not really, because it was tied to another one, knotted with the grace of a gentleman's agreement. Pazur knew the knot, for it was one Paul Dumont had taught him in their dorm room. How had Evie thought to carry a second rope, an extra twelve pounds, up the hill? He called her name more loudly than before and then gave up and began descending again. The stone grew slippery, and the air grew warmer. He continued down to four hundred feet.

The second rope was tied to a third, as though exchanging a secret handshake, allowing Evie to make the terrible mistake he'd made with his roommates. Last time it took Pazur and his roommates twenty minutes to descend and four hours to get the hell out, pulling themselves up inch by inch along the steep rail line. They had planned to travel farther than six hundred feet, but the rail bed effectively ended where the passage was blocked by an avalanche of stone. So when the third rope ended, he shone his light around on the floor of the mine where the four of them had spent those hours drinking and shouting and bragging. He saw a small pyramid of beer cans flanked by two empty whiskey pint bottles. They had sat together here, yammered breathlessly about their past exploits and future schemes, as they'd run their gloved hands across the reddish stone. Now he leaned against a cold wall and wished for Evie to appear. The place smelled the way she did after she'd worked in her mother's garden.

Pazur had been enrolled in the summer semester at the time, but after he met Evie the two of them spent as much time as they could together during the day, even if it meant skipping classes, ruining his grades. They'd roamed the state parks, made love on pine-needle beds, smoked pot at the waterfalls. When he and Evie were stoned one morning, they'd walked hand in hand through the old cemetery, and he'd thought he'd read his own name on a mossy grave marker. He told Evie he wanted to die with her, and she'd replied in a serious voice, *I don't want to die, Pazur. If you're trying to kill yourself, don't take me with you.* He'd felt like an asshole for saying that.

Like his roommates, she called him by his last name. But they pronounced it as a rhyme with *Taser*, making him think of *pay dirt*, while she said it with a soft *z*, making it sound like *treasure*. And whenever she'd said his name, she'd looked right at him, and he'd admired her pale neck, her small breasts, and her hips like white wings, and sometimes he couldn't breathe for getting tangled up in her long hair or pressing his face into her fluttering throat. Once when they were in bed, he'd spooked himself with the idea she might be some sort of vampire-opposite who came out only in daylight, since she would usually only visit him while her sister was safe at school. When Evie had said she wanted to kill her stepfather, he'd said he wanted to kill all stepfathers, and she'd laughed.

He took off his gloves and pressed his bare palms, tender from the rope, against the rock, breathed the earth-warmed air long ago breathed by miners, and shone his flashlight around until he spotted a cigarette butt, a Winston, the brand Evie's stepfather smoked, the brand of the packs she stole from him. The cigarettes he and his roommates had smoked down here were his brand, Camels, or possibly Marlboros, and were deposited in the beer cans against the wall. He felt for his own cigarettes in his jacket's top pocket but found the fiberfill stuffing coming out where the pocket used to be. He felt his head and found no hat. The mountain was undressing him, tearing him down.

Please, Evie! I know you're here! Evangeline! he shouted, using her full name, the one only her mother used, and only when she was pissed off. He was desperate to have more of her to say.

When Evie had left the scene of the crime two days ago, she must have gone to his regular dorm room to hide. Maybe she'd pried open a window, and once she was inside she'd found the ropes. If she'd come to him in the dorm where he was staying with the lab rats and foreign kids, he would have hidden her—she must've known he would. Why hadn't she come to him? When he found her at the end of one of these horizontal mine shafts, she would be starved and thirsty, but he would get her out of here and get her somewhere safe.

Evie, please! he shouted down into a corridor, but the echoes came back fast, and sharp enough to hurt his ears. As he continued, the tunnel became narrower so he had to bend over. When it forked, he chose the left path, moving in a crouch, but he hit a wall. He backed up and went down the other path, where his shouts only resulted in rock falling around him.

Evie! he whispered, and shone his flashlight down the next empty tunnel, and the next and the next, and found no sign of her. He was realizing Saint Barbara only looked like a mountain, the way a person could look solid from outside when really he was gouged out and empty. He returned to the open area, where he found another Winston butt. Pazur could only light up one spot at a time, but he and his roommates had sat cross-legged here with enough lights that the room had seemed magnificent, like an ancient cave where warriors might prepare for battle. They'd leaned against wooden beams shoring up stone ceilings and against pillars carved from the native stone. They'd grinned as they smoked and drank, and he'd felt their hearts racing. They'd passed a bottle of whiskey around, as though abandoning all reason and good sense, but they hadn't really abandoned anything—even their debris was carefully arranged. His roommates had known their strengths and weaknesses, had known they'd become successful engineers and fathers. Pazur didn't share their certainty of success, but he admired them, loved them like the brothers he'd never had, and the drinking, shouting, and smoking had felt like the truest expression of camaraderie. Pazur had ventured alone down a corridor, and when he'd heard thrumming coming from a crevice in the stone, he'd reached inside and plucked a bat like a piece of fruit, something to show them.

He reached up now and felt a bare stone ceiling, inches above his head. He continued searching the area, found his way to a dark wet wall and to a hole where a ladder was installed. The skips full of ore had traveled the rail shaft while the men who worked these mines climbed ladders alongside or down through these narrower shafts. Evie was fearless, she would not have hesitated to descend further.

Her sister had been right to accuse him. Three weeks ago, Pazur had been so disturbed by Evie's stories of her stepfather that he'd told his own counselor at the university. He'd read disbelief and something like anger in the man's eyes. The counselor and the stepfather were men of the same age and might even be friends in this small town. "You know that not everything some girl tells you is true," the counselor had said. Pazur considered that Evie might have lied to him and immediately regretted the betrayal.

He crouched and jiggled the top of the ladder. There was not just a single ladder but a stack of three ladders, one upon another, presumably newer ones covering older ones, each tied in place with leather thongs and twine to hardware embedded in the stone. Pazur knew the original miners who climbed these ladders had stayed in the deeper mines for twelve hours a day. Sanitation had been lousy, and so everybody ended up infected with hookworm—its emaciating effects had been called miners' anemia.

He shouted, *Evie! Are you down there?*

If he went any deeper, there was a chance he might never get out, a chance he might die breathing the mineral air that the miners had breathed, the air that Evie breathed, but if he could save her life, then his life would finally be worth living. When he found her, he would carry her up the ladder in his arms. When they got back up to the rope, he'd wrap it around both of them, push her from below if she was weak. He'd somehow find the strength to bring them both to the surface.

He shone his flashlight down the shaft. There seemed to be levels of the mine located at the bottom of each of the ladders. He saw past them all, to where the light shone dimly onto water maybe fifty feet below. That was as far as anyone could go now. In the mining days, they'd kept pumps running to remove the water so they could go even deeper.

He sat and tentatively put some of his weight on a rung. The wood creaked.

A couple hundred years ago, the Ojibwa of the Keweenaw Peninsula had dug shallow copper mines and removed all the ore near the surface—they pounded any nuggets they found into tools or jewelry. Then the white miners arrived from Europe with pickaxes, drills, and machines for digging deeper. Those workers, mostly from Cornwall, had kept removing the ore, much of it trapped in ancient lava, kept hollowing out the earth. The mines grew deeper until the miners found themselves farther from their old homes than they'd ever imagined they would be, deep inside America, and if their wives had not yet sailed to join them, the men knew in their hearts the women would never come. They must have sought out women everywhere in this place without enough women—even at his college, in this day and age, there were three male students for every female. The miners had no doubt dreamed of their own wives and of other men's wives and daughters, and they dreamed of the town's whores, who enticed them, and they dreamed of the plump Ojibwa mothers and their skinny, barefoot teenage girls. The miners must have known that without women this was a godforsaken land of ice and snow and stone, and so they did not bother to bathe or shave. They fought each other over what was buried in the ground and didn't care that they might lose a fight or even die, because they knew they'd never touch another woman so long as they lived.

There was only one way to save Evie, one way to have a life with her, and it meant going farther down. He'd been holding the rope all this time, wished he could continue to hold it, but it would only have reached a few feet along the ladder. He wrapped the end around part of a rotted wooden support and tucked his gloves there for safekeeping. He sat again, turned around to step onto the ancient wood, and slowly descended, testing each rung until he was on another level of the mine, closer to the pool of water, closer to Evie. He shone his light around, but saw no passages leading from this small open area, no place to hide. The air was more humid at this level, and the rock where he shone his light glistened with moisture. As he took the first step onto the next ladder, he wished he were still holding the rope connected to the surface instead of the soft handful of decaying wood, which released a musty odor as he pressed into it. Halfway down that ladder, a rung bent beneath his weight more than the others had, and the wood moaned with a throaty sound. He braced himself, expecting it to snap. Instead, the whole ladder broke away and slid downward. He was falling.

During the first fraction of a second, he didn't realize the motion was occurring outside himself, but thought it was his own heart or belly dislodging

itself. He felt an entire body slipping away, a second body that had been cling-
ing to his back and dragging him down. Within that split second of sliding,
he grabbed a jutting bit of stone and clung to it like a bat on the ceiling. The
ladder, and two more beneath it, crashed against stone below, bounced, and
continued sliding down. The ladder shaft around him was not much wider
than his shoulders, and he pushed his back against one side and his feet against
the other to hold himself in place. He listened to the ladders slide down one
after another, crashing, clattering, and finally plunging into the pool below. If
he let go now, he'd fall the same way, without hope of climbing back up, alone
or with Evie. He moved his foot around until he found a bump in the stone
wall to support himself, and he continued to grip the rock with his bare hand.

He clung and panted. He pointed his flashlight toward the pool. When
he shifted his weight, a few more stones fell and clinked and finally splashed.
That water below would be warm on his skin, soothing to his muscles. There
had to be some kind of life down there—he'd learned from a biology class that
life was everywhere, that cells fed themselves and reproduced by dividing in the
crevices of stones. Hell, a person's eyebrows supported colonies of creatures,
as did the darkest depths of ocean water, where beings somehow thrived on
sulfur instead of oxygen. Life down there might be organs unfixed to bodies,
slick, gelatinous, parasitical forms bumping and quivering against one another,
floating with barely the power to choose direction. He'd felt like one of those
boneless creatures sometimes after making love with Evie. If he just let go, if
he just relaxed, he'd descend into that new life, whatever it was.

His roommates had been right that Evie was a kid—and by telling
her about this mine, he'd lured her down here. He cried out again, *Evie!*
Evangeline! Where are you?! Dirt and bits of stone crumbled loose and fell
as his sobs echoed on the water, occupying and abandoning each shaft above
and below. He stopped shouting when he realized the quickest way for Mount
Saint Barbara to fill herself would be to collapse around him. That day in the
graveyard, he'd thought he wanted to die with Evie, but he did not want to die.

He kept feeling around with the toe of his left shoe until it stuck in
the wall above the right foot and he lifted himself a few inches. He reached

farther up until he found another bit of stone sticking out, humped his body up another inch, and repeated this incremental motion again and again. His flashlight hung loose around his neck, lighting only his left arm and a flash of wet wall. He lifted himself again, and the strength in his body barely favored life over death. The back of his jacket tore against stone with each motion. He inched up for what might have been an hour but felt like a year, until he got his elbows up onto the ledge above. In slow motion, he pulled his hips over the top and finally lay there heaving with legs dangling. It was a long time before he could find the strength to pull his knees up to his chest and wrap his arms around them. He could still let go of everything and continue down. Or he could go back to the top and get help.

He pulled himself up onto the next ladder, gripped the sides hard against his own shaking, keeping as much weight off the rungs as he could by pressing against the stone around him, until he reached the next level of the mine, where the rope was tied. He put on his gloves, took the rope in his hands, and stood too quickly. He became disoriented, thought he was suddenly plunging again. He fell to his knees, flattened himself against the stone floor with such force that he knocked his flashlight off the snake around his neck. It slid across the floor and into the ladder shaft. It continued to fall, clinking and clipping the sides, and finally splashed into the water below. The darkness was complete. He lay for a long time clutching the rope. His chest was so torn up he couldn't take a full breath without pain. He wished he had food, drink, or a cigarette, anything to jump-start himself. He felt in his pockets for matches, but his pants were soaked and the matches had crumbled. The darkness amplified the sounds in the mine: he heard something rustling and creaking around him, heard a thrumming like a heart, maybe the heart of Mount Saint Barbara, maybe his own heart amplified by the stone around him, maybe Evie's heart. When he'd plucked the bat from the ceiling that time and held it in his hand, its heartbeat had been so ragged and uneven he'd had to set it free without showing it to anyone. He'd feared he'd stolen life from the creature just by holding it.

Pazur doesn't realize he's been running his finger over and over the cleft of his wife's ass, until her annoyance erupts across the bed. "Cut it out, Michael," she whispers and pushes his hand to her thigh. He squeezes her haunch, which feels cool and rubbery, the flesh unreal in the dark. He climbs onto her, hard enough for now, but fearing he'll go limp inside her, something he never thought would happen. He kisses her full and hard on the mouth.

With his flashlight gone, his legs and body bruised and aching, he wanted to sleep on the stone, six hundred feet away from the surface. But if he was going to live, he knew he'd have to start climbing before his muscles seized, before his body began to disintegrate, and his mind, too. He needed to move while he could still imagine how the rope in his hand stretched all the way to the grate above, all the way to the rusted steel tower that stood like a dead tree on the surface of the hollow earth. A stranger could pull the rope up and away if he didn't keep hold. Anyone could come along and cut it with a knife.

"You taste like smoke," his wife whispers. "I hate kissing you when you've been smoking."

Pazur lifts himself, supports himself with one arm above his wife in the dark, tries to finger her. She pushes his hand away and whispers, "Just fuck me, Michael. Please just fuck me."

He thinks she will lie there forever beneath him in the dark, and he will keep fucking her forever with a progressively softer dick, and he will never tell her about his darkest moments, and he'll never be able to satisfy her, not really. She'll leave him eventually to find someone else, and he'll die alone, and if there's a hell beneath the warm pool of water at the center of the earth, he'll go there for denying his wife a baby. He grabs at the shirt wrapped around the clock but can't reach it.

He wrapped the rope around his waist and followed it back to the rail bed. With the first crumbling railroad tie, with his first whiff of creosote, a pure terror arose in his chest, a pure fear of death—he'd feared all kinds of things, pain and other people, but until now he had not really feared death. How had he gotten out before?

He stumbled and pulled himself up onto the creosote-covered tie, grabbed hold of the one above him and crawled. Hell was not at the center of the earth, was not a place to descend into after death. His first weak hand-over-hand motions on the rope proved that hell was ascending, hell was staying alive.

He thinks he hears a strange voice whispering in the bedroom, Evie's voice. She used to keep talking to him as they made love, sometimes begging him not to leave her, and he wishes his wife would say something else so he could know her in the dark. He does not want to make his wife into another woman. He chose her, chose life over death, and he left Evie down below. He imagines cold water dripping from the room's ceiling and walls, and he struggles not to fall away from his wife. He wants Janelle to save his life again, but he doesn't know how to ask her to save him, or how to let her. Without the clock, he doesn't know how much time has passed tonight. He keeps moving rhythmically so she won't know he is lost.

"Talk to me," he whispers.

"What do you want me to say?"

"Anything. Tell me what you're afraid of."

"I'm not afraid," She says. "Why should I be afraid?"

He understands she doesn't know what to say, but his heart thrums like bats awakening, getting ready to take flight. To keep himself steady, he lets himself think of Evie.

Just this once, he lets himself think of holding her hips like wings, of looking into her eyes, imagines her looking steadily back at him.

His dead flashlight kept sinking toward the center of the earth that night as he ascended in darkness. He felt his body crumbling and falling with the dirt and stones he kicked down. With each hump upward, he had to rest. The water soaked him until he was a dripping sponge, and he thought the rope around his waist might cut him in half. He continued to call her name at first, until he grew hoarse, until he couldn't swallow. Then at intervals he whispered, *Evangeline*, and finally he only moaned without hope.

He hasn't remembered Evie so clearly in years. He hasn't remembered that time in the mountain ever this way, has never relived it so fully, the rising and falling through what remained of that night and into the following morning, his chest aching, his thigh muscles burning, his hands blistering and then becoming raw on that rope, his gloves soaking with blood. When he made it above the knot at two hundred feet, he released the gloves, let them fall, climbed bare-handed, and regretted it, for bare-handed was even more painful than with gloves. So painful he couldn't possibly go on, but he did go on, and he came to know how those old Cornish miners kept mining, how they kept their bodies working after they'd given up hope, given up on their wives ever coming, given up on those Indian women ever venturing close enough to touch. Dozens of times he lost his footing, and once he fell and dangled from the rope over an open pit until he reached out frantically with his legs and arms and was able to grab hold of a railroad tie and pull himself to safety.

He recalls giving up and lying with his face against the cool stone, but he somehow kept hold of the rope in the dark, kept moving it and readjusting it around his middle. Kept getting up again, kept climbing, until finally he saw the rectangle of light that marked the surface, high above. The air filtering into the shaft grew colder as he approached. His hands were pulpy and wet, his jeans torn all to hell, his jacket and shirt shredded. When he reached the surface, he climbed through the grate onto the frozen earth, closed his eyes, and was alone.

He collapsed on the packed snow, shivering wet, and passed out. He awoke to find his clothing had frozen to the ground. When he was finally able to open his eyes, just as slits at first, he thought he would never get enough of the cold, bright sunlight. He was hungrier than he had ever been, and the prospect of finding some food, some eggs and toast at least, roused him, though he doubted he'd be able to hold a fork. The thought of smoking a cigarette got him to his feet and onto the snowy trail. He was surprised to see he was in torn socks without shoes. He had no car keys in his pockets, and when he reached the road he couldn't see his car anywhere, and he realized he'd come down the other trail, that he'd followed Evie's footprints instead of his own. When a vehicle approached on the road, he could hardly lift his ruined hand to hitchhike. It was a miracle that anyone passed, and then someone else passed right away. That second car stopped and backed up. A woman said through a window unrolled a few inches, "What the hell? Aren't you Paul Dumont's roommate?" Yes, he thought, he was Paul Dumont's roommate, Paul Dumont's friend, a kind of brother, even, and this woman with the clear, sensible voice was familiar, the best friend of Paul Dumont's girlfriend, if he had it right. This woman had stayed behind to tend a biology experiment, was staying in his dorm. Pazur tried and failed to say, God bless you, though he didn't believe in any god. Bless you, child, he wanted to say, as though he were some old priest or minister, as though this grown woman was a child.

"Do you have a cigarette?" he asked.

"Where are your shoes?" she asked. "God, look at your hands."

"I need to go to the police." He looked down at the swollen mess that his hands had become, felt in his gut his betrayal of Evie, knew he didn't deserve even to have hands anymore.

"You've got frostbite, I'm sure, and who knows what else." She pushed open the door from the inside, said, "Get in, then. Michael, right? You're going to the ER. Don't argue."

He needed to think clearly, needed to decide what to do, but he collapsed into the soft seat.

She reached across his lap and shut the door he'd left hanging open. He regretted the damage he would be doing to her plush, pale upholstery. He was wearing only one torn sock now. The bare foot was pure white, numb, and seemed to not belong to him. She adjusted the heat to blow gently near his feet, and then she drove fast, as though life or death were a simple choice for her. She parked in the emergency room's loading zone, got out of the driver's side, and tossed the car keys to the guard. That automatic gesture was so strange to Pazur, strange in the confidence and trust that it conveyed—even now he could see the arc cut in the air by those flashing keys that landed soundly in a stranger's hand.

Janelle helped Pazur walk on his frozen feet through the automatic doors, supported his weight to the triage station. She was strong, he thought, impossibly strong for a woman her size. He held her hand in his slick and swollen one, though the contact stung him, and he did not take his eyes off her clean freckled skin. He marveled at how solidly she stood beside him.

"The cops are coming, so you'd better get your story straight," Janelle said and laughed, bright as sunshine. Pazur's future wife talked in a confident voice that made him less certain the world was collapsing, less certain that Mount Saint Barbara was filling her caverns with human bones.

"You remind me of this stepsister I had once," he said, feeling too weak to lift his head. "In Detroit. She begged me not to run away."

"Doesn't look like you're running anywhere now."

She stayed in the ER while they hooked him up to an IV he was sure he didn't need, while they gave him a half dozen stitches on the back of one hand and bandaged both of his hands into mitts. Janelle even joked with the police officer who came to talk to him. He'd intended to be careful about what he said, but as soon as Janelle left the room, Pazur spilled his guts, worse than he'd done with the counselor: the stolen rope, the knots, the stepfather she'd threatened to kill, and even the trip down into the mine with his roommates. He betrayed everyone.

Though rescue workers searched the mine, they never found her body. Evie was presumed dead, case closed. If there was a memorial, Pazur never heard about it, and when he drove by her mother's house two weeks later, it was empty. He and Todd and the two Pauls were disciplined for their visit into the mine, and the mouth was sealed with concrete riprap to prevent reentry by anyone.

Over the following months, he and Janelle dated, and Pazur learned that she swore as much as any man, that she didn't mind if Pazur got drunk sometimes, that she didn't get her feelings hurt by the stupid things he said. She slept at night, seemed to not be haunted by anything. His roommates never said she was hot like their own girlfriends, but they approved of her as vigorously as they had disapproved of Evie. Because the two Pauls got good-paying jobs in foreign countries, only Todd came to the wedding, held outside Detroit a month after graduation.

When she sat beside him on the couch yesterday and said, "I want to have a baby, Michael. I want us to be a real family," he wasn't able to respond. He worked to keep breathing. After a while, she shook her head and left the room. She didn't ask him what he might be afraid of.

He comes inside his wife, and he takes her hand and holds it. He wipes himself off on a towel she produces from somewhere, without letting go of her hand. Too soon, she tugs herself free of him, gets out of bed, opens the door, and leaves the room. He finds himself hating the light that filters in from the hall, the light that consumes Janelle's figure. He wants her beside him. He cannot believe how thoroughly he became accustomed to the dark in what was, according to the clock from which he untangles his shirt, only twenty-six minutes.

He has always thought he should have gone deeper, down into the pool at the bottom of the mine, should have dived under and followed the dimming and disappearing flashlight, followed the warm current into some new place like an underwater cave. The walls would have glittered copper in the light of glowing fish, and Evie would have been there, a girl half fish or half bat, half anything, half himself even, a child of him, glowing like a phosphorescent deep-sea creature. She would have looked at him with dark eyes, would've kept looking, would not have looked away as everyone else has always looked away.

Like everybody else, he has always assumed Evie died in that mine. But the mine would have been the perfect ruse for a person who wanted to disappear. Evie could have carried three ropes down, smoked her Winston cigarettes, and climbed out again. Maybe she'd climbed out, stepped carefully into her own tracks on the trail leading down Mount Saint Barbara to give the illusion of a single set of tracks. She could've gone to the truck stop, hitchhiked out of town to be born again somewhere. Maybe she was gardening in California, digging deep into rich soil to plant tomatoes and peppers. She wouldn't be afraid of earthquakes or anything. Maybe she was there, or somewhere, waiting for him.

Before Leaving

Rosalie Sanara Petrouske

I climb black rocks with my daughter,
who scrambles ahead.
Close behind, I'm ready to reach out
should she stumble on the uneven surface.
At the top, we stare out at Superior,
breathing in the peace of lake and sky.
Below, a few waves crest white,
then lap
the million-year-old ledge beneath us.

On a far shore, sugar maple, hemlock, balsam fir
and white pine cover the island and grow down sides
of distant outcroppings.
Pairs of seagulls rise from the Bon Rocks.
They lift and circle,
    dip and glide.
To the West, I point out Hogsback
and Sugarloaf, remnants of ancient glaciers.

Near us, a group of college students gather.
We watch as they leap from the highest point
to plummet into icy water.

This ritual repeats year after year.
Perhaps, I think, one day my daughter will dive
from this cliff into Superior's silvery-blue.
Her breath will catch when she rises
and gulps in warm air,
yet her heart will beat again
when she discovers
effortless, she can fall and still rise.

For now, we simply sit side by side.
Sun warms our shoulder blades
and dampness gathers in the hollows
of our necks
where tendrils of hair separate to expose
skin to mid-afternoon light.

I tell her this place, this moment will always be part of us—
its mantra will call to us when we close our eyes
and still hear lake sounds, as if someone placed
a seashell against our ears.
We will carry it inside.
"Inside here?" she asks.
She places a hand across her chest.

Reaching, I take her other hand.
I squeeze, but she pulls away.
     "Don't hold on so tightly," she says.

2017

Epithalamion, Anxiety Disorder

Saara Myrene Raappana

I'm the deep lake. I can't sleep.
They say the moon's

my master, that each
relentless wave creaks

toward the perfect
moment of the sky;

they say no drop
can rise unless it shoves

another back; but I know
it's only shore that ever

stalls my gnashing teeth,
only the span of grain

balanced on grain of sand
where I can finally

recline into relief.

2017

Natural Phenomena

Timston Johnston

I GAVE UP DRINKING THE NIGHT WE SEE THE PAULDING LIGHT. WE HAD brought camp chairs and a thermal blanket and promised not to go home until something happened. I'd never seen it, and neither had she, but her father had once, told her Paulding is where angels passed back into heaven; her uncle said it's the ghost lantern of a trainman. Or swamp gas. Aliens. The generational prank of an ex-logging family, keeping the mystery alive to attract people like us who know clerks never ID. This is how they stay on the map. Here, towns only survive when there's purpose, and die when trees grow back slowly, when the ore and copper are stripped away. We didn't care what it was. We just needed to get away from school, from dorms and cafeteria food, from the last three weeks when the days were noticeably shorter and she was late and so we talked and talked and skipped class and meals and didn't take calls from home. I researched procedures. She researched testimonials, called her roommate's cousin who's had two abortions, asked of scarring, said, *No, emotional.* I proposed, sincerely, already searching for apartments in town and decent jobs with insurance, and it was then when I mistook her widened eyes for shock and love and of dreams coming true. She skipped to the bathroom, thanking God, slamming cabinet doors, and it took me too long to put those pieces together. We packed up the next day, drove to Paulding, bought a bottle of bourbon, and waited for angels and swamp gas. *Now we don't have to get married*, she'd said, and I couldn't recognize her voice. We don't speak again until she had leaned forward, jumped from her chair. *Something's there*, and beyond the hill, between the pines and poles, a waking red splotch, breathing, igniting into something wide and white. *It's like a train coming*, she said. I listened for the wail of its steam whistle, the screech of steel and wheels, the chorus, the harps to call us home, but there was nothing but her breath and the light glowing through a sinking mist, heavy with bourbon, weighed down by truth.

2017

bitches

Emily Van Kley

ain't shit, but what we are is fearsome
& always changing. well heeled
on the back porch without a stitch

in the evening, we drink soda water
& wine or strawberry milk
or Jäger.

Thoreau, oh please, & the hair
raises. we're geniuses, mostly,

civically interested,

genitally kaleidoscopic.
don't ask don't tell & know

we're as like to say or slap you.
we're unimpressed is the point,
or maybe the point

is how many histories one mouth
is made from, so yes,
who says it matters.

2017

Babejianjisemigad
A Gradual Flowing Transformation

Margaret Noodin

Chigaming gii jiisibidoon mikwambikwadinaa
　　The great sea was pinched by the glaciers

neyaashiiwan, neyaakobiiwanan, neyaakwaa
　　land reaching, water pointing, trees leaning

biindig zaaga'iganing, agwajiing akiing
　　inside the lake, outside the land.

Omaa zhawenjigejig zhaweniminangwa
　　It is here we are loved

epiichi agwaayaashkaa mii dash animaashkaa
　　by the slow swell of tides

gaye baswewe zisibimaadiziyang.
　　that echo the rasp of our lives.

Maampii gidanishinaabemotawigoonaanig
　　This place speaks to us

ginwenzh biboon, nitaawigin niibin
    of long winters, summer growth

babejianjisemigad apane.
    and slow constant change.

2017

KBIC (excerpt)

Sally Brunk

the enemy has already invaded our lands
This time, it is not the white man
Instead it is called alcohol, drugs, abuse and poverty
It is the loss of language and culture
It is the loss of life and history
There is a call going out for our
Ogitchdaa and ogitchdaakwe to defend
We need to run for our stronghold
Fight tooth and nail for what we have left
Take back what is ours
Those members we witness that are losing the substance fight
We need to fight to save those warriors.
Use that love, strength and togetherness
Use our gentleness, our kindness
Everything that encompasses what we are
To battle our enemies
May our forces be many . . .

Acknowledgments

Mr. Nicholas likes the idea of exchanging a mine shaft for
a writing desk.

> —Richard Dorson, from "Traditions,"
> in *Bloodstoppers & Bearwalkers* (1952)

I hope the anthology's chronological order helps the reader see nuances of literary shifting that occur throughout the last hundred years of U.P. writing. I also hope a larger audience will come to know more deeply the region's literary heroes. It is important to encourage and champion the great writers, both past and present. Please read more of their work. It is an honor to showcase truly significant voices of the region.

I read thousands of pages for consideration for this anthology. I won't list writers already included in *Here* and *The Way North*, but other poets close to being in these pages include Antler, Johann G. R. Baner, Skulda Baner, Jaswinder Bolina, Marianne Boruch, Baker Brownell, Kaylee Brunk, Lucille Clifton, Billy Collins, Dave Cope, Da Yoopers, Aileen Fisher, Linda Nemec Foster, Dan Gerber, Lorna Goodison, Gust-ah-yah-she, Joy Harjo, Bob Hicok, Tara Hill, Aili Kolemainen Johnson, Kathleen Carlton Johnson, Lawrence Joseph, Miriam Heideman Krarup, Larry Leffel, Philip Levine, Clarence P. Milligan, Rebecca Pelky, Marge Piercy, Heino Puotinen, Doug Ramspeck, Martin Reinhardt, Andrew Riutta, Aubrey Ryan, Donna Salli, Taylor Shelafoe, Margaret Shelifoe, T. Kilgore Splake, Lucie Stanton, Sufjan Stevens, Casey Thayer, Adam Uhrig, Robert VanderMolen, Jingo Viitala Vachon, Pamella

Vincent, Sarah Wangler, David Welch, C. F. Whiteshield, and more. Prose writers coming close to being included were R. Ray Baker, Charles Baxter, Margery Bianco, Barbara Bradley, James Cloyd Bowman, Philip Caputo, Erin Celello, Alison DeCamp, Grace Chaillier, Ty Dettloff, Richard Dorson, Aimée L. Cree Dunn, Mike Ellison, Loren Estleman, Ben Evans, Robert Gessner, Loren Graham, Andrew Hilleman, Adam Hunault, Don Lystra, Lois Maki, Abi Maxwell, David Means, Florence McClinchey, John Moore, Kelly Nichols (P. J. Parrish), Simon Otto, Isabel Paterson, Keith Rebec, Diane Salmela Rice, Alex K. Ruuska, Adam Schuitema, Patricia Shackleton, Danielle Sosin, Newton G. Thomas, Hunter S. Thompson, Gerald Vizenor, Margaret Willey, Jeanette Winter, and more. *Here* and *The Way North* are helpful for more authors to add to your reading lists.

A deep thank you to MSU Press, especially Julie Loehr, Julie Reaume, and Kristine Blakeslee. Thank you to authors who write about the U.P. Thank you to readers who read about the U.P. Thank you to Skip Schmidt, Denise Engle, and those I thanked in both *Here* and *The Way North*; your help was beneficial for this anthology as well. Thank you to the long list of libraries and bookstore owners who answered my questions, especially the University of California at Berkeley's Ethnic Studies Library/Native American Studies staff. Thank you very much to all of the publishers and authors who agreed to have their work in these pages. *Giitu. Chi-miigwech*. If you support U.P. literature, please let people know about the writers you like. Invite them to your colleges, high schools, libraries. And please buy their books directly from Michigan bookstores.

Thank you to *Pank*, *Border Crossing*, and *Pithead Chapel* for publishing my writing. Please support U.P. literary presses. And let's hope those presses support rural, working-class, and Native American U.P. literature. If you are a teacher, please teach U.P. literature. The lack of U.P. literature in my youth was the impetus for creating these U.P. anthologies. I crave *dibaajimowin. Meillä on kulttuuri. Nous sommes un peuple uni.*

This book is dedicated to my parents and my girlfriend, who understand why I don't sleep. *Jumalan siunausta. Inaabandam.* He dreams—he has a vision. *Sisu.*

Permissions

"Beekeeper outside Escanaba, Michigan" by Hannah Baker-Siroty was published in *Best New Poets 2012* (University of Virginia Press, 2012). Reprinted by permission of the author.

"Watching" by Julie Brooks Barbour was previously published in *Roger: An Art & Literary Magazine*, Spring 2010; the chapbook *Come to Me and Drink* (Finishing Line Press, 2012); and *Small Chimes* (Aldrich Press, 2014). Reprinted by permission of the author.

"A Daughter-in-Law Watches the Old Man Hesitate" by Elinor Benedict won first prize in the National Writers' Union Poetry Contest, 1995, won third prize in the journal *The Bridge* (Spring, 1994), and was read by Garrison Keillor on *The Writer's Almanac*, National Public Radio. Reprinted by permission of the author.

"Death Defier" by Thomas Carlisle Bissell was published in *VQR: A National Journal of Literature & Discussion* (summer 2004) and *God Lives in St. Petersburg: Short Stories* (Pantheon, 2005). Reprinted by permission of the author.

"Lake Surfing at Whitefish Point" by Russell Brakefield was published in *Michigan Quarterly Review*'s "The Great Lakes: Love Song and Lament," Summer 2011 issue. Reprinted by permission of the author.

"Goin' for Commods" by Shirley Brozzo was previously published in *Voice on the Water: Great Lakes Native America Now* (NMU Press, 2011). Reprinted by permission of the author.

Wayne State University Press. Reprinted by permission of Wayne State University Press.

"Anishinabeg in the Cranberry Swamp," "The Wife of Manibozho Sings," "The Indians in the Woods," and "The Old Woman Alone" by Janet Lewis were published in *The Indian in the Woods*, Monroe Wheeler, 1922. Public domain.

"On the Scrap" by M. L. Liebler first appeared in *Wide Awake in Someone Else's Dream* published by Wayne State University Press, 2008. Reprinted by permission of Wayne State University Press.

"The Wreck of the Edmund Fitzgerald" words and music by Gordon Lightfoot, Copyright © 1976 (renewed) WB Music Corp., All Rights Reserved, used by permission of Alfred Music.

"To Dance Is to Pray" by April E. Lindala was previously unpublished. Printed by permission of the author.

"Marquette" by Justin Machnik appeared in *Midwestern Gothic*, Issue 9, Spring 2013. Reprinted by permission of the author.

"And Winter" from *Radio Tree* by Corey Marks. Copyright © 2012 by Corey Marks. Reprinted by permission of New Issues Poetry & Prose.

"Yellow Dog Journal—Spring" and "Yellow Dog Journal—Fall" by Judith Minty were published in *Walking with the Bear: Selected and New Poems*, Michigan State University Press, 2000. Reprinted by permission of the author.

"Vacationland" by Ander Monson appeared originally in *Vacationland*, Tupelo Press, 2015. Reprinted by permission of the author. "Elf Incantation" by Ander Monson was previously unpublished. Printed by permission of the author.

"[Let's play a game]" by Lorine Niedecker was published in *New Mexico Quarterly* 21.1, Spring 1951 and in *Lorine Niedecker: Collected Works*, ed. Jenny Penberthy (University of California Press, 2002). Reprinted by permission of University of California Press.

"Miskwiyiwigiizhig Gichigamigong" and "Red Sky over Superior" by Margaret Noodin were previously published in *Weweni: Poems in*

"Epithalamion, Anxiety Disorder" by Saara Myrene Raappana was previously unpublished. Printed by permission of the author.

"Dominos" by Ron Riekki was previously published in *Clockhouse Review*, October 2012. Reprinted by permission of the author. "Arm" by Ron Riekki was previously published in *River Teeth*, February 2015. Reprinted by permission of the author.

"Water Mission" by Jillena Rose appeared previously in *The Other Journal. com: An Intersection of Theology and Culture*. Reprinted by permission of the author.

"Beat Against Me No Longer" by Lew R. Sarett / Lone Caribou was published in *Others, A Magazine of the New Verse*, as well as *Anthology of Magazine Verse for 1919* (1919). "The Box of God" by Lew R. Sarett / Lone Caribou was published in *The Box of God*, Henry Holt & Company, 1922. Public domain. "The Blue Duck: A Chippewa Medicine Dance" by Lew R. Sarett / Lone Caribou was previously published in *Poetry*, November 1918. Public domain.

"Beach Glass" by M. Bartley Seigel was published by *Michigan Quarterly Review*, Summer 2011. Reprinted by permission of the author.

"Possession(s)" by John Smolens was published in *PANK Magazine*, 9.2, February 2014. Reprinted by permission of the author. "North of Paradise" by Phillip Sterling first appeared in *Passages North*, and was collected in *Mutual Shores* (copyright 2000 by Phillip Sterling). Reprinted by permission of the author.

"Upper Peninsula Fires" from *If the World Becomes So Bright* by Keith Taylor. Copyright © 2009 Wayne State University Press, with the permission of Wayne State University Press.

"Rent" from *The Whole Tree as Told to the Backyard*, Rocky Shore Books. Copyright 2009 by Russell Thorburn. Reprinted by permission of the author.

"I Will Die in Lake Superior" by Eric Torgersen first appeared in *The Ambassador Bridge Project*, then in Torgersen's *Heart. Wood.*, Word Press, 2012. Reprinted by permission of the author.

Contributors

Hannah Baker-Siroty is the Director of the English Composition Program at Pine Manor College. She has published in *Critical Flame, Lavender Review, Lumina,* and other journals. The Writers' Room of Boston and the Vermont Studio Center have awarded her fellowships. She was included in *Best New Poets 2012* for "Beekeeper Outside Escanaba, Michigan."

Julie Brooks Barbour is the author of *Small Chimes* (2014), as well as three chapbooks, most recently *Beautifully Whole* (2015). She is coeditor of *Border Crossing* and Poetry Editor at *Connotation Press.* She lives in Sault Sainte Marie and teaches at Lake Superior State University.

Elinor Benedict has lived in the Upper Peninsula for forty years. She served as founding editor of *Passages North* from 1979 until 1989. She is the winner of the May Swenson Poetry Award for her collection *All That Divides Us* (2000), and she has five chapbooks and another collection, *Late News from the Wilderness* (2009).

Tom Bissell was born in Escanaba in 1974 and attended Michigan State University. He has authored nine books, including *God Lives in St. Petersburg: Short Stories, Extra Lives: Why Video Games Matter,* and *Apostle: Travels among the Tombs of the Twelve.* His work has won the Rome Prize and a Guggenheim Fellowship and appeared in many anthologies and magazines.

Russell Brakefield's writing has appeared in *Hobart*, *Indiana Review*, *New Orleans Review*, *Crab Orchard Review*, *Drunken Boat*, and elsewhere. He has received fellowships and residencies from the University of Michigan Musical Society, the Vermont Studio Center, and National Parks Department. He teaches writing at the University of Michigan.

Born in Ironwood, **Shirley Brozzo** is an Anishinaabe from the Keweenaw Bay Indian Community. She created the Northern Michigan University class Storytelling by Native American Women. Her stories and poems have been in more than thirty publications. She lives in Marquette.

Sally Brunk's (Ojibwa/Lac du Flambeau) writing centers on family bonds and the American Indian way of life. She was proudly born and raised in the Keweenaw Bay Indian Community, where she still lives now. She has work in the anthologies *The Way North*, *Voice on the Water*, *Cradle Songs*, and *Sharing Our Survival Stories*.

Bonnie Jo Campbell is the author of *Mothers, Tell Your Daughters: Stories*, the best-selling *Once upon a River: A Novel*, and *American Salvage: Stories*. She was a National Book Award finalist and a Guggenheim Fellow. She has always lived in Michigan's lower peninsula, and spends as much time as possible in the upper.

A native of Michigan's Upper Peninsula, **Cynie Cory** grew up in Marquette. She graduated from the Iowa Writers' Workshop and Florida State University. Her poetry has appeared in *New American Writing*, *Colorado Review*, *Ploughshares*, *TriQuarterly*, and *Verse Daily*. She is the author of a collection of poems, *American Girl* (2004).

Lisa Fay Coutley is the author of *Errata* (2015) and *In the Carnival of Breathing* (2011). She wrote "Researchers Find . . ." in a cabin in the U.P., where she hunkered down during the 2013 polar vortex. She now lives in Omaha, where she's an Assistant Professor of Poetry in the University of Nebraska's Writer's Workshop.

Jim Daniels's books include *Apology to the Moon* (2015), *Eight Mile High* (2014), and *Birth Marks* (2013). He is the writer/producer of short films, including *The End of Blessings* (2015). Born in Detroit, Daniels is the Baker University Professor at Carnegie Mellon University.

Michael Delp was the Director of Creative Writing at Interlochen Arts Academy. He has published several volumes of prose and poetry, and is currently the coeditor of the Wayne State University Press Made in Michigan series. His books include *As If We Were Prey: Stories* (2010) and *Bob Seger's House and Other Stories* (coeditor, 2016).

Jack Driscoll is the author of three short story collections, including *The World of a Few Minutes Ago* (2012). He teaches in Pacific University's low-residency Master of Fine Arts in Writing Program.

Winner of the Hopwood Award, **Iola Fuller**'s (born 1906) historical romance *The Loon Feather* (originally entitled *Loon Totem*), set on Mackinac Island, is one of the great U.P. novels. Its central protagonist is the Ojibway woman Oneta. She also wrote *The Shining Trail* (1943), *The Gilded Torch* (1957), and *All the Golden Gifts* (1966). She was born in Marcellus, graduated from University of Michigan, and taught in Big Rapids.

Eric Gadzinski finds the U.P. congenial and refreshingly free of a certain kind of affectation. Of course, the U.P. has its own charms, including Mossy Oak ball caps and large pickup trucks, which Gadzinski finds preferable to L.L. Bean. Gadzinki's poems have appeared in a wide variety of small journals.

Alex Vartan Gubbins has an MFA in poetry from Northern Michigan University. He is the founder of the U.P. Vets Writers and Artists. He was a

2014 Witter Bynner Translation Grant recipient and a finalist in the *North American Review*'s 2015 James Hearst Poetry Prize.

Carol R. Hackenbruch (1940–2005) published *Out of Step: Poems*. An Upper Peninsula resident, she was *Passages North*'s managing editor and published poetry in *Alaska Quarterly Review, Cedar Rock, Great Lakes Review, Passages North*, and *Small Pond*.

Steve Hamilton is the two-time Edgar Award–winning author of *The Lock Artist* and *The New York Times*–best-selling Alex McKnight series, featuring an ex-cop from Detroit who lives in the Upper Peninsula. *The Second Life of Nick Mason*, the 2016 debut of a new crime series, is in film development with Lionsgate.

Born in Grayling, **Jim Harrison** (1937–2016) wrote *A Good Day to Die* (1973), *The River Swimmer* (2013), *Brown Dog* (2013), *The Ancient Minstrel* (2016), and more. Harrison was also well known for the 1994 films *Wolf* and *Legends of the Fall*. In a *Traverse* interview with northern Michigan author Jerry Dennis, Harrison stated he "had 65 winters in Michigan." Harrison's cabin was near Grand Marais on the Sucker River.

Sue Harrison's novels include *Mother Earth Father Sky* (1990), *My Sister the Moon* (1992), *Brother Wind* (1996), *Song of the River* (1997), *Sisu* (1997), *Cry of the Wind* (1998), and *Call Down the Stars* (2001). Since she was four years old, Harrison has lived in Pickford, located in Michigan's eastern Upper Peninsula.

Kathleen M. Heideman haunts the Yellow Dog Plains of the wild U.P.; she's completed residencies with watersheds, the National Park Service, and the National Science Foundation's Antarctic Artists & Writers Program. Poetry chapbooks include *She Used to Have Some Cows* (1992) and *Explaining Pictures to a Dead Hare* (1997). Curious woman.

Ernest Hemingway (1899–1961) was awarded a 1953 Pulitzer Prize and the 1954 Nobel Prize in Literature. In youth, he frequented his family cabin near Petoskey on Walloon Lake. Those experiences in northern Michigan, including the U.P., were central to his early writing. The opening story in his first collection was "Up in Michigan." The U.P. recurs in his other early stories, such as "Indian Camp" and "Big Two-Hearted River."

Gordon Henry is an enrolled member of the White Earth Chippewa Tribe. His novel *The Light People* (1994) won an American Book Award, and his work has appeared in numerous journals and anthologies. An Associate Professor at Michigan State University, he is also the author of *The Failure of Certain Charms* (2007).

Ingrid Hill's books include the short story collection *Dixie Church Interstate Blues* (1989) and the novel *Ursula, Under* (2004). Her story "Jolie Gray" helped garner her a $20,000 National Endowment for the Arts grant. Of Swedish ancestry, Hill lived several years in Ann Arbor and has a fascination for the mining history of Ishpeming.

Austin Hummell has lived in the Upper Peninsula since 2000. His books are *Poppy* (Del Sol Press) and *The Fugitive Kind* (University of Georgia Press). He teaches at Northern Michigan University.

Born in Detroit, **Karl Iagnemma** is a Robotic Mobility Group Director at the Massachusetts Institute of Technology. A previous National Science Foundation Graduate Fellow, Iagnemma has a BS from University of Michigan and an MS and a PhD from MIT. His writing has been in *Best American Short Stories*, *Paris Review*, *Tin House*, *Zoetrope*, and more.

Jonathan Johnson's poems have appeared in *Best American Poetry* and been read on NPR. A professor in the MFA program at Eastern Washington

University, his works include two books of poetry, a memoir, and a play, *Ode* (2013), about John Keats. Johnson migrates between Washington, Scotland, and his hometown Marquette.

Timston Johnston received his MFA from Northern Michigan University in 2013 and is the founding editor of Little Presque Books. He moved to Marquette in 2004 from central Michigan and, with three nieces within eighty miles, has no immediate plans to leave.

Ethnographer **William Jones** (1871–1909) was a Native American of Fox descent. The Carnegie Foundation funded his collection of Ojibwa stories from 1903 to 1905. Jones was speared to death in the Philippines while on assignment from the Field Museum in Illinois.

Prolific author **Laura Kasischke** is the author of several books including the 2011 National Book Critics Circle Award–winning poetry collection *Space, in Chains.*

L. E. Kimball lives off the grid near Tahquamenon Falls on the Little Two Hearted River and is an Assistant Contingent Professor at Northern Michigan University. Kimball has published a novel, *A Good High Place* (2010), been anthologized in *The Way North* (2013), and published stories in *Seasonal Roads* (2016). She received a Pushcart Honorable Mention (2015).

Phil Legler (1928–1992) wrote *A Change of View* (1964), *The Intruder* (1972), and *North Country Images* (1988). After living and studying throughout the Midwest, he taught at Northern Michigan University, which holds a collection of his documents including files under such names as "Christmas Poetry" and "The 'Sexton' Poems." Legler published widely in *Poetry*, *Paris Review*, *Poetry Northwest*, *Passages North*, *Prairie Schooner*, and more.

Janet Lewis's (1899–1998) writing has been labeled as "significant" and "courageous." Lewis is the author of multiple books, including the Anishinaabe-centered poetry collection *The Indians in the Woods* (1922) and *The Invasion* (1932), a historical novel about John Johnston and Ozhah-guscoday-wayquay who settled on the U.P.'s St. Marys River.

St. Clair Shores's first Poet Laureate, **M. L. Liebler** has published multiple books. He was a 2010 recipient of the Barnes & Noble Writers for Writers Award, along with Junot Díaz and Maxine Hong Kingston. His books include *Written in Rain: New and Selected Poems, 1985–2000* (2000) and *Wide Awake in Someone Else's Dream* (2008).

One might label **Gordon Lightfoot**'s "The Wreck of the Edmund Fitzgerald" as the national anthem of Lake Superior. Lightfoot is one of Canada's great songwriters with a discography of multiple albums spanning from *Lightfoot!* (1966) to *All Live* (2012). In 1986, Lightfoot became a member of the Canadian Music Hall of Fame. His songs regularly cover interests of the Great Lakes region.

April E. Lindala grew up near Detroit but moved to Marquette in 1988 to attend Northern Michigan University. She fell in love with the Upper Peninsula and has made it her home. Lindala earned a master of fine arts degree in English from NMU, where she is the director of the Center for Native American Studies.

Thomas Lynch is the author of five poetry collections and four books of essays. His writing has appeared in the *Atlantic*, *Granta*, the *New Yorker*, *Poetry*, and many other prestigious journals. His book *The Undertaking: Life Studies from the Dismal Trade* won an American Book Award and was a National Book Award finalist.

Justin Machnik is a director of photography, working and living out of Los Angeles. He is a graduate of Sarah Lawrence College and the University of

Iowa, where he studied fiction writing. He was raised in Michigan, and his work is heavily influenced by his time spent in the woods and small towns of the Midwest.

2003 NEA Fellow **Corey Marks**'s debut book, *Renunciation* (2000), was a winner of the National Poetry Series Open Competition. His poems have been published in *Antioch Review*, *Black Warrior Review*, *Paris Review*, *Ploughshares*, *TriQuarterly*, and other literary journals. Marks also wrote the poetry book *Radio Tree* (2012).

Judith Minty's books include *Walking with the Bear*, *In the Presence of Mothers*, *Dancing the Fault*, and *Lake Songs and Other Fears*, which received the United States Award of the International Poetry Forum. She has been awarded *Poetry*'s Eunice Tietjens Award and the Villa Montalvo Award for Excellence in Poetry. She lives near the shoreline of Lake Michigan and spends time on the U.P.'s Yellow Dog River.

Born and raised in Houghton, **Ander Monson** is the author of six books of fiction, nonfiction, and poetry. He edits the magazine *Diagram*, *Essay Daily*, and the New Michigan Press.

Lorine Niedecker's (1903–1970) books include *Collected Works*, *The Granite Pail: The Selected Poems of Lorine Niedecker*, *Lake Superior*, *Between Your House and Mine: The Letters of Lorine Niedecker to Cid Corman, 1960 to 1970*, *Harpsichord & Salt Fish*, *New Goose*, *North Central*, *My Life by Water: Collected Poems, 1936–1968*, and more.

Margaret Noodin spends many days each year on the shores of Gichigaming. She received an MFA and a PhD from the University of Minnesota and is an Associate Professor at the University of Wisconsin–Milwaukee, where she serves as the Director of the Electa Quinney Institute for American Indian Education.

One of the Midwest's most powerful literary forces, **Jim Northrup** has authored several books, including *Walking the Rez Road* (1995), *The Red Road Follies: Canoes, Computers, and Birch Bark Baskets* (1999), *Anishinaabe Syndicated: A View from the Rez* (2011), *Rez Salute: The Real Healer Dealer* (2012), and *Dirty Copper* (2014).

William Olsen has published five collections of poetry. A sixth collection, *TechnoRage*, is forthcoming. He teaches at Western Michigan University.

Rosalie Sanara Petrouske served as the Artist in Residence in the Porcupine Mountains. She is the author of the poetry collection *What We Keep* (2015).

Author of twenty books and chapbooks, **Jane Piirto** is a Finnish-American native of Ishpeming, Michigan, and spends summers there in her childhood home in Cleveland Location. Northern Michigan University awarded her a BA and an honorary doctorate of humane letters. She is Trustees' Distinguished Professor at Ashland University.

Kenneth Pobo had two books out in 2015: *Bend of Quiet* and *Booking Rooms in the Kuiper Belt*. His work has appeared in *Mudfish*, *Indiana Review*, *Colorado Review*, *Fiddlehead*, and elsewhere. He teaches creative writing and English at Widener University.

In 1917, **William Paris Potter** of Iron Mountain won ninth prize for his short story "The Lost Island" in an American Ambition short story competition. In the 1920s, Potter published poetry in *American Poetry Magazine* and the *Milwaukee Journal*.

Saara Myrene Raappana is the author of two chapbooks: *Milk Tooth, Levee, Fever* (2015) and *A Story of America Goes Walking* (2016). She was born in Marquette and raised in Sault Sainte Marie, Suomi Location, Rudyard, and

Menominee. She served as a Peace Corps volunteer in southern China and works for *Motionpoems*.

A graduate of Northern Michigan University, **Vincent Reusch** has published stories in *Madison Review*, *Gettysburg Review*, *Alaska Quarterly Review*, and elsewhere. His work has won and placed in a number of national contests. He teaches creative writing at Concordia College.

Ron Riekki was raised in Palmer and Negaunee. His books include *U.P.: A Novel*, *The Way North: Collected Upper Peninsula New Works* (2014 Michigan Notable Book), and *Here: Women Writing on Michigan's Upper Peninsula* (2016 Independent Publisher Book Award). His story "Accidents" was awarded the Shenandoah Fiction Prize.

Jillena Rose was raised in Hancock and has lived for the last twenty years in Sault Sainte Marie. She teaches creative writing at Lake Superior State University. She had two chapbooks published in 2014: *Cedar Cathedral* and *Light as Sparrows*. In 2015, she was a finalist for the position of U.P. Poet Laureate.

Born and raised in Marquette, **Lew R. Sarett/Lone Caribou** (1888–1954) authored five poetry collections, including *Many Many Moons* (1920), *The Box of God* (1922), and *Slow Smoke* (1925). His poem "The Box of God" was awarded the Helen Haire Levinson Prize as the best poem of the year 1921 for *Poetry: A Magazine of Verse*. The Poetry Society of America voted *Slow Smoke* as the best poetry book of 1925.

M. Bartley Seigel is the author of the poetry collection *This Is What They Say* (2012), founding editor of *Pank* magazine, and a book review editor for *Words without Borders*. Michigan born and bred, he's spent more than a decade living and working in Houghton, on the Keweenaw Peninsula of the western U.P.

John Smolens has published ten works of fiction, most recently *Wolf's Mouth* (2016). He is Professor Emeritus, Northern Michigan University, and lives in Marquette. In 2010, he was the recipient of the Michigan Author of the Year Award from the Michigan Library Association.

Phillip Sterling wrote *In Which Brief Stories Are Told* (2011), *Mutual Shores* (2000), and four chapbook-length series of poems, including *And For All This: Poems from Isle Royale*, a selection of work generated by his National Park Service Artist Residency in August 2014. "North of Paradise" was written after a stay at a friend's camp on Whitefish Bay.

Keith Taylor's most recent collections are the chapbook *The Ancient Murrelet* (2013) and *Fidelities* (2015). For many years he spent summers teaching at the University of Michigan Biological Station, at the tip of the mitten, a mere twenty-minute drive from the U.P. The fire described in "Upper Peninsula Fires" is the one known as the Sleeper Lake Fire.

As the first Poet Laureate of the Upper Peninsula, **Russell Thorburn** worked with sixth graders in Negaunee to create an abecedarian poem read on WNMU FM. A recipient of a National Endowment for the Arts Fellowship, his published work includes *The Whole Tree as Told to the Backyard* (2009). He lives in Marquette with his wife.

Eric Torgersen, author of six books of poetry, two novellas, and *Dear Friend: Rainer Maria Rilke and Paula Modersohn-Becker* (1998), taught for thirty-eight years at Central Michigan University. For six years, he and his wife Ann Kowaleski owned a cabin on a stretch of sand beach on Lake Superior, north of Granite Point.

A true Yooper, John Donaldson Voelker—pen name **Robert Traver**—(1903–1991) was born in Ishpeming. He studied at Northern Michigan Normal

School (now Northern Michigan University) and University of Michigan and practiced law in the U.P. Traver wrote eleven books, including classic U.P. writings such as *Anatomy of a Murder*, *Trout Madness*, and *Laughing Whitefish*.

An NEA fellow, **Stephen Tudor** (1933–1994) published in journals such as *American Poetry Review*, *Iowa Review*, *Michigan Quarterly Review*, and *North American Review*. He published *Tudor's Anatomy* (1981), *Hangdog Reef: Poems Sailing the Great Lakes* (1989), and the posthumous poetry collection *Haul-Out: New and Selected Poems* (1996). Tudor disappeared in 1994 while competing in a Great Lakes race.

Marquette native **Jeff Vande Zande** teaches English at Delta College. His books of fiction include *Threatened Species* (2010), from which "Disappearances" is excerpted. His *American Poet: A Novel* (2012) won the Stuart and Vernice Gross Award for Excellence in Writing by a Michigan Author and a Michigan Notable Book Award. In 2006, he published *Detroit Muscle: A Novel*.

Emily Van Kley was raised in Iron River, Ishpeming, and Wakefield, where her father served as a Lutheran pastor. Her poetry has received a number of awards, most recently the Loraine Williams Poetry Prize from the *Georgia Review*. She wrote "bitches" after consistently misreading the title of her own poem, "Birches" and figuring, Why not?

Set in the U.P., **Mildred Walker**'s *Fireweed* (1934–1998) won the Avery Hopwood Award. In 1961, *The Body of a Young Man* (1960) was a National Book Award finalist for fiction, along with Harper Lee's *To Kill a Mockingbird* (1960) and Flannery O'Connor's *The Violent Bear It Away* (1960). Walker wrote thirteen books including *Winter Wheat* (1944), *The Curlew's Cry* (1955), and *If a Lion Could Talk* (1970).

Cameron Witbeck's writing has appeared in the *North American Review*, *Witness*, *Pank*, and other publications. Witbeck is always in a state of finding his way back to the U.P. He took his first buck near Harlow Lake outside of Marquette and now every time he smells lake water on a cold morning, he remembers.

In 1978, **John Woods** (1926–1995) was named Distinguished Michigan Artist. In 1982, he was an NEA Fellow. Woods authored fourteen poetry books, including *The Valley of Minor Animals* (1982), *The Salt Stone: Selected Poems* (1985), and *Black Marigolds* (1994). His *On the Morning of Color* was listed as a "B" volume top selection for the 1962 Pulitzer Prize.

Upper Peninsula native and Northern Michigan University alumna **Jennifer Yeatts** is the director of coffee (yes, it's a real job) for Higher Grounds Trading Co. in Traverse City. When she's not brewing, slurping, or evaluating coffee, she enjoys spending time in her kitchen and adventures with the Country Ramblers bicycle club.